CRYSTAL ROOMS

CRYSTAL ROOMS

Melvyn Bragg

Hodder & Stoughton
LONDON SYDNEY AUCKLAND

British Library Cataloguing in Publication Data

Bragg, Melvyn
  Crystal rooms.
  I. Title
  823.914 [F]

ISBN 0-340-56409-1

Copyright © Melvyn Bragg 1992

First published in Great Britain in 1992

A version of the first five chapters
was published in *Esquire* in 1991

Published by Hodder and Stoughton,
a division of Hodder and Stoughton Ltd,
Mill Road, Dunton Green, Sevenoaks, Kent TN13 2YA.
Editorial Office: 47 Bedford Square, London WC1B 3DP.

Photoset by Rowland Phototypesetting Ltd,
Bury St Edmunds, Suffolk

Printed in Great Britain by Butler and Tanner Ltd,
Frome, Somerset

To
Anthony Pye-Jeary
and
The Eighth Day

"And this is the eternal law. For Evil often stops short of itself and dies with the doer of it, but Good never.'

Charles Dickens

"O that 'twere possible
After long grief and pain
To find the arms of my true love
Round me once again! . . ."

Alfred Lord Tennyson

CONTENTS

Part One

LONDON CALLING

ONE

I

THE angry howl of the wind pursued the sleet through the cardboard which had replaced the window-panes. Harry woke violently from the terror of his worst nightmare mouthing the word LONDON. He wanted his mother to be near, but in the same split instant he knew that he would never see her again. There was still the inexpressible pain of that parting, an open wound in his heart, which he must bear secretly.

The boy was confused by the whine and rage of the gale unleashed in the bare room. There was comfort, even a certain pleasure in listening to its sound outside but now it had broken and entered, seeking him out, threatening to suck him into the storm which was spinning from a bitter South Atlantic over the turbulent Irish land and sea. As if finding its target, it battered the most wasted streets of the wasted estate in this industrial ghost-town near the north-west coast of England.

For a moment Harry thought, or felt, "Good! I'll go with you. Yes. Take me away from this. Let me disappear on the wind." Then he saw his sister, asleep, beside him on the mattress, and he remembered his tearful promise to their mother, that he would look after her.

He switched on the bicycle-lamp and hurried to stuff the sodden cardboard and some of his clothes into the gaps which had once held glass. Quite suddenly all the force was shut out; the wind, denied, swung away and he was uneasy in the silence. He played the light around the room looking for intruders, taking care not to direct the beam on to Mary breathing evenly, undisturbed. He

3

knelt down on the floor and tugged the two blankets and the coats over her, wishing he could do more. From downstairs the voices started up and as he edged on to the narrow landing he heard again the word LONDON.

Harry crouched against the wall, his feet chilled by the bare boards. The row – it must have been a row if he could hear them from upstairs; it usually was at this time of night – appeared to have stopped, but he lingered on, listening. They would kill him if they caught him spying on them. His aunt – who hated and despised that word – Fiona certainly would and Jake, the new boyfriend, in the end had to do her bidding. Jake was still too enthralled by her to let loose his own blind temper yet. The boy strained hard to catch the next word.

At first there was only the wind which attacked the flaking houses on this high and most exposed part of the estate, shaking the boarded-up windows, scattering overfilled dustbins, making a mocking dance of old wrapping papers, takeaway cartons, the litter of daily survival. Inside the house the wind boomed down the narrow uncarpeted hall and clattered the remaining window-panes. He came out on to the landing.

"Get him off my back!" he heard. The boy knew the vicious power of that tone and dread tensed his body. "We've had the money. The money's gone. It's all bloody spent!" His aunt's next words were drowned under the wind which surged through the house as if determined to invade, possess and destroy it. The boy found that he was edging down the stairs. He had always known that she meant him no good.

"London." Again the word, the name.

"Take him . . ." Once again, Harry could not catch the rest of the sentence which the wind took and gobbled, leaving him fighting down his panic. They must not catch him. "London." Jake this time. Jake went to London with a "fresh load" in a van now and then. Jake's London was a wonder which he flaunted, boasting of it to the boy. He had promised to take Harry with him one day. London was Jake's superiority.

Their voices were still too low and the boy slithered down a few more stairs until he was opposite the door. "Money spent!" recurred and "Take him!" Then Fiona began a litany which always came back to "Life of my own! Life of my own!" Although Jake's replies were too murmured to be intelligible, Harry sensed that he was on his side and felt a gush of near-tearful gratitude to Jake which helped hold back his panic. His heart bumped strenuously

4

against his skinny chest; he took three deep breaths and froze, bottling up the last gulp of air as the door was flung open. Jake. Jake with his black oiled hair now looping over his brow, his lumberjack shirtsleeves rolled up to his tattooed biceps – a butterfly on the left, a cobra on the right. Jake with a can of beer in his hand. Harry cowered into a foetal position which absorbed punishment least woundingly. Recent bruises seemed to become alert and tender, especially the cut under his left eye where Jake's signet ring had caught him. It was so finely balanced that a breath could decide it – would Jake strike? Or would he decide to be a pal, a good guy? – and so Harry took no breath, held on.

It was resolved.

"*You,*" said Jake, stabbing his forefinger at the fragile bars between them. "Upstairs." Unnervingly, he winked. "Move." Harry found that he was backing up the stairs, his eyes trapped by Jake's drunken, abstract gaze. "Move!" Jake repeated. Harry turned and scrambled away. "Stay!" Jake commanded. Harry stopped dead.

Jake looked back into the room. Harry could imagine Fiona, white-faced, blood lipstick, tumbled jet hair, messed clothes, cigarette burning apparently unnoticed between stained fingers, a can of beer to match Jake's. Then the whirlwind.

"That fucking boy! Spying on us! See?" From her invisible lair the venom-tipped words thudded, hurting him to despair. "*Do it!*" Jake turned from the door to Harry and back again. "*Do it!* Or else. Nothing for you. You can sing for it. How would you like that?"

"You!" Harry, fearful of catching Jake's eye, was compelled by the man's suddenly vicious stare. "Tomorrow. Four o'clock. London. OK? *Move!*"

Harry fled into his bedroom, across the bare floor, crawled on to the mattress and endured in silence what was almost a seizure of shivering. Fiona's words scared him as spitefully and as darkly as the wind. His eventual sleep was a shipwreck. The hand on his shoulder was gentle enough but he was startled, untrusting, when Jake coaxed, "Off we go, pal. London here we come, eh? Pal?"

He switched on the bicycle-lamp and dressed with the experienced speed of someone used to peremptory and absolute commands.

He was undecided about whether to wake Mary – still breathing evenly in the burrow of warmth he had created for her. But he was tugged by an instinct he could not yet unravel and he tapped on her cheek in the usual way. She was awake immediately.

"I'm going to London with Jake," he said.

"Now?" She glanced into the dark outside the thin arc of bicycle-lamp light.

He nodded. He must not let her see his fear. Although she was only nine – two years younger than he – she was quicker to scent a mood and she could comprehend him in a moment.

"What's wrong?" she asked.

"Nothing," Harry whispered. He heard Jake moving downstairs and was aware that his time was running out. He made a brave effort. "I've always wanted to go to London."

"You have." Mary had divined the fear and the desperation of her brother, but she knew also that he must conceal it from her. "I'm glad you woke me up."

"I'll bring you something back." She saw the misery beating against his white, thin face. He saw the face of their mother in her expression. He wanted her to kiss him. But she merely nodded. Awkwardly, Harry reached out and touched her cheek, unable to kiss her but unable to leave without touching her. "You take care now," he said gamely. "You look after yourself."

She waited until the door banged, even until the van started before she let herself cry. One day she would make Fiona suffer.

The wind buffeted the van and rocked it and Harry sensed that Jake was scared. Jake had told Harry to get some sleep but the boy was too alarmed to sleep as they left the desolate estate, sleet its natural element, and turned south, yellow lights lancing the enemy dark, hounded by the demons in the wind, making for London.

II

"Oh do shut up!" she said. Silence. Ah! The power. A few minutes later the noise started up again. This time her comic raspberry had the same silencing effect. But it was not long term and, at the third reminder, she flapped a hand and detonated the alarm which gagged the clock. Now it was willpower alone: the first test of character and so soon and every morning.

Although she knew that Tim, her husband, had left an hour before, she stretched a leg over to his side of the bed but it was cold and she lingered only for the moment in which, to her hardheaded embarrassment, on this as on most mornings she experienced a gulp of thanks for her docile, loving, ineffective, unsuccessful, good-looking, almost-upper-class, what-does-she-see-in-him? or how-can-he-put-up-with-her? husband of now four years. As she swung out of bed and came face to face with herself in the large florid gilt wall mirror, placed to enhance her sexual relish but simply ignored by Tim and now kept on as punishment, she met the second hurdle of the day. What did she look like? She was merciless.

Feet, too big, legs egg-white, hairless and stocky, topped by sumo thighs. Belly folds that cascaded over a crotch once boasted as (and still) insatiable but now stabled in monogamy and pre-served for Tim's increasingly absent-minded outings. Breasts formerly her glory now sagging? flopping? pendulous? – there was no kind word for them – and needing all the technology of old-fashioned bra engineering to turn into what Martha called in others "lovely tits there". Face – forever pale, once thought strangely attractive – she could make no comment on it. Nor, alas, did many others these days. Thus stood Martha Potter, successful metropolitan journalist, in her forties, aching for fame and, as was not unusual, badly hung over.

She was vaguely aware – behind the creases of pain (sitting up was always a mistake) – that outside her madly over-mortgaged, small but perfectly positioned terraced cottage in deeply smart Holland Park, there was a gale, a storm, a hurricane, a tornado, a killer Force Ten or the Big Wind, depending on which of her six daily newspapers she picked up first. But contact with anything except her own reputation was fleeting. Volcanically through the alcohol, which had served its secondary purpose as a blocker-out of serious disturbance, came the clear and undeniable memory of that bloody interview by that bloody bloody man in that bloody American magazine. The relevant pages had been faxed over from New York by an old friend.

Martha had told him it was off the record. Strictly. Before, during, after lunch, and anyway did it matter between two hacks, even if he were a USA superstar hack ("I've adored you for years," she told him, rather loudly, intending others to overhear, res-taurants were her stage) and she a mere UK wannabe? But – God! Help! He had printed the lot. Who could be trusted? Stitched her up. Screwed her. Was this because she had not made a pass? (Or had she? At about four-thirty the maître d' had cautioned against yet another port: she refused to remember the precise wording of her reply. After that was blank or patchy at best.) Didn't matter. Deed done. Damn. Damned.

For it was of the Royal Family they had talked. He the disappointingly Quiet American (Martha wanted cowboy boots and coke, raw bourbon and a deeper drawl – he was nothing *like* his PR), she become the eager-to-please (was this yet another penalty of the convent education?) English girl insider who wanted to sprinkle England's own stardust gossip over this ex-colonial Prince Hunk of the prints. Social suicide. She stood up, an act of some boldness, and unfolded the faxed sheet whose contents could well nobble her in the peculiar and often spiteful machinery of the British class and media labyrinth.

"Two things about the Royals get my goat," she read herself saying, in anguish at the deception of that American bastard, that *Man*! – "the *family* rubbish and the *loot*. We're supposed to revere them as the model family. A Holy Family for a Godless age, but just look at them! Ask any junior Foreign Office brat about Phil the Greek's appetites abroad." The language here grew lurid and Martha groaned through it. "As well as slaughtering the other birds –" Oh no! No! They would mug her in the streets. And it went on. "Charles and Diana, yawn one and yawn two, scarcely meet; the poor sods have a busted marriage and can't find the bottle to say so. Her brother, just married at great expense, is back with one of his old girlfriends. Anne's on a divorce which is a shame and nobody knows what Fergie's *for*. Edward's just plain curious and Margaret is a sport but where *are* we? Royal Family? Holy Mary! Royal cock-up more like." Martha had to admit she liked the restrained innuendo there. "What is this ridiculous sham *for*? I'll tell you: tourists, snobs and the lower orders."

And then she slammed into what she called "the loot". The Queen on more than a million pounds a day. The family not paying *any income tax*, not using its state-subsidised wealth to "set up an orchestra, found a college for inner city kids, put its money where its mouth always is. Even the Maundy Money the Queen doles out comes from the taxpayer. What *is* this? When did we vote to make her the richest female on the planet? As for style and taste – forget it." Martha took several deep breaths. It would be all over town by dinner. It could be nasty – people could get very unpredictable about the Royals. Was she damagingly out of step or cleverly ahead of the game?

The best way was to affect to ignore it. Head down. Get on

with her own work. Get her byline on to a talked-about piece a.s.a.p.

Mark Armstrong had agreed to see her. Riding so high after yet another dramatic programme on Northern Ireland, Mark was a major talent in the television land in which Tim, Timmy, Timmo, as a gallant independent film producer, was being handed such a rotten deal. Armstrong was late-middle-aged, his own man. There were few rumours about him and none damaging to that central nervous system of professional integrity and effectiveness, widely admired as much for his occasional column in the quality newspapers as for his dominating television work. Just the target she needed.

Something like a sigh of pleasure crept into the wracked misfortune of her morning mind. She would get him. That could do the trick. She would nobble him. A diversionary tactic. She yawned at full stretch – her morning exercise. If only she had a personal fitness coach to visit her every morning. Some Aussie hunk.

The bottle of Sancerre was about a third full. The wine was warm but it did the business. Martha picked up her new see-thru black knickers and laughed aloud: they were in a twist.

III

Mark Armstrong was feeling indescribably content and fully aware of the danger of such an enviable state. He subscribed to the ancient gods. The older he became, the more sense their mythology made of his life, just as Romantic poetry made more sense of love. Now just tippling out of his sixth decade – could it be true? When did it happen? – Mark Armstrong was a pagan, a Scot, a democrat; intellectual but uncorrupted by elitism, wilful, butterhearted, about-to-be twice divorced, childless, hippo happy in his bath, and broke. In the still warm water he sang "Oh what a beautiful morning" practically in tune. Timing it well, Prue, his secretary, who came in three mornings a week (and he was pushed to afford even that), she of the easy, lean figure and of the consuming boyfriend collapsing in Venture Capital, put on the kettle in the "surprisingly tiny, really" kitchen. The kitchen was not out of proportion with the rest of the Bloomsbury flat. Prue was a touch embarrassed for him. Mark considered he was lucky to have landed up with quite so much.

9

The profound source of this inexpressible contentment was, he knew, hidden, out of reach of any analysis or memory he might have brought to it. It was a delicious euphoria, like the first gobfuls of glazed mountain air, like the first kiss after too long a parting, like the crystal glass of cheap champagne he had childishly allowed himself on this morning of a day of no formal work. The contentment made his almost tuneful song an anthem of joy. How could such a mood be held? Was that what gurus taught you? Was this what saints felt? Or Mozart? Or Galileo? "Oh what a beautiful day!" Or was this simply (*simply!*) a flood tide of anticipation? "Oh what a wonderful feeling!" An inkling of paradise.

Prue smiled as she slit the envelopes. One of his good mornings and goodness he needed one, she thought. Working far harder than anyone she knew, and the stresses, poor man, the problems, and the threats, nobody guessed. Prue was proud of him. Very good-looking too, she *had to admit* (a favourite phrase) in a "craggy, untidy, intelligent, amused way" (the memorised description had been in her weekly magazine). Prue had often pondered on the unfairness of nature which allowed men to age better than women: it was a recurrent point of conversation with her girlfriends in the wine bars of Fulham, and Mark was her prize, her personal example. She hummed along with his bathroom-booming melody.

Oh, just give me a moment or two more of this gliding feeling, total freedom, no past, no present, no pressure, Mark prayed.

The previous night's programme on Northern Ireland had been his best. It had snaked through the censors, it had nailed the IRA in a way he had aimed to do for years and it had made a nonsense of the government's more stubborn claims. Bagshaw, his departmental head, had left a negative message on his answering-machine requesting a meeting – in a bureau-speak tone of command, the prat. (Why did Bagshaw provoke the worst in him?) The reviews were generally good. Useful ammo.

His second divorce was now down the slipway. He had insisted on a gallant settlement, despite her reservations, and it had left him skint. But, he thought, she was probably as relieved as he was. The wounds were already healing, and perhaps in a year or two they would meet for a rueful lunch. It had not been a passionate marriage and it was not a lacerating split: there were no children.

He would see Rudolf Lukas, media mogul and husband of Jen, the love of Mark's life, with whom after lunch he would almost certainly enjoy complex, detailed and audacious sex. Lukas would offer him serious money to take part in a television franchise bid. Mark, in his irritation with Bagshaw and all the bureaucratic Bagshaws who now roosted in his television world, was more tempted than he ever dreamt he could be. And the day was full of other goodies.

There would be Nicholas his close friend – at a lunch which would reek with some of the freshest political and media gossip if they bowled up at the Garrick and joined the corner table or lingered in the bar. Cabinet-level insider-information would be on offer. Or, if Nicholas decided on the latest fashionable watering-hole, the chat would be more personal and more amusing. Mark was fashion-blind and a non-starter in what he considered was the foodie farce and Nicholas enjoyed taunting him. There was nothing like a semi-drunken lunch to set you up for an afternoon's intense sex, he thought. The only thing better was for the partner to be with you at the lunch, but Jen, alas, was pre-booked.

The grey bathwater was indisputably tepid, the last wisps of the euphoria fading into the light of an ordinary naked bulb – there was only the afterglow, but that would do, that was better than most days. He heaved himself out like a suction pad leaving an obstinate gripping surface and towelled himself down to the growling words of his favourite Big Bill Broonzy.

Breakfast and letters dispatched, he took his third cup of coffee and his first small cigar into the sitting-room and settled blissfully into the corner of the large sofa to indulge himself on the phone. First the strictly business. Then the postmortem with the producer – to include the reviews and other reactions. Mark passed on some of the pleasing messages he had found on his answering-machine. Dave, the producer, returned the ball with praise "from inside the building". The coolness and knuckle-rap from Bagshaw was thoroughly anticipated.

Dave had read in the morning gossips that Mark had been at a political pre-Christmas party, which had "starred Margaret Thatcher". Mark confirmed this and, answering Dave's eager question, said, "The odd thing was that you had to fight against feeling quite sorry for her. She looked so isolated and shorn, even, ridiculously, shorter – as if she had lost a few inches. No longer a power of the land, clout gone, authority gone, aura gone. The cabinet ministers there seemed to be edging away from her when once they would have pressed towards her. Perhaps they were just embarrassed but it was all a bit sickening."

Mark, in fact, had thought it a textbook example of the essential significance of the Office itself. All of Mrs Thatcher's real and vaunted strengths were of no account at all now that she was no longer Prime Minister but a rather dumpy backbencher in a burgundy two-piece suit. Mark would have been shy to say it, but he considered it a substantial tribute to democracy. He reassured Dave about Bagshaw's reservations, took a slug of cold coffee and steadied himself to return Fred's call.

"Any news on the Dorothy front?" Fred would not dissemble. He wanted Mark, whom he had known and tagged since university, to open a door for Dorothy, his sole child, in what he called the "Meeja". "None," said Mark, cringing with guilt – why? Why did Fred Nightingale, author of two slim glum volumes of poetry, lecturer in English and American Literature, put the pincers of guilt on him? Perhaps that's what old friends were for. "It's a bad time, Fred. BSB collapsing. All the ITV companies going in for redundancies. BBC in a dither. The recession. Slimming down for the franchises. But I'm trying."

"I'm engaged in a rather interesting piece on the Thames," said Fred, sweeping on, as he always did, into his own immediate concerns. "They've sent me a spurious book to review but the idea of Thames as source and symbol rather appeals. You know – Spenser's silken meadows, Defoe's cure for the plague – the river had a rather similar function in the Blitz, actually – Dickens' decay and death, Conrad's imperial longings, Eliot's waste – one wonders if it is possible to use the river today as source or symbol – and if not – what does that say about the state of our mythology? I'm thinking of Nietzsche here –'without a myth every culture loses its creative natural power'."

I'm thinking of Nietzsche here! Why did Fred not buy an away-day return, stand on Waterloo Bridge and work it out for himself? Mark thought, and then chided himself. Fred was a speaking encyclopaedia. That was his pitch. Fred's had been a life of the mind. And Dorothy, Mark's god-daughter, was a sweet unambitious young woman, blissfully enthralled by Greens, peace, anti-vivisection, rainforests, whales, dolphins, wild geese . . .

Abruptly, as usual, Fred rang off, and Prue brought him another mug of black, no sugar, instant. The euphoria was all but gone.

Nick – Sir Nicholas de Loit, MP – called to arrange the lunch. Drinks at the Garrick – "You must meet your critics – oh yes! *Not* a safe programme – and then move on smartly" – and lunch at The Ivy – "the boys from the Caprice have not tarted it up at all – very wise. I thought of Green's but I don't like feeding with my own kind. And the division bell is such a tug on the conscience." Mark rather liked the division bell in Green's, liked to see the MPs scuttle away from their Parker Bowles Olde English Tuck. He was impressed. But Nick was the arbiter. His restaurant guide in the heaviest of the glossies had for ten years been "a bible" in the reverent vocabulary of the foodies. Even now that he had abandoned it, he was received with undisguised ceremony by the best restaurateurs in the metropolis.

Mark failed to pick up the anxiety, even the desperation, in Nick's tone, and yet Nick put down the phone in his Albany flat still sweating from the fear of what he might do, the crime he might commit that afternoon, as his homosexuality, which had for years been comfortably enough closeted and recently unfussily acknowledged in quiet ways, found itself horribly possessed by an urgent, shameful lust. Mark must help him; Mark alone could and would.

Before ringing Jen, Mark, as he knew he would, heaved himself to the kitchen to take another glass of champagne. And one for Prue: rule of the house with drinks before ten.

Mark contemplated the next call with the deepest pleasure. Jen would be full of talk or tap him expertly for what he most wanted off his mind. The gale would prevent her going flying – he liked to think of her in the air, soaring over the Home Counties in the paths of the wartime Spitfires. What bored him in others intrigued him in her. Even the flying seemed more a mysterious act of desperation than the leisured affectation of a woman with too much time on her hands. He could not believe she still wanted him. Her dizzy wealth – her unique, understated, connoisseur's beauty and her acknowledged independence from her second husband, Rudolf Lukas, made her one of the most attractive women in London, in New York, or in any city she decided to visit. She was always visiting.

More than twenty years before, when Jen was a wild creature just turned adult, orphaned in London and landed up in television, more passionate for the moment and more forgetful of anything previous to the moment than anyone he had known, she and Mark had burned through an obsessive, outrageous affair which she had ended abruptly by disappearing to America where a year or so later her great reputation had begun. Mark now knew that he had never recovered from her departure and that this was a wholly unexpected and undeserved second chance.

She was back in London and, the miracle of his life, back with him.

He lifted the phone affectionately and tapped out the seven singing numbers. He hummed as he waited, happier, he knew, and luckier, than he had any right to expect. Oh what a beautiful day.

IV

Jake was excited and proprietorial. "Nowhere in the world," he boasted, "is there anything like this. No way." His arm swept magisterially around Leicester Square and solemnly he recited the names: "The Empire, the Odeon West End, the other Odeon with the tower on it, the Empire plus Dancing, the Prince Charles up the side street there . . ." Harry fought to overcome the shivering but he too was impressed and very cautiously warmed by Jake's good humour.

Men were drilling to lay new paving stones. A barricade of large boards, a wall of hoarding, was painted with cowboys and old movie stars, bigger than lifesize and unrecognisable. Less than two weeks to Christmas and mid-morning shoppers passed through with parcels and holly in plastic bags.

But the Square was a night place. Cold mornings found it bare. Even the winos had retreated underground to the Gentlemen's, where Jake had, as usual, been outraged at the ten pence entrance charge and the turnstile. "What if you're caught short and broke?" (He had lifted Harry over.) Standing around the washbasin with their green cans of lager, the winos had talked loudly, without any apparent communication – "Five times thirty that's a hundred and fifty pounds – right? Am I right?" This was repeated at the same level of aggression and met not with a response but with equally monotonous, adamant assertions. The policy, the fashion for releasing the mentally unwell had put on the streets a diaspora of sick people. Harry had scented violence and was glad to have Jake push him back through the turnstile and up into the cold, gusty Square. The wind was less angry than in the North but still bitter, shaking the litter along the pavements.

"This is it," said Jake. He had led Harry to a corner building. The three windows on the ground floor had Amusements, Amusements, Amusements glitteringly painted on to the glass. "This is class." Harry caught the awe in Jake's tone and looked up. Jake

14

was gazing up at the words blocked out in yellow metal above the tall windows. "Crystal Rooms," he read out. "Gold. Nowhere like this anyplace – no argument." Jake was someone stepping into his kingdom.

It was so warm that for a second or two Harry almost swooned. Jake flashily changed a ten-pound note in the machine. The place was almost empty and the machines neither clanked nor ground as they did in the tinny amusement arcade of Harry's home town, they murmured: the sound of luxury. Yet he spotted some of his favourites – Space Invaders, Hotshots, World Cup, OT Zone, Carrier Airway, Pitstop – but in this room they were different. The walls were striped with mirrors, the floor was wall-to-wall carpeted and, most wonderful of all, were the chandeliers.

There were seven: six with twelve lights on – arranged in tiers – these six reflected and doubled in the mirrors. The lights on the seventh and largest chandelier were hard to count – one hidden behind the other – but he got there: four lights on the top tier, ten below and ten again below that. The lights were in cups, a bit like tulips opening out, Harry thought, as he concentrated fiercely, his sense of privilege clutched at with the grip of drowning fingers. These cups were cloudy and he knew that crystal was supposed to be clear, but the place was so obviously royal that he had no doubt there was one crystal which was especially expensively clouded and this was it. Never in his life had he been in such an opulent and beautiful room; even the ululation of the machines was not yet a temptation as he shivered out of his stiff coldness and gazed at the chandeliers.

Scarcely aware of what was happening, he found himself ushered out and back on the street with Jake, who was rattled. A man wearing a black bow tie stood at the door. "Got to be eighteen. Sorry son. We don't make the laws. More than my job's worth. Trocadero, down the Circus, just keep going." He pointed and disappeared. Jake slapped the hard flat of his palm on the back of Harry's head. It hurt but Harry understood. It was for not being eighteen and humiliating Jake in London. "I'll be back," Jake said, menacingly, though to himself, and he repeated it louder, defiantly, as they passed what seemed to be a café devoted solely to ice-cream.

They walked in silence, Harry absorbed in the vision of the crystal chandeliers, Jake glancing nervously at the boy. As if to emphasise a sudden decision, Jake threw his arm around Harry's shoulder in a manly fashion and said, "You're OK, Harry. You're

15

like me. You're OK." The economy of words carried what appeared to be a genuine strength of affection. Harry knew that he ought to be wary, even distrustful, but he was so starved that he looked up gratefully.

Entwined, then, in the common mood of young blades on the town, they turned into the Trocadero, walked past the parade which included, Harry noticed rapidly, a sweet shop where you could *serve yourself*, and a shop with toys where he could get something for Mary, up the escalator which led to the Guinness World of Records and doubled back from that to Funland Luna Park.

The noise was the crowded clanking of boy toy public technology. The Crystal Rooms were a dream apart but here was the usable stuff. All the machines he had ever seen, more than he had ever imagined, lights flashing on the low ceiling, from the walls, from the floor, blue, red, white, strobing, chrome glittering, transparent plastic lit up with neon, and, unbelievably, a whole dodgem car track in the middle of the room on the upstairs floor of a building! Jake gave him five pound coins in a neat little stack. Harry was overwhelmed and waited for them to be snatched back, but Jake indicated one of the most complicated machines – a pound a go – and Harry got into it.

He leant back in the seat and, with two levers, piloted the spacecraft through enemy lines, manoeuvring and firing as the seat dipped. The whole machine swirled and danced, it was real *Star Wars*, not just a game on a machine, just like Luke at the controls. It stopped, but Jake reached forward and put a pound of his own money in the slot, pointed to Harry's vast score – 195,700 with a 298 energy bonus – gave him the thumbs up and once more Harry drove through the fantasy, thrilled to his heart. And yet again Jake paid, a third turn, Harry's reserve all gone, Jake's goodness unquestionable, and he nodded as, the second before it began, Jake gestured down the room to the TOILETS sign, pointed laughingly at his flies, and grimaced comically before he walked away.

Harry carefully considered a fourth go, but there were so many other treats. He walked past a pair of young girls who were hitting squawking rubber crocodiles on the head with a mallet and came to an airplane cockpit. He waited his turn, went in, closed the door behind him, entered his pound and saw before him what the voice called "The Majestic City of London". He pulled at the wheel and the plane took off. He was climbing, he banked, he climbed higher. It was night and he saw the stars sharper, bigger, than he had ever seen them and the plane soared faster than twice the speed of sound, headed for New York. Harry was captured in his dreams.

At first he was not surprised that he could not find Jake. He drifted, the three pound coins a talisman in his hand, his own small stash still wrapped in the handkerchief in his jeans pocket, somehow not caring to linger and spend. He was not in the Gents, although Harry hung about in case he was in a cubicle. Not around the dodgems. Not along the big-money fruit-machines. Harry's throat tightened and ached a little. Although the Funland Luna Park was hot, there was a cold seepage of sweat on his brow and clamminess in his stomach. He did not drift but began to half-stumble, half-trot. He went out and looked up and down the escalators. No Jake. Convinced that Jake had suddenly returned to Funland and would be waiting for him beside that first machine, he rushed back inside and crunched into a Japanese man who smiled and bowed. Jake was not there. Again he was not in the Gents. The dodgems. The change centre. Harry ran down the escalator to the Parade. Jake must have gone shopping. Not there. Not there in the café. Harry was breathing fast and with difficulty. The three pound coins were a nugget of hope, a prayer in his sweating palm. Back to Funland. Not there.

Not there.

And then Harry realised. Of course! Jake would surely have gone back to the Crystal Rooms. He said he'd go back to the Crystal Rooms. Crying with relief, Harry went out into the cold and ran, pounded along the pavement, did not see a red light and ignored the honking car, past the Kentucky Fried Chicken and the Swiss Bells he had tried to count, past the Empire and the ice-cream café to the golden letters which said CRYSTAL ROOMS, where Jake must be, will be, has to be, please, oh please.

V

About half an hour later, Mark walked through Leicester Square on his way to Maugham's Hotel where Rudolf had set up a temporary HQ. Mark was still stinging with pleasure at Jen's description of a scandal which could well break at her very exclusive charity lunch and relishing her barefisted description of Martha Potter whom she had known many years ago. He put to the back

of his mind the telephone call from New Scotland Yard and managed to keep in touch with that rare rainbow mood of the morning.
Outside an ice-cream parlour he saw a huddled, thin-faced boy on
his hunkers eating an ice-cream and staring intently at the rather
posh amusement place. Something about the boy made Mark want
to flick him a coin but he desisted. The ice-cream betokened no
poverty. There would be plenty of other more deserving cases as
he walked through the day. He felt cold. He wished he had worn
a coat: perhaps the boy's ice-cream triggered it off, more likely
the wind roaring meanly across the Square.

And so Mark Armstrong entered the day: a white, overprivi-
leged, overweight, late-middle-aged Englishman – with, according
to Fred, no symbolic significance on a world stage which now
belonged to women, blacks, Muslims and former members of the
Soviet Empire – sometimes gently satirised as one of the chattering
classes, trying to concentrate on Rudolf and the franchise bids, his
future, the desperation in Northern Ireland, the situation in the
Gulf, a tone he had not quite resolved in Nick's call; but dreaming
only of Jen.

Another man had his eyes on the boy with the ice-cream and
his mind on the party he had promised to arrange that afternoon
in a discreet hotel off Oxford Street for a few distinguished and
monied men of particular tastes.

Harry knew it was hopeless but the crying inside had left him
feeling weak and he could not move from the Crystal Rooms,
trapped in the Square.

Two

L ONDON was choking on its pre-Christmas traffic but, by walking, Mark arrived at Maugham's Hotel in Mayfair punctually at eleven. Half an hour, Rudolf's secretary had warned, would be quite enough time for what she called "this preliminary encounter". Her self-importance had amused and relaxed Mark. It was a preliminary encounter which might better have been avoided. The deciding factor had been curiosity. Its object beckoned him into a large drawing-room in the Victoria Suite, waving a fanciful silver pot of coffee, offering that or nothing. At a meeting with Rudolf Lukas you drank what Rudolf drank or you went thirsty. Noting that, Mark again was amused and thought he might even enjoy the "encounter".

Great issues surfaced immediately. Rudolf considered small talk to be the indicator of small minds.

"There will certainly be a war in the Gulf," he announced apropos of nothing at all. Mark glanced around to see if there were a drinks cabinet. He was on a roll. It was nowhere to be seen. "The Brits will enjoy that. Take their minds off things like the economy which they don't understand. They like wars. Best army in the world nowadays. Keep it simple. It's what they're good at. You thrive in wars. When the old Brits can't find real wars, the young Brits invent them at soccer games or in those street marches which turn into battles with the police. Or they just riot for the hell of it."

Much against his preconceived judgement, Mark found that he liked Rudolf. Liked his raunchy growl, liked the bulk of him which avoided fat, the coarse pinkish face, restless, fast on the smile with the shark teeth, liked the appearance of the English Gieves Hawkes gentleman, muted grey double-breasted pinstripe, over-polished brogues, lightly patterned blue and red silk tie, modestly mono-grammed gold cuff-links, which effectively covered up the con-flicting stories of his origins and early days.

Rudolf Lukas was a self-made man highly pleased with his creation.

Money was suddenly on the agenda.

"Everything's too expensive. Social systems are too expensive. Schooling, public transportation, old age is too expensive. Educat-ing the young, feeding the world, war, a real war not a Third World canter, that's too expensive. And of course debt is ridiculously expensive! We need a new sort of money for the third millennium."

For his part, Rudolf had done his best to amass it in the second. He was one of the most successful of the new moneyed fliers who had soared up through the Sixties, Seventies and Eighties dazzling the world with their skills. The happy few. How did they do it? How had they come by this golden knowledge as magical as the gift to Midas? In America, in Europe, in Japan, in Australasia, see how they burst through the antique gravity of the accepted finan-cial atmosphere and found a space of their own. And then, as sure as retribution, one by one they were burnt and melted down and over the past few years had plummeted back to earth, screaming with excuses and re-gearings as they hit the ground. But Rudolf would not be grounded. "My Mogul", as Jen called him, was too granite for that. All had seemed lost. He had become a famous, buoyant millionaire, yet here he was, cocky, bright-eyed, muscled with energy. The debt was soundly recon-structed; the banks had obliged yet again; heavy new investment had been made in computer technology – his core business. Where Mark would have been dizzy or in despair, Rudolf was full of bite. The one-to-one meeting was Rudolf's great skill: this sort of encounter was his drama. He was the main player and nothing could throw him.

Still, Mark thought, even in these times it is a touch odd to be courted by the husband of the woman you will make love to after lunch. Mark wished he could find a way to tell him – Jen would not mind, he was sure. Perhaps, though, it would come better from her. Perhaps Rudolf knew. Just possibly. That thought partly excused his duplicity, which he saw as a failing.

The phone provided the next item on Rudolf's agenda. "It's

Alfreda," Rudolf said, assuming that the name alone was sufficient excuse and explanation for the interruption to their vital "preliminary encounter". His open affair with Lady Alfreda Kennersley clearly elated him. It was his first venture into the heartland of London social and snob life. So far, it was a ravishing new toy. Alfreda was putting together the final list for the evening's dinner-party which would follow one of her famous six until eight At Homes for grateful metropolitan opinion formers.

While he was on the phone, Rudolf alternately picked his teeth with an Asprey's gold toothpick and pawed his groin, gleefully all the while and dangerously swinging on the genuine Chippendale chair, threatening its ancient joints. Mark got up to hunt for the drinks, disguising this quest by pretending to gaze at the tasteful modern paintings which decorated the walls. Names were launched across the room like announcements from a tannoy on a railway station. "Nureyev, Gore Vidal, Princess Margaret" – Mark ambled over to the large Victorian chiffonnier and tugged open the door. Crockery for the dining-room and crystal glasses. He took out a tumbler – "the Douros, the Waldegraves – who? Oh yes. Good" – found the fridge behind a low-slung cabinet and extracted a small bottle of champagne. It was one of those with a screw top but it would be serviceable. He waved it at Rudolf, who waved back, overcome by good humour. Mark poured out most of it into his tumbler – "Lucian Freud – *got* one! – And her! Oh! Great! Great legs! OK. OK? You are. Yes." He put down the phone indulgently. "Know Alfreda?" Mark shook his head. "She likes all this social shit."

"Do you?"

"Zoo time," Rudolf answered and the shark's teeth clashed in the "boyish grin" so often referred to by the press. "I expect you're a busy man, Mark," said Rudolf, instantly serious. "Let's cut the niceties. I want a British television station. Now's the time to get it. You're the man to get it for me. Here's how we do it."

Mark took a swig and set down his glass.

Rudolf leant forward and delivered a concise, lucid briefing, very like the great battle briefings Mark had heard about during his time in the army. Rudolf, a few years older than Mark, had fought in World War II with conspicuous gallantry and, as he went over ground Mark knew so well, he could imagine the glee this piratical figure would have taken in zapping the enemy.

It was franchise time in the UK and outsiders could bid for existing commercial television companies, ousting the present occupants, and, in one move, give themselves a prime stake in British, European and, if they managed things well, world television. Rudolf had long been thought of as a prime predator, unencumbered as he was by the ownership of national newspapers which was legally blocking one or two of his financial peers. He was going for one of the biggest companies of all and spun Mark visions of Empire.

"I've got my chairman." Rudolf mentioned a name which surprised Mark – he had thought the man too deeply snug in his Establishment foxhole to be teased out. "I've got my chief executive." Another name well known to Mark but not such a surprise. Neither man had been rumoured. Mark was impressed that Rudolf took it for granted that he would be discreet. "But I need a man who can impress the arse off the creative types – somebody who *is* the business – somebody who everybody knows can pick up the phone and talk to the best writers and actors and comedians and all the stars and they'll listen and come along for the ride. For the fun of it. It's got to be fun, Mark, hasn't it? Or, what the hell? You could do that. You're my man."

Mark had to resist the almost physical impulse to lean forward and grasp Rudolf by the hand, swear then and there to follow him into battle. He had badly underestimated the full force of charm exercised by Rudolf Lukas, his powerful ability to seduce. He could see now why Jen had married him.

Yet what did the man know or care? Would he ever have seen one of Mark's programmes or, if he had seen it, understood why it was there? Rudolf's intense confidentiality had an aphrodisiac quality which teased out conceit. Underneath the flagrant temptation was mere flattery. Mark told himself that he was being head-hunted to plug a gap in Rudolf's master plan. If he turned it down – someone else would serve just as well. It was not man-to-man however much it looked like that. It was nothing personal.

"What sort of programme mix would you tolerate?"

"That's up to the chairman, the chief executive and yourself. Your shout, I would guess."

"What if I wanted a more upmarket, a less popular, mix than they have now?"

"As long as we win. As long as your mix will deliver. I'm not fannying around but I'm not Santa Claus either."

"If you agreed a programme mix and then interfered I'd resign."

"If you produced a mix that bombed you'd be fired."

Mark desisted from taking a sip of champagne much as he

wanted one. He was rather critical of himself for enjoying the meeting so much.

"This is an entertaining game of ping-pong, Mr Lukas —"

"Rudolf."

"— but what guarantees am I able to give the people I invite in? British television has sometimes been able to claim the best writers and directors and journalists and actors because there have been implicit guarantees of security for adult programme-making. By adult I don't mean X-rated."

"Mark. Why did you have to say that?"

Mark smiled, unimpressed by Rudolf's reproach. For Rudolf, reproach was just another arrow in the quiver.

"I would need a three-year written guarantee for myself and about — up to a dozen programme people."

"Done. Subject to the chairman et cetera."

"I'd want to talk to him, of course. And —"

"The chief exec. The money men. Your lawyer. Our lawyers. Accountants. Done. Money is not a problem."

"What do *you* get out of it?"

Rudolf hesitated and Mark was again tempted to believe that something close to the truth was on the way. When it came he was both surprised and impressed. Like others of his liberal, non-scientific, non-economic, verging on unworldly education, Mark was vulnerable to the mathematics and politics of high finance. This was the dazzling thread Rudolf spun. Current media barons were merely the torchbearers lighting Rudolf's inevitable progress before him and Mark was somehow at the heart of it. Once more Mark had the sensation that he was being physically drawn towards this smiling predatory man.

The situation was not complicated. Mark was almost sixty, with most awards that British television could give. He was also broke; a man who had rather waywardly enjoyed a much-acclaimed television career with little material reward, so far resisting offers to climb the executive greasy pole. Yet, as a recent *Independent on Sunday* piece had said, "his influence among his peers is considerable; his contribution to hard-edged political and investigative television on a par with the very best. His work in Ireland alone is widely acknowledged to be a serious contribution. He has kept his independence and that has guarded his integrity."

Rudolf offered a new world, wealth, and the chance to continue and consolidate Mark's own work through others. There would be uncertainty and it would be a gamble, but what was really going on was the last lap of his life. What was the power of his rediscovered love for Jen? What must he achieve now that she had come back? Rudolf and Rudolf's offer could be central to that.

"By next Monday if you can," said Rudolf, suddenly catapulting out of his chair.

"Monday," Mark repeated, and nodded. The men shook hands.

"Jen told me about you," Rudolf said, while holding Mark's rather slim hand in his bear-paw. "Used to work with you."

"Long time ago," said Mark, shovelling the words up a dry throat.

"Great girl."

"Great girl," Mark laughed. *Girl?* Rudolf squeezed Mark's hand very hard and bared the large teeth. The grin was not boyish, Mark thought. It was the camouflaged sign of the happy killer. Rudolf Lukas was not a nice man at all.

Leaving Maugham's, Mark strolled into Piccadilly and across the West End rather more slowly and certainly more thoughtfully than he had done earlier. Piccadilly Circus, once nominated the centre of the British Empire, of all that pinkish-red which had blurred the spinning schoolroom globes of Mark's youth, was still seized up with traffic. He weaved between the cars, one of many pedestrians tauntingly leaving the pavements to flaunt their freedom. Next to Eros a baglady stared into the cloud-scuttling sky and ranted words of hate.

II

"Go swim with dolphins," said Cally, "believe me."

"Any old dolphin?"

"Better if it's wild, you know, not zooed up or aquariumised. But they can do it also. Just takes longer."

"Why dolphins?"

"I read about it. I'll send you the cutting. They can cure cancer. How? I'll tell you how. They are the most intelligent beings on the planet and they *know*. OK? They *know*."

"Darling, are you a little stoned, a little drunk or just tired? It *is* two in the morning over there, isn't it?"

"My best time, Jen, you know that."

"I do."

"You are my best friend, Jen, you know that?"

24

"I do. And you are mine too, darling. You know *that*."

It was crucially important to Cally that she heard Jen assert that regularly. A few months earlier, Cally had headed for the West Coast and embraced all the psycho-babble as if it had been invented yesterday just for her. She was taking classes in a multitude of disciplines and when she was good and ready she was going to go for it! Jen phoned her every day. Cally was her best friend. Until Mark's recent re-emergence, her only friend. Occasionally this struck Jen as a bleak reflection on her own character, too much in love with solitude. She imagined Cally now, marooned in L.A., the black fringe heavy on her brow, the large-boned figure crammed into a designer dress that somehow didn't . . .

"Your turn," said Cally. "London working out? Yet? Hold on. Lemme getta . . . I'll just be a minute . . . don't go away . . ."

This was a regular ploy. Was Cally lighting up, off to the loo, or just testing? Jen waited. She stretched out on the spartan bed she preferred, hunched the telephone between her shoulder and her ear and prepared to speak as in a confessional. Conversations with Cally were very useful, even refreshing at times. Sometimes she felt a pulse of guilt that helping Cally should benefit her, herself, so much. For some time, Cally had been her sole confidante. Even so, Jen was careful: some things she told no one.

Jen felt deeply relaxed. Her masseur had made her spine crackle and his remorseless Aussie hands had left her muscles satiated. He had unsinkable pretensions to Art — "You are my greatest creation," he said. "You are my David. I am the wave, you are the surfer." Her Anglo-Saxon riposte had no effect on this antipodean cultural nightmare. But she was in fine shape — he was a good coach — and the mild December climate of London seemed to tone her skin perfectly; just as the subtle northern light brought out the shades of subdued blond and red in her hair and reflected the mesmerising grey purity of her eyes. After lunch there would be sex with Mark. She could pretend that the twenty years since she had fled to New York had never happened.

In New York, Jen had made a remarkable reputation on television. After that — the marriage to Robert Butterfield Junior, eccentric heir to an oil empire with houses everywhere — Dallas, Paris, the Pacific Atoll and Tuscany . . . She had passed through London and stayed the occasional weekend at a stately pile, but this was the first time in more than twenty years that she had taken it on again. In truth she was looking for refuge. Mark was the first surprise. Her affection for the city itself the second. She discovered charms she had overlooked or taken for granted before. It was with these that in the dead hours she regaled Cally, curled up in Los Angeles.

Most of all Jen loved the obvious things that she had scarcely noticed in her youthful conquest. The great indulgence of parks dominating the centre of the city – sometimes she walked from Westminster through St James's Park, Green Park and Hyde Park to Holland Park just to relish the doing of it. She described other parks and the squares and then the commons and heaths, all landscaped intelligently, as much a pleasure for the mind as for the limbs. She loved the steady mix of a city that London still was. Paris, everybody's favourite, was becoming a cultural theme park; New York, which had its own song and would never be relinquished by Jen, whose greatest triumphs had been there, was increasingly a city where you were turned off or warned off; Tokyo, Rome, nowhere had the combination of money, power, the Horseguards, the galleries in Cork Street, the theatre, the street markets, and still remain a place you could, as Jen did, walk around feeling safe, along the Thames, through the cream-sculpted squares of Pimlico and Kensington, in and out the gamey alleyways of Covent Garden and Soho.

Cally came back on the phone, as usual with a question which denied that she had left her post for whatever fix.

"You still go out walking alone? Like *on your own?*"

"Yes."

"No gun?"

"No gun. Nobody carries them over here."

"Weird."

Cally was definitely on something, but Jen let it slide. If you could not turn the occasional blind eye at two-thirty a.m. Pacific Time and eight thousand miles away, what sort of surrogate mother were you?

"You mean it's like Disneyland?"

"No. No. It can be dirty. Litter and the traffic and –"

"Let me get this right. You walk alone, right? On your own, OK? How long, three months you been there – NOT ONE INCIDENT? Come *on!*"

"OK. One."

"Ha!"

"But it wasn't . . ."

"No! The truth. Lemme have it."

Jen knew that it would be a disappointment but she did her

26

best. This was the part of the ritual where she went into free flow and Cally said "Uh" or "Uh, uh" every so often. Nevertheless, as she was talking, she wondered why Cally did not switch on the horror movie channel for a much better frisson.

It had happened in the second week of her return to London. She was staying at the Savoy while her house was being revamped and, on a perfect early evening in September, decided to walk across Waterloo Bridge to meet Mark who was taking her to the National Theatre. The river flowed smoothly, ripe under the sun now lowering itself into position for the full blood Turner sunset over the Thames. River, country, life, all was well. The Houses of Parliament were glowing; to the east the dome of St Paul's soared miraculously, still resisting the concrete siege towers which threatened it. An unusually long hot summer and the aftermath of a warm autumn had given the Brits an infusion of tranquillity and they drifted across the bridge most amiably, some still dressed in holiday clothes, holding on to the last.

"Any change?"

Jen was startled. She had scarcely noticed the youth sitting on the wall halfway down the steps leading from the bridge to the theatre. There was an aggressive tone which triggered her resistance. Then she remembered that she had no cash. Merely a few ten-pound notes and that was out of the question: too showy, disproportionate, and the youth looked neither gaunt nor cowed.

"I'm sorry. I've no change."

"Bastard!"

Jen had stopped and faced up.

"Bastard! Rich bastard! Shit!"

Jen looked more closely and saw that the youth was a young woman, a girl. Eighteen? Nineteen? She would have been quite striking had the hair been washed, the face drained of its venom. Jen herself had arrived in London at about that age.

"Where does this hatred come from?" As soon as she uttered it, Jen was aware of the provocation the stilted question could cause, but she stood her ground as her enquiry set off a further jet of obscenities.

Cally's "Uh, uh" intensified. "So you walked away?"

"No. For some reason I opened my purse and pulled out the notes, the money I was carrying."

"Oh my God!"

"She lurched for it. I was going to – I *think* I was going to peel off a single one of the notes but she grabbed them all."

"Oh my God!"

"And she shouted, 'You rich bitch! You rich bitch!'."

"She was a dangerous person, Jen."

"Then she ran away."

"You were lucky."

"I was furious with myself."

"What did you do?"

"Nothing."

Cally pressed her to go over it again, which Jen did, increasingly puzzled and angry that she had simply watched the girl leap down the steps towards the river and disappear into the concrete maze.

After Cally had rung off, the events of that evening continued to play on her mind. "She had an out-of-town accent," Jen told Mark, as she retailed the experience in the interval, "not unlike my own when I first landed here."

"We could never quite place yours," Mark said.

"I took good care of that."

After the play Jen had wanted to go and hunt for the girl in Cardboard City, just behind the National Theatre, next to the biggest complex of cultural buildings in the world, across the river from the Mother of Parliaments and, ponderous irony, more than a stroll to the City of London, spinner of fabled wealth . . . Under the Waterloo Bridge roundabout was a last refuge for the homeless, a shanty-town pummelled by juggernauts.

"It's a sad place," said Mark. "And a dangerous place. Not a place for sightseers."

Jen had blushed. "Don't go to Harlem in diamonds and pearls?"

"Something like that," Mark had said, and she nodded.

"I'm getting fat," Jen said. "Getting dumb."

As if to make a point of not rubbing it in, Mark walked across the bridge with her. Arm-in-arm, they strolled down the Strand taking the long route to the small restaurant in Soho where he had booked for dinner. Jen had noticed the young people begging and the old people huddled in misery. In Mark's company, though he said nothing, she felt it involved her.

They had stopped just before Charing Cross Station as an old woman had laid and re-laid newspapers, muttering aloud all the time. No arrangement, it seemed, would satisfy her. All the while she muttered, the words barely distinguishable. Her face was patched in scarlet, the lips blubbery as if turned inside out. Jen had been hypnotised and the woman had begun to direct her ravings at her. On top of several layers she wore a lilac coat styled long ago. "What a lovely colour," Jen found herself saying.

As part of the ritual, the phone rang once more.

"Did you see her again?" Cally asked. "The girl. The thief."

"No."

"Did you *look*? Real hard look, I mean. C'mon, Jen."

"No."

"She threaten you?"

"She certainly spoke in a threatening manner."

"Yeah, yeah, but I mean *threaten*. Like – in there. I'm pointing to my brain."

"Perhaps she did. Clever old you. Rather tame by L.A. standards, I'm afraid."

"Don't let it worry you," said Cally. "I'm tired now. Remember the dolphins, OK?" The conversation was over.

The dolphins were Cally's solution to a "problem" which Jen had been unwise enough to hint at some time ago. That was the danger of letting Cally dictate the confessional terms of their conversations; and yet Jen realised that now and then she had to, or resentment would silt up their relationship. The "problem" was her primary reason for settling in England, although as yet she had made no move to solve it. She lay perfectly still, breathing deeply, holding her breath, breathing out slowly. Perhaps it was no bad thing for Cally to know that she too had a problem. And perhaps dolphins *were* the cure.

She snapped herself upright, dressed briskly in the minimalist Art Deco bedroom, and spent the next hour on the phone – first to Rudolf, who amused her – unwittingly – with his description of Lady Alfreda and her social cavortings, then to accountants and brokers in London – New York and Dallas would be contacted at the end of the afternoon.

The wealth of Mrs Lukas (her second marriage), still better known as "the tragic widow, Mrs Butterfield Jnr.", was a subject of gossip and concern in all the magazine pages which gnawed at people with money. Jen never gave interviews. She had been on the fringe of the list of the world's twenty richest women for the last two years (she would pay to be excluded). Her initial independent fortune had been zero. Her earnings in television in New York, startling by ordinary standards, were piffling by the standards of the seriously rich. The Butterfield marriage and the tragedy that followed had left her heir to a substantial fortune but thereafter it had been consolidated by her own luck and skills.

Two major decisions had sent her into that revered, moneyed stratosphere – both questioned heavily at the time, the latter still regarded as very dubious. She had sold out all the Butterfield holdings in oil at what proved to be precisely the right time; and, through a personal contact with the fastest trader on the junk bond track, it was estimated she had at the very least quadrupled that fortune in a wild gamble. Recently her "personal contact" had appeared in a much publicised fraud case: another Eighties Icarus. But Jen had sold out some months before. Now, with the best advice, she played the world's money markets and the cash grew somewhere in the region of half a million a day.

These daily rounds on the telephone were her real society. She had made no friends among the rich. Mark's funny, loving call was all the personal contact she needed at present. Afterwards, as the weather was against flying, she went to the Vanderbilt for an hour's tennis, where she was lucky to find her new (strictly tennis) acquaintance, a leggy and taciturn English aristo, who was about the same standard as she was. The two women enjoyed a real game after half-an-hour's grind of professional coaching.

Lunch was to be her second attendance at the committee which was arranging a charity function to benefit Cardboard City. She had sought it out and tried to give a sum of money only. But the committee would have its day. Jen was *selected* to join and given to understand that this opportunity to give her time, money, energy and public commitment to the cause was a privilege. She had no wish to join. She had avoided all clubs and cliques, all groupings and select orders. She was the cat who walked alone. But the obscenities of the young girl under the bridge and the memories of the old woman making a home of newspapers had persuaded her. And if she disliked it, she told herself, she would put down more money and leave without any further explanation.

The first meeting had been more intriguing than she had anticipated – because of the people, as Mark had forecast. But she was not looking forward to this second round. They met in a house in Royal Avenue, Chelsea. There was a real lunch, not lettuce as would have been the menu in the States. At least four of the ladies were in their sixties, admitted it cheerfully, were comfortably stout, a little jowly and not unduly worried by it. They drank. One was a parrot-nosed marchioness of ancient Highland lineage – who had taken a great liking to Jen – and whose chief preoccupation was breeding and painting falcons, out of which, through

30

browbeating her friends and mercilessly exploiting her title, she made what she called "an honest penny". She, like Jen and one other, could have signed a cheque for the full amount targeted by the charity without a blink. She was given to imperious pronouncements. "Jews and Muslims give easily," she had said at Jen's first meeting, "Christians have to be tortured into it." Another was the retired Mistress of a Cambridge college, "wildly intellectual" according to the marchioness, who teased her slyly. Another the wife of a newly-knighted businessman whose business – she predicted hysterically – would fold spectacularly if the interest rates stayed as high as they were for one month longer. Her chainsmoking was not objected to: in New York, Jen thought, it would have been regarded as socially outrageous. They would have called the health department, alerted the fire department and contacted the gossip columns. There was the reconstructed wife of a retailing baron, now a Conservative, elected to the Lords by the Labour Party and lost in a jousting scrum of teasing Tory peers; the hostess, a hugely successful crime novelist with a policing conscience; a secretary-organiser; and Jen. The task would be to organise a gala evening for Cardboard City at Covent Garden which would raise between £100,000 and £150,000, to acquire temporary homes. Jen had enjoyed the mixture of sincerity and hypocrisy, the purely social and the social conscience, the Lady Bountiful and the hard-nosed modern businesswoman, the spread of good charitable feeling, the sense of society, the whole glorious shambollocks of it all, as she called it privately. But once, she thought, would prove enough. This second appearance was for London manners.

She put on her Burberry. That hit the tone. And sensible shoes. She told the chauffeur she would be down in three minutes. Remembering the dolphins, she smiled and began to hum. Perhaps London *would* be home. Perhaps Mark *was* the solution. Perhaps the fear would be met at last. Perhaps the sex would melt it down.

III

"'Ere! You. Quick!" Harry turned to see a boy not much above his own size but somehow elegant and fashionable, in a knowing way, outside Harry's experience. "Quick!" the boy repeated, and added, dramatically, "The pigs!" Harry did not move. "The

31

Ole Bill!'' The odd boy pointed at two policemen strolling across Leicester Square towards the Crystal Rooms. "Cops!"

Harry scrambled upright and ran after the fast-retreating stranger. They came into a small square which was another world: Chinese writing above the shops, Chinese shoppers, an Oriental pavement congestion. Harry passed a shop out of whose window, hung with a score of bright brown varnished ducks, came such a strong waft of heat and tastiness that he wanted to stay there and feed on it but the older boy hurried him along, down through Gerrard Street and into Wardour Street where he stopped, looked around with exaggerated circumspection and pulled out a cigarette.

"Close fing," he said, careful of a Cockney accent which Harry suspected to be fake, although he was too confused to be able to identify why. "Use 'ese?"

Harry shook his head. He tried to memorise the way back to the Crystal Rooms.

"Mine's Doug."

"Harry."

"Nu te Lunnen?"

"Yes."

"From ve Norf? Yeh?"

Harry nodded, unable to enter into a conversation, pains in the chest, breath short. The threat of the police had lifted the scab which had begun to form on his panic.

"Hello, young fella."

"Deuce!" Doug gratefully acknowledged the arrival of a man who seemed to Harry to be about Jake's age. Although it was still morning, Harry thought this man Deuce was dressed for a Saturday night out – glossy black shoes with a silver chain across them, a sharp grey suit, white shirt, tie and a scarf. His nails, Harry noticed, were gleaming clean. On the little finger of his left hand was a ring, like Jake's but much golder and heavier-looking. A neat moustache gave him a rather sinister look, Harry thought.

The wind scuffled along the street, bitterly attacking ungloved hands, chapping cheeks, a warning wind – but Harry was too numb to feel it.

"I bin lookin' at you," the man said and Harry's confusion deepened. "Down there. Outside that . . ."

"Crystal Rooms." It was the first time Harry had said the words.

32

They gave him comfort but also threatened to make him cry.

"Was you waitin' for that . . . ?" Deuce paused, seeking, it seemed to Harry, to repair a temporary forgetfulness.

"Jake." Harry checked a sob.

"Right. He was, correct me, about . . ." The man raised his hands expressively.

"Yes," said Harry, "your height."

"That's right! And hair . . ."

"Black," Harry nodded, helpfully.

"That's the customer. From the North. Right?"

"Yes," Harry said, his voice almost pleading for Jake, whom he knew had tried to do him harm. "That's him."

"He come to me. Didn't he, Doug?"

"Yeah." Doug pulled on his cigarette and coughed. Was the cough also a fake? Again Harry buried the suspicion but caught the eagerness to please in Doug's manner, which in some way made him feel both equal and uneasy.

"He says, 'Keep your eye out'. Right, Doug?"

"Right."

"'There's this boy', he says. Then he describes yourself – just as you are standing there. Doug?"

"To a 'T'," Doug confirmed. He's afraid, Harry sensed. Afraid he'll be struck. But Doug's presence was secondary now. Deuce was the salvation. Deuce would decide his future.

"He says –" Deuce reached out, Doug passed him the cigarette, Deuce took a short puff and handed it back. "I'm giving them up," he grimaced. "He says keep an eye out for that boy and tell him . . ." here the man hesitated, as if straining to recollect the precise message. Then he nodded, satisfied that he would not perjure his conscience.

"Yes?" Harry's sob now broke through in his eagerness for this message from Jake.

"He says, 'Tell him to be outside that –'"

"Crystal Rooms."

"Right! 'About six' – was it six he said, Doug?"

"Six it was," Doug echoed, stamping vehemently on the remains of the cigarette.

"After he's dropped his load?" Harry offered.

"The very thing," said the man. "*And –*" from his pocket he brought out a clutch of coins "– he gives me . . . a pound, no, I tell a lie, two pounds for you to feed yourself up." Two warm

33

coins which stuck together were passed into Harry's cold hand. He nodded his thanks. The relief was inexpressible.

"Well, Norf," Doug had decided against Harry as a name. "Ever 'ad real Chinese fish 'n' chips?"

"No," Harry replied.

"Foller me," said Doug.

"Follow Doug," said the man, "an' I'll follow the both of you."

Harry's emotions were in such turbulence that he feared to do anything but smile. The man's gloating return attempt at a smile alerted him, but Doug was already dancing through the drifting crowds in Chinatown, as if blown by the wind, a small packet of human litter bowling along the gutterless street.

"C'mon, Norf!" he shouted. "Follow me!"

Deuce watched them go and then strolled after them, glancing in a shop window here and there to check up on his appearance. "A chicken," he murmured to himself. "Deuce has landed himself a chicken. And the price of chickens, my friends, my lords and gentlemen on your way to a certain rendezvous this afternoon, the price of little fresh virgin chickens with little sweet faces is very high at this particular time."

THREE

I

CHOOSING a restaurant always tormented Martha. The one certainty in her intensive experience was that the action would be somewhere else. It would be in the restaurant that she had *almost* picked that the hot TV alternative host would turn up, or the coven of fashionable younger novelists slope in to complain about their publishers, or a segment of the metropolitan radical chic meet to deconstruct the menu and most likely order Chablis! (Or were they all avoiding *her*? Pride and paranoia jostled uneasily.) Not that her choice was unlimited: cost, geography and the narrow parameters of her career ambition ruled out swathes of Chelsea, all hotels, Langan's (the former proprietor had once parked himself under her table throughout lunch and woken up to bark and bite her ankles), most of Mayfair (snobs), all Belgravia (worse snobs) and anything south of the Thames. That still left a considerable pasture and it was a bothersome dilemma especially when she was taking along her favourite protégé and, unusually, paying for the lunch herself, which meant that it had to be reasonable. (She had come out badly from a recent internal audit on expenses; chilling smears about "theft" had begun to circulate.)

Kensington Place was undoubtedly the "in" spot, and she loved the two gallants who ran it, but better for dinner than lunch and a little too far from the office. Groucho's would be full of her own kind and she wanted to avoid her own kind thank you very much until the temperature had been taken on her unfairly reported outburst against the Royal Family. The Academy was an original hidey-hole but presented the same problem as Groucho's, and there was never enough for Martha to eat. The Gay Hussar (politicians on padded benches), L'Escargot (media munchers) – better keep out of Soho altogether today: hacks plying for trade in every corner; executive media Mafia in corner-table conspiracies about the new television franchises; who cared who won as long as they put her on one of those screamingly naff panel shows?

Covent Garden was likelier ground and there, where Wellington Street charged towards Waterloo Bridge, was the bearably fashionable, subterranean, undemanding Orso's. They would give her a table beside the wall so that she could enjoy some privacy and a good view of the place. The waiters were young, wore white aprons down to their ankles, and reminded Martha of her ripest trip to New York. There was thick gaily painted peasant crockery and a menu she could both afford and accommodate to her (secret) diet. Provided she denied herself ice-cream.

Young Stephen – Desperate Stephen, she called him, her ploy boy – was already at the wall table under the gallery of black-and-white photographs of fast fading stars. She herself always sat under Richard Burton. She agreed with Marlene Dietrich that Burton was "the perfect man". Ah! If only she could have interviewed him.

Martha cased the place thoroughly as she was escorted towards the table. The ex-editor of *Private Eye* with a very attractive woman in a Dior jacket, but damn she knew the woman and damn it was unimpeachable; an actress well known this month for a fab ad; a hunky writer and editor from Faber & Faber with an apprehensive author she recognised from television – must be a contract breaker; *that woman* from Chatto with the mega-biographer of the decade; a female editor of a national paper whom Martha would never forgive for beating her to a key post, and whose clay image was like a hedgehog in Martha's mind. By no means a bull's-eye but not a complete washout. The actress and her companion could be the story.

Stephen was drinking a Campari "for its herbal values". He didn't really drink properly; Martha was determined to put it down to his being Jewish. She liked to tease and mock him about that, interested to discover when he would wince. She ordered a fully spiced Bloody Mary. Stephen was never without a strategy for these liaisons and he handed her a cutting. It was the offhand response of a playwright to something Martha had written about him recently. Martha's first reaction was to puff with pride that her importance was even so whimsically recognised. Then she studied the few lines in silence as a great scholar might bend her skills to decode Assyrian tablets.

"I don't mind him saying I'm a nasty piece of work —" Martha did not even bother to conceal the lie and waited — in vain — for Stephen to contradict her.

"He *did* say you were quite good at what you did. He just didn't rate what you did," was all he said. They could be very unfeeling, the young, she thought. But Stephen knew his strength in this bargain of mischief and need.

"But to say I'm archetypal Eighties. *Eighties!*" Martha moaned the word aloud; her voice was rather attractively deep, causing one or two of the less secure in Orso's to throw her a gratifying glance.

"Well, you *are*," said Stephen, bravely. "Do you wish I'd not brought it?"

"That's why I take you to lunch. But I am *not* Eighties, Stephen. That prat is too Sixties to know that. The Eighties were material-ism. I'm above all that. I am malice." Martha ordered for both of them: insalata campese and gnocchi twice, a bottle of Frascati and a bottle of Crodo.

She smiled — Stephen smiled back as if she had said something witty and fed yet more bread into his lean and hungry face. Martha's patronage could be wearing but he valued it, although he was still irked that she had picked on him not for any of his devastating reviews or brilliant (occasional) features, not because he was if not the brightest then certainly the hungriest young critic in town, but because in a moment of true anguish at the most fashionable publisher's Christmas party the previous year he had blurted out to her the fears he had for the progress of his career when "in three years I'll be thirty!". That phrase sold him. Every so often she took him out for lunch and mined him.

He had roughed out his spiel on the walk up the Strand from Charing Cross. First there was the rubbishing by clever dissection of an over-prominent piece written by her greatest female rival. Very good. She took out her first fag of the day. She did not like the taste but it was wickedly unfashionable. (But it would become smart again — Martha had written a column predicting this.) Then there was some quite fresh stuff from the literary stock market: insider dealing, nepotism, creative accounting of the reviews, all serving — as Stephen knew she appreciated — to portray to Martha a world she wanted to believe in, a world of bookworms turned book-dealers, back-scratchers, brown-nosers, tossers, creeps, trendies and wimps. Stephen was at a stage when to perceive those who had "made it" as part of a hypocritical, self-serving, talentless clique was much the preferred option. The major crime was that, so far, he was excluded. He let his guard down enough to allude to a metropolitan Mafia. Martha pounced.

"Your lot are the biggest Mafia on the planet," she said.

"I wouldn't say that." Why did he tighten up so? Why was he so instantly chilled into deep defensiveness?

"You wouldn't dare."

Martha punched out the jab of a sentence and waited. Stephen licked his lips. "You mean Jews, Martha, so say it. We damn well need to be organised against the rest of you."

"*We're* mongrels. You want to be pure-bred. What does that make you?"

"Very careful. With cause."

"Oh yeah, oh yeah, I know. George Steiner, blah blah."

Should a century, a thousand, two thousand years of history and tragedy come to this? From an educated woman in a London restaurant in a country, the land of relative tolerance, perhaps even the most tolerant of all? Was it just "blah blah"?

"And I've been to Yad Vashem," she said, pouncing again. "The Nazis were shits."

"You can be a bit of a shit yourself, Martha. Now and then."

"Good!" She beamed. "*Good!*"

"I'm glad you approve," he said. "That's all I ask." The deal was that now and then he acted seduced.

Sometimes his looks were just too sexy, Jewish yes, but anglicised in a way that made them Renaissance Italian! That nonsense made some sense – in truth she thought it brilliant (and she had studied Art History for a term) – but she had schooled herself not to fancy him. Yet that smile . . .

"So?" she said, taking mere titbits of the delicious bread, still in game pursuit of her figure. "Is it . . . ?" Was everybody talking about her blurtings on the Royals? *Please*.

Stephen nodded gravely. It was quite exciting: she actually depended on him for reassurance.

"And?"

"The jury's out." He lied. He had not heard a word, not a dicky bird. But he knew his Martha well.

"Thought so." A mild flutter of vexation made her take a bigger swig of the Bloody Mary than she had bargained for and she coughed loudly. A passing waiter over-attentively banged her on the shoulder blades. Martha looked up at him murderously and he fled. She drank more to sort things out and beckoned for the wine.

"I think you'll get away with it." Stephen was annoyed that he had agreed to her suggestion that they eat the same food. Besides, it was always *her* they talked about; what about *him*? He made a lunge at honesty. "In fact I think nobody'll notice much." Martha's look made him wish he had left that unsaid.

"*Everybody* will notice."

"My lot won't."

"That is because your lot is still a bunch of acned wannabes slavering up the greasy pole."

"Who cares about some scandal or slagging off about the Royals?" Stephen knew that to be her doormat was to be dead. He told his friends that his value to Martha was that of a provocateur.

"My editor. His friends. All those middle-aged, so-called opinion-forming men who want to be 'sirred', or who say their wives want it for them. And all the wives who *really admire* the Queen and think she does a *good job* and are preparing for the advent of Prince Charles who is *very nice*. Don't be an out of touch little prick, Stephen." The Frascati arrived. "Just pour it," she said.

"My lot . . ."

"Most of you are already in a predictable little rut and the joke is you think it's the motorway to stardom."

Why don't you *really* speak your mind? Stephen whispered to himself, but said nothing. He feared she might be right. The problem – which Martha would never understand – was that in his generation there were just too many *very* bright, talented and ambitious people. It made it *very* hard. He made a note of the way her eyes hunted down newcomers to the restaurant, the way her hand had trembled on the tumbler.

"Cheer up," she said. "The axe job you did in the *Spectator* on the television coverage of the Fall of the Great Thatcher was funny, very good."

"Really?" He wanted more. There was never enough praise, there never could be. That was the first lesson of his writer's life.

"Really," she reassured him and then relented and talked about his career. Her suspender belt was biting into her belly, which seemed to swell up with the gnocchi and the Frascati. Why had she wanted to feel sexy on a worrying day such as this? Perhaps to poke it in the eye. Or in hope? No. No more of that, only her husband now. Only Tim, Timmy, Timmo was the object of her desire these days, or so she excused her failure to incite any but end-of-party drunks. If only chastity could be a turn-on. Wasn't Germaine Greer into that now? She would love to do or do over Greer, but she had been turned down contemptuously. Greer had been an early idol. The rebuff stung. Now she talked of Greer as the elephantine Aussie with the kangaroo comic intellectual pretensions. A vicious review of the next book would have to do, but that was sitting-duck territory – no special skills needed there, Martha thought, child's play, the yapping of the journalistic yuppies, a great shame.

"Do you think I should write a novel?" Stephen blurted out. "Everybody I know is doing non-fiction. My generation doesn't really have a seriously successful novelist yet."

"Another bottle?"

He hesitated. But Martha did not like to drink alone. He wished he did not want her approval so badly; he did not rate himself for this compulsive weakness.

"Sure." He would have to suffer for the answer to his plea for advice on this career move. Her glare across to the bar targeted the waiter and the order immediately. He noted that.

"Now then," she said, and it was as if he had never spoken. "First I'll tell you why there could be a serious stink over the Royals for yours truly from certain influential quarters. I'm stuck with it now, part of the profile. Could be a nuisance, never mind – that's another matter. And then I want you to tell me about Mark Armstrong. How long did you work for him?"

"Nearly a year. The year I came down from Oxford. Not exactly *for* him but I was a researcher on that fantastic trilogy about the origins of the IRA. I'm glad you're doing him. He's *great*."

"That won't do at all," said Martha grimly. "Not at all." The second bottle arrived. "Just pour it."

Stephen was alerted. His mind scampered eagerly for pleasing information.

"I saw him a couple of months ago at the National with a terrific woman."

"So?"

"He introduced me to her."

"Name?"

"Jen," said Stephen. He had been daunted by her beauty and the syllable had stroked his mind for some time afterwards. "Jen," he repeated.

Martha described Jen Butterfield, now Jen Lukas.

"That's right," said Stephen. "Her."

"Very good," said Martha. "Would you say that they were bonking?"

II

Mark badly needed to take a leak. The Garrick Club housed one of the most agreeable urinals in town. He sped past the coat-cluttered corridor which led to it, past the polished jockey scales opposite the famous painting of the Derby Day Outing. It featured Barker, a club servant, long dead, a harmless old homosexual whose acquittal before the courts on charges of importuning had nothing whatever to do with the vain gossip that the courts' most senior persons were all members of the Garrick. There was something very clubby and Merrie England about that story which appealed to Mark Armstrong, who often felt out of his milieu here even after so many years' membership. He arrived in the place of ease just before his tightening bladder burst.

"Age and the Bladder" – a melancholy essay. Such relief. A Mafeking of a pee. Why did writers not dwell more often on this? Mark pondered, as he stood in front of the porcelain looking at a period sketch of a picture hanging. The urgent crypto-erotic sensation of release, the potent surge through the lower middle swamps of the body, the reliable comfort of this daily draining process, the curve and splash of the little waterfall, kinetic art on tap, the guaranteed pleasure of that post-urinal moment, *sans tristesse*, even the obstinate tricks of the final dribbles; and the afterglow. Surely there was a poem or a couple of paragraphs there? Mark nodded amiably to his co-leakers and decided to keep his thoughts to himself.

A final shake and he was through. He washed his hands and wandered back, glancing as he never failed to do at London's only convincingly intelligent bust of Shakespeare, loped up the broad oak stairs two at a time, and entered the bar, which had the brass and geniality of a crowded country auction.

Nicholas was already there and he waved his silver tankard of champagne to the smiling hitman behind the bar, thus summoning Mark to get a drink and join him. Nicholas was chatting with a group which included a controversial ex-cabinet minister, the editor of a beleaguered broadsheet, a hawkish political columnist, a newly-knighted novelist and a marooned young actor whose host had not yet arrived. Mark, waiting his turn at the bar – he would switch to whisky to kill off all those bubbles – was nobbled by a breezy gap-toothed pink-pated chap. Was he an actor? A barrister? A hack? The man sported the Garrick's salmon and cucumber colours in a bow tie and instantly attacked Mark in the most genial tones for what he called "that disgraceful bloody show of yours last night on the telly". The burden of his case was that by calling in IRA supporters Mark was giving the "oxygen of publicity" to a "bunch of murdering swine". Mark's rather more complex opposing view was difficult to transmit over the conversational clamour, but he did his best. Very soon a quorum had formed around the two of them.

"We should get out the army altogether," said a thoroughly three-piece-gold-watch-chain Establishment suit, who unblushingly sided with the far-left tendency currently under-represented in the Garrick. Before the cries of "Nonsense!" drowned him out, he explained his reasons in clipped judicial tones. Those who knew that his brother, a serving officer, had been paralysed in an IRA bomb attack in Northern Ireland listened with especial attention. "We should have a five-year plan," he concluded. "We withdraw a fifth of our forces every year and the UN makes good that fifth – especially with Americans. Alas, one or two murdered Americans along the Falls Road or in Derry or out on the Antrim border would soon slow down the flow of funds from over *there*. After five years it would be all UN. Another three years and then they too could begin to withdraw. Otherwise it is nothing but a blood feud without limit or end."

"We should wipe the bastards out," said pink pate imperturbably. "Chase them out of Ireland and bugger the Dáil."

"Withdraw," said the suit. "Tomorrow morning. Cheers!" He moved away.

Yet if one conversation united the bar that lunchtime, it was not Ireland or the takeover of East by West Germany, nor the fate of the Baltic States, nor yet the future of Eastern Europe or Iraq's occupation of Kuwait, but the inner workings of the Conservative Party which by its extraordinary act of throwing out a powerful Prime Minister between elections had baffled the world, brought to bear on the UK as many headlines as vastly superior crises and proved that Planet Earth was once more on the right course: that is, taking its political salon excitement and its constitutional mean time from Westminster.

Mark played his part in this until, as occasionally happened, he felt claustrophobic and went into the adjoining room where members could catch up with all the week's magazines and newspapers. It was here that Nicholas found him. "Time to miss the school lunch," he said, and led him down the grand staircase rather in the manner of a Busby Berkeley star making a significant musical entrance. Nicholas came from that generation and that selective part of society which had never disguised itself in home waters, and a slight queening it up was part of the tease, as were the over-thought-about ties, the Tommy Nutter cut, the remote Wildean references. This was a well-manicured act and its gentle daring amused Mark as much as it entertained Nicholas himself, but both were rather relieved when it was put off as soon as they were alone together.

They strolled around the corner, past a fashionable nightclub, to reach the Ivy restaurant. It stared at them like a very large wedge of cheese, and very appropriate too, Nicholas commented, as it was directly opposite *The Mousetrap* – the world's longest-running play. "If only Maggie could have employed Agatha Christie," Nicholas said, undisguised in his delight in her fall, "she too might have run and run." Apart from his disapproval of some of her policies and all of her style, she had not seen her way to give him preferment and, naturally, he resented her for it.

"Good," said Nicholas, as they came into the quiet diamond-paned restaurant, "no one here I work with." Mark saw a small, dark-haired, intense television hierarch (male) talking to a small, dark-haired, intense media editor (female) and concluded, correctly, that the future of British broadcasting was the menu, and more particularly the immediate future of the small, dark-haired, intense male hierarch.

Nicholas liked the smattering of film and theatrical names in the place and was always amused at Mark's total and unaffected indifference. "I might just as well take you to McDonald's." Similarly with the menu: Mark chose in half a minute – split pea and ham soup and salmon fishcakes with chips – while Nicholas wrapped himself in a thoughtful exchange with the waiter over the texture of monkfish. They drank a sensibly priced Sancerre. "Lunchtime drinking is so unfashionable as to be fashionable now," said Nicholas, "and so, at last, you score, Mark. Cheers!"

The two men knew each other well and were greatly fond of

each other. Their several obvious differences in politics and personality often confused others but served only to spice their deep mutual affection. Each had confessed to the other what had seemed at the time the most painful personal confidences. Yet, the tilt of the morning, the fact that it was lunch and in such a sprightly place, some combination of mood and circumstance meant that on this day opportunities were not taken. Mark did not reveal his meeting with Rudolf and the temptation of the franchise offer. The call from Scotland Yard he suppressed completely. He found that his interest was satisfied by the easy old-shoe talk between them, talk which drifted lightly from politics to scandals to a new television play, a new movie, a novel, friends, enemies, fools, jokes.

It allowed Mark's most pressing thoughts to steal away and concentrate on Jen, on the unabashedly seductive antique silk rugs and the late-nineteenth-century black, scarlet and gold flaring French bordello pleasures of the bedroom they used, of the satiation of their lovemaking, the compulsion, the care, the fury of it. Nicholas also kept to the surface – a surface on which the two of them could play so warmly and so well. His anguish would not be spoken – not even to Mark. It was hugged in terror and secrecy, daring not to speak its name yet having a power which he did not know if he could possibly resist, after this lunch, the name of the hotel in his breast pocket, neatly folded behind the bouffant of his Paisley silk handkerchief.

III

Two more boys had turned up together, about the same age as Doug, Harry guessed, but not as nice. They made Doug nervous, Harry could tell that. They seemed to work as a team, to taunt him. Like Doug, they wore posh gear and were always seeking out mirrors. All three ignored Harry as they played on the sole Sky Raider in the mean Soho café while Deuce monopolised the phone in the corner. Harry wanted to play the machine but he held on to his money. He still had three pounds from the morning, one pound from the two Deuce had given him and two pounds sixty-five of his own. Six pounds and sixty-five pence. If he could find the bus station, it would probably be enough, he reckoned, to get him the fare home. For Jake would not be at the Crystal Rooms at six, would he? Deuce was lying, wasn't he?

44

But what if it were true?

After more telephoning and heavy peering at his glittering watch, Deuce called Doug over and the two got entangled in a discussion in which Harry's name figured prominently. Through the music and the clatter of the machines, Harry picked up half-sentences which made little sense.

"I don't *want* to be a bait," Doug said, in a voice markedly different, much less crude than the accent he affected with Harry. Deuce was attempting to soothe him down. "Fresh chicken" were the words which seemed to come regularly from Deuce's lips. "Fresh chicken". Harry was puzzled and alarmed. Unhappily, he was well taught in the intimations of terror and he knew that he was in danger. But from what? As Doug came towards him, smiling easily, and Deuce looked on, pretending (Harry was not fooled) benevolence, he was on his guard – but where was the danger?

"Well, Norf. We're all off t' 'o'l." The Cockney was back in place and Harry wanted to ask why. "Comin'?"

"Doug doesn't describe it very well," Deuce said, smiling as he shook his head. "What he means is we've taken a liking to you, Harry, and, seeing you are on your own in the big city until six o'clock when your Jake comes to find you, we thought, Doug and me and the boys there, we thought – he can fetch up with us at this here hotel where we intend to have a little party."

"That's if you really fancies it, Norf," said Doug. Harry could feel that this was a signal, a fleeting act of friendship: but what was going on?

"Why should he *not* fancy it, Doug?" Deuce was a little testy. "We're doing him a kindness."

"Yes," said Harry, helplessly bewildered, "thank you."

"You dow nav to –" Deuce grabbed Doug's neck in what could seem a playful grip. The other two boys came towards them to listen to the discussion and giggled happily. Harry was surrounded.

"He's coming along. Aren't you, Harry?"

Fresh, innocent, lovely little face, slim: could be very valuable, a definite shortage on the market at the moment.

"Yes," said Harry.

"That's all right then. Now then you two, away you go. We three will stroll along together. Do you mind a walk, Harry?" They nodded and left as briskly as soldiers.

"No, not at all."

45

"Tough in the North, you see, Doug. We should send *you* there. Toughen you up a bit. Shouldn't we, Harry?"

Harry tried to smile but his expression revealed his fear. Yet, helplessly, he followed, walking quite swiftly between Deuce and Doug. Harry feverishly tried to memorise the route as they turned up Oxford Street, where they passed a Salvation Army band playing a mournful carol, and crossed a mill of traffic which seemed to swallow them up as they made their way to the hotel named on the slip of paper which burned in Nicholas de Loit's breast pocket.

Four

I

JEN'S London house was in one of those half-hidden little streets behind the Albert Hall. Even in such a discreet location, Jen had found yet greater anonymity and it was easier for the cab to drop him off nearby. Mark walked swiftly along a short alley, rang at a small black door which could have been the tradesman's entrance to any one of a terrace of houses, and was buzzed into the high-walled garden of a remarkable detached early Victorian villa. Again he was buzzed in and this time he ran, up the stairs.

The bedroom was his own fantasy. The night that he and Jen had been reunited, in the commanding languor of post-coital and alcoholically eased gratitude, she had encouraged him to describe his adolescent dream of a sexual pleasure-dome. The next morning she had moved out of her home, taken a suite at the Savoy, and overpaid an imaginative decorator to tailor a special bedroom, swiftly, to Mark's younger self. It was uncharacteristic behaviour, but meeting Mark again had triggered such impulses. She saw a past she could recapture and perhaps resolve and no characteristic behaviour would help her.

They had laughed at the place, and still did, and called it vulgar and French and brothel and obvious and ridiculous, but Mark's fantasy had been a true one, youthful though it was, and they enjoyed it. Jen had thought back on her own fantasies and although they were dominated by the need to give men no quarter, nevertheless she found satisfaction in the lace and silks, the sheathing of allure. Now after a few weeks the place no longer seemed

47

vulgar, no longer brothel-obvious or ridiculous, or only insofar as that was part of their joke, their private life and secret folly, somehow strengthening them. The overlaid rugs, the long scarlet and gold velvet curtains, the tuliped Art Nouveau lamps, the gilt mirrored headboard and the vast crystal chandelier were merely the setting for the urgency of their sexual passion. Here they sought to recapture what they had once had.

She was lying on the white silk sheets in scarlet and black.

He sat beside her and stroked her face. His hands glided on the skin, slowly traced the line of her cheekbones, drew around her lips, stroked her hair, letting his fingers filter through its red and gold, parting it into strands. At times his need for her and her equal fury for him spurred a violent passion which was disturbing but comprehended. Today, despite the pitch of his longing, he sensed she needed this quietness. His control reassured her; hers gave him confidence.

Every now and then she reached up for his fingers and rubbed them or just held them. He would lean down and brush her earlobe with his lips, kiss the wide unguarded throat; she loosened his tie, unbuttoned his shirt. The clumsy act of a man's undressing was smoothed and even made erotic in the intensity of her attentions.

Her gaze was too intimate to hold for long: either she herself broke it with a smile or Mark looked away, unable to fathom the depth of question she was asking him. The flicker between pain and pleasure in those startling eyes.

They would sometimes talk about their past, as if they were discussing the adventures of their adolescent children, searching for the point of hurt and ease.

"So?" he said.

"So." Her eyes were too steady for him. He pivoted and looked down her body, his hand trailing across its form, the tense white skin and the textures and shapes of provocation. She stirred, gently. His hand strayed from the silk and stayed on the satin-fleshed inside of her thigh.

"Let's talk about nothing that matters," she said, "just for a minute or two."

"Your charity lunch?"

"They're an odd bunch but never again. I'll send another cheque and if that disgraces me in all London society – tough. Yours?"

"Nick made efforts but his mind was somewhere else. But then, so was mine."

48

Jen smiled at him and pressed her thighs against his hand. His index finger brushed against the edge of her vagina. But not quite, not quite ready yet.

"He's a real friend, isn't he?"

Mark nodded.

"I can see why." She closed her eyes and tilted back her head in what might have been construed as a pose. Mark knew better. There was not a grain of affectation in her. That gesture could indicate abandon or the terrible descent into despair which he could not follow. What was it that took her so far away from him? He had to rediscover her.

He stood up, completed the undressing and knelt on the bed above her. She put her arms over her head and clenched them into fists, as if holding on to something. He bent over her and kissed her face, stroked her face, kissed her neck, her breasts, with his right hand opened her moist vagina and slipped fingers rapidly into it, working them sensuously around the contours and dark opening flesh which yielded and undulated very slightly. Her tongue licked at the palm which covered her mouth and, as his fingers sought out other openings, Jen reached up and took his hard penis in her hand. Moving gently so as not to excite him too much too soon, but enough for it to swell and gorge to a bruised helmet, she began to graze on him and he on her, the cue and the unleashing fierceness in some balance as he probed and drew on her orgasm. She held him just, just until the two bodies, stimulated beyond enduring, seemed to jackknife into coupling-combat; his arms wrapped around her parted thighs stretched wide as she came to a climax; she feasting on him, greedily kissing, tearing at him until the piercing moment when she shuddered on and he turned her, pushed in deep as she lay face down, hair down her shoulders, fists clenching and unclenching as Mark drove in long after he too had come, drove into her even savagely. "Yes," was all she said, and repeated the word over and over again. "Yes. Yes."

He lay on her and she bore him on her back. His brow was filmed with sweat, her hair was damp. He felt her shape stir beneath him and the distant response promised another coming together – but first this close drowse of spent contentment. She reached behind her and with one hand cradled him: his lips murmured in her hair – he too could not quite let it go. Both the bodies felt light but swollen with whatever force had coupled, welded and, for those minutes, transformed them. And to both of them it was, at that moment, the most valuable part of their lives, indeed

49

life itself, with the power – as nothing else had, it seemed – to change and lead to a new life that mattered. Minutes went by. It had been like this before, Mark thought, and he had let it go.

"That was good," she whispered.

"You were good."

"We were good."

She turned her head and he saw the face he had seen more than twenty years before – the same irresistible complexity of innocence and experience, of wildness and control, of independence and wanton compliance.

"And very sweet," she said.

"Nothing for the censors."

"Later."

"Please."

Jen mimed a kiss and he rolled over bringing her with him so that she now lay on top of him, her hair curtaining his face. She straddled her legs and shrugged herself into a more comfortable position. She took his right hand and sucked the fingers carefully, one by one.

"This little piggy . . . Gentle fingers."

"You are the –"

"Ssshh! Ssshh!" She sucked deeply on his middle finger. "I mean it. The way you touch me. Maybe fingers and hands are the most intimate things of all." She examined his hand as if she were about to read his fortune. "There must be connections between touch and touch. You could always touch me – you know, move me, affect me. And you were the first man I loved to touch me, however you wanted to, because I knew you would be, I trusted you would be, gentle when gentle was right and hard and really hard when that was right and sometimes draw blood, patterns on my back, I loved it all. Do you remember?"

"Oh yes." Mark nodded. Her light weight on him was a completion of himself. He wanted his body to be so imprinted by it that he would be able to summon it up at will, like the taste of her or the expressions or the inconsequential words which came after their strongest sex.

She looked at his fingers as if for the first time. "Just touching. That's how it starts, doesn't it? Hands touching hands or a shoulder, or an elbow or whatever it is, just the touching and somehow you make a decision at that moment. It can be negative. It always is with me now. I came to hate Rudolf's touch. Not Rudolf. Whatever you think – you haven't told me but I can guess at least fifty per cent – I like him as a buccaneer and a mogul – a failed mogul, I think, but we'll see – and his energy and the cold way he sees life. I like that. It might worry you if we really talked about that, Mark, but soon after I married Rudolf I started to get ill and so on, all that, and it was his touch that I couldn't bear. And he never touched – moved – me. I think you are the only man who did." This last sentence was said reflectively although she smiled to take the weight off it. "So you see, it's all in the hands. Lovely hands."

Her eyes closed as she nested her face in his hand and Mark felt as embarrassed as a guilty boy, but moved by her openness, touched.

"The very first time . . ." she began.

"Witch."

"Did you warn me?"

"I gave you every chance."

"And I didn't listen, did I?"

"You were unstoppable."

"I *was*."

"You were shameless."

"I just wanted to be with you. Put it another way. To fuck you."

"I was nervous as hell," said Mark.

"I was shameless."

"I warned you. I said it would be complicated."

"Yes." She kissed his nose.

"And difficult."

"Yes." His forehead.

"And out of the question."

"Yes." Full on the lips, her tongue reaching out for him, her body slowly moving against his. "Yes," she repeated, as she slid down and drew her nails lightly down his sides.

"Too much," he murmured. "Too too solid flesh."

"Every bit of it," she snapped her teeth mockingly. "I could eat every bit of it."

"Surely –?"

"No." Her voice was smudged, her face buried on his belly. "Hate all the athletics, hate all the vanity –" She looked up and he, peering down, saw what he loved most – that indescribable merriment in her eyes, at once shy and bold, lit by inner joy yet seeming to scoop up all that was light about it – "love all this." She took a wodge of belly fat between her teeth and worried it before letting it go – "Not too much but enough. Says 'living', says 'don't care', says 'more important things than exercise' . . ."

"You exercise."

"Of course. But I'm rich and bored. I do it instead of an occupation."

He folded his arms behind his head to get a better look at the beautiful foreshortened creature now halfway down his flabby belly.

"I warned you off this time as well," he said complacently.

"You did."

"I'm old, I'm broke, my present job is not secure, I hate my little filofax boss, I am in a game which favours youth –"

"Youth's blown it. The oldies are back in the saddle. And you sound too cheerful to be believed."

"I'm a bad bet for marriage."

"I don't want marriage."

The same thought occurred to both of them.

"You would have stayed faithful to me."

"I would," Mark said, quietly, in a tone altogether different from the banter. Jen chose to ignore it.

"And if you hadn't," she said, punctuating every phrase with a dig in his buttocks, "I would have gone to her house – whoever she might have been – and broken the windows, glued up her car locks, made phone calls in the middle of the night, and then raced away, and flaunted myself, and made you so jealous you would have gone insane."

Instead of which, he thought but did not say, you took me to the edge, you led me over the edge, and then you went away, went clean away, and left me to fall, and I fell until now. He knew the same thought passed through her mind too but she chose not to say anything and levered herself up, kneeling above him, hair tumbledown, glowing in her red and black basque sculpted splendour. She fondled her breasts, lifted them out of the unlaced cups and leaned forward so that he could suckle her nipples. As he did so he unhooked her and finally she too was naked.

The lovemaking which followed was dark and often violent. Not the violence that seeks to hurt, but that which cannot restrain desire while still holding like a lifeline to the deep law that love must not be fed on pain. Before that, there was far to go and, in the multi-mirrors of the fantastical low-lit afternoon room, Mark saw himself standing, Jen knelt away from him, his body shuddering into her, she pulling him down on to the floor where it was harder, wanting the impact of his thrusting which seemed in this

52

struggle of love to take power from his own need and, although they would pause, clasped drowning in the overwhelming lust for each other, soon the quickening stab of yet more, yet more, would begin again and the room became the lair in which they hunted each other. Against the wall, skewed across the bed, rolling over and clinging to each other almost frantically to discover more, to find more, until she straddled him and pinned his arms and rode him relentlessly so that he cried out for relief but held until she too found her consummation.

Jen slept. Deep, even breathing. Mark leant over to tug the embroidered counterpane from the bed and draped it over them, a many-coloured shawl. He looked at her and kissed the face he thought he had lost for ever, wondering whether this was a return or merely a visit. If she left him again then this time he would not deny that his heart was broken. Over the years he had missed her far too much and far too often to be able to deceive himself again. Without Jen he had been forlorn.

In some way he was afraid of her, he now realised. He was afraid of the hurt he detected inside her, sensing that she herself did not understand it; and yet the hurt was a burden and an obsession. He was afraid of what she had become in those years away from him, years which had changed her, externally, to a giddy, fabulistic extent and left the former self more lonely, more isolated even than she had been in the solitary wildness of her youth. It was hard to lead her to talk fully, openly, of that time in America and yet he must because it had both made and destroyed the person the world's curiosity savoured, the other woman he had to get past to reclaim her as he longed to do.

He was afraid he would come as a pauper and though he knew her utter indifference to that, his own clumsy, disabling pride made him look more kindly on Rudolf's offer than he would otherwise have done. In truth he was not altogether convinced that part of the job's attraction was not the rather perverse opportunity it gave him of getting to know the man who, for four of those years, had been her husband, however nominally, had known her become what Mark did not know. Most of all he was afraid to lose her. And afraid to confess that.

Could you whisper a spell on a sleeping lover? Could ancient stories of binding love be trickled into a couchant ear? What did he have to be to make her stay with him?

No force, none. No falsity either. Nothing but the truth. But what truth? And whose?

Eventually she stirred and moved closer and they mumbled in soft tones tenderly. And then, as he knew she would, and of course she had to, she stretched herself, yawned deliciously and it was over.

"This place is absurd," Mark said, as he drew the curtains and the serious twilight of an English December afternoon came chasteningly into the room of fantasy.

"It is, isn't it?" she agreed happily. "I'm growing very fond of it."

II

"What Martha wanted, Martha got" had been her fun motto in the old days and never mind the plagiarism. Things were not so much fun now. Although her answering-machine was satisfyingly laden with enquiries about the Royals, it was not enough: support which was too easy and not from people who counted, so damn them; commiseration and gentle criticism from two or three self-righteous bastards who might know what they were talking about, so damn them; a deeply insulting jolly from the Gossip King himself telling her not to worry because, although the phrasing was hot water, and certainly the sentiments were ripe, she herself was not important enough (he used *important*! Was the man mad?) to justify a scandal. Certainly not by him, so cheer up! So double damn, damn and blast him! Only one reply to her messages to friends of Mark Armstrong who might be prepared to talk to her about him. Stephen had revealed pathetically few indiscretions even under threat. And a note on her desk, private, from the editor. Could she see him at four? Half-an-hour. It was not handwritten and no endearment, no jokes. And all around her was the nightmare of the new open-plan, we-are-all-public-property office which depressed the hell out of her even in the best of times, wherever they had gone.

Martha went to the loo.

Even the loo was no consolation. For a start, instead of having words on the door – it was a newspaper office after all! – even simple words like GENTS and LADIES, there were those ubiquitous stick-person graphics easily confused by someone who, like Martha, had been forced to lick the second bottle of Frascati almost single-handed on account of Desperate Stephen's modish moderation. And then they were not cubicled in the kind of privacy that allowed a bonk but were designed deliberately anti-bonk like the rest of this aesthetic anti-erotic disaster. Martha mourned the days of squalid offices in Fleet Street before the newspapers had allowed themselves to be swept down the Thames to factory farms. She mourned the twisty little corridors where you could get a good grope; the many culs-de-sac which led to rusted fire exits where you could go quite far if you were at all aware of the flow in the building and kept an ear open; the forgotten little rooms, dusty with files and archives, cluttered with obsolete typewriters and broken chairs, where you could make a camp better than any in *Swallows and Amazons* and screw the afternoon away. It was the afternoons she missed most since Timmy, whom God preserve. But who would preserve her when she was as randy as the proverbial and faced only with the mini-door of a Scandinavian loo while contemplating the termination of a most desirable contract?

Sex in the afternoon used to sort her out.

Now she sat contemplating the cheap bog door in that most unbecoming posture – knickers round the ankles, gnocchi-filled stomach straining at the belt, thighs folding over the green stocking tops, skirt exposing too much, oh much too much tile-white bum already glued to the cheap pink plastic seat, and she was left with what had become an increasingly regular alternative. It need not feel failed, she told herself, as she found the spot and got down to it. It was a liberated act, it was certainly a necessary skill, it could be a craft, and most of all it did away with men. Bloody men. Not Tim, Timmy, Timmo, not him. Whose footsteps? Never mind, don't moan, not much cause for ecstasy today, that was it, hit the spot. Who needed men? Not Timmo, she really loved Timmo, yes, but not. Who? Someone there, out there. Yes. New York. That, that, *that* tiiiime! The Prince of Wales! Yeeees! A squeak could not be suppressed. Where had He come from? It was a little worrying – a Royal fantasy?

She must get some of those extra-strong mints from the machine. If the bloody thing had been mended.

III

"The two most successful species on the planet," said Rudolf to Alfreda as they took off their clothes and folded them quite tidily, "are scavengers and parasites. I am a supreme example of one, you of the other. Together we are unbeatable." He turned and beamed, pointing proudly to his erection: not often was the timing so good. Alfreda took off her spectacles and became instantly myopic, patting the bed like a blind woman, fumbling fingers peeling back the sheets. "Bloody good idea this, Alfreda," Rudolf did all he could to encourage her. Not that she was shy, indeed her enthusiasm on occasion was so hearty it rather squashed his own interest. But he liked her to think she was original. That was what she most wanted to be known for.

Despite his ferocious schedule, he had allowed about ten minutes for this business. Anything less, he argued, would show a lack of respect especially on a day when she was making so many efforts for the dinner-party.

They did it.

As soon as he had finished he promptly rolled off and she in the same instant sat up as if their two actions were connected by the one lever.

"Do you think twelve is too many?" she asked. "Sometimes I think ten is the absolute limit for a small dinner."

Rudolf itched to leave but, sportingly, he joined in. There were still more than six minutes to go. Perhaps he could cut the overall time period to eight: Alfreda was too preoccupied with the dinner-party to worry or to notice.

And then, unaccountably, a mood came on him, a message from another age, as strong as the smell from a dearly loved moment of childhood. Jen, those early weeks, even two or three months, if he lied to himself a little: the demands she made, the compulsion he felt to satisfy her, the power and turbulence of it all, never mind if she had been on drugs then, the sheer sexiness of everything she did. How had he let her go? How could he? What was all this social crap and sexual exercise which he pretended had replaced her?

He slid out of bed and went over to dress.

"Darling," said Alfreda, putting on her glasses. "I accept that you are a scavenger but am I really a parasite?"

"Of course not." His pace was picking up as he fell into the purposeful routine of dressing. Socks first. "Of *course* not."

"But I rather like the idea."

Rudolf turned and she opened her arms, her breasts well and knowingly displayed. He blinked as if suddenly he did not know her or as if he hoped that in that blink she might vanish.

"Don't look at me like that," Alfreda said, firmly, "I don't like it." Alfreda was not to be underestimated.

"Sorry."

He shook his head to dislodge the troublesome thought and smiled full-toothed and rapaciously at the woman he had just penetrated. But the troublesome thought would not be dislodged. Jen rich, rich Jen, his legal wife, Jen had to be won back.

"Twelve will be just fine," he said. "Good enough for Jesus Christ, wasn't it?" He laughed at his wit and departed ahead of schedule.

IV

Bought sex, forced sex, sex fantasised, imagined, sublimated, mourned; soft porn on the high racks out of reach of the children, hard core inside bazaars of bright sexual implements and accessories. Sex the promise of the full life, sex the excuse – for faithlessness, for failure, for despair. A religion with its prophets and texts, its corrupt readings, its litanies and now its curse. Sex the killer. Joy become the murderer. Pleasure-finding victims. Desire culling young life. Sex trade, the sell, the product, the penis and vagina on the altar of commerce. Sex talk, sex scared, sex scarred, starved, sickened. A hurt. The pockets and dives of the metropolis hiding the misery of a brief, brutal stab in the dark. A god become a monster stalking the December city cold. For some a dead deity, but greedy still. Needing sacrifices. Needing innocence. Needing virgin flesh most of all. Hungry for that.

And Harry almost there now, where he would be offered up for sex, where he would be changed utterly.

FIVE

I

IN the triumphant glass atrium of the bullishly refurbished hotel, one small boy felt very cold. He was frightened, despite the encouraging winks of Deuce and the occasional smile from Doug. He was disoriented amid the tropical-forest-sized plants, the silent, ceaseless escalators, the glass walls, the glass lifts, the pageboys in scarlet and green livery and all manner of sights which would normally have thrilled him and been companionable to his mind and stored for his sister. And cold, very cold, despite the hothouse temperature of the atrium. The two other boys were sitting neatly on a sofa in the distance but they failed to acknowledge the main party and Harry was disinclined to acknowledge them. He wanted to be gone, even though Deuce made reassuring promises and Doug could one day turn out to be a friend. He wanted to be hundreds of miles away, even in that bleak house in that wasted corner of the sleet-driven estate. But he was in thrall to Deuce who now reappeared in the distance followed by a green-liveried porter who was carrying two large suitcases.

"Only lef' them 'ere this mornin', did'n' we? Less suspicious, see? Class," Doug confided admiringly. "Now, Norf. You and me's 'is nefyews up 'ere for a 'oliday, OK?"

Harry nodded, or perhaps it was the threatening chatter of his teeth which caused his head to simulate assent. Certainly it was only the even greater fear of being altogether abandoned among this intimidating luxuriance which pressed him to follow his new fellow-nephew and his new uncle across the black and white mock-marble floor to the glass lift. Deuce attempted no conversation and the porter, a man of about Deuce's own age, who looked cannily at his guest as if to say "I know *you*. You can't fool *me*", offered none either, save for saying "Here we are, sir" when they reached the eighth floor. Here again Harry experienced a sudden lethargy of the lower limbs, once again only overcome by the thought of a greater paralysis, this time of being trapped in the glass lift, for evermore exhibited up and down the tropical conservatory.

"Suite 817," said the porter as he opened the door and now, with a tip in prospect, he did stir himself and pointed out the televisions, the radios, the mini-bar, the bathrooms, the telephones, the heating, the wardrobes, the list of amenities and the double lock on the door "advisable even in daytime, sir, and even when you are in residence", delivered with the straightest of faces. Deuce's calculation of three pounds was the correct amount to encourage reticence without seeming to indicate anxiety. Outbluffed, the porter left courteously.

"Now then," said Deuce, looking critically around the large sitting-room, which seemed to Harry to be the sort of place the Queen of England would live in, "this won't do at all." He looked at his watch. "Go down for the boys, Doug, and *be smart*, right? Then I want this lot livened up." He opened one of the suitcases and took out an expensive tape recorder and a neat little package of cassettes. "Chop chop," he said. Doug left.

"You," said Deuce, frowning. "You are cold. Yes?"

"Yes." Harry almost clenched his teeth to put this syllable through them without rattling it and shaking it.

"Right, my son. A bath."

Harry followed Deuce into a bathroom. He was overwhelmed. Thick pink towels were stacked on a rack, other pink towels were over a rail, the washbasin was surely made of marble and the taps, gleaming as gold, were surrounded by a platoon of little bottles and cases, all matching, saying shampoo and conditioner, soap, hair gel, sewing service. There was a pink carpet on the floor, pink tiles everywhere, and a bath with a curtain half drawn across it and behind the curtain, a shower. Deuce leant into the bath and turned on more golden taps which fed water through a central feed at a prodigious rate.

"Get undressed!" he yelled. Harry obeyed, slowly.

Deuce found a circular box of highly recommended herbal bath powder and smelled it deeply.

59

"Just the ticket for a cold boy," he said. "Clothes off. Chop chop."

Once again Harry's deep reluctance was overcome only by a deeper fear of what Deuce might do if he disobeyed. He slid out of his clothes and the crumpled pile of cheap garments curled around his ankles like litter. While he was doing this, Deuce was gaily cascading powder into the bath, now and then yelling out "Just a little bit more! And a little bit more! I'm forever blowing bubbles!"

The bath was soon drawn, the foam white and thick, the mirrors steamed up and Deuce gazing at him in a way which made Harry cover himself as if ashamed.

"Very pretty," said Deuce. "Thin but not skinny. Nice set of shoulders. Lovely little chest. Prime chicken. *In* you go. *Nice* little bot." He slapped Harry lightly on the buttocks and, as the boy shivered down through the foam into the hot stinging water, he clapped his hands. "A bubble bath! Who'd have thought it?"

And with that he disappeared.

For some minutes Harry sat extremely still to leach the sting. It was somehow too much of an effort to lean forward and turn on the cold tap, and besides he wanted the heat. The discomfort would go, and it did, and he slid down, his head resting just above the thick lace of foam. He looked at the minute bubbles intently: they could be frothed-up frogspawn or snow just fallen; they could be clouds; they could be millions of crystals, tiny, almost invisible bubbles of crystal. Would Jake really be at the Crystal Rooms at six? Jake had loved the place, he knew that for certain, and he could understand why. There was nothing, not even that hotel sitting-room, to compare. Harry remembered the crystal chandeliers and, as the warmth began to work through him, he dozed, dreaming of a multitude of chandeliers, all lit up with candles, coming slowly down from the ceiling, while he and Mary watched. Somewhere there was his mother's voice and music, music making the chandeliers clink and shiver in tune.

"She's in here!" Harry looked around, startled. Who? Who was *she*? At the door one of the boys said, "Hurry up, mate. Duty calls," and then slammed the door.

Harry clambered out of the bath urgently, still pink from the piping hot water and covered in foam as if he had been tarred and then feathered with it. But where was *she*? The bathroom was now a spooky place. He rubbed himself briskly, but not too thoroughly, and put on his clothes with all speed. The music came from next door and, when he left the bathroom and turned into the sitting-room, he felt a little dizzy.

The two boys were wearing white underpants and nothing else, dancing to the music coming from Deuce's tape recorder. The curtains had been drawn, furniture rearranged, lights seductively positioned. Two men were dancing, or rather standing and twitching a little as the two boys danced round them, brilliantly, Harry noted. The men were old, Harry thought, in dark suits, and one was bald and wore glasses. Nevertheless they smiled and waved at him as he came in and Deuce, at the tape recorder, came over, arms open, as if he had been away for weeks.

"Harry! So pink! So clean! So *hot*! Why don't you take something off? At least your anorak — eh? Look at them," he pointed to the young dancers weaving self-absorbed and intricate patterns around the stiffly stamping men in dark suits, "they appreciate the central heating. So should you."

He helped Harry take off his anorak and tugged at his pullover, but Harry resisted and Deuce backed off.

"New," he murmured, it seemed to no one in particular, "just in from the North and fresh as fish."

The two men waved to him again and one of them pointed to a table which was labouring under a monstrous number of bottles. Harry went across and picked up a Coke. He looked across at Deuce and held it up.

"Of course! Help yourself! Compliments of the house! New! From the North, gentlemen!"

The Coke was cold and Harry drank it gratefully even though he could feel that it brought him out in a sweat.

Then he saw one of the boys turn his back on the man he seemed to be dancing with, hook his fingers in the skimpy underpants, wriggle them down to reveal his bottom and then wiggle the bottom until it shook like a jelly. The man, it was the bald one with glasses, knelt down on both knees, grabbed the bottom and began to kiss it ardently.

Harry felt a jolt of pre-panic breath pump out of his mouth. His chest tightened, his head ached; he knew he could not, dare not go out of the main door, so he went slowly across the room past the bathroom he had just relinquished and found the door beyond that. He could not open it. Perhaps it was just stiff. He pushed hard.

"Who *is* that?" A cultivated, indisputably boss-voice, a voice of authority, arrested him immediately.

61

"S'me in 'ere, OK?" Doug's voice. He sounded a little disturbed. "Thank you *very* much."

"Bugger orf, will you?" said the older voice. In his panic, Harry waited for a moment and in that moment Doug screamed in pain.

Harry fled into the bathroom and locked the door. There were no windows.

II

Nicholas kept telling himself that as he had never done this before, he was somehow engaged in research and thereby exonerated. But he could not deceive himself. He was wittingly going to meet young prostitutes, most likely aged under twenty-one, and so still outside the law – dangerous for one of Her Majesty's legislators. And wearily distasteful for Nicholas's romantic view of himself, now shrivelled to bought sex in a turning off Oxford Street. He never had been capable of self-delusion which, in sprightlier moments, he thought might have been the true cause of his notable lack of advancement in politics. Now he walked with a sense of fatefulness which he would have mocked had it not felt so inescapably dangerous. No lies could help him now. For it was, in truth, as if his legs followed a route from which he could not turn them back, along the sales signs in an Oxford Street occupied by a bedraggled army of Christmas bargain-hunters, and up to the grandiose frontage of the hotel. A phone call from the house phone, the sound of throbbing popular music and a number – 817. Into the glass lift.

Nicholas's private emotional life had been neither happy nor successful. One intense affair at Oxford had drifted through almost a dozen years into an indeterminate relationship and ended in a brutal rejection. Caution after that, caution even after the criminal penalty for homosexuality was ameliorated; caution even when the social stigma was reported extinct, and in that caution only the occasional pleasure of a chance taken and soon regretted. Once love for a woman but hopeless from the start and perhaps needing to be. Companionships easier with heterosexuals and few enough of those; Mark by far the closest. Occasional flings, but Nicholas was inept at all forms of promiscuity except gossip. He did not see the point of it. He was a liberal, conservative gentleman from a line of such who had cultivated their patch of Wiltshire since one of the first gentrifications four centuries previously. Homosexuals must have occurred in the family but, like women, they were not seriously recognised. Judges, two bishops, a general, a few MPs, a colonial governor and assorted Establishment males were the recognised de Loits. Sir Nicholas de Loit, MP, was well inside that tradition. Save for . . . but he refused in his quaint but thoroughly determined way to evade or to apologise any more. Save for nothing. But the big emotion had eluded him, the great love, the true passion. In his romantic intransigence, that is what he wanted more than anything.

And he had come to this. He had seen in many countries the objects of commercial desire and Nicholas was no prude. But he disliked the exploitation, and could not suppress a colonising guilt on expeditions abroad. It had unmanned him. Rarely had he followed up and never had there been measurable satisfaction. Just sex. Bleak holiday sex. But, until now, never paid-for sex. Even the sighs seeking a tip. Fine if you could chop it away from feeling and treat it as a mere sensation. But if you could not, if you wanted affection and love, if you wanted passion above all, the great thing, then such forays left scars: they were unworthy skirmishes on the path which must be pursued to that greater passion, however distant and unattainable it seemed. There had been a handful of young men, so why the horror now? Why the desperate fascination? By what despairing route had this new and unexpected compulsion carried him through semi-tropical plants in a glass lift to an afternoon such as he would have sworn never to attend? He did not know. But he seemed helpless in its grip.

The door opened and Nicholas gave a name, not his own, to a natty young man he detested on sight. Inside the room, half-dark and pumped with drubbing pop music, he saw two all but naked slender youths writhing before two stout pinstriped gentlemen and decided to walk out immediately. Christ! These were children! That was not the deal. But the door was bolted and chained behind him, his host had darted across the room to bring him a drink and, as he looked around, he saw other doors, other lights.

"Bubbly," said Deuce, offering a slender glass, "compliments of the house." The entrance fee, a large one, had been paid in advance in cash through the contact.

"Thank you." Nicholas took it and sipped. He was too shocked to refuse.

"Coat?"

It seemed a ridiculously important point of decision. Did he want to take off his coat? He heard in his mind the catchphrase of a long-forgotten Northern radio comedian: "I won't take me coat off, I'm not stopping." Was he stopping?

Deuce did not press the point. He never did with his clients. That was his golden rule. "I have a lad might suit . . ." His "instant portrait" – on the accuracy of which he prided himself excessively – was that the client was most likely a beginner, most certainly a married man, children off his hands, time on his hands, going back to his old public-school days – the velvet collar on the overcoat was a giveaway – and the "boys will be boys" bit, or had just realised very late that what he really fancied was a bit of the other and he had the wallet to get it. Probably one of the tarts later on but not to settle him in. The new boy could do that. "New," he said, "not a hand laid on him. Where the hell . . . ?"

"Harry." He shook the door quietly and spoke quietly but Harry clamped his hands to his ears and backed away.

"Trouble with this door," Deuce explained to Nicholas, who stood a few paces away sipping his champagne too quickly, working out his retreat and ignoring the come-on of one of the dancing youths. "Poor boy can't get out. Shoddy workmanship wherever you look. Can't very well send for the house carpenter, can we, eh? One, two, three." As he counted he stood back and then launched his shoulder at the door with surprising force. It cracked, the slender bolt was wrenched out and Harry's face contorted in terror. He curled up to avoid, if he could, the worst of the blows.

"Harry, Harry my boy," Deuce was very calm, "what a silly lock. Dear me. We was worried about you. 'Where's Harry?' they all said. 'Maybe he can't get out. Fetch him,' they said, 'he's missing the party.' So here I am. Eh? What do you say?"

Like a trapped animal being crooned out of its last redoubt, Harry, his mind all but blank with the terrible force of an unnameable fear, allowed himself to be coaxed out of the bathroom and into the small hall where he turned and saw a tall blond-haired man holding out an empty glass.

What Nicholas saw was a sweet-faced young boy, wet hair plastered across his forehead, eyes wide, shining with alarm, face flushed with heat or panic, posture that of a wild thing alert and trembling, searching, frantic for escape from this intolerable pressure.

The guilt and shame switched instantly to love. A feeling which would have grown slowly was enormously accelerated. A load was not only lifted, it was transformed into a spirit which bore him up. Perhaps the fact that he was so finely wracked made him helplessly susceptible, but there was no mistaking it.

Nicholas wanted to hold him and say – you are safe, you will be protected. He wanted to hug the damage of fear out of his body. He wanted to soothe and calm him and in the same instant tell him that he would never in his life want for anything, not as long as he, Nicholas de Loit, MP, had anything to give, because, in that most strange place and in that short moment, Nicholas lost his heart and knew for certain that at last, at very last, without doubt or question, he had fallen in love for ever.

III

When he reflected on that moment, as he did so often, he saw his whole world there. For that instant appeared suspended and enlarged. He realised that this was the great love he had been hoping for, his quest fulfilled. His despair fell away. This was the grand passion, this boy. In all its unmistakable force it was before him now. He realised in that same moment that it would be chaste, that he would never physically consummate this love. And that was fine. It was a passion that could live and stay without that. He realised that his entire life would be changed utterly – that this was no sentimental longing, no passing fancy or phase, this was a feeling he would live by, whatever the costs. And he realised the boy's terror, he could feel the imprint of the boy's feelings as strongly as if they had been his own and he knew that the next few minutes could lose what chance or fortune had so miraculously delivered up to him at long last. His happiness depended on the next few moments.

IV

"He looks as if he needs a drink," said Nicholas, planing his voice into a gentle neutral tone.

"Good idea. Yes? Harry? Wake up, chop chop."

Harry's gaze was fixed on the stranger and still looking at him, he nodded. Deuce slipped away for the drink. Nicholas, although

65

his chest was threatening to burst from the pounding within, was sadly well studied in the art of disguising his true feelings and the tested experience just saw him through moments when the boy could have slid away from him for ever. Above all, Nicholas prayed, above all in these moments which matter far too much, let him not be frightened of me; let his fear stay outside of me. Let me be the one who protects him, the one he trusts; that will do.

"It is noisy here, isn't it?" said Nicholas, "there's a room over there, I think" – the second bedroom. Deuce arrived with a Coke and the champagne, which he poured too quickly. The head spilled over the glass, soaking Nicholas's hand, but he dismissed Deuce's apologies and explanations abruptly. "We could go in that room, couldn't we?" He pointed. "Much quieter."

"Certainly," said Deuce. "Certainly is. Now then, Harry. Got everything you want?"

Harry nodded, not trusting himself to speak, clutching the neck of the bottle, not trusting himself to drink. He looked from Deuce to the man and back again. Deuce would hurt him – he knew that for certain. Deuce was bad. Harry could not get Doug's cry of pain out of his head. He grabbed his anorak and followed the tall man across the dancing-room and into what proved to be another bedroom. Nicholas locked the door absent-mindedly.

"Would you like to watch the telly?"

Without waiting for an answer, Nicholas switched on the television and handed the zapper to Harry, who flicked from channel to channel. If he said nothing, perhaps it would all be over soon. Afternoon programmes were not designed for him, but he stayed on a black and white film which included sailing ships. He sat only a few feet from the screen, perched on the edge of the bed, a study in confusion and misery. Nicholas's arms ached to hold and comfort him but he kept his distance, literally, sitting in an armchair with all but maximum space between them. He watched Harry watching television for a while and then, cautiously, opened the mini-bar and took out a bar of chocolate. There were a couple of splits of champagne but he would drink no more until this was resolved.

"Chocolate?" Harry turned and focused on the bar of chocolate. He took it with a courteous "Thank you very much". "Are you hungry? Would you like something more substantial? Sandwiches? I'm sure . . ."

Harry shook his head and just as well. It would be impossible to whistle up room service. The noise from the next room grew louder, more threatening. Harry turned and looked at the man, desperate for comfort.

"So you're new to London?"

"Yes." Harry had eaten a square of the chocolate and somehow felt bound to answer questions by way of thanks. This man did not frighten him, but he was cautious. "This morning," he added. "First time."

"How did you get here?"

"Jake." Harry swallowed hard on the chocolate as the rather unattractive figure of Jake surfaced in his mind as a lost friend. "He brought me down." He hesitated. "He had to bring a load. Then we went to some places. Do you know the Crystal Rooms?" Nicholas shook his head. Harry's expression softened slightly and Nicholas was intrigued at how it could have such a powerfully affecting influence on him. "Deuce says Jake'll be back there at six."

"Deuce?"

"Out there." Harry was puzzled that Nicholas seemed not to know him. "The man with the drinks."

"How did you get to know him?"

"This morning. When I couldn't find Jake. Doug, that's a boy, and Deuce, they passed on Jake's message."

"I see."

A few more offhand questions and Nicholas had the full picture of Harry's day in London. He knew also which town he came from and of the existence of a younger sister. He had formed his view of Jake, although Harry had not coloured his description with any comments other than the barest fact. It was enough to know. Nicholas had a suddenly furious need to get the boy out of this place.

The bedroom, when not included in the suite, was an independent unit. Its door could be opened from the inside and led directly to the corridor. Harry returned to watch television in which Nicholas knew he was not interested. He sought for the right phrase.

"Tell you what," he said, "rather than sit about here – why don't we wander down to those Crystal Rooms now? Where are they?"

"Leicester Square."

"That's it. Then if Jake has come back earlier – so much the better. If not, I don't know – we could go to the cinema."

Harry's expression began to relax for the first time in Nicholas's company.

"There's a stack of cinemas in Leicester Square," he said. "Jake says nowhere else like it in the world."

"Good. Good. Well then?"

Nicholas stood up as if all had been thoroughly discussed and decided. Harry glanced at the through-door.

"Don't worry about – Deuce and the others. I'll phone him up later. Unless you want to go in there?"

Harry shook his head and looked clearly at Nicholas. It was a look of pure and honest questioning. Nicholas held his gaze for a moment. I won't fail you, said Nicholas to himself. Believe me, I won't let you down or let anyone else hurt you again.

"Shall we go?"

He opened the door and ushered Harry out. He closed it carefully behind him. He saw that Harry noticed his care and smiled, put a finger to his lips, all a bit of fun at Deuce's expense. Harry was marginally reassured.

The glass lift took an interminable time arriving and as they descended, Nicholas felt as exposed as Saint Sebastian. They walked out of the warm lobby and gasped, both of them, as the December wind whipped down the street and slapped them into the open air. Nicholas welcomed it; the tension across his chest was severe; he took some deep breaths.

He walked slowly down towards Oxford Street, as if he were walking aimlessly. Too many thoughts, plans, obstacles and emotions blurred his mind.

"I believe there's a fair in Covent Garden at this time of year," he heard himself saying, "not a very big business but there's a Big Wheel, I've certainly seen that, and – sideshows – it's almost on the way – would you like to see it?"

Harry looked up at him, twisting his neck suddenly like a sparrow, Nicholas thought, and giving such a grateful, sweet, longing look; nobody should look like that. Nicholas's heart lurched violently.

"All right," the boy said, the flat tone making more poignant the transparent eagerness.

"Let's grab a cab," Nicholas said. "This wind's bitter, don't you find?"

Harry was puzzled at being addressed in such a laconically adult way, but pleased. He looked around as Nicholas did and peered out behind him as the man hailed a taxi. The black cab drew in to the pavement a few yards ahead of them. Nicholas went to the front window. The driver pressed a switch to bring it down so that he could announce his destination.

"Covent Garden, please. The fair. The best way is probably down King Street."

"*Norf!*" Doug's voice pierced the wind. "Norf! 'Old on! 'Old on!"

He raced up to them and grabbed Harry's arm.

"What you mean, 'oppin' off like that?"

"Leave him alone," said Nicholas. "Harry, get in the taxi."

"No you don't. 'E's none o' yore bizniss."

"Harry. Ignore him."

Nicholas held out a hand to encourage and if necessary to help the boy up the high step into the cab.

"You don't touch 'm, mister!" Doug's cry alerted the taxi-driver, who turned his full attention to the scene. Nicholas felt himself flushing despite the bitter day.

"In you go, Harry, and you – leave him alone!"

"'E's my cousin. Ask 'im, mister." The appeal was to the cab driver. Doug looked distraught: Harry could tell he had been weeping. "This man 'e jus' come an' take off my cousin. We don' know 'oo 'e is from Adam. 'E could be anybody. 'Oo are you, then?" Doug was throwing himself into the part. Two pedestrians gathered at a suitably spaced distance. The taxi-driver knocked off his engine.

"This lad your cousin, son?" he asked Harry.

"Course 'e is!" said Doug, "jus' down from the Norf, is'n'e? Right?"

Harry nodded at that one and the driver looked suspiciously at Nicholas.

"This is ridiculous," he said. "Harry – come on. Now!"

"Hold on, hold on." The taxi-driver, a soberly spoken older man, was clearly worried and would not have it brushed aside. "Let's get this sorted first."

"I am a Member of Parliament," said Nicholas, panicking, flushing even more furiously and unable to repress this dangerous admission, "I have identification. Just a moment."

He put his hand in his inside pocket, searching for his wallet, and, as he did, Doug, serious now, yanked Harry towards him and whispered in tones from which all traces of Cockney were absent.

"Member of Parliament. Run, North, run! Just run like hell. Go *that* way. *Run!*"

Nicholas, dishevelled, his expression in disarray; the taxi-driver ready to condemn; Doug truly alarmed –

"RUN!"

Harry hesitated.

"RUN!"

"Harry!" Nicholas's voice checked him for a moment but he saw that the taxi-driver was getting out of the cab.

"Harry!"

"RUN!"

The boy could take no more. He ran. Twisting into the first side-street and then a smaller street off that and along its full length he ran and ran as fast as his legs would carry him, ran across streets and squares, ran past swerving traffic and Christmas shoppers and commuters thronging to their stations; ran, ran away from it all, sobbing until he thought he would choke.

V

Never in the long span of their friendship had Mark heard Nicholas so strained and upset. Yes, he agreed, he would come to see him at once. No, it was no trouble. He would be there.

He rang Martha's office to cancel the appointment but he was told that she had already left. A note pinned on the door and an apologetic drink on the step were the best he could manage.

The lift was out of order and he found himself running down the three flights of stairs which would later dissolve a tired and emotional Martha to despair.

Nicholas had said, "I need serious help."

Six

I

"I hate to be formal," said Bagshaw, who liked nothing better, "but the fact is that if you want to write articles or books on the back of programmes you have to get written permission from myself. And if I wanted to be really constitutional, from the legal department as well." Bagshaw chuckled nervously to indicate that of course he would never go that far but he did know his stuff and had prepared his ground thoroughly for this interview. He did not enjoy what he had been encouraged to call one-to-one situations, much preferring the cover of a larger meeting, the distance of the telephone or, above all, the control of the memo. But his new elevated position as departmental head made certain demands. Not very many, but one of them was to keep a watching brief on "all aspects of programming touching on Northern Ireland".

"What about vice versa? Programmes made on the back of books and articles?"

"That is not the point at issue. That could be described as research and fair dealings." Bagshaw bit his lower lip for a moment as if in doubt and then released it as if the doubt had been nipped in the bud.

"Well, I've agreed that I'll deliver two or maybe three articles and there is a publisher interested, so what do we do?"

"I must ask you to reconsider," said Bagshaw promptly. "I don't want it to become an either–or situation but it may have to."

"What is all this?" said Mark, meaning to keep it to himself but speaking it aloud. "There never used to be this fuss."

"New structures have been introduced," said Bagshaw primly, "in response to criticisms which could no longer be ignored."

Mark sighed and stared around the large office. Bagshaw, in his very late thirties (if you mentioned that he was forty he got rather tetchy: his generation seemed to watch their years like diet freaks watching the scales), was a fast-rising broadcasting executive hopelessly impaired, in Mark's view, by wholly undistinguished service as a programme-maker and no discernible talent save greasing. But he was being talked up as a Coming Man. He managed the Establishment hierarchy game with tunnel vision, which could be admired: he was careful, even fearful, which could be understood at a time when broadcasting institutions were under political, financial and competitive strain. No doubt he had his endearing private weaknesses like other men. Mark was at a loss to fathom why he resented him so much.

Especially at this particular time. A late December white light afternoon, London, never better, making efforts for Christmas, lights benignly on the Thames, the favourable comments on his programme grown into a storm of praise by the time he had reached his desk in the office he shared with a couple of other contract staff, the memory of the afternoon with Jen . . . He was still basking in the erotic aftermath, nursing the fresh memories.

Bagshaw had his list, of course, and began to itemise what he saw as the *constitutional* (not critical, he insisted) shortcomings of the previous night's programme. It did not take great intelligence to have anticipated all these and so Mark appeared to be listening, switched to neutral and got on with his own thoughts, as he did when dragooned to the ballet or the opera. Despite the notice saying "Thank you for not smoking", Mark lit up almost immediately and, to his credit, Bagshaw scarcely faltered. The unravelling of the Bagshaw, Mark thought: discuss. Was he ever thus?

The world of television was increasingly full of Bagshaws, it seemed to Mark, but so, he had the impression, was the world of hospitals and schools and ministries and business, a world of administration always vulnerable to Bagshawism but now increasingly possessed by it. A world where meetings were the agenda of the day the whole day, and a conference was a week's achievement. A world which seemed to attract those whom Mark had suspected throughout his life, the penpushers in the army, the toadies at school, the brown nose specialists. A world of slogans and piety masquerading as imagination and public responsibility. A world made safe for Bagshaws, he thought, who manipulated it with Bagshaw precision for Bagshaw ends, which were what?

The perpetuation of the Bagshaw, of course, and to perpetuate the Bagshaw everything must be controlled by the Bagshaw, modelled on the Bagshaw, not allowed to deviate by any unBagshaw jot or tittle that might show initiative from the line laid down by Bagshaw, which was what? To please the Bagshaw superiors who wanted first, no trouble, and second, men beneath them who could deal with the departments and ministries of governmental Bagshaws on whom they depended for franchises, funds, preferment, approval, the continuity of their own upper-Bagshaw existence. So there was nothing that moved below Bagshaw which would threaten the serenity of all that moved above Bagshaw, and why? Because Bagshaw himself aimed to become a super-Bagshaw as soon as possible. He would then arrive in that floating category of hierarchs, hierarchs the land over who now enjoyed the fruits of leisure once inherited by aristocrats alone or bought by great entrepreneurs.

Super-Bagshaw would then be chauffeur-driven, boxed at Ascot, Wimbledon, Cheltenham, Lord's, the Royal Opera House, the Albert Hall, Wembley, fed and stabled like a thoroughbred: he would rove the world to encounter foreign Bagshaws; he would be first-class flown, coddled, feted, be full of unimpeachable and risk-free judgements over late and long dinners in European cities or American resorts or Japanese hotels, asserting the necessity of this bit of Bagshawism, the importance of that other Bagshawism, traversing the world like a nobleman from a previous century and all this on behalf of, and in the name of, the non-Bagshaws who did the job back at the factory.

And all of it declared to be *pro bono publico*. That was the rub. The pious mask of self-advancement and self-aggrandisement. Mark could see the attraction. Perhaps the whole of Britain from being an ideal playground for aristos and bucks, and the ideal money-machine for grinders and sharpers, and the ideal casino for entrepreneurs and con men of all variations, was now evolving through the centuries into a land of Bagshaws and this particular Bagshaw was the voice and face of the future. Perhaps private gain had always been made through public piety and there was nothing new, the Bagshaws were Luther's indulgent monks, Thomas Cromwell's heirs. This Bagshawed isle, this Bagshaw land.

Mark could never be a Bagshaw for, although he spoke very little about his job, Mark thought that the journalism which investigated in order to throw some light on an obstinate darkness was worth doing. Especially in a society such as the British where, through tradition and by collective Establishment, instinct as much as possible was concealed from as many as possible for as long as possible. Bagshaw would sympathise with that but not fight for it. And Ireland was the sort of hot potato a Bagshaw feared most.

Yet Ireland mattered to Mark very much. Over the years he had spent a great deal of time and energy there. In his rather more alcoholic moments he saw almost a personal link – his own family, the Armstrongs, was a Border family and it was the feuding, recidivist Border families exported by the shipload across to Ireland, since the late Middle Ages, who had taken their vicious and hopeless family wars with them. Indeed to some limited extent – which he wanted to investigate – it was still family warfare, using religion and politics merely as reinforcements. The Irish Question was one of the world's insoluble problems, a murderous testing epic put on the back burner by so many Brits who appeared to have ceased caring. Or was it the deep and wise tolerance of the tribe? Its complications had ensnared him. He had no illusions that he could solve anything or achieve anything more than be one of those who tried to bring in an honest account; one that was not cowed by the IRA nor muffled by the RUC nor fudged by the British or Irish governments. If he could continue to do that – that would do. Bagshaw would never understand or support that and Mark would never forgive him for it.

Or was it the jealousy of an older man for a younger who held the reins of employment and clearly enjoyed too much the driving? The curious fleeting thought of his being of an age to be Mark's son again appeared. No. Much less significant than that. Maybe the real source of irritation was irredeemably trivial – the way Bagshaw shaped his fearful words, the way his fingernails were so correctly cut and cleaned, those cherished cuticles, the hushed tone when he mentioned a superior, the whole maddening persona of this man who would ordain whether or not Mark and his producer got the funds for their next programme.

"Tell you what," said Mark, stubbing out his cigar rather messily – another thing, it would never occur to the man to offer a drink outside opening hours. In fact, had there not been some lunatic move to stop all smoking and drinking in the place? "I understand your anxieties and, although you can't expect me to go along with them, I know that that's the situation and you have to abide by it – or you choose to abide by it. There is the beginning of a nastier new phase over in Ireland now. We need a little development money. To make it a touch difficult, I'd rather not be specific because it is better you don't know at this stage. You'd rather not know, believe me."

Mark had given Bagshaw the chance to behave boldly and well, to back his men, their track record, their persistence, to be a leader. Bagshaw did not hesitate.

"I'm afraid that's out of the question," he said. "Under the new dispensation."

"You *are* the new dispensation," said Mark and laughed. "I *am* the vicar." He paused. "Never mind." How could one so young be so old? Bagshaw had been born middle-aged and now was about to enter his destined kingdom.

"I would much rather we cleared up the matter of these articles. That is the agenda for this meeting."

"Is it not possible to cast your mind elsewhere?"

"I'm afraid not."

"You never fail to astonish me." Mark said this so gently that for a moment Bagshaw did not know whether he was being praised or mocked. "So it's no."

"I would like us to settle the matter of the articles."

Mark felt a rush of anger which he tried to staunch or divert but it would not be stopped and the fury which unhappily but sometimes effectively came over him burst through the usual office courtesies, loosened perhaps by the champagne, the courting from Rudolf, the time with Jen.

"I'm writing the articles and that's that. If it means I break my contract here – fine. In fact, why don't I break it now? Consider it broken. I'll make the fucking programme on my own and write any bloody article I want to write. Sorry, but I'm leaving before I start kicking the furniture."

He left, taking care not to bang the door, the anger still muzzling his thoughts, fog thick in his brain, swarming over his feelings. He walked swiftly along the corridor and down four flights of emergency-exit stairs – which helped – to his own shared cubicle. It took fewer than three minutes for him to grab all that he would ever want from the place, wrap it up in a copy of the *Independent* and, with his ungainly hobo bundle under his arm, head down for the reception area and into the street where he found a taxi and headed for the flat.

Only when he was in the taxi did the anger subside and, as usual, he felt embarrassed and ashamed. His instinct was to call

Bagshaw and apologise but, although that would rectify an act of bad manners, it would not resolve the problem and would undoubtedly pass the initiative wholly to Bagshaw, which was unwise. Besides he was beginning to experience that inordinate sense of relief which tells you that you have done the right thing. To apologise to Bagshaw would implicitly reconstitute their contract. He would have to absorb the embarrassment but he made a note: on some occasion he would find a way to square it with an apology.

As the taxi-driver played the brake and accelerator game and jolted him through the dark London streets, Mark considered his position. He had been on a loose contract with the company – which at the moment was unsigned. It was an indication of his cavalier attitude that he had not bothered to sign the contract but the carelessness was now an asset. The previous night's programme meant that he had no immediate obligations. He would set up an independent company – i.e. himself – run it from his flat – he could not afford anywhere else – and attempt to place the work as and when he did it. There was nothing but risk in it, especially for a man near pensionable age (who had no pension arrangements), whose interest in finance alternated between the lordly and the incompetent, who deeply resented spending on plumbing or painting in the comfortably crumbly flat but felt that money exchanged for a first edition of Graham Greene or Conrad or Malcolm Lowry or Robert Louis Stevenson was well spent. But the risk exhilarated him.

It was a time for changing tack, burning bridges, striking out: Jen had to be won and he knew enough to be aware that his old self could not do it. She could spring him into a long-overdue liberation. And Rudolf's offer? It had to be considered urgently. He over-tipped.

In the flat he threw off his clothes and imagined, correctly, that Bagshaw would be composing a Ciceronian memo justifying the Bagshaw line at their meeting and laying out Mark's hasty resignation for the ill-considered act it most certainly appeared to be. Yet Mark had never used that threat before and he sat down, shorts, socks, dress shirt on but unbuttoned, and typed off a resignation letter which was neither whingeing nor bitter nor threatening. It sounded rather apologetic and explicitly underlined that it was nothing to do with Bagshaw. To have done so would have been petty. Just "time for a change", he wrote, which was probably near enough the truth. Then he turned on his answering-machine and flinched at the call from Nick.

*   *   *

Bagshaw had finished dictating his memo into one of the machines which gave him disproportionate, even a sort of substitute sensual pleasure. Then, as was his custom and practice, he sat and went over the consequences of the meeting; the consequences for him. Would his reputation be enhanced? Would his career be in any way halted? Would his judgement and man-management be questioned? Bagshaw gave himself a clean sheet on all these points.

There was, however, the question of the imminent battle for the franchise. The company was powerful – as he had told management at his last board – very well managed, as he had said, well stocked with effective programme-makers, valuable copyrights, excellent sales force, but perhaps come the heart of the bidding in May of the following year, a bit short on starry names. Armstrong was to some degree a starry name. In fact, Bagshaw forced himself to recognise, although it alarmed him to do so, that in his own sphere Armstrong was the starriest name in the business. His dedication and record of delivery were unparalleled.

Bagshaw did not think – I must retrieve this fine programme-maker. Bagshaw did not think – we as a company have led the uneasy, uncertain pack in television reporting in the unprofitable but profoundly important Northern Irish issue and ought to keep the man who gives us that lead; Bagshaw thought – will my bosses blame me for letting this man go at what is approaching a crucial time? Bagshaw feared they might. He drafted another memo.

He was a true Bagshaw.

II

Martha clumped along to the editor's office wishing her bum were smaller. It is a mistake to sleep with someone who could become your boss, she thought. But how the hell were you to judge? When she had banged Geoffrey a few months before Timmy had presented himself as a possible domestic male, he had seemed rather pompous, ridiculously solemn, under-experienced and tactically primitive. (So why had she banged him? That was a miserable period in her life and besides she hated his wife.) Now he was editor of a quality newspaper and, of course, looking for a way to dump her. She knocked on the door rather sarcastically, she thought, pushed back her hair and entered the editor's office boldly.

"Hi, Geoff," she said. "How's the sex life?" Why did she have to say that every time?

Geoffrey had a Roman nose – first brought to his attention in the Lower Fourth at a public school distinguished in his time for a sex scandal exclusively revealed in the *News Of The World* – and he used it now as he had used it before to express disdain. This was achieved by turning half away with a repressed sigh so that the onlooker observed the profile which photographed very pleasingly. His deep brown hair waved with an undulating neatness which suggested the primping of an adoring mother's fingers, his lips puckered sensually, the jowls were on the prowl but there was no denying the nose and its overall dignifying effect. Big noses, Martha thought mercilessly, were supposed to indicate big willies. So what went wrong, Geoff?

She sat down and once again winced at the bite of that too-young belt.

"How's the girl?" He referred to her only child, a daughter by her first marriage, now fourteen and parked in a layby of education at a girls' public school somewhere in the Home Counties. Typical of bloody Geoff who had met the child only once.

"Bored," Martha said. "But being fourteen is boring."

"*Ergo* normal."

Ergo! Martha checked her tongue. Geoffrey was clearly pleased with *ergo*. Probably slept with it these days.

"Do you get easily bored?" Geoffrey was being the grand editor at leisure. Perhaps it was even worse than she had dreaded.

"People who say they get bored very easily," she said, steadily, "usually accompany the confession with a sad smile which says either – my mighty brain is just too fast, too voracious, too intelligent for this foolish old world to keep up with, or – I am too deep and melancholily profound to take this trivial passage through life seriously. Yes. I do get easily bored now and then."

Geoffrey came briskly to the point.

"This Royals business . . ."

"I was pissed."

"The – what you said about them – were reported as saying – sounded very like you . . ."

"It was off the record. I was pissed."

"This – American reporter, he seems to be . . ."

"He's a shit. It was off the record. I was pissed."

"Martha. I am interested."

"It's a great subject," she said promptly.

"Is it due for a complete rethink?" And are you the person to undertake that? Martha spotted the thought and moved with care. There was a real chance going here.

"The tabloids have been on the job for years."

"Sometimes I think of you as my little bit of tabloid on the side," said Geoffrey musingly. He had said it before: three times. He was very pleased with it. Martha was as the sphinx but it was logged in arsenic. "But they don't really tackle them, do they? It's pin-ups of the girls, rather like page three but with those absurd clothes on" – his wife was a fashion writer – "or a bit of high-mindedness from Charles and the supporting cast rolled out at holiday times."

"It's more than that." Martha scowled. "It's very clever. The tabloids own them. Or they act as if they do, which comes to the same thing. The young Royals, the ones who *count*, are addicted to publicity. They mainline on it. It's their job-substitute. The tabloids spotted that and over the years they've cultivated it until it's an unbreakable habit. They are publicity junkies. The tabloids are what makes being royal different. Both sides know that. And both sides play up. It's mob 'n' yob royalty nowadays and the tabloids understand that and they feed the habit."

"I don't altogether see how we come into it."

You wouldn't, you prat, trained in the political pages and promoted in an accountant's takeover, what do you know? She said sweetly, "Why would you choose to come into it?"

Geoffrey had prepared his ground and began one of his famous *tours d'horizon*. What did the monarchy realistically represent today? The fact that the Queen, for instance, paid no income tax – as Martha had so tellingly remarked – and received munificent gifts made her not only one of the richest women in the world but also a figure dramatically cut off from her subjects and, however hard she tried to seem (and perhaps she was) a normal enough suburban wife and mother, her extreme financial eminence cut her off as surely as her great predecessor of the same name's Divine Right. Why did so many of them have to be given public money when the family was more wealthy than two-thirds of the nations on the planet? Why did everything bend so easily to them? Traffic stop in London when they went to the theatre; universities be "proud" if a minor royal sprig turned up to present degrees far more suitably presented by a great scholar; their social round be presented as relentless charity work? Why were they always the emblem and never the substance? Most importantly – Geoffrey at this stage once more offered the profile as he looked out of the window and drew on his deepest resources, thus enabling Martha to yawn, scratch, make a belch – the Crown represented all that was keeping this country back. It represented and tacitly encouraged the drive for landed wealth, for acres of time spent in country acres on sports and exclusively expensive pastimes. It was the keystone in a wealthy, bright elite which spurned science, industry, technology, teaching, learning, research, engineering, all manufacturing, scoffed at all that which would make the country a better and richer place for future generations to live in. He grew quite heated on this theme and Martha ceased to yawn: Geoffrey was never to be entirely dismissed.

"So we do a stitch-up?"

"*Comme çi, comme ça.* I have my knighthood to think of."

Was he joking? Martha said nothing.

"I regard you as a bit of a weathervane," he said. He had always found it difficult to pay Martha compliments. His respect for her was not as high as it was for her rivals – Barber, for instance, who was so much cleverer and with whom he had not (unlike with Martha) had an "affair". Perhaps he should poach Barber.

A bit of! Martha said nothing.

"You may well be on to something," he continued. "What I want you to do is not to follow this up – in word or deed, young Martha – but let us both have a brood. I have asked Simon to brood also. In the goodness of time we three shall meet and decide. So, not a wigging, you see, but not full marks either. You of all people should know better than to get pissed while talking to a journa*list*." He was pleased with the rhyme. "It won't have burnished your reputation in the Garrick and the Home Counties, but that is not why we give you house room."

Once again, heroically, Martha was silent. But to herself, she said: "Thank you, kind sir," and kneed the patronising berk in the goolies.

"So who do you have lined up for your next little case of assault and battery?"

"Mark Armstrong?"

She had not wanted to bring the subject to him yet – usually it reached him through the features editor whom Martha had trained to SAS standards. But her bottled resentment at Geoffrey's hauteur had to have some outlet: the name dared him.

"He does some good stuff," said Geoffrey. "Last night's programme – I didn't see it myself, but James – did you read him?" She nodded: James was Desperate Stephen ten years on, but he had made it. "James gave it ten out of ten. Why him?"

Martha shrugged. If he was going to cast her as the weathervane of popular taste, the tea-leaves lady of Quality Street, then a shrug was as good as a thesis, she thought. He seemed not unimpressed.

"Do you remember that leader we wrote – I wrote – about Northern Ireland – nine months ago?"

"No."

"He was lined up to do a couple of articles for us but he pulled out because of that. Didn't make a fuss. Just pulled out. That's when the other lot signed him up." He paused. "I thought it was my best leader."

Good old Rule One, thought Martha, exultantly. Good old Rule One! *Nobody ever forgets a personal slight!* She was home on this one. God bless Rule Number One.

"Take care," he said.

"Don't I always?" Martha gave him her first, her only level look of the meeting. Her reply carried guns and he blushed just a touch, nodded and turned once more to allow her a final glance at the Roman profile.

III

Rudolf loved to talk nationalities and their sub-groups. He considered himself a, if not the, world expert on the characteristics of the British and their few subdivisions, especially the Scots; the Germans, especially the Bavarians; the French, especially the Parisians; the Italians, New Yorkers, Texans, Australians, Japanese, Taiwanese, Koreans, Arabs of all definitions, Israelis, West Indians, Czechs and Sikhs. With others he would occasionally let the conversation flow uninterruptedly for a few minutes but soon be in there showing off. He moved peoples around as, in his glory days – before his crash – he had moved money around the world, chasing time zones, beating the clock, switching from currency to currency on a wing and a prayer, happier than anyone could imagine, he thought, and always ahead of the game. If only . . .

but there were no 'if onlys' in the life of Rudolf Lukas. Regrets were for losers. Excuses were for failures. Failure was for cowards. For the right man, Rudolf thought, every flag of failure on the map of his life would later be seen as a milestone on the inevitable march to victory.

Yet, if challenged, he would have been hard put to understand why anyone in his or her right mind turned up to Alfreda's early evening thrash. True, Lady Alfreda was a prominent hostess and the party had cachet: politicians and one or two average big-money players knew that they would meet a selection of their kind and encounter newspaper editors, good journalists, television people, assorted arty types, fashionable writers and a guaranteed turn-out of the less thick young aristos. True it was a fine drawing-room often featured as the ideal place for this sort of entertaining, with its Picasso lithographs, rare Gwen Johns, early Hockneys, one of the best of Bacon's Popes, those interesting Schnabels, a Braque and a Magritte that was out of this world. The magnificent large rug was Aubusson, the furniture handpicked of course by David Hicks, the decoration accomplished by the brilliant new man from Japan, the champagne reliable. True, no gossip columnists allowed, no photographers permitted. Alfreda would have none of that. Her party was private – not aimed at "coverage" in some newspaper or glossy magazine. Rudolf had some notion of the lure and the seduction of all that. But still, he thought – look at them!

Crushed together, fearful to lift an arm lest the gesture send a drinks tray flying, stuck against the wall, bent over the furniture, handcuffed to the first similar unfortunate they had lurched into, yelling out basic information often as not to total strangers, desperate for a second drink, a first drink, anything, no ashtrays, the woman they wanted to see imprisoned in thickets of suits, the man nobbled by two terminally deaf older ladies who would not be denied, the noise like a cattle market in the Outback, a bar in a Northern town at closing time on a Saturday, no windows open because of the central heating which operated at full force at this time of the year. Who, which one, which single person was actually enjoying this? Alfreda wasn't. She did it as an amusing act of patronage, as near as she got to meeting "the people", and anyway it had become a habit: Alfreda had her party twice a year. None of her guests for the later dinner in the best hotel in town had turned up. Except Rudolf himself, now trapped in a corner, being questioned by a plain but impressively flattering woman who was somehow too good with the footwork to let him out. But where would he go? Into that yakking mêlée? Better stay – and there was something about her.

He cut across her questioning and said what was on his mind.

"How can the Brits – this crowd, well-educated, superbly educated, best universities in the world, well-heeled Brits, most independent nation on the planet, a land of eccentrics, how can they come to something like this and stay?"

Martha was about to reply when she saw the gleam in his eye and once more – it was the day for it – called on what she called her Trappist exercises from the ever-helpful convent concentration camp which had made her what she was. She was silent. He flowed on.

"Can it be," Rudolf leant against the wall which took the weight off his feet and left him feeling instantly relaxed (Martha glanced down at his thighs: massive, no other word would do, massive it had to be, like pumping machines, she thought, he would go on for hours!), "that the British gene pool has finally exhausted itself?"

Again Martha desisted, but this time more happily as she had grabbed a bottle at the entrance and was feeding herself Tattinger while mentally undressing this gorgeous man – she knew who he was – and power was an aphrodisiac – sod the liberals! – and if he had left his amazing wife for crud-like Alfreda (or had she left him? But whatever), who knows, who knows? Look at those thighs!

"You know," said Rudolf, rather taken by the intensity of attention this somewhat intelligent-looking woman was giving him, "there is a limit to a gene pool. It has been scientifically proven. Now consider how many people the Brits have exported in the last few hundred years. Exported and lost, I mean in battle. It is only a very small island and yet it had the biggest Empire ever known – everybody's so ashamed of that these days that they've practically forgotten it – and young Brits went out to Canada, to India, Australasia, Africa, the Far East, the West Indies – generation after generation – the youngest and the strongest. Most of them died there, or they stayed there, and look at what other nations have got from here. The USA – founded on Brits; its constitution, its politics, its farming, its religion, its crime. The Aussies, the New Zealanders – toughest bastards in the world – what are they? Transplanted Brits. They're in the Canadian mix, Brits are still lingering everywhere else, especially the Scots, greatest travellers in the world – and on top of that this century –"

Why did he keep saying "*Brits*"? Martha wondered, as she peeled off his shirt and clawed at that weightlifter's chest, was he not a Brit? There was a muddle about his origins, wasn't there? Who cared? Another swig. Not too hairy: she was not into orang-utans.

"– the Brits lost the flower of their youth twice in two world wars. Maybe that explains this whole thing."

"We come to this because we have been invited and we want that to be registered," said Martha, who had gatecrashed. When she had got back to her office – her Roman march through the open plan had been spectacular – and after Armstrong's let-down, she needed action and here she was.

"You know," said Rudolf, "you're not too full of shit."

"There – you see? You can be charming when you try."

"So why are you at this pigswill?"

"I'm a bit of a pig myself. And I like to look at the other little pigs with their snouts twitching away in the trough and their curly little tails exposing their vain little arseholes."

Rudolf laughed. He loved women who swore. (Martha had sussed that out.) Jen could swear. Alfreda could curse in a rather hearty manner.

"Whose arsehole are you most captivated by tonight?"

"Do I have to do this without turning round?"

"You can have one quick squint. Pretend you are trying to catch a fleeting Filipino with the bubbly. That'll give you time. I'll take care of that bottle of yours."

Martha did as instructed. She had always been good at Kim's Game. She forced the thighs out of her mind but his buttocks, what motoring masculinity there – no, no – buttocks out! She turned back and took a draught of the champagne which Rudolf had poured for her. "OK." And oh, she had a wonderful time. She asset-stripped the three cabinet ministers huddled not five yards behind her until Rudolf, who had seen impeccable pinstripes, meaningful ties and authority's insouciance, saw a trio of mistress-driven, avaricious, stiletto-bearing heels naked in their need for power. She skinned alive the most famous editor at the party, flayed his philandering taste in women, suits, society and employees and then revealed that he was on the look-out for a job swap; a young novelist was praised – Martha took care to keep an appearance of balance, it was part of the art – but in such a manner – for the creasing crapulousness of his snap-crackle prose and for bearing his illness so jokily – that Rudolf suggested his books be held with tongs; a rather simple country-faced balding early-middle-aged man was sliced open as the demon wit and mimic of Fleet Street, alas losing his own talent in the undergrowths of imitation; this woman was dumped on as a slag in wolf's clothing – was it of her, Martha asked, that the story had just gone round in New York about the fur coat? "Do you know how many animals had to be killed so that you could wear that fur coat?" an activist had screamed at her. "Do you know how many men had to be fucked so that I can wear this fur coat?" was the reply – Martha hoped it was her, she admired that. She rattled off the names of some of the young aristos restless already to heave into Chelsea for a night's honking and bonking: and there could have been more – Rudolf was clearly impressed, but suddenly he became distracted. Alfreda was semaphoring to him from across the room.

"I have to go."

"Duty calls?"

"It does."

"And you – *you* – hop off just like that?" What was there to lose? "*You?*"

"Enjoyed talking to you."

"Can I come and interview you? I do it for a living?"

"After that performance? You must be mad."

"Can I just come and see you then? One afternoon?"

Rudolf did not say no. The bared teeth clashed in a smile. "You know – you are one helluva girl."

"I bet you're one helluva lay."

"Nice to meet you."

"Duty calls."

Martha pitched the sneer just right. Rudolf nodded meaningfully at her and left. She watched him open up the scrum of a room as he went towards the myopic Alfreda. Just look at that arse. Of course she would have to do all the running, all the commuting but – no! Oh Tim, Timmy, Timmo! Overwhelmed with guilt and self-pity, what was Martha doing?

Very precisely she sidestepped her way to the door, eventually found the right coat, went down the steps without falling and sucked in the slap of winter air. It would make her feel drunker but she did not mind that at all. She would walk for half an hour or so and then grab a cab and back to Tim. Why had she fallen for that brute? She had, he was, but alas she had. Her deal with herself over Timmo was clear and tough. No messing about, not even pretend messing. But, as the square was walked, the great terraces envied, the glowing comforts of deep wealth, the sense of all that you wanted available immediately, she knew that somehow Rudolf had wedged in. She could – and would, she promised herself – avoid him. She could try to forget him; she could attempt an exorcism by her particular witchcraft of compulsive denigration. But she could not pretend that she had not wanted to be unfaithful to her loving husband. She had tried to pick up Rudolf. Why didn't she just go for him? The fumes rose into her brain and she fought off the weariness and self-reproach with spite against this world of wealth all paraded about her.

A police car slowed down, the two young officers looked carefully. But it was a very exclusive part of town and there were always eccentric ladies puttering around at night. Usually there would be a small dog defecating at a distance, nothing to get excited about. They moved on.

When Rudolf and Alfreda passed by in the Daimler on the way to the hotel, Martha was leaning against the railings of a house which had lately been purchased for £10.5 million. The new owner, too, had refused to be interviewed. She had been sick on his doorstep.

Rudolf did not spare a glance. He was bracing himself for more socialising when what he really wanted was to be back in the hunt for Jen. How could he get her? Alfreda noticed his silence and stroked his thigh which irritated him but he said nothing. The champagne repeated itself, sour.

"Those poor bagladies are everywhere," said Alfreda, glancing briefly out of the window at Martha. "It's appalling. Something really ought to be done."

IV

Mark hesitated. What should he do? He was due at the opera in about an hour and a half. Nicholas had sounded very strained. He could need time. Mark rang up his host for the evening and apologised. The host – one of London's few truly philanthropic millionaires and even rarer a genuine opera buff, a man born and bred in Ulster, which had brought him and Mark together – understood promptly when Mark said "I think a friend's in trouble". Saying it aloud reinforced Mark's gathering anxiety.

86

Quickly he took off the dress shirt, found a clean set of clothes, remembered his coat and set off on the same route he had taken that morning, this time through inky streets spotted by glowing lights, the surge of the end-of-day crowd moving into place for a night in the West End. He forged through the side-streets and was outside the Hippodrome with a couple of minutes to spare.

"This way," said Nicholas.

He walked fiercely along the short street into Leicester Square and stopped outside an amusement arcade.

"We'll stand over there," said Nicholas, "otherwise he might spot us and get scared." Nicholas looked at his watch, went across to the other pavement and then stood, hands deep in the pockets of his coat, staring at the Crystal Rooms. Mark stood beside him and took out a cigar. Once again Nicholas looked at his watch.

They waited.

Harry was brought back to the Square on his last lap by two young Swedish students who had responded generously to his appeal for directions. They were unwilling to leave him until they could see that he had made contact with this Jake – but Harry's dogged repetition of "I'll be all right now. Really. I'll be all right" finally prised them away with many good wishes and greetings.

The Crystal Rooms were still there. Harry felt tears of relief press against his eyes but he held them back. It took an effort. He was scared, shocked, tired and hungry but determined to spend none of his money on food. He would need every penny for the fare back home.

He looked in the Crystal Rooms, staring through the windows one-by-one, working his way around the exterior. At night it was even more of a paradise. The whole of the inside seemed golden and those chandeliers so warm and magnificent. No wonder Jake thought it was the best arcade in the world! Jake knew.

For about half-an-hour Harry wandered and looked, never more than two yards from the Crystal Rooms. There was a dread inner certainty that Jake would not come there. There was the sound of Fiona's voice in the far past and the foreign country that was this morning in his own house that had murdered the heart of hope. There was the knowledge that the worst happened and then worse followed and life was about not falling into the pit by day or the horrors and terrors of night. But there was also the inexplicable resilience of youth, something in the growing, in the blood, in the air which said "Life could be better, it will get better", and it was this that kept him going, this and the golden warmth of the Crystal

Rooms as his feet blocked to stiff cold and his face froze, his hands saved only by the pockets of his jeans. The certainty that life would be bad and the prayer that it would not struggled for supremacy in his exhausted mind.

Nicholas watched all this for a while and made no move. Mark stood beside him, occasionally stamping his feet and walking in a circle like an old dog bedding down, but always returning, just behind Nicholas's left shoulder. The object of Nicholas's attention was unmistakable and Mark felt his stomach clench in alarm but he stood alongside and waited.

It was only when the boy seemed to crumble and sat down, back against the wall, in an attitude of despair, that Nicholas drew a deep breath and said, "If he runs – follow him. Don't scare him. He's called Harry. You stay here."

Nicholas strolled across the street as casually as he could manage. A few paces before he arrived, Harry looked up. Nicholas smiled as if his life depended on it.

"Hello, Harry. Sorry about that mix-up. Jake turned up?"

Harry shook his head. Still squatted against the wall, his white face looking up the cliff of Nicholas with an expression of pleading.

"Shall I go inside and see if he's left a message?"

Harry nodded.

Nicholas performed the charade conscientiously, aware that Harry was staring at him through the window.

"They think he may have been here earlier, missed you and – probably – gone back home."

"That what they said?"

Nicholas looked at him and knew that however short and hopeless he would not muddy it with unnecessary lies.

"No. I made it up. They didn't know who I was talking about."

Harry nodded and bent his head. Nicholas leant down and ruffled his cold hair. The fond gesture was too much for the little boy and he began to cry. Nicholas stood above him, looking around savagely as if seeking someone to blame and punish for this and at the same time guarding the boy's private grief. He wanted, wanted more than he could ever remember, to put his arms around another human being and comfort him. But that was forbidden.

"Tell you what, Harry. Why don't we go to McDonald's? I saw one around the corner. We could have something to warm us up and then come back and look again. I'll tell the men inside where we're going and if Jake does turn up he'll know where to find us."

The bowed head nodded almost imperceptibly and Nicholas returned into the amusement arcade and delivered the message in his roundest upper-middle-class tones which would make it marginally more certain that it would be delivered.

"OK?" He plucked at Harry's shoulder and the boy stood up and then, like the parting of the waters, like the touch that heals, like a miracle for so it seemed, Harry slipped his hand into Nicholas's cold palm. Nicholas held that moment, that sensation, that open gate of love, there and then and burned it in his mind for evermore. It could well be the finest moment he ever had: all he ever had.

"We're going down to McDonald's," Nicholas said to Mark. "I'd like you to come with us. Mark, this is Harry, Harry this is Mark. McDonald's here we come!"

"Do you want to go to the loo first?" he asked Harry when they arrived there. "Mark – you take him, will you? I'll just pop out to make a call."

Nicholas was much longer on the phone than Mark had antici-pated and, by the time he returned, he and Harry were almost finished. Nicholas squirted a few delicate blobs of ketchup on to his Big Mac and took a couple of thoughtful mouthfuls.

"Not at all bad," he said. "Tell you what, Harry, you look whacked. Why don't you just put your head down and have a nap while Mark and I chat a few things over. When you wake up, everything will be taken care of – you have my word."

The food, the heat, the confusion of kindness, tired, tired. The boy obeyed the kind voice, pushed his food away, folded his arms, dropped his head on their pillow and was asleep in a moment.

"These seats were not made for the middle-aged spread," Mark said. "Can't we move?"

"I would rather stay. Easier for him. Not very busy, anyway." He took off his coat and draped it over Harry. "He needs a sleep and we must make plans."

"Nicholas."

"Yes?"

"If you want me to help, and you do and I will, then before the plans, the explanations or at least the story – please? And Nicholas – you'll tell me the truth, I know that. I'll tell you exactly what I think as well – that *is* the deal, isn't it?"

"Of course."

Nicholas took another mouthful of his food and then took some heavily scribbled notepaper from his pocket. After pressing the sheets flat he peered through them, every now and then casting a look at Harry which was in no need of interpretation.

"I see what the case is," Mark said, gently, "but . . ."

Nicholas explained, fully, what the circumstances were: the hotel, his fears, the awful compulsion. And then the shock of seeing the children, the terrible "party", the appearance of Harry. He did not dwell on his feelings for Harry, but Mark helped him simply by saying "I can see that". Briskly Nicholas described how he had reassured the taxi-driver, given chase unsuccessfully, and filled in the time between then and six p.m. when he knew Harry would attempt to link up with Jake by finding out the legalities of the matter. He had copied them down just now in the phone box.

"So," he said, "I want your advice. These are the options."

"Hold on. Hold on." Mark held up his hand. "Just a minute. You are saying that you are so – let us use the word overcome – by this, let us call him little chap, that you are determined to forge some sort of association with him?"

"I am."

"You know the risks if you attempt it secretly?"

"Yes."

"And I'm not at all sure I'm your man in that case."

"Understood."

"But you think there is a way to attempt it openly?"

"Yes."

"And I can help?"

"You already have. I have never been alone with him."

"Except in that bedroom in the hotel. They could get you there."

"They could."

"Why the hell were you there in the first place, Nick?"

"I don't know . . . A moment of madness . . . But look what came from it . . . For me – sorry, pretentious – but it seems even – destined. But I must, you are right, make amends for that. This is a start. My hope is that we can forget about the hotel."

"It's dynamite."

"Yes."

"What about him?"

"If the hotel comes into any argument then the game's up for me and it will mean that something has gone horribly wrong, horribly wrong all round. We must prevent that happening and I think we will have a chance. After all, the organisers are unlikely to want it publicised. What's criminal for me is criminal for them."

"Dear God, Nick." Mark leant across the table, took one of Nicholas's hands and shook it gently. "Dear God," he repeated very quietly.

"So I want to do it openly."

"Do?"

"Get him away from people who wanted to abandon him in London." Nicholas fought back his indignation. His anger, his furious urgency, his violent longing to resolve everything now and for ever was being held under the severest control: a control long practised in his life, so often the outsider.

"I understand that. But you will have to prove it."

"I know."

"There could be – will almost certainly be – denials, resistance, counter-charges."

"Yes."

"Why can't you just let the police deal with it?"

Nicholas paused and then he looked intently at Mark and Mark could not hold the gaze.

"Right," said Mark, "I understand and that is that. Fine. What did you find out?"

The place was emptying quickly as the customers moved out to the cinemas and other diversions around the Square. The two men were virtually isolated in a corner of the large floor space. Their dress and manner and perhaps the force of their intimacy kept what amounted to a cordon sanitaire around them. Even so, Nicholas spoke softly and Mark had to lean forward to hear. Nicholas put on his spectacles.

"This is what I have found out so far. He's a minor. His aunt is his legal guardian. We should go to a police station with the child. At this time of night they would put the child in a home or with temporary foster parents while they ring the aunt and get him back to her tomorrow. Basically the police will regard the child as lost property to be returned as soon as possible. On the other hand, if the man – myself – phoned the guardian directly and said 'Do you mind if he stays?' – or whatever tale was to be spun – then should she agree, there is no legal process which can prevent me from holding the child for twenty-eight continuous days. In effect this could be described as a holiday. After twenty-eight days the child must be returned or legally fostered."

"You have to go to the police," Mark said. Nicholas continued to read from his notes.

91

"For the child to be privately fostered – even though it is an arrangement between adults – the local authority must carry out checks over six months into the medical history of the foster parents, their general worth, and attention must be paid to the child's wishes. A big factor here is whether the child would be at risk with his existing guardian: and, equally, will he be at risk with his foster parents?" He looked up. "Obviously my homosexuality would be an obstacle – most probably, though not absolutely, it depends on the authority, on the region, and so it's not entirely insurmountable. I could become a legal custodian which again takes six months and might with certain local authorities offer more of a chance. My age would probably tell against me as well: and the boy, being pre-pubescent, would certainly be given all the protection available by any conscientious social worker. In London, I am told, it would be very difficult indeed: in other parts of the UK it could conceivably happen more easily. I am also told that all this could be in the air as the Children Act is going to change many regulations next year. So."

Both men paused and hesitated. Mark spoke first.

"Before anything else you have to get him home."

"I know. But when?"

"As soon as possible," said Mark, firmly. "You know that too."

"Why?"

"You have to play this absolutely by the book, Nick."

"Whose? Whoever it was tried to dump him must have had the co-operation of this aunt. Why should he be forced back to her because of some 'book'?"

"Because the alternative is worse."

"Is it? I ring her up. She agrees to let him stay – of course she will. She won't want the police sniffing around. She'll see a bob or two in it for herself. I'll be with him for a week or two."

"Nicholas . . ."

"Mark. I will say it because you won't. Perhaps – indeed, I think certainly – you are not even thinking it, but I will say it. I won't lay a finger on him."

"I accept that."

"I never will. *I know that.*"

"Yes."

"That is not the point. I just want to be with him. Just for one, uncomplicated, unthreatened piece of time." He hesitated. "Forgive me, but you had that once – years ago – with Jen. When I thought you would marry her. You were so amazingly happy –

not just happy – more yourself in some indefinable way, more your true self, I think, more at ease *and* at full strength, more just the lovely man you are than ever before or since. It is the only time in our lives that I have envied you." He took a sip of Harry's Coca-Cola. "I have never had that. I realise now, I realised today that it is all I ever wanted. Don't you see? You had that."

"Yes I did."

"I was surprised –"

"That I lost it? She went away."

"And now you hope she has come back?"

"Yes."

"More than hope?"

"Oh yes."

"So?"

"Say everything is as you assume," Mark began, wrenching himself away from a sudden, panic thought that he might lose Jen again, "say that he has been dumped – he could, of course, be fantasising, just a little, just enough to skew the facts that damaging degree off true, but say that his story is the truth, the whole truth – then what? You obviously intend to go down the line – all the way down the line?"

"Yes."

"Fostering, legal guardianship – and if that causes political difficulties –?"

"I'll resign."

"Personal, financial, social difficulties –?"

"It doesn't matter save for two things. If he – after he knows me better – wants me to go, to leave him, then I will. I will still settle what I have on him – that will not change – but I will go out of his life. Secondly, if I think any – notoriety or scandal threatens which will bring him into public view, do him harm, in any way, then I will leave. But with care, and patience and luck – with lots of luck – none of this may happen."

"So you want to take him away from his aunt? And let us say she is willing . . ."

"Yes."

"Where will he go?"

"If not with me – and I admit that is a remote, the remotest possibility – then there's my sister, she lives in the country. I would try to persuade her to take him. And I would be nearby. Another thing. The boy has a younger sister. If she too wants to be moved from this aunt, she is also included. That is not in question."

"Things can't work like that today."

"They can and they will. One advantage being an MP brings you is that you can see how terrible life is for many people in this country and how unexpected and downright unbelievable some solutions can be. This can be made to work."

"So let me ask you the one terrible question."

"No one told me there would be children," said Nicholas, quickly.

"Who would believe you?" Mark did not hesitate. "And why did you go to that hotel in the first place?"

"I don't know."

"That won't do."

"Truly, Mark —"

"I must ask this until I'm satisfied, Nick. Why did you go?" He waited. One last time would do it. He all but whispered, "Why did you go?"

Nicholas nodded, looked at Harry and unnecessarily adjusted the coat around his small sleeping form.

"Perhaps I went to find him. I have never been to such a place, event, whatever it was, before. It is not as if I have the excuse that I was desperate. In this regard I have been nothing else all my life. It was the way the coin spun, the way a leaf fell, an opening, I thought I'd take almost idly and yet as soon as I took it I knew that there was something in me that burned to know where it led. Maybe to know more about myself, maybe at last to face this thing I am . . ."

"Maybe to find a boy to go to bed with. That's what they'll say."

Nicholas rode back his head as if taking a punch.

"No. Believe me. Believe me. As soon as I walked into the place I knew I had no appetite for it. It was nothing to do with me. I swear. It was a moment of madness. I repeat that and I hold to it. I would have walked away immediately and never turned and never regretted it, regretted only my going there in the first place — do you believe that, Mark? But then I saw him. He is why I went."

"I believe it. I do. But it is a very private truth, Nicholas. And I know you very well. And I trust you."

"It won't arise," he repeated.

"Take him back."

"Mark."

"Take him back."

"Not to the police."

"Nicholas."

"Phone this aunt. Get her permission for him to stay at least one night. *Then* we can go to the police if she wants it."

"Where will he stay?"

"Wherever you decide. Not with me, of course."

"I still think you should play this one strictly by the book."

"I am, Mark. A good researcher did these notes. What we are about to do is legal. But I want a woman to make the call."

There was Jen, of course, although he was reluctant to draw her in. Prue would be willing but impossible to get hold of. Dorothy would be eminently suitable but somehow Mark had a qualm about involving her in the matter – and perhaps a suspicion that her earnest, open, innocent green-ness could foul up the situation. Jen would be at home – she had turned down the opera but insisted that Mark go to acknowledge the friendship.

"I'll phone Jen."

Nicholas nodded. He trusted Jen absolutely.

The phone call was necessary good manners: there was no hesitation.

Mark almost turned away as Nicholas gently woke Harry, the touch was so tender and terrified, so nervous and breath-held that it was too intimate to watch. Yet all he did was softly rock the little boy's shoulders until his sleep-puffed face emerged from its pillow of arms and looked woefully at its marauder.

"C'mon, Harry. C'mon. Away we go. Nice warm bed. C'mon." Harry's alarm was palpable. Nicholas was immobile. Mark, after a pause, pushed the Coca-Cola towards him and the boy took a sip and stood up.

Nicholas left his coat around the boy's shoulders and its elegant length swept behind him like a bridal train as he walked, again, in silent answer to Nicholas's longing, his hand in that of this unknown protector. The wind in the Square attacked them the moment they walked into the street and Nicholas shivered as he wrapped the coat more firmly around the boy.

Mark hailed a taxi and they were away.

95

V

But not before Deuce had seen them in the spotlit doorway. So, off they go. He noted the number of the cab because you never knew and Deuce's philosophy was that success was a matter of getting all the details right. Item one: he had a Member of Parliament with a good strong face easy to recognise – that should be no trouble. Item two: he had a face, a telly face, should come to him soon, would come to him, work his way through the TV magazines, a bonus. Item three: the chicken, his chicken, somehow not in danger, Deuce intuited, still up for grabs, then, his property after all, his discovery, Columbus and all that, findings keepings. Way of the world. One thing most certain. Money around. Piles of, stacks of, could be even mountains of the lucre. Seeing those two old queens in McDonald's, you could tell, the way they sat and owned the place, not letting anybody else within a mile of them, too good for the common herd. Money there, my son, no question.

Deuce drew his Aquascutum double-breasted British winter warm about his spare frame and began the nightly amble around his parish: down to Piccadilly, up through Great Windmill Street and tacked up to Oxford Street, a bit of in and out and back down Greek Street where he might take a light dinner at Le Fournil, very select: the vegetable terrine pâté followed by the turbot and a green salad, Pouilly Fuissé, half a bottle.

Oh yes, there was money there. He walked crisply across the Square, ignoring all the pleas of the beggars who should be shovelled away, idle sods, usually Scottish, or barmy. Should never let them on the streets, kept respectable people out of the district which was bad for trade, besides which who really cared whether they snuffed it? Oh yes, there was money in McDonald's! Loved the sound of it. Said the Jews had a nose, said the Arabs had a nose, said the Japanese had a nose, but Deuce's Bethnal Green hooter could outsniff the lot when loot was concerned. Deuce was going to be a main man and one Member of Parliament and one television person were going to be very helpful along the way.

The Swiss clock performed its elaborate gavotte on the hour. Deuce paused to admire it. Craftsmanship. Going out these days. Think of the work in it. Craftsmanship.

Isabella, Jen's housekeeper, took Harry from them as if they were restoring her long-lost child. Clucking noises accompanied her progress up the stairs, a journey which would go via a swift bath to a cosy bed in the spare bedroom of her housekeeper's flat at the top of the house. Milk, biscuits, and a few chocolates were already prepared; an electric blanket had been inserted just a few minutes before but at maximum temperature. That was the last they would see of him that evening.

While this Mediterranean festival of mothering was being performed at the top of the house, two floors down Mark filled in on the sketched telephone call and Nicholas took up the story to give a brief but accurate account of himself and his present action.

Harry, who had not dared phone, fearing Fiona's rage, had offered up her phone number to Nicholas as they had sped through London in the cab, fighting hard to keep his eyes open to record the big buildings, the lights, the flash cars, the endless shop windows. He had failed to buy a present for Mary . . . After they had taken a drink, Jen telephoned.

It had been agreed she use her own name.

"Mrs Abbots? My name is Jennifer Lukas. I am calling from London. I want you to know that Harry is fine. He seemed to have got himself lost and, anyway, he landed up practically outside my front door looking so sorry for himself I've put him to bed. He gave me your phone number – of course – otherwise how else . . . ? The police? No – I hadn't thought of contacting them. I suppose I should. Should I . . . ? As it happens I'm coming north in a day or so, I could drop him off or pop him on a train, whatever you wish . . . Thank you. Well, I'll let you know tomorrow but he should be perfectly all right. Good night . . ."

Jen put down the phone and breathed out loudly.

"That was not pleasant." She took out a cigarette from a heavy silver box.

Mark lit it for her. She inhaled deeply.

"Do we still contact the police tomorrow?" Nicholas asked.

"She was not interested in him and scarcely disguised it," said Jen. "When I suggested how he could be returned she made it clear that any time – no time – was all the same to her. Bad."

She stubbed out the barely smoked cigarette.

"If I took him back, tomorrow, would you come with me?" Nicholas asked Jen.

"Of course."

Mark asked, "Nicholas, are you sure this is right? Are you sure you know what you're doing and why you're doing it?"

"Ask Jen."

"Jen?"

"You understand, don't you?" Nicholas said.

"Yes," she replied.

Jen poured more drinks and Nicholas, as if winded, suddenly bent over, his head to his knees, his hands clasped behind his neck.

"Leave him," said Jen, "he's just beginning to believe it . . ."

VII

Fiona could spot a phoney a mile off and Jennifer or whatever she called herself was a phoney. So what was her game? No pressure for the police. No threats. No do-goody laying on a guilt trip. Just an old friend, as might be, talking about a bit of shopping. So where was the catch? Jake should be back soon but he wouldn't be able to help – pump him as she might, he'd be gormless. Good in bed, thick in the head, more front than Morecambe. Let him know nothing. If there was anything in it why cut him in?

There was something in it, she was certain sure of that. When Mary came into the kitchen to get herself some cornflakes for supper, she found her aunt humming, smiling, strange.

"When's Harry coming back?" She was bold to ask a question she had somehow feared to frame all day.

"Soon. Tomorrow or the next day. Oh yes, he'll be back soon! And things will change. Mary, things will be a bloody sight better. I feel it in my water."

"Was that him on the phone?"

"Were you snooping, you little bugger?"

"No. Please."

"It was sort of him. The people he's staying with. Very well-spoken people. Very well-off. Very clever. I expect you'll see them when they bring him back."

Mary sometimes dreamed of stabbing her aunt.

The last breath of a dying wind rattled the kitchen window-pane. Fiona felt comforted by the sound and hummed along with it.

VIII

Harry woke up crying, silently, so as not to disturb anyone. His mother had been there. She had taken him by the hand and they had walked in this wonderful place full of lights. Then as they crossed the road a black car had cut her off from him and when it passed she was gone. He ran back to find her. He ran until his chest ached as it did now and the tears came as he turned into a cul-de-sac and saw the high black wall. A man stepped out of it and struck the boy dumb.

Harry put on the bedside light and saw the glass of milk, the two biscuits. The room was white as snow. Even the curtains were white. He could not quite remember where he was. There was no sound at all and the luxury seemed too grand for him. Had he any right to be here? When would they come for him?

He got up and rubbed his eyes dry. Isabella had found a shirt for him, and it hung down almost to his ankles. The door was ajar and opened without a murmur. He went along the deeply carpeted landing and down the silent stairs, guided by the moonlight which came in through a large window set in the roof. As he went down the stairs he heard a voice and paused outside the room it issued from. There was light coming from under the door and Harry felt comforted by that. He sat down, leaning against the banister, lulled by the company of the voice within. Why was he crying again? He could not stop the tears coursing down his cheeks.

When Jen opened the door he was all but asleep.

"I thought I heard someone," she said. "Do you want something?"

In his half-unconsciousness he nodded and she bent over him to catch his whisper: "My mother".

"Oh yes," she said. "Oh yes, darling – oh yes." And she sat beside him and hugged him, remembering when this was all she needed, all she ever wanted, all that could help.

Part Two

BEFORE THAT DAY

SEVEN

FOR her first free Saturday in London, Jen dressed like a warrior. The cream skirt was flick short, a loincloth or a Roman tunic, lean legs bare and brown from the month's beachcombing in the Mediterranean, clean boots supple, built for speed, light-brown blouse satin-like, loose-armed, buttoned at the cuff, encouraging a ripple of shapes as the soft material swung with the sway of the breasts. The belt was crude: broad Spanish leather, buckled like a scabbard, slung on the hip; the Mexican glass beads draped totemistically in rainbow layers matched by the run of cheap bright Indian bangles. Around her forehead – too much but she would not resist the temptation – the Apache band in scarlet. It held back – like a dam – the flood of blond hair and threw into disconcerting relief the voraciously slim face, the pure, even cold, grey eyes.

She stared at herself for some time in the full-length mirror of the attic bedroom. The music of the time danced through her mind. She was part of it. Out there the world had changed. The young generation understood that. There were marches to be joined, wars spiked, icons destroyed, music made, women rein-venting their roles, myths junked, men tamed, the moon was no longer the limit. Her lot ruled. Out there in London where she had arrived so auspiciously that she still could not believe her luck, out there in the city so different from the clenched Northern industrial steel-and-soot city of her childhood, out there was all that she could want, all that she could imagine, all that she could fantasise.

Without knowing why, she raised her right fist in a salute to her image and punched the air. Into battle: the enemy was waiting to be captured or slain.

She avoided Helen, despite what she owed her or, for Jen though just twenty was wise already, because of what she owed her. She left a note, drank a cup of water, took an apple and, wild in her heart, entered into the lists of the streets of London.

She remembered the dream, the same dream, but pushed it down, far down. This bright summer Spenser Faerie morning, full leaf and lulling warmth, was to entertain no shadows, no death.

With a sense of the symbolic she tacked her way through the Victorian and Georgian roads and avenues, hills and crescents of Hampstead and on to the Heath itself, where she mounted Parliament Hill and looked across the city. There it was, this Saturday morning, quiet below her in that river basin which had cradled the dominating history of her race. It was where you could be unlicensed, where you could be anonymous, unencumbered, no past, free. Free. It was waiting to be plundered. Ready to yield up its infinite variety. All you had to do was to be bold.

She moved to her own hummed music through the genteel urban villagey centres of South End Green, Belsize Park and England's Lane and on to Primrose Hill, where the grass had just been mown. The sweet explosion of that scent, its possession of her lungs and throat triggered such a rage for sensation that she ran, flew up the hill, legs stretching easily, betraying the girl she was, and arrived too soon at the top, scarcely a pulse count up, her eyes hunting over the territory before her. Parkland: the true grandeur and power of a city which could take away so much of its centre from its natural elements of bricks and mortar. Down the hill she raced again, through Regent's Park, and followed the curve of Nash towards Piccadilly Circus.

Jen sat under Eros with other students, Dutch and German, and breathed in the dust of the city as eagerly as she had sucked at the tang of new-mown grass, surged to the noise of traffic as enraptured as she had been in the silence of the earlier morning on Parliament Hill. It was all good. London was her place. It would never do her harm. She would own it.

She was thirsty and a little hungry, but decided to postpone eating and drinking for a while, keen to heighten the experience of the first full lone day in the city she wanted. East was jolly Leicester Square, Covent Garden Market, Fleet Street, St Paul's. She had seen from Parliament Hill the City of London, the Docks, the East End, Crystal Palace – even signpost names such as these, to say nothing of the yards and squares, the passages and alleys which had irrigated metropolitan letters – gave her a feeling of scope, of adventure, foreign destinations, Babel, dark ships of wealth stealing up from Tilbury. South and west were the great twins of Westminster Abbey and Parliament, then the Tate, the arts and parts of Chelsea and on by boat to Kew, a penny for the Gardens, Richmond and the rock clubs "Richmond and Kew undid me", to Hampton Court on the fat suburban Thames with a louche riverside life slouching alongside like a fat freeloader. She had already been to some of these places and been obliged to memorise a map of London in her whirlwind of work over the past weeks: work which had leavened the school and university reading and far outstripped the Northern yearnings of her youth. She eased herself up, ignored the good-natured guttural invitations in a language whose words were opaque, whose meaning was transparent, and set off along Piccadilly, the flick of her skirt, the lift of her mane, the jangling of her beads and bangles magnetising male attention.

The exhibition at the Academy would have interested her on another occasion but today she was too excited for contemplation. London was to be gorged, not considered. She turned into New Bond Street and soon, to her surprise, found herself absorbed in the artifacts of wealth. From shop to shop she moved like a hungry waif. What would it be like to walk down a street like this and be able to buy anything that took your fancy? What would it *feel* like? Shoes that cost a month's wages; necklaces, rings, bracelets glittering with legendary stones, priced out of all reason; clothes anciently styled but cut from material you could rub through the window glass; paintings with the mint of museum about them; small porthole windows boasting a single pendant. She went into Asprey's and entered a tomb of rich objects, gilded trinkets, polished, dazzling, profuse, costly, desirable. She browsed as, until that morning, she had only browsed in bookshops, and explored it as closely as an archaeologist might have explored a treasure vault.

Jen was puzzled by the intensity of her reaction. She would have judged herself unexceptional in the matter of acquisitiveness, and without avarice. Yet there was no doubting that the wealth of objects in this hushed and burnished shopping palace seized her as directly as the smack of the grass, the high view over the city, the hub of Piccadilly. Like someone open to all infections, she was open to all the powers of London and this cavern of preciously wrought metals and minerals was a power.

She was aware that she was being closely observed by the formally dressed staff. Was she a shoplifter? A call-girl or a dyke or a millionaire's stray doll or daughter? Her clothes were no sure clue in this new world permissive age, nor was her cool manner. "Can we help you, Madam?" – a mere shake of the head brought silence and a courteous retreat. Jen was shocked by the force of the place: but not, as might have been expected, outraged. The shock, she thought, as she wandered down Piccadilly towards Hyde Park, the shock, she finally decided, was the shock of recognition she had been told about by the enthusiastic lecturer at Sussex University who took a few of them for a special class. The recognition of a world planets removed from tight Northern thrift and all the combinations of lower-middle and middle-class comforts coupled with anti-materialism which she had encountered in her couple of years in the South with friends around the villas of Brighton. The recognition was of her own lust for such objects. In that shop she had caught the virus of curiosity about the feeling of power over possessions. What *would* it feel like to stroll down New Bond Street and pick out those objects as easily as picking blackberries?

The thing was to admit it, she thought, first and most importantly to herself. No need to be ashamed of it. No need to lie. She needed to be everything she could be and London would provide for that. Freedom, Truth and all of life!

Hyde Park was a green beach strewn with sunbathers. Deckchairs striped like summer blazers lolled in clusters or singly in English attitudes summoning up cricket, seaside postcards, strawberries and canvas-bottomed sloth. Jen had spent her first summer vacation peddling deckchairs on Brighton beach and the memory of that larking student time, though only a year old, seemed as distant as puberty. She had said goodbye to all that.

Beside the still waters of the Serpentine she lay down and slept. Waking up ravenous, she bought a giant ice-cream, Italian, soft on the tongue which could carve into it, shape and let it lob around the mouth. The clumsy boats, the occasional bob of a swimmer's head, the, as she thought, Seurat dots of light on the grass, on the water, the urban ease and stroll of the day, reassured her. All very ordinary matter and herself very matter-of-factly part of it – a relief after too much *Zarathustra* earlier in the morning. This was also her town; not particularly well-off tourists, Londoners on a free outing, cheap and cheerful communal recreation. A place for free trips. She wanted to be part of that, too.

In the middle of the Royal Park, itself in the middle of the ancient and modern city, anonymous, twenty, without money, on a temporary job, irretrievably alienated from her past, planning to abort her university career, infused with a savage sense of exhilaration, Jen felt she could and would and must do everything she wanted in this city. The sensation of charged, sunburnt, healthy youth was only part of it. There was no question in her mind that there was the anger and the energy and the will to burn the pain and find a place in the refuge of ambition; safety in the isolation of great success. She hunched up her knees and stared at the grass in front of her as if she were making a medieval vow or chastely dedicating herself to pursue the impulse which throbbed through her so fiercely that she wanted to stand and stretch and shout aloud "Here I am! Watch out world! There is nothing I cannot do!" She held on to that, tried to pull together all her reserves, wished and willed an unimaginable future.

"Another ice-cream?"

For a second or two Jen failed to register that the question, which was repeated, was being addressed to her. When finally she turned to face the voice it was with a palpable wrench, like being dragged out of the deepest sleep or the most compelling dream.

"Who are you?"

Simon smiled. That usually did the trick. "Just someone who wants to buy you an ice-cream."

Jen looked away from him, back to the grass sod which had been her altar. The rare moment had passed. But it had been there, she told herself, it could be revisited.

"Who *are* you?"

She made no attempt to conceal her irritation. Her question clearly meant 'Who do you think you are?'

"Simon," he said. "And you?"

She did not reply.

"Let me guess. Apache? Great-granddaughter of Geronimo? No? Stray hippy on the turn? Wrong again, I see. Walking personification of current erotic fantasy, male that is? Am I getting hot? As it were?" He smiled again, harder.

"What happened to your arm?"

Simon's left arm was in plaster from the hand to the elbow. It was slung around his shoulder in such an elegant way that it seemed a fashion accessory. He was the most elegant young man she had seen: a beautifully cut sports coat; white Indian cotton shirt; tailored jeans; bare feet in white tennis shoes. Black-haired, athletically slim, in absolutely no doubt about the prevailing force of his charm.

"Cricket," he said. "Failed to see a medium fast ball. Should be playing today. Perfect." He looked at the sky, mostly blue, clouds few, white and wispy. Jen noticed his lean chin – was that why he had looked at the sky? She was beginning to like him.

"I can't bear to watch it so I wandered along here."

"To see what you could pick up?"

Simon laughed.

"Looking for a flying shag in the afternoon before jumping your girlfriend later on?" Jen smiled throughout the sentence.

"I know you now. You're a radical feminist tease. Well: that's a relief."

"Could I have the one with the chocolate flake in it?"

"The pornographic one?"

"That's it."

"No problem."

He was conscious of the way he moved, too, she observed. But she liked the way he moved. She liked the way he talked.

Later, as they walked together as slowly as pensioners around the pond, he said, "What brings a gorgeous creature like you to a landlocked seaside nightmare like this?"

"You sound a hundred and six –"

"Inherited."

"Snobbish –"

"Fully paid for: expensive training. Very gruelling."

"And a *passé* prat."

"You know. You really are a find."

"Want me in your collection?"

"Yes please."

"Do you think of anything else?"

"Not much. No. Work and that sort of stuff, money, interferes sometimes. And there's cricket, of course, and booze and horses. But basically – no. Should I?"

"You're not getting anything from me today, Simon, and perhaps never. So if you want your daily dose of instant gratification you'd better hop off."

"Has anybody told you about your fantastic eyes? They should have done. But you never know with your dumb hippy lefty types. Have they?"

"I see. A little more market research."

"I mean the legs are A1 terrific and I bet the butt is randier than

Nijinsky's. I mean the horse, of course. Were you on him? Don't answer. Your type don't go racing. I must take you. Where was I? The butt. Well –"

"That'll do."

"The butt stops there?"

"That was a really terrible pun."

"Didn't you love it?"

"Not much."

"They *are* the most fantastic eyes. A bit creepy in some respects. Like those kids – a science-fiction thing – they all came from the same planet – anyway – there was a film, or a telly, *they* all had the same rather beautiful, rather weird eyes. Yours are just a bit like that now and then when they aren't just wildly sexy."

"Thank you, Simon."

"Ah. The lady mocks me."

"Afraid so."

"Damn! What's a chap to do?"

"There's a bit of Bertie Wooster in you, Simon. I think that's one of the bits I could like."

"Other bits are eager to please."

"No doubt."

"Certificates have been won."

"And pinned no doubt like knicker-trophies to your bedroom wall."

"You mistake your man. Truly."

"Perhaps. Even so. No go. I want today to myself."

She stopped and held out her hand. Simon took it and drew it to his lips where he butterflied the lightest kiss.

"Not even a farewell drink?"

"Sorry."

"But may we meet, sob, see each other, sob, again?"

"I'll give you my number at work. You have no pen, of course."

"I'll remember. Shoot." He dared her.

Unfazed, she delivered it and smiled as he mumbled it over several times.

"And yours?" she asked.

"I'll ring *you*," he said. "Monday."

"I see. A call from me would embarrass you. Is that it?"

Simon hesitated and then he made the right decision.

"In the present circumstances, life being what it is – yes."

"Fair enough."

She turned and walked a few paces. Inevitably, as she knew he would, he called out.

"Hey!"

And she turned.

"The bandanna." He pointed to his forehead. "Take it off. It doesn't do for afternoons."

He really did look good, she thought. He would be fun. She took it off, whirled it around and launched it at him. Without waiting to see what he did, she walked on.

"I'll put it on my lance," he shouted. "I'll nail it to the wall!"

Over into Notting Hill Gate where the drift of the young Saturday crowd enticed her into the Portobello Road. A jazz band, playing Dixie, trudged between the stalls of silver, brass, jewellery, all manner of superior junk and easily portable antiques. Shops too, and she was soon leaning against a bookshelf of calfbound volumes, absorbed in a luridly illustrated second edition of Foxe's *Book of Martyrs*. How much religion meant then, how violently and wholly people believed in what, to her, was at best a tradition of cruel or charming superstitions of no more than historical interest. But look – and read: people every bit as intelligent and thoughtful as herself – more so in most cases, she had no doubt. And such a short time ago, a few centuries, less than a dozen lives at three score years and ten. Such sacrifice, such faith, such will. She admired them. To be as determined as that, as tunnel-visioned, if you like, but as flat out for all they believed in – anything else was selling it short. It was a wonderful book.

"Twenty-two pounds," the yellow-moustached old man said. "I'm afraid I can't reduce it further. I'll put it aside for you if you like."

"I would have to pay in instalments and I don't like that. So."

"You could change your mind. I'll keep it until this time next Saturday."

"That's very kind of you."

"I saw you reading it," he said, by way of explanation, and Jen felt her heart leap a little: another recognition. He could become a friend.

They talked a little more and he offered her a cup of tea but she was tugged back on to the warm pavements. She wanted to keep moving and soon she was out of the easy swarm of Portobello and drifting through streets of stately serenity. Tall houses, usually white, composed, terraced or in pairs, handsomely windowed, testaments to a level and spread of wealth and expectation of leisured comfort of which she had no experience.

There was a quietness about these streets, a security, no sense of strain, goods were never a problem, merely a choice; here were paintings on the walls, she saw clearly as the twilight began to stain the air and the bulbs lit discreet corners of rooms with undrawn curtains, books lining shelves, pretty furniture, house after house. As she criss-crossed Holland Park and moved across the park itself into Kensington and then Chelsea, the accretion of those deep domestic fortunes, the solidity of the achieved metropolitan life, the privileged trick of such rural-seeming relaxation in the centre of the urban stronghold, all impressed themselves on her.

It was a lesson showing the true nature of that part of English society that ruled: the officer class, living in houses grouped around the parks and palaces like an urban guard, loyal, largely monarchist, having fashioned an enviable laager of continuing civilisation which was neither feudal, baronial, *nouveau* nor piratical, although it had connections in all those strains. These were the settlements of the well-to-do middle- to upper-middle classes and, only by drifting through them, often through deserted streets, the sense of placidity as crushing as cathedral silence, could she understand the strength and attraction of it. This too was a London she would conquer.

She had reached the river – the river that had given London its shape and history, now winding slowly down with the ebbing tide, and turned east. She was drowsy, leg weary, soupbrained with the wandering, a little light-headed from lack of food, but, as the Thames glittered under the setting sun, she had no wish to do anything else, be anywhere else, than in this city. The summer job she had so flukily landed in television had shuttled her across London in the finding of the artists, "characters" and celebrities necessary to feed its greedy magazine formula. That had taken her into pockets and places she could not have expected to reach unaided by the Aladdin's lamp of the television camera. That alone had excited her appetite: this day, though, had uncovered what might even be called a vision.

It was as if she had always had knowledge of the city. Or perhaps she had always had an intimation of the multitude of possibilities available to her in some place. Like the theories which suggest that all knowledge is there, simply waiting to be uncovered, like rubbing an old brass until you reveal the words and the patterns – London, the city, the rich contradictory variety of it, was deeply calming. It could transform any pain, a great ocean to her hurt. Always somewhere to hide, always somewhere new to turn, always something to make. For making it was vital: it was the essential distance between a past which still threatened to trap and wound her, and a future in which she could invent herself. Making it was necessary if she was going to be free. More than that, it was, she recognised now, a compulsion, in itself a pain as severe as the childhood pain, as if only pain could drive out pain. My God, she was going to do it!

This theme recurred between stretches of blackness as she wound by the river. She would have appeared a lonely figure, even pathetic, abandoned by a circus of style and fun going on elsewhere, in the way she trailed along, intent in a way which could have been misinterpreted as self-pitying. Not a likely figure – without money, without that spread of connections which gives such a rocket launch to so many successful careers – to take on the heft and welt of a bruising city. But she would do it.

"Or bust," she said to herself quite solemnly. "Or bust."

At Westminster Bridge she turned north and went into Soho. She was looking for a cheap nightclub with her sort of music where she would have a beer and a sandwich and maybe, if there was a band, sing a few songs. She was a confident rocker with a bluesy voice and loved to sing, loved the sensation of being possessed. But she was too tired to hunt the place down – if it existed – and too full of the wonders of her day fully to appreciate the Soho quilt of sleaze and glamour, the village in the fast lane, the crime and nourishment.

Suddenly she knew that she could not make the haul uphill to Hampstead and went across to Charing Cross Road for the 24 bus. By the time she reached Helen's house she was all but asleep on her feet.

"Your parents called," Helen said. "They sounded rather anxious."

"Whom did you talk to?" Jen was immediately alert. "Dennis or Marjorie?"

"Your father."

"Did he say anything?"

"I think they would appreciate a call."

Jen nodded.

"You can use the extension in my study."

"I'll phone them tomorrow."

To Helen, the reaction seemed unnecessarily cruel and impolite. She restrained her impulse to comment. She felt that she had already overstepped her relationship with Jen by using 'anxious' and assuming the mothering role. She saw Jen as a wild foal and knew that she would race away at the first touch of the bridle. Yet she longed to be the one to break her in.

"Would you like something to eat? I was going to make myself an omelette."

"I'll make it."

"Why don't you have a bath?"

"Could I?"

"Take a clean towel from the airing-cupboard. A yellow one."

"You want me to phone Dennis and Marjorie now, don't you?"

"I am only the messenger," said Helen.

"But that's what you want."

"Perhaps you could turn your psychic powers to real advantage and tell me where I have mislaid a silver christening spoon which I polished along with everything else this morning."

"I won't be long."

"Very well. Six minutes."

Helen could lift her mood more successfully than anyone Jen had ever known. Nothing she said was without acute interest, nothing was wasted, no quarter was given. To have landed a summer job in Helen's television department was the greatest luck: but to have been offered 'the attic' in Helen's house and thereby enjoy the company of this remarkable woman was, Jen thought, almost a freak of fortune. Helen made her feel not only that she could but that she *would* achieve everything she wanted to do. Helen made her want to sing. As she ran the deep old-fashioned bath and stripped off, longing for the water, she began to sing. Her voice was good and strong and the sound – she sang the blues – shivered through the house like a charge.

In the kitchen, Helen listened to the singing and felt the thrill of its life. What was she to do with this remarkable child? Quite the most remarkable girl she had ever encountered, but wild as a hare. Something *had* to be made of all that energy and fury – if not, Helen thought, the girl would implode. There was danger there. To use it or to be destroyed by it. Helen could see the dilemma and, after almost six weeks, she was still uncertain how to proceed.

Normally, Helen Fraser, CBE, had very little difficulty in deciding on and expediting a course of action. In the world of television and, before that, radio she was famous for her decisiveness. Her first-class mind (Cambridge: Classics), her background (several generations of high-ranking Colonial administrators), her flair for spotting new talent and giving it its chance – these qualities added to her utter rectitude and amused determination that had made her the leading woman in British broadcasting and a very rare female eminence in the British Establishment. Her husband had died many years before: she had never remarried. A discreetly conducted liaison had almost drawn her back into matrimony but she had decided against it. By then her career, her solitude and her control over her own life mattered too much. There had been no children and she would often let to students one or both of the attic bedrooms in the overlarge Hampstead house she could not bear (or be bothered) to quit.

Jen puzzled and excited her. She had sailed through the interview for this short summer training-scheme, totally outgunning Oxbridge contemporaries whose advantages and paper achievements were in a different league from hers. Within a few days it was clear that she was a natural for the sort of television work required of her. But it was the force of the girl, the glow, the anger just under the skin, the aura. Helen reached out for these words. She did not like them but felt drawn to them. She did not want to think of Jen as being too strange.

"Too leathery," said Helen of the mushroom omelette.

"Better than too squidgy," said Jen.

"Would you like a glass of wine?"

"I'll get it."

Jen went to the sideboard and took the half-full bottle of 'cheap Italian' of which Helen expressed herself very fond, although she never drank more than two glasses. The girl was wearing a flowing white robe in cheap cotton, a cross between a sari and a dressing-gown; her hair tumbled every which way; health and pleasure pulsed off her; the blaze in her eyes was best avoided.

It was not unusual for them to have a snack at the end of the day. Jen's involvement with her job was such that she could not bear to leave it and would have motored through the day on a couple of sandwiches. Helen rarely arrived home before 10.30 p.m. The office, the theatre, the opera or a dinner-party would claim her. In a very short time the two women had come to look forward to this informal event.

Generally Helen would extrapolate on one of the more testing programmes coming out of her department. She was a passionate

Liberal, widely tipped to be elevated to the House of Lords. She found Jen's contempt for politicians both bracing and worrying. Such ruthless distrust, she thought, boded ill. Jen, however, would not be shaken.

Helen had set herself the task of prising the younger woman away from what she regarded as her wilfully immature absolutist attitudes and would devote much of the meal to goading her with arguments which, while they could leave Jen like a picador-quilled bull, had not yet brought her to concede Helen's basic points. These were to do with the essential and necessary conservative nature of all democratic institutions, the relative goodness of men and women in politics in Britain, the inefficiency inherent in democracy, the variability of human nature, the necessary difficulty of harnessing the weak and the strong, and the importance of trying, though acknowledging the perpetual certainty of failure, to move huge masses of people for their betterment through such varied aspects of life as health, education, reward, work. Jen fought her corner fiercely but Helen knew that she was winning. The prising loose was under way. She knew that Jen was not what she called "a silly person" and relativity would prevail.

Jen loved to hear her talk. Loved to hear that mind at work. Loved its range of reference, its worldliness, its incorruptibility. Kept the argument going just to listen to it.

Still perhaps a touch perturbed by Jen's reaction to the phone message from her parents, Helen took what she would usually dismiss as the facile option. A gambit used only by poverty-stricken conversationalists.

"Tell me what you did today?"

Jen was jolted back to her schooldays. It was the only question that Dennis and Marjorie seemed capable of asking. They had wanted to know everything – above all, how she had 'done'. In other words, had her work been commended, had her work been as good, even better than anyone else's, had she been praised by this or that teacher, was she going to do well in exams, was she near the top, would she get good results, might she be university material, how had she "done"? Very soon a cold stone wall of silence had tormented them to wounded exasperation.

Helen was either plotting or tired. She could not possibly be so banal. Jen made an effort.

So, although Jen began slowly, with no omissions, she rekindled her day until it blazed across the table to Helen, whose eyes narrowed at Asprey's, laughed at Simon, sympathised with her affection for the bookseller and felt herself walking along the streets, some sort of fellow pilgrim, as Jen beat the bounds of her new territory.

"And then the bus, the bath, the omelette, perfect. London. Perfect." She raised her glass, toasted and drank.

Helen paused, yet again puzzled as to the cause of the strength of the impact. She pulled herself together. If it would not come through intuition then she must take care not to stalk it too clumsily, or it would surely take flight.

"If you had pushed down Ladbroke Grove when you were at the Portobello Road you might have picked up something which would have bruised your idea, a little, of a perfect London. This race question is going to be very hard to deal with. And the next time you go wandering, take in the Docklands. That's where British industry and the style of life of ordinary people are both in the melting-pot. It is falling apart – possibly for ever. I can understand that London is something of a dream to you: I remember not dissimilar feelings myself when I came down in the Thirties. But it is a nightmare for others: that helps make it powerful. You ought to read Mayhew. I'll lend it you."

Jen smiled. Helen was forever adding to her reading list. Moreover, she expected Jen to go and read the recommended books. Discussion would follow.

"You ought to have read History," Helen said. "Or PPE. Intelligent people read English literature by themselves, as a matter of course."

"Perhaps you're right but it doesn't matter now. I'm not going back."

"What *are* you saying, child?"

"Geoff said there was a PA's job going. I've applied for it. Even if I don't get it I'm not going back."

"Geoff," said Helen, being scrupulously fair but with difficulty, "has every right to tell you that a PA's job might be available, although in the circumstances he could, for courtesy's sake, have consulted me, and a PA's job is well below the level of your ability."

"I don't care. It'll get me in. Then you'll see."

"Will I?" Helen's flow of thought was tripped up by Jen's boast.

"Yes," said Jen, smiling. And emptied her glass.

"I suppose you consider it pointless for me to explain the importance not so much of a university education, although you have need of it every bit as much as anyone else, but of finishing something you started. You have in effect a contract to take your degree over a three-year period. To opt out after two years could be construed as evidence of unreliability."

Jen was silent. She prided herself on her honesty and knew that Helen shared this characteristic. Should she, then, admit that at sixteen she had left school, to the despair of Dennis and Marjorie, and been persuaded back only by the persistence of the English teacher, aided by the realisation that the job opportunities available to a sixteen-year-old were tedious, arduous or rough?

"I know what I want to do," she said quietly. "I've found it. Why should I spend a year in Sussex just hanging about waiting and then perhaps there won't be an opening? I've been lucky to land this summer scheme. I see no point in leading my life in segments just because somebody else laid it out like that. I want to be in television in London. I like everything about television. I think it's wonderful. It can do anything. It can go everywhere. It can light up the world. A PA's job *may* be below my ability and indeed I may not even get it, but I'm putting in for it and I'm going flat out for it and, Helen, I *want* it."

Helen was struck by the hunger in the face. A disturbing paradox. A girl as healthy as it was possible to imagine and yet there, undoubtedly, was the expression of hunger. Of hunger and behind that something which now surfaced for the first time. Hurt. Perhaps beyond healing. The hunger driven by the hurt. Whatever pain it was, it drove her. Helen wanted to uncover it.

"How long have you called your parents by their Christian names?" Helen asked.

"Since I was sixteen."

"Do they object?"

"They did at first."

"Dennis seemed very concerned."

"He always does. He's in insurance. That seems – unfair. He's – he can be – no, he is – lovely."

Helen held her tongue and did not ask 'And Marjorie?'

"Marjorie and I hate each other."

Helen was shocked at the force of this sudden quiet lash of vitriol.

"Oh?"

"I wish we didn't." Jen hesitated and then was fair. "So does she. But we do. I'll clear up."

There was a moment before she did so when the two women looked at each other as might have been across a gulf. Of knowing

– so much to recognise; of unknowing – so much to discover. Helen experienced the glowering energy of the younger woman and decided that she would not be threatened by it nor could she be bullied by it. She would try to absorb what was hurting Jen, use and build on what was strong. What was strong was extraordinary. She had encountered many young people: this one was rare indeed.

In bed, the sheet cast aside, the gown taken off, naked and looking at the mix of citylight and moonlight coming through the open attic window, Jen felt the heat of the day and of the house press into the stillness of the room: heat trapped under the pitched roof, heat which she felt she could stir with her finger. A light silk of sweat cooled her just a little. Traffic sounds were a pleasant ripple on the somnolent back of warmth.

Jen lay calmly, the day's hunt done, the terrain explored, the object of desire identified, the plan and the path crystal clear. She hummed the music of the moment, felt the purr of it on her half-open lips, quietly enjoying a strength of enormous satisfaction.

The dream began to filter into her mind, but she tried not to be afraid of it, the wind howled in this dream, the small room, the woman crying . . .

EIGHT

IF he caught the late-afternoon train he could be in Edinburgh
by ten. He phoned home but there was no answer. Still a new
boy to television, he had a vague feeling that he ought to ask
permission to skip Friday, but whom was he to ask? The system
appeared to work in three stages: research which could be done
anywhere and for which there was a gratifying amount of time;
shooting the film which was careful and steady work on location;
and cutting it and finishing it back in London which began as an
elegant game of jigsaw and accelerated very rapidly to a panic
dash for the deadline. Then the slump of relief. Everybody evapo-
rated. He was in that slump now, after making a film on the
campus view of Vietnam which had raised a storm of comment
and slapped his name and style on to the screen in one. "Mark
Armstrong," *The Times* had written, "in his first television report,
has proved to have the natural authority of the born communicator. His commitment is clear and his integrity is undeniable. He
is a valuable addition to our rather jaded gallery of television
investigative reporters." The critic was an acquaintance but the
opinion was generally shared.

Mark wished it were not so. He had been deeply contented with
his job on the newspaper's Washington desk. Sylvia's urge and
then her determination to return to Edinburgh had given him little
choice. Of course there was some sort of an option and, as he had
stayed on alone for the two months to see out his contract, he had
considered it. But Atlantic commuting was out of his league and
in every way impossible. What he had not bargained for was the
depression he experienced. It was more than a forewarning of
withdrawal symptoms. In those last weeks in Washington he felt

that something altogether terrible was going on, a hauling up of roots which would never be replanted.

Mark had idolised foreign correspondents ever since he began in newspapers. To be the Washington correspondent was such a combination of fantasy fulfilment, profound achievement and delight in the scope and detail of the job that he knew there could be nothing to match it ever again. Thirty-eight and peaked. Sylvia thirty-four and childless – that was undoubtedly her anguish and he understood it, he respected it. He thought he could divine why she wanted to be back on home territory to square up to the middle passage of her life.

The despair was like homesickness, bad flu and drunken self-pity all compressed into a palpable object which now lodged in his head, now in his stomach. He made no effort to take up the reasonable but unexciting offer made him by his newspaper on his return to London. After several weeks of 'resettling', better described as mourning, the offer to do two television documentaries on American foreign policy as seen through its universities appeared like the miracle in a fable. He had been offered a twelve-month contract and he had taken it. It would never match being a correspondent but the reach, the influence and the difficulties of doing it well, finally drew him into the new world of television and refreshed him. Professionally, his move to television had been justified and the first job well done. He caught the train north as well off, he thought, as anyone had any right to be.

He had a cheap pad in London which he shared with a doctor and a television director – both of them, like himself, needing to get out of the city as often as possible. Edinburgh was a mite far for a home address but until now the peripatetic demands of the job had made it defensible. And Sylvia was deeply comfortable there.

So was he, he thought, as he strolled up the ramp out of Waverley Station on the fine, still light mid-September evening. The Old Town crept into view. Bastions of stone, fortress-windowed, huddled together in battle formations and there, floating on its rock of basalt in the yellow electric light, the castle itself. Mark had loved the castle from the moment he had clapped eyes on it – a moment he could remember clearly when he had been hauled across the Borders with his brothers for Christmas 1938. A treat for them all. His mother to see the shops of Princes Street, the children to the zoo and the Castle, tea in the Roxburgh. His childhood imagination, full of Rob Roy and Robert the Bruce, Wallace and famous Reivers of the Borders, was ignited by the walls and the cannon, the waterfall of frozen rock scaled only once by a successful assault in all those years – and those men Scottish! He wanted to rip the claymores from the walls and defy all Scotland's enemies, let them do their worst, he would never surrender.

As the years went by and he came again – to play rugby, to watch the Internationals – he rarely failed to go to the Castle for a visit, however hurried. It was like a hawk on that rock, he thought, or a kite with the long tail of the Royal Mile drifting down to Holyrood Palace. Kinks in the tail now and then, like the great square stone fortress cathedral of St Giles. But what he came to love most about this descent was the multitude of little doorways, entrances, the closes or wynds, courts or stairs often leading to steps which rattled down towards the valley which divided the city. Bull's Close, Boswell's Court, Stairs Close, Baillie Maude's Close, Carribers Close, Fountain Close, Flesh Market Close which funnelled down to the bowels of *The Scotsman*, where he had gained his first serious job as a journalist; scores of these entrances home of lawyers and Jacobins, philosophers, prostitutes, scholars, thieves, merchants – in his three years at *The Scotsman* he had become an expert on the intrigues of the place. It could give him a sense of being in a different country, bawdier, stinkier, more cruel, crowded, unjust, intolerant but somehow, Mark felt, more alive – more alive to the sort of simple feelings he could still summon up when he saw the castle again and heard a skirl of the pipes. As now.

He strolled over towards the New Town in which Sylvia had managed to secure a flat. R. L. Stevenson, one of his favourite authors, who caught yet another side of Edinburgh in *Dr Jekyll and Mr Hyde*, had called his city 'this dream in masonry and living rock'. The dream in rock was the castle. The dream in masonry was this astounding New Town, born of a civic and national rediscovery and planned by a young man, Craig, a twenty-two-year-old whose dream of Classical grandeur, Graeco-Scottish terraces, circuses and crescents for the leaders of society had been executed by others, but retained all the simplicity and force of a young man's clinical dream. Mark had come late to an affection for this part of the town, preferring for years the narrow side-streets, especially Rose Street, full of writers and pubs. But it was where Sylvia hailed from and the place to which she had determined to return. And in the calm sweep and style of it, the rectitude of the stone and the gravity of the plan, he now found much to admire. Their flat was just below Queen Street.

It was empty. He had taken a snack and a couple of beers on the train. He was restless without quite knowing why. Sylvia would be safely out with a friend. Although he had failed to make contact with her, he was still disappointed that she was not there to meet him and dismayed that he should still be so emotionally feeble. Washington was over, Edinburgh and London would be the places now. *The Scotsman* had even asked him to contribute an occasional piece which would settle his itching hand. His life was on track.

Yet after skimming through the letters and taking a second large Bell's, he retreated to his armchair by the unlit fire more like a tired old dog than a vigorous young man on the verge of a fine new career. There was the shadow which would not leave him and he could not continually direct it at Washington. It was much, much closer to home than that.

And so when Sylvia came into the flat with Alexander he was almost relieved. He heard them murmuring in the hall; then silence; then they came in. They were holding hands. Alexander dropped his hand instantly. Sylvia, after a pause, took it up again.

"I tried to ring," Mark said. "I mean, I *did* ring. No one was here."

"We drove across to Melrose," Sylvia said. "It was a glorious afternoon."

"Well," said Alexander, "I'll be off."

"Have a drink," said Mark.

"No. I'm —"

"Have a drink."

"Have a drink, Alexander. Let's all have a drink," said Sylvia, firmly.

Mark found he was having difficulty drawing in his breath. He turned his back on them as he poured out the drinks and inwardly muttered commands to himself. "Shoulders back!" "Deep breath!" "Deeeeep breeeath!" He felt as if he were about to shake so violently he would fall to pieces.

"Here we are," he said. "Here we are."

Alexander took a sip of the whisky and set it down. He glanced at Sylvia and squared up.

"Look, Mark. I'm in love with Sylvia. I have been, I realise, for a very long time. I tried — we both did — to ignore it and hoped it would go away but it hasn't, it didn't and over the past few months —"

"Is that why you were so determined to come back from Washington?" said Mark.

"Yes," said Sylvia.

"I understand."

"It's terrible," Alexander said. "The worst of it is you are a friend, which is dreadful. But it's happened, Mark. I wish we'd told you earlier instead of your finding out like this."

"So it wasn't that you hated Washington?"

"No. I rather liked Georgetown."

"I'm on my way. No," Alexander raised his hand, "you two need time together. I've said my piece. I'm desperately sorry, Mark."

"Yes."

"I'll call you later," said Sylvia.

For some moments there was silence which was broken by a strange and unattractive sound. He looked up and saw Sylvia looking at him with apprehension and pity. The sound grew louder and more crude, a heaving even a snorting sound, crude and even disgusting. When he realised that it was himself, sobbing, he was ashamed but by then he was caught up in it and the sound became a howl. Sylvia came over to put her arms around him but he coiled like a foetus and she retreated and waited until the noise, which had grown intolerable, and filled the flat, ebbed, quietened, declined to an exhausted whisper of sobbing, even whimpering. He took out a handkerchief and dried his face, hid behind it to prepare an expression to meet his wife.

He had met Sylvia when he was twenty-two and both of them had been inexperienced. He had never once been unfaithful to her nor she to him, he would gamble, until now.

He found that he was taking deep heavy breaths and this continued for a minute or so.

"There's something I have to say."

"Please." He held up his hand like a policeman stopping traffic. "There's nothing to say. I – er – I do – I understand and there will have to be arrangements. Just tell me what to do and I'll do it. Nothing more to say."

"Mark, I'm sorry, but there is."

He feared what she would say and he looked like someone waiting for the axe to fall on his neck.

"I'm pregnant." Sylvia tried but could not entirely keep the joy out of her voice.

"What was that?" he whispered.

"It's so unfair," she said.

123

Mark was too full, too stunned to speak. But after he had stood up, driven himself up like a very old man seeking his uncertain balance on the frailest of legs, he forced himself to say, "I'm sorry it couldn't happen to us – you know – between us."

"So am I." Sylvia wept now, but silently. "Oh, so am I. I still love you, Mark, but I'm thirty-four and I am in love with Alexander and –"

"Of course. You want . . . You must. Now then. I need a little air."

"Mark. You do realise . . ."

But she saw his expression and stopped.

"You'll be all right, won't you?" he said. "Get Alexander round."

"I'll go over to his place. It's something we haven't done but – you must have the flat to yourself tonight."

"Whatever you say."

Holding up his hands, rather like a blind man but also as if he feared she might touch him, something which at all costs had to be prevented, Mark moved past her and went down the hall, down the stairs, on to the empty street and began to walk.

He did not return until dawn. He walked through the night city like a man seeking a resting place in the catacombs. Often the streets before him were utterly deserted of people and of traffic. The sound of his unflagging footsteps was his only company. Up to the castle, below the bridges, down towards the palace, across to the monuments to the dead on Carlton Hill, in and out the New Town, he was like Aeneas or Orpheus seeking a spirit in the underworld, except that the spirit he sought was irrecoverable. Although he would never be able to, never want to, cut out his love for her, she was now dead to him, as surely as a claymore thrust to the heart. There would be no finding it again, ever again, he thought, and what was life without it?

Back in the flat, birds singing in the garden, pearl light sweeping through the classical windows, he stood in the kitchen waiting for the kettle to boil and shivered. The shivering grew so intense that his teeth began to chatter. It was as if the protective layer around a vacuum flask were being jarred and shaken, shaken until it splintered, fell away, leaving him utterly exposed, without protection, without form. He knew, and the knowledge was terrible, that a life was over.

The tea scalded his tongue.

NINE

IT would be a lucky year, she had thought, because the numbers added up to her age. Eighteen and never been kissed! She blushed even though the phrase was often in her mind. It was curious how certain phrases just crept in there and could not be brushed off. Eighteen and never been kissed! As if a parrot were repeating it. Still, it would be her lucky year; her mother had been emphatic on that. Her mother was always right about such things. Before the illness her mother had been such a force. That was the vicar's word: a force. Even now there were times when Valerie quailed, when she felt crushed. Mother put it down to Valerie's illness – the tuberculosis – and the weakness which followed, but Valerie remembered well enough the times before that. Her mother was a force. Her mother had had too much to bear. That was how she put it. Just too much to bear.

When they had all arrived in the little Cumbrian market town about fourteen years ago, everything had seemed rosy. Her father had got a job in the local branch of a building society – a job which almost matched the one he had left and was very much better than he could have hoped for. They had soon found a bungalow on the West Road which suited them adequately. Mother had found the church to her liking, the vicar sympathetic, the small social circle which grew out of that connection perfectly satisfactory, and the town, though rather common, acceptable. For some years they lived as a devoted family. Indeed it was remarked on by the few who knew them that they appeared altogether self-sufficient. Mrs Thomlinson was to do with the church, soon on the flower rota, a willing hand at jumble sales; Mr Thomlinson also attended but declined to be nominated as a church warden or to stand for any office, join any club. Valerie was the most biddable of daughters. They kept themselves to themselves and people thought well of them for it.

Sometimes Valerie wished she had more playmates. School was a treat but she was rarely allowed to do anything outside school hours. If she did go anywhere, Mr Thomlinson would be waiting for her outside the gates, at the house where the party was being held, at the bus stop. Mrs Thomlinson would greet her like a prodigal returned and the guilt would grow. But at least there was school and although she was timid she was sufficiently conscientious to keep up. She loved school: sitting in the same room as thirty others, yet being left alone. Able to feel safe because so many milled around her in the playground yet able to enjoy the peace and quiet of unmolested solitude. A smile from another girl, the offer of a sweet. Sometimes "Well done, Valerie". Not often but often enough. She dreaded the end of the fifth year when she would have to leave – it had been made clear to her that she was not "sixth form material". There was some consolation in getting a nice job in Mr Rigg's office but that only lasted until Christmas. Her mother fell ill.

It had been coming on for a few months but at Christmas it became worrying. At first they thought it was the strain – the church bazaar, the carol services, the rush and fuss of the time. Then she had caught a very nasty cold which would not budge. But on Boxing Day she had a "turn". The doctor advised rest and quiet and prescribed some red pills.

For a few weeks there was great unease in the house. The illness could not be diagnosed or defined. There was no mistaking its effect. Mrs Thomlinson was lethargic, she was tired, as she said, "before I wake up". She had been a woman of great energy in a little space but now that was gone. Like a light being switched off, her husband said, just – click, and she was an invalid. It was accepted, soon, that was it.

Valerie left her job to look after her mother.

Mr Thomlinson had always been the lesser power between them. He attempted to meet the challenge of an invalid wife but even in her lethargy, in her tired large-eyed heaviness of debilitation, she was too much for him. His dependency grew, his helplessness matched hers: Valerie ministered to both of them. The radio or television provided the backdrop for long days, long evenings of service.

Still, there were features which could be enjoyed. Valerie did all the shopping and found that the shopkeepers became very friendly and supportive after a few visits. She looked forward to that enormously. She had to take driving lessons as her mother was too weak to drive and her father became increasingly fearful. Valerie was a nervous driver but underneath the anxiety there was pleasure and she loved it when her instructor bowled out of the little town and went some way into the fells. She had been into the Lake District a few times on school trips or on Sunday runs with her parents and had loved it from the first moment. And there was church. Her mother had insisted on being taken to the evening service and Valerie could occasionally pop out to help at a church function.

It was not the life which had begun to open up in prospect in Mr Rigg's office, nor was it anything like as enjoyable as school, but there were many much worse off than she and, besides, it was only right that she should give something back to parents who had given so much to her. Everybody in her own small world thought that she was exemplary in her duty and one or two of them praised her to her face, which flustered her.

What made it difficult and then intolerable was a growing competition, a struggle for her affection between her parents. If she made her mother comfortable on the sofa beside the fire then a little whinny from her father would indicate that he too needed attention. If she offered to go for a short walk with her father – whose helplessness had now turned to declining health which kept him at home more often than he was at work – then a baleful look from her mother shortened the walk even more or stopped it altogether. Four greedy eyes gobbled at her. She would plead tiredness and go to bed very early to be alone. There she would read, guiltily aware that her light was visible under the doorway. Whenever they came in to say goodnight, she would apologise for the book and feel even worse at the protestations of understanding. "You need all the rest you can get! We're a terrible burden on a young girl."

Eventually, the silent struggle became articulated. Remarks, threats, references, jibes, only some of which passed her by; low words of reproach, whispered words of anger, looks of hatred. Valerie was constantly upset, but she had no strategies, no resources other than persistent attention. She prayed with all her might but there was no response. She had to watch and attend while her parents waged war. Sometimes she stared at them in disbelief and they turned away from the clarity of her open blue-grey gaze.

Her father collapsed one day and was taken to hospital, from which he never returned. After the funeral and the mourning, Valerie suggested that she might go back to work. She could easily come home at lunchtime and the housework was nothing, a good clean through on Saturday and an hour or so every morning before the office. Her mother would not hear of it. Careful planning and frugal living would satisfy their needs: her husband's pension, a small income of her own and their savings would be quite sufficient. She would miss Valerie and preferred her to stay at home. At least for a few months or so. But next year, she assured her, would be different.

The bungalow was small, set back from the road which was becoming busier by the month as the nuclear plant developed on the west coast and bigger and bigger lorries went to it. There were days when Valerie counted every one of them from the moment she woke up until the moment she fell asleep. The death of her father had brought undisguised contentment to her mother but Valerie tried to block that chilling realisation out of her mind. There was still the shopping, the occasional trip into the Lakes and Sunday, of course, Evensong. Now and then she bumped into girls she had known at school or boys who had begun to come into focus just when she was leaving. They always seemed so full of life. She longed to be with them, not necessarily to talk, just to stand beside them. But she always hurried on, not to bother them, not to get in their way. And her mother did not like her to be out for too long: fretted. Besides, she was becoming attractive, the school mousiness remained in manner only. The tuberculosis which had impaired her childhood and left her weak, now seemed far behind her.

If she spent too much time alone she could get into a panic. She did not know where it came from or why it came but she would find it difficult to breathe, her palms would sweat, her stomach clench with cold spasms of sickness, her brow feel hot. Once or twice her mother saw her like that and said that she was prone to asthma. It ran in the family. She would stop there. The hinterland of family was unknown to Valerie. Occasionally an Uncle Jack had been referred to and grandparents, now dead she assumed.

She had always been a little frightened of her mother and now that she was alone with her she was frightened all the time. Evensong was her refuge and her strength.

$18 = 1 + 9 + 7 + 1$. She wrote it on a slip of paper and hid it in her prayer book.

TEN

"THREE passions have governed my life," Nicholas read. "A longing for love, the search for knowledge and unbearable pity for the sufferings of mankind." Beside those words from Bertrand Russell's autobiography were a tick, a question mark, a date, Sept. 18th, 1971, and the name of a city. He wanted to unravel his past and this was as good a starting point as any.

He was reading the Russell autobiography in order to steady himself for the selection procedure. Russell's death the previous year at an immense age had pulled Nicholas back to those parts of his bookshelf neglected since university and he had laboured through the *History of Western Philosophy*. In truth, an act of piety had become a weekly pleasure as the lucid Edwardian prose had so elegantly arranged centuries of thought into convenient and digestible morsels. Now he looked for the man behind the masks of others' thoughts.

Nicholas, just into his forties, was dissatisfied with himself and his life on every level. His rather belated decision to 'go in for politics' appeared, even to himself, as much a surrender as an advance, more a gesture to give some public point to his life than a vocational urge or career move. He had sidled up to it crabwise but to his surprise Tory Central Office had welcomed him. The old family name, of course, its fine record of public servants, his own laconic success in business in the Sixties, that seductive independence of means, the irreproachable education, the wit and well-preserved, though apparently carelessly cultivated, appearance. The rather unlikely Northern seat was his first test and he boarded the train with heartsinking recognition of the feelings generated by going off to prep school and then public school for a term's enforced absence from otherwise beloved parents. Russell had been his rod and staff. It had been a transforming experience.

Thinking back on it, as he often did, kneading that time into pliable presences, his first clear sensation was of the smell of leafsmoke, woodsmoke. As a clue to take him back through almost twenty years, into the kernel of a northern industrial city, it seemed unlikely to yield much. But the smell persisted. He could even persuade himself that he could hear again the soft crackling of dry leaves, see the small leaps of flame on pale blocks of sawn wood, have the tang of it in his nostrils.

The primary purpose of the expedition seemed unimportant – he had not been selected although his performance before the committee had been highly commended. He remembered some members of the selection committee, ranged behind a table around glasses of water and niblets to eat, something between the Last Supper and the Last Judgement he had thought. One port-purple-nosed man wearing a yellow polka-dotted bow tie who was determined to trip him up on his economics; one slim no-nonsense head-girl-type who asked him briskly about his matrimonial intentions and moved on briskly when he replied, "Unrequited, alas, as yet".

What he most keenly remembered was wandering about the place the day before the selection committee. He had given himself some time to get the feel of it. The industrial North was more foreign to him than the Continent, further away than the Mediterranean, as curious as India, as menacing as the worst stories of Chicago. Nicholas could make no sense of it in the designs of his life. He understood the idea of the Two Nations and Disraeli was a model; he knew about the division of North and South and had smiled at the Bradford Millionaire, where there's muck there's brass; he had enjoyed the rock and lolly mirage of Sixties classlessness which had brought the background of mean streets, coalmining, steel-furnaced, factory-grimed ordinariness a little way into the foreground with plays and films and unforgettable popular music. It was a loving creation and mockery of the life which then seemed the life of a nation. But he had never exposed himself to it in any way which made him feel vulnerable, until his first venture into politics, in that bleak town.

What was the key to the place? Where was its grace, its art, its heart? He had wandered past grimy Victorian piles which had undoubted strength but, he thought, no charm, no lightness, no

130

wit. He strayed down shopping streets populated by people he could feel nothing for save pity. This one so fat, that one so ill-clad, that one so pale, the other so harassed, that one so clenched, the other so bent with strain – so rarely, it seemed, did he catch a smile or an attitude which announced joy on the streets. There were sales in many of the shops and the goods on sale seemed to Nicholas – well aware of his privileges – to be tacky. Was this the best of it?

Away from the city centre but still within easy strolling distance, he came to the acres of factory brick which occupied so much of the city and led to the railway lines and beyond that to the river. Here he experienced some alarm. How was he to represent people who worked, endured and somehow lived out of what he saw as oppressive, grinding soullessness? He felt pity. He felt inadequacy. He also felt shame. He had taken too little care of this. Did he now want to enlist it to prop up a middle-age crisis? To use and exploit it once again?

Guilt, he remembered and flushed to remember it, guilt was what he had mostly felt. That those in this town, his countrymen, whose patriotic allegiance so many of his friends and his party took for granted at moments aflush with English St Crispin pride, that so many of them should scurry out of such mean walls inside which they were condemned to cobble the wealth of this nation like the dwarves in the opera . . . What sense was there in an order that gave him so much and so many of them so little? Oh, of course people were much worse off in parts of Africa, South America, in Asia and no doubt in every substantial patch of the globe – but these were supposedly "his" people. He was aiming to represent them and be their spokesman in Parliament. These were the people whose dwelling below ground, before the open fire of furnace doors, in tough shipyards and amid the hellish racket of ancient machines, had fed the coffers of the Commonwealth which had been so generous in its return to himself. In Nicholas the benign policies of the squirearchy had survived intact.

But there was a prodigality of self-indulgence in the inflation of shame which he wished to avoid and so he hurried and turned through the factory streets, as if trying to shake it off.

When he went down a narrow alleyway – by now he was completely lost – in the general direction of the noise of the trains as if the tracks would give him his bearings, he stopped dead at the sight which met him. It was like a smile, it was like a little Eden of thoughtful pleasure: a swathe of allotments. A quilted spread of ground descending an easy slope to the railway lines. Fences marked out individual stakes. Paths pottered through the site like the twisting streets of medieval hill towns. Shocks of blooms – chrysanthemums, blowsy peonies – sat beside neatly drilled lines of vegetables. Pigeon lofts painted white or green were like tents on this encampment. To each plot of land, it seemed to Nicholas, there was a man, digging, tying, mending, cultivating, dreaming. Woodsmoke drifted low on the light westerly wind and on the railway tracks great trains clanked by rhythmically, somehow accentuating the serenity of the place. Nicholas breathed out a sigh of relief – more, of gratitude – that such life went on.

"Lost?"

His questioner was a wiry man, most likely in his late fifties. A bounce of thick, curly, sandy hair gave him a rather clownish appearance. He wore the dark trousers and waistcoat from what once must have been a formal three-piece suit and the sleeves of his shirt were rolled up to the elbow, revealing a dramatic cut-off just above the wrist where weathered brown hand met sheltered white arm.

"I fear I am, rather."

"Where do you want to be?"

Nicholas paused.

"To tell you the truth, I'd rather like to stay here for a few minutes and smoke a cigarette."

"You're welcome to my porch."

Nicholas thanked him, and the man set off down the slope, nodding at one or two, not all, of the men on other allotments. His own proved to be one of the biggest, well kept. The porch he had referred to was on his pigeon loft. Two small canvas chairs were produced. Nicholas offered his host a cigarette but he declined.

It was the next hour or two that he remembered with such intensity. He was able to summon it up for the rest of his life. Soon he had explained why he was in the city and how he had stumbled on the place and so, having exorcised natural curiosity about his dress, his accent, and his appearance among the allotments, he was drawn in by the man's warmth and ease. Eventually they were joined by two other men who sat on the ledge of the porch, making way now and then as a pigeon landed with a great batter and rush of wings. The chat was of politics but without rancour, of the city but without resentment, but mostly, Nicholas remembered, they told stories. The anecdotes themselves slithered down a black hole of forgetfulness but he recalled laughing and smiling when he knew his leg was being pulled, being moved when a sudden twist of story exposed a raw plight.

He did not want to leave, nor, he sensed, did the men who were as much beguiled by his openness, his accent, his difference and his decency as he was by theirs. The cut of his expensive cloth was remarked on and laughed off; his address at the town's one grand hotel amused them. All said they would not vote for his party in the election but all of them seemed keen to encourage him, happy to give him information and tips, on his side in some protective way, not at all wanting favours, tugging forelocks or seeking the comfort and glamour that the craven seek from what they see as superior beings. There was, Nicholas thought, and he held on to that despite the accusation of sentimentality and its distorting lens which mocked him, a feeling of ease, of equality, above all a warmth.

It was the warmth which lulled him. The men had worked hard all day in the steelworks, sweat-stained; gone home, washed, changed into "old togs" and come out to their allotments. Here they were independent, on their own ground, in contact with soil and roots, and at leisure. The boundary of the railway lines was not seen as a fence against their ambition but as a track of adventure, steel parallels of excursions into dream worlds. The factory buildings at the upper end of their clearing were ignored, kept at bay by the flowers, surmounted and made light of by the swooping, circling pigeons. It was a tribal warmth, almost a body warmth which Nicholas, to his joy, found could accept him.

Not until it was dark did they leave the porch. As they wandered up the twisting mud path back into the mass of brick, Nicholas pretended he needed to tie a shoelace. What he wanted to do, he would remember, with passionate nostalgia, was to look back and catch sight of the speckled glow of the embering fire, take in the last whisper and scent of woodsmoke, let the train surge past and draw a firm line under this encounter: feel wholly at peace and alive.

ELEVEN

HELEN was amazed with herself for being so fussed about the choice of restaurant. Her usual method was to go where asked, go to the nearest place, or take the first recommendation offered. The whole business of eating out in restaurants she considered a worryingly overrated activity. Intellectuals simply did not bother about such matters: no apologies or explanations. It was self-evident. There was a small bistro near the television studios which suited her perfectly. The canteen was jolly good value. In Hampstead there was a cheap and cheerful Italian around the corner. Everywhere else was rather a blur.

Yet she had allowed herself to become rather fussed about taking Jen out to dinner. At first she had thought of inviting her home, but the memories of those first two years of Jen in London were too unsettling easily to allow her to slip back into the kitchen for those late-night dinners so often raging, so often profoundly happy. Her bistro seemed too workaday; the Italian too noisy for comfortable conversation *à deux*. Finally, after a desperate rummage in her memory — for although she had lived in Hampstead "for ever" and defended its Georgian architecture against vandalising shopkeepers, its crowded streets and sly-stepped alleys against over-organising councils, she was peculiarly blank on restaurants — she identified a rather fashionable place where the steaks were supposed to be good and the atmosphere cosy, candles stuck in Chianti bottles and quiet corners where you could talk privately.

Jen burst out laughing the instant she walked in. (About fifteen minutes late, Helen noted.)

"Helen," she said, after she had pecked her cheek and sat down, "are you trying to tell me something?"

The vixen was on to her right away! Yes. Helen wanted a significant encounter. Guilty!

"You are late," she said.

"Is that unusual?" Jen asked.

"No."

"So?"

"You have a perfectly reasonable excuse," said Helen and
sighed. She had been put on the defensive in less than ten seconds.
"Very well. Have some of this Chianti."

"Do you think they would do a Kir Royale?"

"You'd better ask."

Jen turned and a waiter all but galloped across to her. It was not
only that she had so quickly become so well known on television –
Helen knew how dim the light of so many onscreen faces could
be bereft of the focusing box – it was the impact she had. The
restaurant was less than half-full and yet as soon as Jen had
invaded it, the place buzzed with crowded special excitement. The
waiter, Helen thought, was only waiting for the nod and he would
turn cartwheels. Everyone spoke that little bit louder. Helen was
grimly pleased that their corner table was further cut off from the
rest by a barricade of two empty tables. Impulsively she said, "Do
ask the young man if he can fill these two tables last of all, Jen,
would you? When he brings you your Hollywood drink."

"Oh dear," said Jen, "a wigging. A telling-off. Groan – groan.
Mea culpa. I'll have the Chianti after all."

"Don't be silly. It's just . . ." Helen stubbed out her cigarette
ineptly. Nerves! "People," she concluded.

Jen relented and did as Helen had requested – the waiter assured
her that only if the most exceptional circumstances arose, circumstances impossible to imagine on a slow winter Monday evening
in Hampstead, then and only then *might* he sacrifice those tables
because he knew how much people like her needed privacy, needed
to go around without being plagued, needed to be left alone. It
must be terrible everybody recognising her but he had to say he
thought she was great and the chap who did it with her – what
was he called? – he was very good too. What was he called? And
the time when, the other night in fact, or the week before when
she had – it was amazing – when she had –

"We're ready to order," said Helen. "*Now*. I'll have *steak au
poivre, à point*. With a green salad. Jen?"

Jen had not looked at the menu.

135

"Fish of the day," she said. "Or whatever fresh fish you have. And a selection of vegetables."

"And a jug of water," said Helen. "Tap water. With ice. *Thank you*."

The waiter grinned conspiratorially at Jen and hopped away on one leg.

"Sometimes I think that television has a great deal to answer for," said Helen.

"He's sweet."

"He strikes me as being quite alarmingly backward."

"*Lovely* to see you, Helen. Really. *Lovely*."

Helen looked away. She knew that Jen meant it and that made it worse.

"Tell me about your day," she said.

"You always say that when you're stalling for time," said Jen, smiling.

"It's a very good way to relax into a serious conversation."

"Yes. We must."

So Jen unwound the day, not unhappy to be obedient. Helen had given her so much and she had no problem in showing her gratitude. Moving out of Helen's home had been a trauma – her word: Helen would never allow such exaggeration – but by that time she had to go. At present she shared a flat with a colleague, a television researcher her own age, and, although it had worked out reasonably well, Jen now wanted her own place. Having the time to look and the money to afford what she really desired had held her back for almost a year but now she had it in her sights – a wonderful mansion flat overlooking the Thames at Chiswick.

The day she outlined to Helen as she toyed with her sole and sipped the Kir Royale would have astonished and delighted the girl she had been on her first arrival in London five years ago. In the morning she had poached a short and cheeky interview with the woman just elected to head the Conservative Party. Lunch had been at the *Spectator* where the easy manners and bright efforts of the "hacks", as they called themselves, had entranced her as much as her directness and beauty had caused middle-aged swooning among them. The cutting-room in the afternoon had been a dogged three hours of haggling and jigsaw repatterning of a mini-documentary on Petticoat Lane – she loved the aggro and the detail involved in that. A catch-up at the office, mail, calls, running order for the next day's programme, gossip. Then time with Mark. He was her excuse for being late – which she knew she would never be called on to confess: too vulgar, Helen would have thought. And now dinner with wonderful Helen and a clock ticking inside her head which said that down in a bar in Covent Garden up until 1 a.m., Mark Armstrong would be waiting for her. The thought of it made her shift as if uncomfortable in her seat.

In her crisp, precise and rather brutal way, Helen anatomised and commented on Jen's programme. It was a thrice-weekly early evening magazine introduced by Jen and one of the Grand Old Lovable Bores of British television. Walt Davidson had begun a long broadcasting career on BBC Radio during World War Two, truculently butted his way into television (which he despised) after Suez, been a pillar of its output for about twenty years, and was now deflecting senility by playing on the lower slopes. In truth he was about to be sacked when Helen, with one of her flashes of inspiration, saw that he was just the old warhorse to put in harness with Jen. "Father and daughter, you see," she had said, cuttingly, and gone on to add, "Teacher and pupil, male and female, youth and age, innocence and experience, Beauty and the Beast." This, of course, had got back but by then Walt sensed that a success, an Indian summer, another last fix of fame might be on the way and he merely smiled and stored it up. Though light and flouncy the show was fast-moving and entertaining. It clicked. The public turned on. Jen, who had been given her role only as a try-out – her previous experience was no more than local opt-out newsroom work – woke up to find herself a celebrity. She was highly amused. "She burns up the screen," said the *Observer* critic, "the camera loves her and so do I. Beauty and brains – this isn't TV, this is paradise regained thrice weekly. A Miltonic."

"But it's not enough," said Helen, staring rather morosely into her large cup of black coffee.

"I'm enjoying it, Helen."

"Yes, you are. And it shows. And that is the programme's strength. But the whole thing has become far too successful. It's got out of hand."

"Too successful?"

"Yes. You may start to believe your own publicity."

"Helen!" Without waiting for a reply, Jen went on, "It was you who encouraged me."

"There was no stopping you," said Helen and suddenly she smiled in recollection, and at the sight of that sweet, happy, almost dopey expression on that stern academic face, Jen's umbrage left her.

"Haven't I done what you wanted?"

137

"Oh, more," said Helen fervently. "Much more. And nobody knows how talented you have to be, how rare it is for anyone to combine in correct measure the qualities of intelligence and wit, the qualities of charm and manners, the gutsiness, timing, nerve – all that you have already to a very high degree, darling, but – it isn't enough."

"It is for me. For the time being."

"What questions did you ask Mrs Thatcher this morning?"

Jen answered.

"So. A four- or five-minute interview on a gossipy level, quite cheeky and witty and charming I've no doubt. But this is a formidable woman, this is the first woman to lead a major political party in this country, this may well be the first female Prime Minister: you could do so much more. So much better."

"Not on *my* programme."

"In that case, leave it. Leave the screen. Become a producer. Make longer, deeper, important programmes that matter."

"Doesn't what I do matter?"

"Not enough. It doesn't contribute to any debate. It never will."

"What's the virtue of contributing to the debate?"

"To give television audiences the best possible service," said Helen, simply. "We are privileged to reach out to millions of people of all classes, all creeds, all intelligence levels, tastes and backgrounds – we have to take this responsibility seriously and not fritter it away. You have an undoubted talent as a communicator and it will not go away. If you keep doing this song-and-dance act you will lose all appetite, I suspect, but more importantly, all possibility of being regarded as a person of substance."

"Thanks."

"Don't sulk."

"I'm not. I'm furious."

"Never mind. You will always be able to come back on screen but I think it is positively dangerous for you to carry on as you are doing for much longer. You are first-rate editor material. You need two or three years as a line producer, a few years editing and after that you could be a powerful voice in broadcasting. You could shape things, Jen, you could influence the way many people work, how they work, and what the mass of the population in this country gets by way of information and enlightened entertainment."

"I think that what I'm doing now does that."

"Only up to a point."

"Helen. Are you saying you are taking the programme off?"

"Not at the moment. I thought of trying out Liz Holmes."

"She's too treacly!"

"She's very popular."

"She's ancient."

"She's reliable. Thirty-four, I believe."

"I helped to make that programme."

"No one denies it."

"For Christ's sake!"

"Jen. Please keep your voice down. Although your village idiot waiter has virtually cleared the restaurant for us, there are still one or two tables straining to follow every word."

"I need another year," Jen said. "Another year, eighteen months, and I'll consider, I'll most probably do what you say. But not now."

"Why not now?"

"Because," Jen sluiced back her third Kir Royale, "I'm having too good a time, Helen. I'm having a wonderful, wonderful time and I want it to go on. I want it to go on because I've just recently begun to enjoy it as distinct from experiencing it. I can do it. Like riding a bike. No hands! See! I don't fall off. I'm having such a lovely time, Helen. Don't be a spoilsport. You can make me a woman of destiny next year. OK?"

"I did not bring you out to a restaurant to be charmed off the branch by one sweep of your eloquence."

"Oh yes you did."

"Jen."

"Helen."

The two paused and looked at each other, each thinking – what a woman! Jen's affection and bubble and undeniable force seemed to flood through Helen like a charge of power: Helen's affection and caring, her indisputable high-minded splendour, ratified the younger woman's life.

"I will not let you go so easily," said Helen, though acknowledging to herself that there were secrets which Jen would never give up to her.

"You will not let me go at all, I hope."

"I am right, you know."

"Don't sound so sad about it."

"You must take care."

"I will."

"Will you? Will you promise me, Jen? To take care."

"Promise. I promise. Just one more Kir Royale."

TWELVE

"I think I can even remember the date," Mark said. "Just over three years ago. January 30th, 1972."

"Bloody Sunday," said Jack and the other two nodded.

"Bloody Sunday. It was a watershed for me," Mark continued. "I'd known about Northern Ireland, I'd watched and I'd read about it, but when I saw those pictures I remember thinking — what *is* going on? What are they shooting *for*? This is supposed to be the United Kingdom for Christ's sake! And another thing," he sipped at the Glenmorangie and hesitated — would this expose him too much? — but it was a night for talk, these were good mates, "the faces of the kids. I seemed to recognise them. I did recognise them. I've seen those faces at Hawick Market and in the streets of Dumfries, not to say Glasgow. But in the Borders especially I've seen that fanatical desperation and suddenly I felt," he paused only slightly, "this will sound a bit far-fetched but I felt it was part of my own patch of history. It was part of my own quarrel with the United Kingdom, a quarrel that's been going on for several centuries and time and again involved lads just like that against soldiers — who could be their brothers — both sides fighting to kill and for what? For what? And how to stop it? How to understand it?"

"All I'm saying," said Jack, equally well oiled, "is that Vietnam it isn't. This is no attempt to establish a pecking order but Belfast is no Saigon."

Mark let it pass. It was, had been, too good an evening to spoil it with a half-soaked wrangle.

They were in Covent Garden in the Zanzibar. It was a club which had become instantly fashionable — heiresses playing at being waitresses, the glamorous and the chattering journalistic dropping in after the curtain came down or the pubs and restaurants closed. The Zanzibar's attraction was its guaranteed good fun and the cheap offer of membership to a self-selected circle who dearly wanted somewhere unthreatening and preferably elegant to flop for a final drink around midnight. There was a long American-type bar with a highly polished brass bar-rail; a rather narrow crowded banquette and a handkerchief space for a piano and singer. It was fresh and new and Mark had been co-opted by a couple of former colleagues from the *Observer* and *The Times*.

Nowadays he liked nothing better than drinking rather too much with journalists, and chewing the fat. About friends of theirs who were filing television, radio and written reports from all over the world; about the accidents and cock-ups in the job; about the close-up hopelessness of it all; the gap between public speech and private experience; the endless fascination of seeking for solutions to problems which appeared beyond recovery. He was reinforced in his conviction – especially after spaghetti and strong house red at Bianchi's and a few golden Glenmorangies in the Zanzibar – that journalists – his friends – were the best company in the world.

The one or two novelists he had met were defensive, furtive, chippy, always somehow holding up a notebook to life. Poets were off the radar, flying so high in their craft of self-confident immortality that Mark felt it was rather like bursting in on a meeting of Freemasons. Other arty types were generally ill-informed. Showbusiness people were much more fun, especially about landladies in Accrington and early days in Oldham, but on the few occasions Mark had been in their company he felt that he had nothing to contribute and became embarrassed at taking without giving. Sportsmen were very like thespians. The professional classes, whom he encountered very little, always made him feel that he ought to be doing a proper job and his unease could turn to intellectual aggression. Politicians were always on parade. No, give him journalists, especially foreign reporters, men, ninety-five per cent in his circle were men, whose pack of cards included the seven continents.

He was still provincial enough to find it exhilarating that world politics, world wars, terrorism, fatalities, epidemics could be discussed so knowingly, so personally. Those men, including himself, had today's magic carpet, the Press Card. They wished and they were transported to meet the power-pullers, the leaders and shakers of the world, and they came back with the loot of a story and a disarray of expenses. Over the past few painful years since his divorce, he had found a life with them, sufficient to itself. Until young Jen appeared.

"Saigon will fall," said Jack, a little overemphatically, "this year, next year. It will go."

"The Americans daren't let it happen. They wouldn't."

"They've lost heart. It will go, I tell you. They're moving on Da Nang now – what odds Da Nang? If that goes, it's just a matter of time."

"The Americans can't allow it. Screw the domino theory, there's the whole question of their world leadership, their prestige, what are they if they are not top dog? All that is at stake."

"'Never march on Moscow'," quoted Jack, "'Never fight on the mainland of Asia'."

"What was it Orwell said about the world wars of the future being fought – was it in equatorial regions or on the extremes of the archipelago of Asia? Something like that."

"That doesn't quite make sense."

"Your round."

Jen came in. The bar was full, it was a few minutes after midnight, the crowd was smart and broken up into self-consumed groups, and yet Mark looked up, as did several others. Her smile reached into him in a way in which nothing had touched him since that night in Edinburgh. She managed to take on the introductions, get herself a drink, settle and yet leave the sense of male camaraderie and cosy booziness intact. Mark noted that.

Soon enough she was telling them about Margaret Thatcher and doing an imitation which delighted all of them.

"I think the Tories have got it right," said Jack. "A woman and a toughie. Two good constituencies there. Ted Heath, as we know, was neither."

"She'll be minced at the box."

"Maybe, but being a woman there'll be the female vote. How will that go? And maybe she'll not be minced. What do you think?"

"She's very, very ambitious," said Jen. "And she won't make many mistakes. And," she paused and twirled the unsipped flute of champagne a little to disturb the bubbles which reminded her when they rose in the glass of those snowflakes in glass-faced Christmas baubles, "there's something else – I said ambitious but what I think I mean is fanatical. There's something fanatical about

142

her – she thinks she has been picked out, in fact chosen, to do great things." She wished she had thought of that at the time and found a way to mention it or make it evident in her piece. Helen was right. She needed more time to think.

"The Messiah," said Jack, "and a female. That's all we need. Same again?"

Mark caught Jen's eye and shook his head. Not much later, with the minimum fuss, they slid off the banquette and down the thinning bar to retrieve their coats at the cloakroom and brace themselves against a winter night threatening snow.

They huddled up close to each other as they walked rather aimlessly towards the heart of the old market. Jen had expected Mark to be alone and so had he but, as he explained, he had "fallen among thieves". She had liked them, indeed felt closer to Mark because she had been so effortlessly absorbed into what was clearly his gang. And he, to be truthful to himself, had been relieved that he was not alone.

She had bombed into his life suddenly and demandingly. Before then he had seen her on her new show: he had enjoyed her and been enchanted like all the other men he knew. A few weeks before, after his report on the fire in the Maze Prison, and conditions inside the prison had finally made it to the screen – very little noticed – she had come across to him in the canteen, sat down opposite to him, and said:

"I thought your Maze report was marvellous. I would like to do reports like that. How did you get the IRA men to talk to you so openly?"

And they had been away. From that encounter she had seen him every day. Although none of his friends would have believed him (not that he made the case), it was he who was being pursued. Jen admitted to it quite cheerfully. He was deeply wary. Even now they had not yet gone to bed together, despite her clear willingness and his equally clear, sometimes rather embarrassingly prominent desire. He had been badly burnt in that first marriage and a couple of desultory brief encounters since then had done nothing to repair the damage.

But Jen. Jen was, as they all said, something else.

"You're twenty years younger than I am, young lady."

"Seventeen. I know. Isn't it great? Think of all that energy waiting for you."

"I'm a thick-waisted, unexercised, born-again unreconstructed bachelor."

"You used to be a great rugby player, didn't you? And squash – for your university."

"How did –?"

"Research. And you like the blues. So do I. And *I* can think of lots and lots of exercise."

"You are brazen."

"You can think of far raunchier words than that."

"You ought to be with someone more glamorous –"

"More glamorous than a Scot? More glamorous than a Border Scot who once rode a horse bareback in a point-to-point?"

"Younger –"

"Boring."

"Man-about-town."

"Yawn."

"Can't you tell when a man is desperate?"

"I love it."

She was emotionally more sophisticated than he was, more experienced, more aware of what was going on. Eventually, one night, he had told her something – not all – of the breakup of his marriage. After that it was inevitable that they would make love to each other. He had told no one else: indeed he had not spoken a word about it to a soul in the four years since it had happened. His gratitude to Jen was considerable, his vulnerability absolute; his dependence, though he did not realise it, just as total.

Still, as they shivered through Covent Garden, Jen was aware that back at her flat a flatmate was sleeping with a boyfriend and back at his flat there was a man called Dave who snored, farted, got up to go to the bathroom several times every night and woke up noisily with Radio Four at 6.30 a.m. So Mark had told her and she believed him.

"I love all the back alleys in Covent Garden," she said, "all the little short cuts and the almost tunnels. We did an item around here a few months ago. You've no idea how many yards there are, and little culs-de-sac, connecting warrens of streets and courtyards. Right in the middle of London. You expect robbers to leap out at you or murders in the dark or prostitution up the lanes. That's what it must have been like at one time."

Mark felt the happy chiming of recognition when someone you love says what is on your mind. He had been silently comparing it with the closes and courts and stairs which had once so besotted him – and for much the same reason – on the Royal Mile. He told Jen about them.

"Why don't we just snuggle into one of them and," she paused, "do it? Out in the cold. Here and now. Get it over with. You want it," she foraged around, "yes, that's clear enough. I want it. We're the only two on the street. Yes?"

Mark felt his throat go dry. They were at the crossroads just up from the Opera House and one of the thoughts which popped into his mind was that Bow Street Police Station was about fifty yards away. Another part of his mind flared up with eagerness at the opportunity on offer. Something about its danger, its stupidity, its bawdy Restoration splash of sex, its Victorian urgency – in short, the thought had crossed his mind several times before. But there was something else –

"I . . . well . . . I . . ." he said, "well, I booked . . . booked in . . . to a hotel. You needn't, but I thought . . . tonight . . . I booked into a hotel and we can go if you like. Now."

"Mark!"

Jen flung herself at him, around him, kissing his cold face with her warm lips, hugging him tightly.

"We're very late," he said.

"So are people arriving from São Paolo. Or Annabel's."

"We have no luggage."

"Which hotel?" He told her. "No problem at all. You say nothing. They say nothing. It's called breeding."

"Are you sure?"

"Come on!"

She took his hand and tugged him, ran, teased him down the fluorescent emptiness of Bow Street, between the police station and the Opera House, past the smart boutiques and the Lyceum Ballroom of so many London romances and out on to the Strand, where they caught a cab – Mark thought it more sensible for the last lap of their journey.

His anxieties did not decrease. Despite Jen's insouciance, he was sure that they were marked out as a suspect couple. The absence of luggage, as glaring as two black eyes, and the unmistakable odour of whisky on the breath added nothing to his confidence when it came to negotiating a reception desk manned by a bright-eyed young tailor's dummy in a morning suit whose efforts to please seemed pitying. Perhaps Jen's act of innocence was a direct provocation.

The room was very grand and Mark longed for modesty.

In the time it took him to scratch his head, open the mini-bar, pour himself a scotch and look down the long chart detailing what he could order for breakfast, Jen had been in the bathroom, the sound of a shower, and returned, bright-eyed, gleaming skin, carelessly wrapped in a soft white towelling gown. She took the glass from him and gently aimed him in the direction from which she had returned.

Mark found the marble bathroom almost offensive. Why did it have to be so flash? So many towels. Such a clutter of soaps, shampoos, sewing kit, shower cap, shoe polisher, flannel . . . There was a matching white towelling dressing-gown hanging behind the door. As he sat rather heavily on the lavatory trying to clear a space in his head which would enable him to think this through, the empty dressing-gown seemed to say, "Wear me! Come on! Join in! Don't be a spoilsport! Wear me!"

He came out still as trussed up in his winter suit as he had been when he went in.

Jen was sitting in one of the two wing armchairs, legs folded under her, feet peeping out under the white towelled hem. She appeared to be absorbed in a glossy brochure but suddenly she looked up and smiled: that open, fresh smile which utterly captured him, the smile coming from the unaccountable grey eyes too, which searched him out, pierced the scars.

"Why don't we just go straight to sleep?" she said.

Mark was relieved, and then amazed that he was relieved, and then curious.

"Why?"

"You're nervous. You've made me nervous or maybe I was already. I'd rather do nothing than have a mess-up. We could just cuddle up and drop off. Couldn't we?"

"I feel I ought to – to . . ." She looked so beautiful. "I do want to – of course I do – it's – in Covent Garden, as you said, down one of those closes, alleys . . ."

"We could always go out again."

"It was very cold. We could have been found frozen in a posture judged to be an affront to public decency."

Jen laughed, got up, came to him, put her arms around his neck and kissed him longingly. He felt the yield and promise of her body and his reaction confused him. What was holding him back?

"Bedtime," she said, dropped off her dressing-gown, and almost dived into the large bed.

Mark never forgot that first sight of her nakedness.

146

Laboriously and in a corner, though he knew she had turned her back to him, he undressed. One of the many mirrors in the room reflected a white-skinned man with broad shoulders, a deep chest, a flabby waistline, bit of a pot and a dangling penis. He got into bed as carefully as a burglar climbing through a window. As far as he could tell, the steady breathing, Jen was already asleep. Twice in the night he heard her murmur – Brother? Mother? Murder? – and once she woke violently, startled, the tension palpable, and said "Sorry", reached out in the dark to touch his face, went back to sleep.

In the morning they made love. As a physical conjunction, as a coupling for pleasure, it was short, awkward and a failure. But it was the beginning and afterwards they laughed, lay in each other's arms and dozed, to wake up to a fierce and passionate sexual savaging, a hungry attack on each other which left both of them breathless and set the pattern for the next few wild months.

Thirteen

"YOU must go," she said. "You get so few outings." Her mother was lying on the sofa and extended a hand. Valerie came across, took the hand and sat on the small stool her mother would use for a table. "Promise me you'll go, Valerie."

The young woman smiled and said nothing. Every protestation that she should go on this outing was clearly a plea for her to stay and resist the invitation. It was already obvious now that if she went to Malvern Festival with the more adventurous members of the choir on a trip very carefully and economically arranged by Gerald, then she would have to hump a weight of guilt up and down England. The question was — could she bear it?

"I know you meet so few people your own age," her mother said. She had become rather fat, white, fatty faced, pasty from her indoor vigil over her own complaints, and the soft white face flesh could threaten tears very readily. "I know that this silly illness of mine — you are so good about it — is such a burden to you. I am such a burden to you. You should put me in a Home. I won't go in a Home! You won't put me in a Home, Valerie, will you? This is my home. This is our home."

And the tears flowed.

Mrs Thomlinson's illness, which some had suspected of being feigned a few years before, had now become a reality. She had a heart condition, the doctor said, and needed constant nursing. Valerie was on hand. Valerie organised all the pills, dressed her, helped her into the bath and levered her out again, dried her down, escorted her to bed, woke up in the middle of the night to minister to her panic, saw that she was comfortable for her favourite

148

television programmes and, when she was tired of those, read to her. Valerie's own occasional relapses were ignored.

Her own life, which had begun to inhabit a slow but encouraging upward curve of activity – principally through joining the choir – had been checked once again by her mother's heart condition; although the rush to the Thursday evening choir practice and the consequent extra attendances at Sunday services had been allowed to stay. Otherwise it was shopping – shadowed a little now by her mother's awareness of the timing of that daily escape; and gardening. The garden had become the greatest liberation.

There was a yard at the back of the bungalow which abutted farm fields which themselves led across to school playing fields. Valerie had a bird table there and a birdbath, and her own, so it seemed, tiny flock of robins, chaffinches, sparrows, blackbirds, thrushes and occasionally more exotic visitors. In front of the bungalow was a patch of garden, about fifty feet square, levelled to a height above the road and split by steps which went down the middle to the pavement. Mr Thomlinson had made a rather ugly rockery out of it. Valerie decided to clear the rocks and make a garden. The excuse for getting out of doors especially on a pleasant evening was unimpeachable. Mrs Thomlinson could watch through the sitting-room window and Valerie took care to go over regularly to make certain that everything was in order. But the pane of glass which separated them was as secure as a moat, as liberating as a channel of sea. She was out there on her own.

Though that was not strictly true. Her gardening efforts drew in the neighbours on either side – Mr Rumney, a retired cobbler, so long retired that his stories seemed to come out of a world now departed; and Miss McGuckian, the music teacher at the Roman Catholic preparatory school. Shy but cordial friendships were struck up, which Mrs Thomlinson was powerless to prevent or subvert. It was Mr Rumney who advised her to plant old-fashioned pinks, aubretia, petunias and "a nice border edging of blue lobelia and alyssum". It was Miss McGuckian who gave her cuttings of hardy fuchsia and suggested a buddleia "to attract the butterflies".

They admired her industry, supervised her efforts and praised the results. Despite the garden's proximity to a road which at times could shudder with juggernauts on their way through the small market town to the industries on the west coast, this became her most peaceful place. And there were times, on weekend afternoons or late on a summer evening when traffic was down to a trickle, that she could linger with the trowel or the fork, look out over the fields to the fells some dozen miles away, reared up like a dream, clouds inevitably capping or cavorting about the tops.

"You'll catch your death in that garden one of these days," her mother said. Or, "It's straining you. Look at the sight of you. It's too much for your strength". There was some truth in this. Valerie tired easily but forced herself to go on, terrified that her mother would begin to insist that she stop the gardening. She had begun a campaign at one stage. "It's too much for you. I'm sure we could get a young man to do it. Put it down to grass. It's too much for your strength."

Valerie changed the subject or kept a deliberate silence. Mrs Thomlinson persisted but not to the point of victory. Perhaps she reckoned that it was a fair deal: Valerie was not wholly out of her control when she was in the garden and, without that little ventilation of freedom, she might be setting up worse trouble for herself. So she tolerated it but with the usual injection of guilt-inducing observations.

The choir had been easier. The vicar, who called on Mrs Thomlinson every week, had requisitioned Valerie openly and firmly and Mrs Thomlinson was no match for him, especially when he had said that, if necessary, he himself would time his visits to coincide with the choir practice so that Valerie could get away, because they needed her voice. The choir was down to five men, six women (two unreliable) and no boys at all. Mr Mitchinson, the organist and choirmaster, had picked out Valerie's voice in a particularly thin, well, seven-strong to be precise, Evensong one snowdrifting Sunday in January and the church needed her. Mrs Thomlinson raised the white flag immediately and sacrificially dismissed the idea of his visit coinciding with Valerie's absence. Valerie's absence allowed her to stoke up all sorts of guilt and self-pity and she did not want to forfeit that.

The choir outing was wholly different. It would occupy four days. Valerie, aged twenty-three, had never slept away from home since they had moved to the town almost twenty years before. Miss McGuckian, who would be taking her half-term holiday at home once again, had offered to pop in regularly; the vicar's wife had offered to make the lunch and prepare a dinner; the vicar said that he would visit every day. All of them stressed that a holiday would do Valerie the world of good. Her doctor agreed.

Mrs Thomlinson was on the rack. It was not so much the four

days, which she thought she could survive. It was the image of Valerie let loose with Gerald.

Gerald Rollinson was a mother's dream. He was in his early thirties, well planted in the office of the longest established of the three local solicitors, neat, tidy, sensible, correct, good-mannered and apparently fond of Valerie. He was the youngest church-warden, as far as records could be brought to bear, in the history of St Mary's and, over the years, he had noted Valerie with increasing approval. She was diffident, which gave him confidence and fed his sense of superiority. She was devout, which as he said to so many of his elders, was "rare in a young woman these days". She cared for her mother in a way he could wholeheartedly commend. He had cared for his mother just as devotedly until her death a year or so ago. She was universally liked but in a quiet way. She did not have a clique or a gang or a noisy interfering outside interest. She was said to be a good cook, a frugal manager, an enthusiastic gardener. Gerald gave especially high marks to the gardening: he could not tell the difference between one flower and another but there was something sound about English women and gardens, something rather classy about it which appealed to him. He had bought her a Reader's Digest special offer gardening book for Christmas, with a free pair of secateurs thrown in. She sang well and here he had a certain inside knowledge, being the bass, the sole natural bass, in the choir. Her soprano was very pleasing although in a bigger choir he thought she might have been better employed as a contralto. And she was very pleasant-looking. Plainly dressed, plainly made up, plainly presented but the sort of woman, Gerald observed, that the other male members of the choir liked to hug around the shoulders.

She was invariably polite to Gerald which was not always the case with young women. Over two or three years he had every reason to believe that a relationship had grown up. He would walk her home from choir practice and Evensong. He made a point of chatting to her at all times. If he saw her on the street about the shopping – and sometimes he could arrange, or rather, would find himself to be out of the office at her predestined shopping hours – he would stop and pass the time of day, always finding something topical to bring up.

He had been to the house: several times.

Mrs Thomlinson was in uproar about this. She was flattered by Gerald's attention and appreciative of his very real concern for her health and her general comfort. His presence brought a new atmosphere into the house. She had forgotten, she said to Valerie, how much difference a man made. Yet he was her enemy. He would take Valerie away from her. Even if they all lived together – and sometimes she caught him eyeing the ample bungalow like a potential purchaser (but that might have been his trade) – she knew that his arrival would accelerate Valerie's departure.

Valerie's views on Gerald were impenetrable. She had learnt very well to bury feelings and whatever soundings her mother took were in vain.

"I won't go if it will worry you and it will, won't it?"

"Of course, but you *must* go." Mrs Thomlinson was vexed. "Everybody's making so much of an effort – making so much fuss really – that if you don't go they'll think it's all my fault and I'll get the blame and *then* where will we be? What does Gerald want to go to Malvern for anyway? Why can't the choir go to Morecambe or Grange-over-Sands as they usually do? You don't have to stay the night there."

"Gerald's very interested in the music festival. Yehudi Menuhin will be playing."

"You can hear him on records or the radio. Much better. That's what they say, isn't it? Much better on records."

"Malvern's supposed to be lovely. Then there's Elgar."

"Well, I'm not educated enough to appreciate all that, I'm afraid. When I was young we just sang the hymns and psalms and didn't bother with composers."

"Elgar," said Valerie, making one of her rare confessions to her mother, "is just wonderful. The cello concerto . . ." She stopped. Had she been able to go on she would have said that the cello concerto pulled at her heart, somehow flooded her not only with a sweet, tormenting, driven sound which could make her brimful of mad pleasure, but also excited her deeply, sensuously, like the smell which could come from the hot earth she turned or the force of a sunset over the sea when she went to the coast nearby. And something more mysterious: a stirring she could not identify; a discomfort which was a membrane away from deep and unknown satisfaction. All of it a thousand miles away from the clammy rectitude of Gerald.

"I'll not go," she said. "And I won't let there be a fuss."

"You can go as far as I'm concerned," said Mrs Thomlinson. "Tell them that."

"I know that, Mother. I'll tell them that."

"In fact," said Mrs Thomlinson, happily, "I'm just about prepared to insist that you go. You need a change. I do insist."

"I appreciate it."

"I'm very annoyed in some respects," she continued boldly, "in some respects very annoyed that you aren't going. I'm quite up to it, you know."

"Are you?"

"But if you've made up your mind," said her mother hurriedly, "and I know you when you've made up your mind, then there's no dealing with you, there's the end of it."

"I'm afraid so."

"Well then. I think I'll have my cocoa now if that's all right."

"That's perfectly all right."

Gerald took it personally as Valerie knew he would. He had planned the trip entirely on her account, he said, and she believed him but was silent. She gave him no sort of sign and, balked by her for the first time and discovering that he could make no impression whatsoever on her will, he turned away, soon stopped the polite escorting of her back to her home, began to rake the town for a better prospect, lost interest and always bore a grudge.

FOURTEEN

IT was as if Mark and Jen had the devil in them that spring and hot summer. He went to Belfast, tried and failed to get a posting to Vietnam as the inconceivable happened and the American Empire was thrown out, but got to Washington for two reports on the American reaction to this dramatic humiliation. Yet none of this external spin matched the turbulence and unlicensed devilry which possessed him when he was with Jen.

She moved into her own flat and they would spend nights there often, as the heat rose to record levels, sleeping naked on the bed dragged to the open windows which overlooked the river. Suddenly it was totally acceptable that two unattached people should be living in what had abruptly ceased to be either sin or socially compromising. And they would dare and push and test themselves with what they did. But somehow, it was not enough.

Jen still felt the sharp, the fine-pointed ache of unsatisfaction. Mark drove and drove her and she in turn exhausted him but even after a night of all but continuous lovemaking, she had that unappeasable pain, the anger, the frantic parched emptiness, the terror of the past she had repudiated so successfully.

As for Mark, although Jen was a revelation of sex and of himself, although she had brought him into a world of sensations he had not even imagined existed, he could still not oust the hurt, still not abandon the lifeline, as he saw it, of caution. Once bitten and the bite had gone deeper, he now knew, than he had ever appreciated. For even with Jen, even when they flung aside from each other bodies poised exquisitely the right side of hurt, there was still the fear of loss.

Unconscious of what was deeply compelling them, they began

154

to take risks. High risks, silly risks, dangerous risks. Jen that spring and summer was probably one of the dozen most vividly recognised faces in London. Mark, too, could be thrown a second glance every now and then. But it was Jen's cathode fame which burst into every restaurant, flashed into every club.

They began to make love wherever they felt like it. They would be eating in a grand hotel, linger over the wine, perhaps order more drinks after the coffee and then hunt through the place to find – anywhere. They would take the lift to the top floor, find the fire exit and discover themselves on a roof – the Thames, South London, the City spread under them as Jen leant over the railings and urged Mark to take her, take her. They would be walking through the streets of Mayfair and suddenly spy a deep wrought-iron staircase into a darkness of unlit basement and down they would go, Jen insisting to be on her knees as pedestrians occasionally passed by overhead. They rooted through the alleyways of Covent Garden. Sometimes they would go into a hotel for a drink, order it, split and, on a floor which was empty, find a doorway and there stab each other into a fierce brief ejaculatory frenzy and then walk back demurely to sip their drinks at the bar. The late-night gardens of Kensington were another haunt with the sounds of parties coming from open summer doors, and music, calls to the dog, the crunch of sole on gravel. Underneath the bridges across the Thames, in the side-streets of Westminster – soon over-confidence and the full throttle of desire led them to see the whole of central London merely as a respectable façade lasciviously undermined by secret places where they could reach that inevitable instant of ecstasy.

They would discuss it sometimes. It was, it had to be, some form of exhibitionism. It was like the compulsive gambler who wanted to lose, the compulsive copulator wanting to be caught. It was an artificial stimulant. It was silly, childish. It was ... But however much they undercut it, and mocked themselves, it was, when they did it, essential. It was hunger. It was as urgent as food. They needed this fucking and they needed it immediately. They needed it to be savage and uncompromising. They needed to fling it in the face of the world and taunt that world to dare to stop them. They needed to fuck each other to bits until the hurt was gone, the fury was equalled and made to bow down and then, on the other side, they would be able to have a life.

FIFTEEN

I

NICHOLAS decided that it would be many people's idea of Hell. And he had been brought there as if to a treat! A new scene, as promised. Four-thirty in the afternoon in a cramped first-floor room in Soho. Champagne with double brandy chasers; placating combinations based on vodka; sailor tots of rum; slugs of gin all slung into mouths in perpetual motion. Words, yawns, gulps for air, retches, belches, mimicked vomitings, gorging, screaming. In charge of the bar a man of scarlet face and furious character roared and insulted in an orgy of camp bonhomie.

Nicholas recognised here a most celebrated painter standing in front of a mirror shaping and reshaping his quiff; there a barrel-bellied writer instructing a youth in the mysteries of the orgasm; a journalist whom he knew from her prominent photograph in a quali-pop tabloid, with, so he was told by his companion, a bisexual Scottish laird, a cluster of East End criminals – the double-breasted set smoking Havanas and sipping Bollinger – stray jeunesse and "the usual crowd". The combination seethed. There was a sulphurous volatility in the place which Nicholas could understand carried a sexual charge, a promise of coarse, violent satisfaction. Smoke from a score of chainsmokers wreathed its funereal patterns. In the corner on a white piano Homer, from St Kitts, probably the only sober creature in the room, played and murmured the blues and, Nicholas thought, who could blame him? Nicholas wanted to go by now, curiosity satiated, but a schooner of champagne had been slotted into his hand, introduction made to a sloe-eyed young man called Derek and he was automatically polite.

Miles Hartford, his companion, was a Conservative MP who had an acquaintanceship with Nicholas's wealthy and well-connected family and had offered to make himself useful in Nicholas's search for a seat. His utility had consisted in letting Nicholas buy him an expensive lunch at Wheeler's and then insisting, with the sort of nod and wink which Nicholas thought had gone out even in the pantomime, that he come for a final snort on him at a little place he might just find amusing. Up a suspicious flight of narrow stairs, through a flaking doorway and into a sty of Hades at the traditional English tea-time.

Though by no means wholly a homosexual retreat, the openness of it, the relieved freedom in it was unmistakable and, while Nicholas admired that and possibly envied it a little, he could not assimilate it. His own self-discovery of being different had been too painful, too crabbed and silently traumatising for him to be able lightly to throw off his mask of slightly Wildean, slightly dandified but wholly oppressed compliance in society's view that he was an oddity. Nor did he enjoy the mass, the open aggression of it, being so used to solitude, to hidden deceits.

His sense of himself had been fashioned quietly and in solitude around writers: glimmerings in Henry James, cultural sublimation in Thomas Mann and the sensuality of Proust, Firbank. Understanding E. M. Forster, and the sexuality of D. H. Lawrence; recognitions in a novel by Gore Vidal or James Purdy, a play by Tennessee Williams, poems by Cavafy, the journals of André Gide, Isherwood's *A Single Man* and Genet's *Notre-Dame-des-Fleurs*. Here in this club he felt Genet was in 3-D. His filleted reading experience allowed him to assimilate details that he could confront in real life. Wilde of course the master, Nijinsky one of the great victims . . . so many others. Indeed, when much younger, Nicholas had sniffed out the homosexual in writers and artists in a manner not unlike that of an Empire builder. Socrates, of course, and Plato and all the fifth-century Greeks who had invented the modern world; Leonardo, Michelangelo and all the great Renaissance figures; Marlowe, Shakespeare – and here he remembered how his pursuit had stumbled one night when he was discussing it with a Jewish friend. For the friend too went through history itemising its geniuses, but this time as Jews, right up to Marx, Freud and Einstein, and he too laid a claim to Shakespeare.

It had been a curious experience for Nicholas, born into such a proprietorial English family, to discover himself an outsider, and the models and examples he had found in art had been central to his self-respect. For although the law had made it legal for consenting adults in private, his sort of love had, during the most formative years of his life, been a criminal offence and as such hunted down with a gleeful bigotry. Not even his own had been immune: Peter Wildeblood, members of the aristocracy, people within the most ancient university. Nicholas knew the extra awareness of the walking wounded at the same time as he took for granted his rights of ownership in the country which his class effectively still owned.

"I knew you was dreamin'."

"Sorry?"

"On another planet. Perhaps you find me boring."

"Of course not. Sorry. It's just so noisy in here. I'm afraid I'm a little deaf in my left ear." Lie. "Middle age, you know."

"I said, first my glass was empty, second do you want to go, you know, somewhere, you know, where we could have a more intimate . . . talk?"

"How rude of me. What is it?"

"Tequila Sunrise, sunshine."

"Tequila Sunrise Sunshine," Nicholas repeated doggedly. The boy laughed and patted him on the cheek.

"No Sunshine, OK? That's you."

Already hot, near scorched from the fumes, Nicholas felt his face redden further.

"How silly of me. Just be a moment."

While he ordered the two drinks, he searched in the small room for Miles, eventually spotting him at the piano talking to a young man who could have been the pianist's brother. For some reason, Nicholas found the vignette touching. There was everything in Miles's background guaranteed to make him unable to talk to any but the most ambassadorial black person on anything but patronising terms: there was everything in that boy's background, Nicholas guessed, which had made him rightly apprehensive of the attentions of upper-class, upper-hand whites. Yet here, in the pursuit of pleasure and sex, a true common ground could be established. What society still called perversion could be the begetter of common decency. Or was it just more colonisation and exploitation at a randy price?

"Here we are. Sorry about the umbrellas. He's rather overdone it." The glass was forested with midget brollies.

158

"She only put them there to annoy me."

"I see. Are you a regular here then?"

"Do I come here often?" Derek was well prepared for this one. "Only in the mating season."

Nicholas suddenly felt very tired.

"What about you?" Derek asked. He reached out and rubbed Nicholas's lapel. "Lovely cloth. You should get it made up into a suit."

"Are you . . . have you . . . ?" Nicholas pawed the air for a polite line, any line.

"So what about it?"

"I – my friend over there –"

"Miles." Nicholas was rather shocked that Miles was so immediately known. "Bit of a cock-teaser, your friend."

"Oh."

"Never mind. Can't come in pairs, can it? What about you?"

"Look. I'm very sorry. I just came here for a drink."

"Don't fancy me?"

"It isn't that."

"It never is."

"I must be – well, I'm late already."

"This place is very quiet at about nine. Very quiet. I'll be here then. On the dot. For fifteen minutes. You look very nice. *Arrivederci.*"

Derek, Nicholas thought, had conducted himself far better than he had. Nevertheless he felt the pressure lift off him as the young man wriggled his way through the crowd. Nicholas caught Miles's eye and indicated, with a jolly smile which signalled "thanks" and "I've enjoyed this a lot but have to dash", that he was on his way. Miles came across to join him, folding a piece of paper on which was a name and a telephone number.

"This should see me all right over the weekend."

Nicholas nodded bleakly.

On the street, Miles said, "Let's go round to my club, shall we? Might just be in time for school teas. Real buttered crumpets and Indian tea stewed *à l'anglaise.*"

"I'm due at your other club."

"The House?"

"Yes. Anthony, you know . . ."

"He's your . . . cousin?"

"Yes. He rang this morning, said he had some news."

"I know him . . ." Miles hesitated; he had been caught out once

159

or twice before with such careless claims. "We've known each other for a while."

In the way of these things, Nicholas interpreted Miles's pause and change of tack with merciless accuracy. Miles was a terrible snob. Miles was still old-fashioned enough to be blinded by the sheer spread and influence of the aristocracy and long-established gentry and wistful to be included in its inner workings.

"He told me he knew you," said Nicholas. Lie two today. "Speaks well of you."

"Does he?" Miles grinned rather foolishly. "He's very nice, isn't he, charming, and his wife, beautiful, she's the younger sister of the Duke of Taunton. His land is near your part of the world, isn't it?"

"Yes. Well – thank you very much for all your advice at lunch. Really – much appreciated your taking the trouble."

"No trouble at all. Thank *you*. If you want to take on this godforsaken job at least you ought to know the worst."

"I do."

"Any time," said Miles.

The men shook hands, feeling a little like foreigners.

But as Nicholas strolled down to Westminster in the last bright moments of a clear winter's day, he felt none of the fatalism which Miles had implied. The House of Commons had become his ideal. He had no doubt there were scoundrels there and hypocrites, time-servers, the callous, the snobbish, the cynical, but that was irrelevant. There were, he also knew, fine people there who would work their days out for constituents, live on a salary far, far less than they could enjoy elsewhere. They would attempt this extraordinary feat of acting as a representative of tens of thousands of people in order to legislate for a democratic society.

From tales of Simon de Montfort to images of Churchill at the dispatch box, Nicholas saw the House of Commons, with all its obvious faults and shortcomings, as a true attempt to bind together an enormous mass of people with interests and ambitions so varied as to be unimaginable. The attempt would always stumble, never wholly succeed, sometimes foul up what it aspired to help, but Nicholas saw it as a noble endeavour. It was something worth dedicating your life to. The more scorn politicians received, the more abusive the satirists grew, the more dismissive some of the commentators, the more Nicholas felt steeled in his decision that here he could play a part, here he could be useful to others, here, above all, he could take part in a great romance, the romance of right governance, the romance of the shaping of a state which always had the right to reject you. You were its servant and yet you served a great cause.

Even the ridiculous décor in the Central Lobby reinforced this idealism. As he waited for Anthony, he strolled around looking at the streaked gilt mock Gothic with unforced affection. There was St Andrew for Scotland, bearded and bald; St George for England, also bearded; St Patrick for Ireland and St David for Wales, a hotch-potch of fantasy, chivalry and saintliness. If the statues of Northcote, John Earl Russell, Gower and Gladstone referred to local politicians now beginning to fade from any general memory, that too was touching, the House remembering its household gods, the piety of a place which could understand honour. "A contrivance of human wisdom to provide for human wants." Good old Tory Burke. Nicholas agreed but would not let go his own romance.

Anthony took him to the Pugin bar where they found a quiet corner protected from the worst of the Pugin wallpaper. Anthony was a brisk man. A brilliant solicitor, prominent in the Shadow Cabinet, only a year or two older than Nicholas but as focused as his cousin was dreamy. As children, though, they had been close friends and both of them remembered that with loyal affection.

"No Sunday collection," said Anthony, after they had chatted for a few minutes. "They end Sunday collections and Saturday afternoon openings of the Post Office and our post bags burst. The Race Relations Bill? Some sick mail but nothing unexpected. The SAS goes to Northern Ireland? Nothing. Wars, slumps, natural disasters – not a dicky bird. But the *Post Office*, old boy! That, my dear Nicholas, is the real stuff!" He smiled. That was the country both of them knew and loved. For the post office was next to the village green, let at a peppercorn rent by the local landowner for cricket, and next to that was the war memorial with the shocking numbers of dead from such a small place, and behind that again was a devotion to a country capable of such equanimity that the decision to close an underused amenity for one afternoon could cause uproar.

"Now then," said Anthony, glancing at his watch, "Basil is not going to stand at the next election. The seat is just right for you. I know you have an attachment to Northern Industrial types and you've done very well in the – is it two? – yes, two seats you've gone for up there. But even if you did snatch a selection you'd be in for a hiding to nothing. If we can get Basil's seat for you, you'll be here for life. It is what we mean by Tory heartland. And I think you can." Anthony sipped his tea, and, after a glance at Nicholas, looked away, dropped his voice and spoke rapidly.

"There's just one thing. This Jeremy Thorpe business has brought up the whole – homosexuality scare. I'm not prejudging Thorpe, of course, and I think the whole affair stinks of a bungle and a vendetta and a silly witch hunt but there it is. It is on the agenda. This place, as you could guess, carries its fair share of those of that preference or persuasion or whatever more inoffensive word I can use. There is less and less fuss. There is still the susceptibility to blackmail and the tabloids are on heat every now and then, but gradually, *very* gradually, it is cooling down. Thorpe brings it back up to the boil. You have to be very careful and plead the bachelor life, which is still perfectly acceptable in Tory circles, although from what you read you would think that the species had suddenly become extinct. Or you have to pretend a female on the horizon, at least in prospect. The latter course is the more reliable. Sorry about that, Nicholas. You know my own feelings." He raised the cup as if he were proposing a toast. "Now let's get you that seat."

In his flat, towards nine o'clock, the memory of Derek's offer focused and intensified his turbulent feelings. Since Ben had left him, some years ago, he had lived alone and, as he saw it, that would be the condition of the rest of his life. It was not easy to accept this and he knew that one of his reasons for attempting to become a Member of Parliament was to employ that part of his nature which needed to help others, to be of use, even invaluable to them, to be in close, intimate contact with their lives, as the good MPs were with some of their constituents.

Yet to be in effect told that he had to deny what he was! To be encouraged to lie and walk away from the person he had discovered himself to be and fought to keep stable and undespairing. To have all that suppressed even for the sake of an ideal and a life that could staunch the daily rot of unfulfilment was very difficult. Why should he hide away his sexual nature? Did it make him less sensitive, less conscientious, less capable, less caring, less able, less tough? If he gave in, was this not just another betrayal at a time when homosexuals were taking great risks? Making great progress? Why could he not come out and stand for what he was and let them choose him or go hang?

Because they would not choose him.

They could not.

Not that all of them were prejudiced or intolerant or vengeful – though a few would be – but because it was an unnecessary complication. A bother. What would be gained by being a bother to the selection committee of a twenty-two carat Tory seat? Could he not work more effectively inside than outside the institution – the old temptation? Could he not make this sacrifice yet again – after all, he had done so many times before?

The image of Derek cleared in front of his eyes. Black thick hair, a little greasy, shaped, unfashionably for these times, in Elvis Presley style. A checked lumberjack-style shirt and tight blue jeans. Were his eyes blue or grey? Rather weak, Nicholas remembered, probably short-sighted. He remembered the shoulders, narrow, somehow touching. He would like to reach out and touch them, make some sort of contact. Derek would be there now, with his Tequila Sunrise. Attention given or sold would be on tap; either would soothe this barren pain, this aching for contact. Hurt would call out to hurt.

Nicholas phoned up Mark. If Mark were at home he would go and see him. If not he would make that date with Derek. Let the phone call decide. It rang, Nicholas counted, ten times. He gave it another five. After four –

"Hello," Mark answered, as if he had just woken up, "who's that?"

"Nicholas."

"It's Nicholas," he said – it must have been to Jen, Nicholas concluded. "What can I do for you?"

"Oh, nothing. Impulse call. Nothing." His mood was instantly caught by Mark.

"Nick says why don't we all have supper together? OK?" Nicholas heard Jen's voice sweet as an echo. "OK. Lovely. Hi, Nick."

"We're famished," said Mark, "how about you?"

"Ravenous," said Nicholas. "Ravenous."

II

"I always want to say 'Earth hath not anything to show more fair' when I stand on Westminster Bridge," said Jen.

"Even at midnight as Big Ben's bongs reverberate in the air?"

"Muggy air."

"Can't be too hot for a Northerner. We kill for heat. Although we go to ice for death."

"This city," Jen said, and went on, "even in the dark, looking down on the river and down the river, feeling it pass under this bridge, under our bodies, seeing the lights in the water . . ."

"Forever changing, forever the same."

"Mark. Because I remember a solitary line of Wordsworth you need not turn this into one of those late-night philosophical bore-ins. Three and a half."

"Three and a half?"

"Bottles. I drank one, or one and a half at most."

"My need was – sorry, another quotation coming up."

"Think for yourself."

"I should say so. Bet that's a quote."

"You were very funny when you were telling me about being a cornet."

"The Cornet in Hawick at the Common Ridings is no figure of fun. I was a high lad leading a cavalry of proud lowlanders around our territory."

"That's what I was talking about when I said I couldn't come on to this bridge without hearing that line. Wordsworth made it his territory. That's a big thing to do."

"Scott and Burns – wonderful names for the job when you come to think – Scotland wet and full of streams – that was my territory."

"Still want to walk back to Chiswick?"

Mark took a deep breath. It was balmy hot this June night, the warm air lapping about his face, the stone returning the fierce heat of the day, the sense of tranquillity this gave in a landscape far more often inimical to such basking.

"No," he said. "We'll grab a cab."

Unusually, as far as Mark could recall, uniquely, they sat a little apart in the cab. Not a sulky distance; not in a posture which indicated quarrel – they had not quarrelled, there was no sulk – but at a distance which indicated a sense of independent self-absorption.

Jen made coffee. Mark poured himself a Macallan and then told himself not to touch it. Still, it would be there if needed.

"So that's it," said Mark, holding the mug of coffee in both hands, massaging the sting of heat from it.

"Yep," said Jen, "that's it."

"I think you are absolutely right," Mark said with gloomy fair-mindedness. "Absolutely right."

"Have you noticed how drunken people repeat themselves?"

"Excuse me?"

"Have you noticed how drunken people repeat themselves?"

"Fifteen-love to me."

"Never underestimate a drunken Scot."

"Not drunk. Alas."

"Worse than drunk."

"I plead guilty."

"I have to go."

"Shall I repeat yourself? I repeat yourself. Change of pronoun constitutes change of sentence."

"You said I had to go."

"I have a clear recollection of that idiot moment of insane self-sacrifice. Of course you have to go."

Which of them was going to tell the truth first? Jen wondered.

Why is it *like* this? Mark thought. How did it become like this so suddenly?

Jen was going over to America for a month or so, that was all. Mark had been on several trips during the last year, though none longer than a fortnight. Jen had been to New York twice, briefly. On none of those occasions had there been the slightest fuss. But this current proposed trip had challenged them to decide on their future.

It was America's Bicentennial and one of the major networks was doing a presenter swap. Jen had been plucked out as the girl most likely to in the USA and she was going to be groomed for one of the morning programmes and allowed to work on it for a week or even a fortnight. In return, an American 'hostess' would take over Jen's show, which now racked up one of the best ratings and the most purring critical response in the television industry. It was an opportunity, it could be fun, it would be testing. Jen wanted it.

The moment it was suggested she wanted it. The instant it became a possibility she went for it. There was no calculation, it was overwhelming instinct. To go and try to be a star in America. "You're only really famous," her co-presenter, the Beast, had said, "if you're famous in America." It was not even as focused as that. What she knew from the first moment was that she was going to do it and she was going to blaze from that screen. That kind of success would surely melt down the lead of anxiety and fear. It would finally make her into a different personality. She wanted to be that different personality. It would kill the past dead. That was one of the most powerful attractions of appearing on television in the first place. There was this "you" on the screen which was only a little to do with the "you" in everyday life. It used other parts of you; it was something which had to be built up and shaped like an artifact. If you went to it, if you accepted it as a second life, then you could be someone else in such a public way that the sheer force of that new recognition would help drive out the old person you were. The Hyde on the screen could take over. That was what she wanted. In America, where no one knew either self, she could carry this through to its conclusion . . .

"You are assuming you'll stay there?" Helen had asked.

"I suppose I am." Jen was puzzled. She had not faced up to this.

"The likelihood is very slim."

Helen cracked a reluctant walnut. Jen had come round some weeks before, to discuss the offer, so she said, but Helen knew that it was encouragement only that was being sought and she was not inclined to offer it.

"Why?"

"Americans like their own. Not unsurprisingly. We suffer from the same smallmindedness. But more important – can you crack this monster? – they have a different system, a different culture. We are divided, as they say, by a common language and we think because our programmes sometimes look vaguely similar that they are alike. They are not. Americans make some very good programmes indeed, especially comedy programmes and news programmes, and in both cases they work from deeply different assumptions. You will appear stiff, rather amateur, cute – thank you, take half – or whatever word they find for you, but you will not be able to muster the chutzpah to deliver the message they want delivered in the way they want it delivered." Helen paused after that sentence and sipped at her herbal tea.

"So what is the core of this difference?"

"Education, references to high school jinks – knowing about them is very very important in America – all sorts of passing cultural know-how that comes naturally to bright people of your age brought up there. You don't have that. You can't have that. You can have a shared international popular culture: I'm sure you do have one in music and films and so on. But that is not the same. Purely national popular culture is wholly iconographic and deeply important to the way in which so many Americans define themselves. You would not be able to take that seriously enough and that would be regarded as typical British snootiness – which it well may be – and consequently they would not be able to take you seriously enough."

"So you think it's a waste of time?"

"I do. Would you crack another nut? They're very good."

"I can't accept that." Jen cracked the nut with one hard movement.

"You'll be very unhappy trying to prove me wrong."

"I want to go there and I want it to work."

"But why?"

Jen shook her head and with a sense approaching despair, Helen realised again that nothing had changed, that still she could not help. If only she had managed to make her face that unspoken pain.

"It isn't for the money. You are sensible but unworldly like all seriously intelligent people."

"Who says I'm 'seriously intelligent'?"

"I do and I have considerable experience in these judgements. You don't crave the carnival rewards of popular success – the waving in the streets and searching for autographs. In fact you are already tired of the little of that you have had."

"You can avoid it if you try."

"But why should you live the life of a spy in your own city among your own friends? Nor," here Helen's voice approached severity, "do I believe that you have any real mission, any real sense of public purpose. Do you?"

"Not in the way you mean."

"Not in the way it is meant. You have shown too little regard for that – but you know my views. So why is America so important to you?"

"Because it's not here," Jen said, slowly, as if the words were coming out of part of her she drew on rarely. "Because I can . . . obliterate myself."

"Don't be ridiculous."

"What if I mean it?" said Jen after a long pause.

"Then I would demand that you explain yourself."

"What if I couldn't?"

"Then I would suggest it was self-indulgent and rather sentimental tosh."

"What if I didn't mind you saying that but still held to that word?"

"Then I would conclude you were behaving neither sensibly nor logically nor particularly sanely."

"You always could pin me to the board, Helen. The pin through the butterfly. Stab! Become a specimen."

Helen sipped at her cold tea and then smiled sadly.

"You let me come so far and no further. You never let me find out what it was, did you?"

"What?"

"You know very well. What hurts you. What makes you so angry. What makes you irresistible."

"I don't know myself."

"Don't fib, darling. That's not allowed . . ."

Jen recollected that conversation now as Mark stalked around the truth in ever-increasing circles of inexact explanations.

The window was open. They were in the bedroom now in the dark, the heat a balm, the river a presence softly running to Tilbury. Side-by-side they lay on their backs like two stone figures in a medieval village church – the Lord and Lady of the Manor . . . Stone they felt too as the evening's evasions accreted like a magical wall between them, a boundary and a limit. It was the first night of their lives together that they had not made love or at least held and enjoyed each other.

In one of those tidal turns happening out in Chiswick Reach in that hour, one of those turns of mood which seem unexpected but can later be traced way, way back, Jen suddenly got out of the bed, snapped on the light, stood at the window and said:

"You have to tell me the truth."

As if he knew he were seeing her as his, as what they were together, for the last time, he looked for some moments without answering. The first time he had seen her naked was in the room of the hotel, and that fact of her body would never leave him. Nor would this, another body, lightly brown now, hair more streaked by the sun and a body known, possessed and possessing, in a thousand shapes and sounds and smells. What was the beauty of it? Yes, the fine curve, the slim shoulders, all the model-speak. But it was just the wonder of the thing itself: a body. It was only in Jen that he had ever been aware of that wonder. That it fitted together in that way. That hair and nails and flesh existed in such proportion, such harmony. That eyes and muscles and skin were there. That the shape of an arm should socket into the shoulder and be pulled and moved the way it was. That the head should be so justly proportioned, the thighs so high riding into the frame. It was the fact of her that made him hold his breath for those minutes. In Jen's body he saw the magnificence of this quite extra-ordinary creation. It was as if he had never seen a body before now. "The truth is, I think you won't come back from America," he said.

"So?"

She stood with her back to him, her arms folded on the terrace rail, leaning into the night. Her back, her thighs, her tender flesh.

"So I don't know what to do."

"Why don't you?"

Why don't you force me not to go? she thought. Why don't you make me stay? Why don't you want me enough? If you think I'll leave you – make me stay. Or what is it worth? What has it been, all this – sex, passion or words? Don't you see that I want you to want me so much that nothing on earth would ever let you accept that I go away from you? Mark, I need this.

"Why don't you know what to do?" She spoke calmly.

"What do you want?" he asked.

"I've told you," she said.

Mark's throat was dry. Suddenly it was all critically important. His life could be changed *now*. He sensed that but could not quite reach it, could not bring himself fully to address it. While he fumbled in the twilight of his confusion, Jen appeared ever more lucid, hard to his soft, light to his dark.

She turned and leant back on the rail, displayed, breathtaking, insolent.

"What *do* you want?" she repeated his question but switched the emphasis, orchestrating the exchange.

"That goes without saying, doesn't it?"

He felt the same disintegration he had felt in his morning flat in Edinburgh, when he realised he had been wholly abandoned. The presence of Jen was like a harsh light in his eyes. He turned away.

"No," she said, after a pause, "it doesn't go without saying. We've been saying so many nothings all night. Why can't we say something?"

"We've talked about marriage."

"Yes. And?"

"Well, of course. But you are so much younger. I . . . there's . . . there's the question of children." He paused. "No children."

"We've been through that."

"But did you mean it? Will you mean it in ten years' time? How can you know?"

"Mark. You have to give me an answer." There was a hoarseness in her voice. He caught her eyes. For once there was not that exhilarating, sometimes chilling clarity. The imminence of tears made her look ambiguous.

Help me, she was crying inside her head. Here I am, naked, yours: please make me want to be with you for ever. Please make me feel that you want that.

"I don't know what else I can say." Conscious of his failure, Mark reached out for a cigarette. Anything to divert this pressure. "Can't we talk about it when we're less tired?"

"Talk about what?" she asked.

Again his throat constricted, was dry. Why did he not dare to follow her? He wanted to, but to be so close would expose him to that terrible pain of loss. He could not bear that.

"About – this trip of yours," he said.

"Is that all it is? Just a trip?"

"I hope so."

"And if it's more than that?" She took as big a risk as her past, her deep and secret reticence, allowed her. "What will you do then, Mark?"

She said that slowly, indicating that he could take his time. He blew out a pant of smoke and, unconsciously taking the cue she had given him, allowed the question to gather its answer. But what was it to be? He sensed, and later, too much later, he was to identify what she wanted, but at this moment cowardice, fear, diffidence possessed him in silence. She waited in vain.

It was as if there were a wall of force between them, and the longer the silence held the more solid it became, the more threatening it felt to Mark, the more ominous, but he was unable to breach it.

Jen yawned and stretched, the stretch of a cat. A huge spread-armed, tip-toe, calves-arched stretch which seemed like some act of exorcism.

Then she smiled, her gentlest, most teasing smile.

"Put out that cigarette, Armstrong," she said. "I am going to do you to death."

Oh, he was such a man! Such a joker and so jolly. Such a rascal. Such a treat to see and he didn't give a bugger for anybody or anything. Even her mother was defenceless. He simply ignored the problem. Sean ignored all problems. Valerie was captivated by him and there seemed nothing her mother could do about it.

It was Miss McGuckian's doing. He was one of her several younger brothers and she had invited him over for the summer. He had come into the unusually hot and sticky summer town like a Zephyr, Valerie thought. She now knew what was meant by a Zephyr. He was so fine and careless, black eyes that would never be still but teased away at you, hair wavy and black and always on the loose. A slim frame but tight little muscles there poking out from under the rolled-up sleeves. And gabbing away like a washerwoman on every subject under the sun. Catholic, of course, "although the name McGuckian," explained Miss McGuckian, "is more commonly found in Ulster. There were branches moved south, it must have been centuries ago now and adopted the true faith, or never left it – I prefer to think it was the latter. We are the McGuckians of –" and she named the village, the county, the sacred ground of the true faith McGuckians.

Sean had seen Valerie in the garden the very first day of his visit and hopped over the fence like a robin to take the fork from her and turn out the weeds as accurately and as delicately as if he had been plucking a rose.

"Isn't this a grand little place?" he said excitedly, looking over the fields, looking up the road which led past the great hall into the town. "Isn't it a smart little number? Just look at the cars on the streets." There were, in truth, rather few cars that summer evening but every one was greeted with applause by Sean, who acted as if he had stumbled into Ali Baba's cave.

It was impossible not to ask him in for a cup of tea. In her recollection of that first meeting – and Valerie revisited it time and again – she was never absolutely certain that he had not just upped and invited himself. It would not have been beyond him. For although he had the most charming manner and the flourishes of great courtesy, he was also a rogue and a rascal and could find his way to a treat faster than a ferret down a rabbit hole.

Her mother was dazzled. It was the first time for years that she had received an unexpected visitor and his puckish strangeness held her gaze like a hare in the headlights. The dour little room of sickness and unspoken stricture, the parlour of malady and constraint was all lit up. He seemed to dance around it, admiring the frames around the photographs, picking out ornaments as if they were jewelled treasures, praising the furniture, ecstatic over the tea service with its little silver sugar bowl and milk jug, deeply complimentary about the hastily assembled sandwiches which he polished off like a trooper. "I like to see a man with a good appetite," said Mrs Thomlinson, faintly, perhaps remembering the line, for by that time her small pocket of energy was utterly spent and Valerie had to rescue her for bed. But there was no checking Sean. It was he who levered her out of the horsehair *chaise-longue*, "Fine piece of antique there, Mrs Thomlinson, when did you last see one of those in the sale room in such perfect condition?", he who shuffled her through the bungalow "what a size for a place without stairs, eh? Doesn't it strike you? The size of it" and would have taken her into the bedroom had she not resisted and Valerie caught her and disappeared to enter into the ritual of preparing her mother for bed.

But her fingers were clumsy that night. Her thoughts on fire with the man who was still there, she could feel it through the walls, waiting for her. Her mother did not refer to him at all and insisted that she read two chapters instead of the more usual one.

Yet he was still there. In the late northern twilight, strewn on the *chaise-longue*, tossing a small china bird from hand to hand and whistling softly to himself.

"I didn't put on a light," he said, "to save – the electricity is terribly dear. And anyhow, looking out the window here at the cars and seeing those hills, purple they looked just before you came in, those'll be the famous hills, won't they? I was better off, I thought, without the light." He smiled and the expression lit up her heart. She all but swayed at the effect it had. "You'll have to come closer for me to see you," he said, "and sit down if we're to talk." She did as he bid.

His talk was a stream which babbled away and it was as much the sound as the sense of it that she loved. His brothers and sisters, his daddy, the poor pickings on the place they tried to work, the wildness of the family, all but Bridie, the eldest, here in England set up as a teacher, "alone of all her kind", he said, "none of the rest of us can hold a pencil". Sometimes dark hints of violence and revenge, merrily-told tales of hare-coursing, which Valerie begged him to stop, and poaching – "there's fine places round-abouts here I'm told, I've met some of your lads". He brought into

172

the fortress bungalow that part of the town which Mrs Thomlinson had utterly ruled out. In the pubs he had met those like himself, who liked to tipple and gamble and bend around the law from time to time. He never became one of them but they all liked him, almost took him up as a mascot – which was the alternative to targeting him as an enemy, which could have been just as easy in the unpredictability of small-town, small-family politics. There was Irish in the town and he was spruce and regular at Mass, escorting his sister with a knightly air.

He had that extra flick of race about him. And there was not a bit of badness in him, she thought. Those were the two strands of Valerie's affection when, as happened, he would be involved in a scrape or an act of laziness which rather perturbed her. She held on to these pillars but in truth she scarcely needed them. With Sean, she floated. She had never known what it was to give all her love and the rapture allowed for no reservations, no insurance, nothing but the joy of falling, falling.

He had come for a month, but stayed on beyond the summer getting short-held jobs here and there – on the roads; once, disastrously, on a milk round; until finally his sister stepped in more and engineered an opening at the big factory where he had regular pay for the sort of work he could do easily. He was a willing enough worker, they all said that, but he never seemed to care enough about the job, lacked that sense of seriousness which gave the thing its meaning. Still, he held down the factory job, gloried in the shifts which gave him all sorts of free afternoons and lie-ins of a morning and, as the autumn deepened to winter, it was clear to one and all that he was courting Valerie and she was entranced. Nothing, from the fair advice of the Church of England vicar and one or two senior members of the congregation, nothing, from the chaffing of the shopkeepers and the scowl of Gerald, would bar her. Her mother saw this and had no resources.

Her courtship bloomed, as Sean touched her body into greedy life. "Look at those breasts, will you? Hidden away under as many layers as your mother has on her bed; just feel these, one in either hand, I'm like a man holding two worlds in his palms. Jesus!" Her mother's health began to decline.

It was hoped that she would last until Christmas and great store was set by that as if she might be blessed with another chance if she managed to make that significant date. But in November she began to fall away. By the end of the month she was wasted and had to be removed to hospital.

Sean was a touch impatient at the time which Valerie devoted to her mother. She would be at the hospital at every opportunity. There was no doubt about who came first, as Sean observed, not quite able to keep the reproach out of his voice. Valerie was alarmed but tried to explain that she had no alternative. He agreed, of course, he always did when he was coaxed. But the reproach remained and she dare not admit that one of her thoughts was that it would soon be over with her mother – the doctor had given her "a matter of months" – and then they would be together for ever. As it happened, Sean was with her in the hospital when her mother died and Valerie sought to interpret in the frightened desperate look of her mother, a blessing on their future.

As soon as was respectable – Miss McGuckian, Bridie, was unyielding in her timetable – they were married, in the Catholic church, Valerie having converted. It was found that Mrs Thomlinson's frugality had been deceptive. There was more money than had been anticipated and the bungalow was unencumbered. "We can live like lords," said Sean. "We can feast off the fat of the land. I'll build myself a shed in that backyard."

Sixteen

THE solution to the Butterfield tragedy was so simple that writers had been constructing mysteries and complications ever since it happened. It had everything which ought to have fed conspiracy, yet it remained obstinately straightforward. A thorough investigation, two exhaustive books, numerous articles and an ocean of bar gossip and street rumour had mowed through the facts, shaved last hours into fully examined minutes, taken on board every test that could be contrived and still the story unravelled clearly and simply. The place had gone up in flames. Jen was out at the time.

The Butterfield family itself was news enough – all the networks led with it; Jen added piquancy. As the survivor, the sole beneficiary, *ergo* the prime suspect, she was hounded, analysed and discussed, very likely, in every diner on the continent. Her American excursion had been triumphant. On the back of the bicentennial opportunity she had struck fast and hard and carved a unique niche for herself on television. The audiences loved the contradiction. Here was an English talent who could not wait to become an American citizen. Used to the Brits assuming superiority, Jen's undisguised passion for everything American surprised and ravished a public which could also appreciate her dexterity as an interviewer, her "tact and tartness tastefully combined", as the *New York Times* put it. As in the UK she managed to captivate the opinion formers and win a loyal mass following. Waved on by a boost of generosity from colleagues and critics alike, "our great new immigrant", as Johnny Carson called her, she achieved a pet status. Her work, though, the zest and detail she brought to it, took her through the mascot barrier and she became a fixture on the small screen, one of a top set of telly celebrities with some columnists talking about her executive future, others predicting a Hollywood career, others just pawing the new kid on the block.

Her name was associated with several men – all eligible, all unmarried – and she was breezily open about her reluctance to "get hitched". In a brilliantly planned and calculated public relations interview which explored the "serious side of her character", she announced that marriage was the most important decision a woman ever took. It involved so much. She admired married women, especially those with children, more than anyone else. It was the hardest job in the world. It was also the most responsible. She was new to this great country and had so much to learn about it. So much to see. So much catching up to do so that she could really feel American, as American as any high school kid because that was the heart of America, the key to the USA. (Thanks, Helen!)

In reality, that was asking the impossible of herself. There would be things about this great and complex country that she would never know. But people had been so generous and kind – Americans were undoubtedly the most generous, the kindest people on the planet – and she just wanted to get her bearings before she took on something as daunting as marriage. There was a whole continent out there – the most exciting continent in the world, she had seen it on the movies and on TV, she had read about it and talked and dreamt about it as a child in England but there was nothing to beat really getting to know the place for yourself and she was going to do that. Take a car. Hit Route Sixty-Six. Or make for Nantucket. Look out the little towns. Smell the desert. Hit the coast. See a stretch of the Mississippi. Go to Georgia and Vermont, places with names as exciting to her as Paris or Venice. All that would take any spare time she had from this job which was very demanding and she was determined to keep improving which meant you had to work that little bit harder. The American way. Everybody knew that was the American way. She had not believed it until she came here and so it was better to have lots of boyfriends, better just to call them friends, a circle of very supportive people and she was very grateful to them. But marriage: she was not yet ready for that responsibility.

Rumours circulated that she was a "wildcat in the sack" but they never surfaced and as juicy bubbles of gossip they did her no harm. Her elegant raunchiness was certainly part of the attraction.

But it was the mutual love affair, innocent and genuine, between a woman who could easily shift into a figure of fantasy and even myth, and a country which she decided was her true home; this was the clincher: the icon and the dream.

Robert – never Bob – Butterfield III, was Antony to her Cleopatra, Menelaus to her Helen – so he saw himself. For thinking grand was one of his characteristics. No comparison was too outrageous. He was short, dumpy and big-nosed; his hair was nondescript sandy and thinning; no suit could stand the strain of his hyperactive volatility for more than a few hours. His manner was brusque on good days, most days rude. He had something of a drink problem and the beginnings of a drug habit. Yet he walked and talked like a matinée idol. He expected and would receive all the superficial applause for the Hollywood stud. He laid down opinions authoritatively and was listened to, and that was the nub of it. Robert Butterfield III was ugly and obnoxious but he was also seriously rich, seriously bright and seriously motoring. The rest followed.

Jen would not go to bed with him. Not the first, nor the second, third, not even after their eleventh date, by which time they had become "an item". Friends who were aware of this thought Jen both shrewd and tough. Robert, the Casanova of the plains, was in a nicely stirred frenzy of desire and frustration. But he was hooked. Jen too was hooked but she needed time.

She feared that the Butterfields were too crushingly grand. Robert's increasingly earnest demand that they marry was coupled with the request, even the command, that she give up her television work. That which had brought her to his attention in the first place had to be destroyed. What defined her had to go. She had to become his. It would be quite enough to be Mrs Butterfield III.

As Mrs Butterfield III, she would be part of one of the wealthiest families in America. As Mrs Butterfield III she could give parties of Roman splendour and chic, cultivate a salon, buy at Sotheby's, pick and choose in the Village, patronise musicians, host charities, feature at all fashionable openings – play on the real stage rather than be confined to television. By implication her work and her achievements were diminished and dismissed and she would not let him get away with that. But when she went to his houses, to the old town home in the Eighties, to the enormous spread near Tulsa, to the cabin in the hills of Colorado where the pioneering

Butterfield had come from at the turn of the century, she saw that Robert could act in no other way.

It was a small family. Intelligence and character had run strongly from generation to generation and control of the vast oil-based empire was still wholly concentrated in family hands. Robert's father was the current chairman, Robert the clearly designated successor. Jen was adopted instantly. She was clearheaded enough to work out why. Robert's father and stepmother thought she would help them control him. Her good manners and immediate affection for them marked her as an ally. Her wit reassured them that Robert would be opposed now and then, if not contained. Her own achievement indicated the sort of will to win that they admired more than anything else in the world.

The problem for Jen was that she was hugely intrigued by the Butterfield connection: it was an arena of life of which until now she had had the merest glimpse. It was not so much the luxury – she was too honest to herself to rule out that lure entirely, but also too honest to pretend that it counted for more than a fraction – as the intriguing, strange new world of power-money.

Jen knew a little about power from television politics and from her journalistic involvement with the real thing. About money she had always been sensible but fundamentally indifferent. The world of the Butterfields welded those two together into a view of life that was as complete and sufficient unto itself as Marxism or Catholicism. Power-money was the way the world worked. All questions were reducible to that, all problems would be solved by that. The money that made trade. The power that generated wealth. The force of the two together was the explanation for everything that mattered.

Africa – rapidly becoming unbankable, they said, chillingly – had lost the power to generate a self-sustaining economy, become a crop resort for the West and from that all its difficulties, ecological, cultural, internecine, political, flowed quite logically. Power-money was the explanation for the dictatorial spasms in the time-warped USSR, where there was no flow between wealth and power, no understanding that they had to be free to find their own channels, dig out their own reservoirs, make their own maps: a case of power without the true responsibility of money. And so they could go around the world and, indeed, the world was the market-place of any Butterfield conversation. Sportsmen were admired for their skill but seen in dollar-pulling terms; artists were ranked according to sale-room prices; the rare was cherished for its money value. Uniqueness was a cash value. Jen was far from persuaded and her arguments were met with courtesy but no concessions were made. The attraction of their closed system was considerable.

The heart of the attraction lay in the feeling it gave her that this was a bedrock world. The television experience was necessarily vicarious, even parasitic, however much value could be added to it by the knowledge that it meant so much to so many. Butterfield was dealing unashamedly with the root matter of the world. In England Jen had met few from industry who had not thought that they were meant to be somehow embarrassed in polite company. Trade continued to carry a stigma. It was swept under the carpet of café society and locked outside the snobby walls of the country house, or country cottage, countrified existence of the old and newly rich. It was as if England were part of a floating island which somehow kept above water by wholly invisible means. For all the Butterfield bleakness of judgement in areas such as painting, Jen felt and was excited by this sense of bedrock. Here was the world as it was: oil coming out of the ground, crops being grown, machines being made in factories, money being switched from Korea to Mexico as trade shuffled in new patterns around the Pacific and Central America.

In its own way – she could see – this power-money club saw itself as a priesthood. They were the true guardians of the vital wealth-producing process without which the entire modern world was doomed. They were its secret leaders, its unacknowledged legislators; it was their world and they ruled. Robert's father gave off that sense of superiority and princely dominion. Robert was Young Hal still, but he would surely come in to his estate. Jen, they told her this, would be of great help to him. Of all the young ladies – the language was often neo-Victorian – he had brought to the house, she was the most outstanding. Her value to them as a family was very high. They wanted her to know that. She could be of great use to them. Her skills were marketable.

It would be a way out. That was what she realised, curiously enough in conversations with Cally. Cally, a teenager, daughter of Robert's stepmother by her first marriage, idolised Jen. Cally had problems – she was slow at school, she was sloppy, she was hope-lessly ill-organised, she was her mother's despair and almost her shame. Part of that tough woman's courting of Jen was to do with her appreciation of Cally's idealising affection for her. Jen improved Cally. You are her role model, her mother said. She has been looking for one for a long time. Cally's daffy, lovesick admiration of the TV star, her assumption that Jen knew everyone in all her favourite soaps and shows and could tell her the most amazing things about them if she chose to, her unremitting star-struck attitude brought home to Jen that this was her life – she had become public property. Just as it had palled in London, so, after she met Robert, it began to pall in the USA.

Robert speeded up the process. Proud at first and glowing a little in reflected celebrity status, he grew bored very quickly with the indiscriminate nature of it all. It had no class, he said. Everybody thought themselves equally entitled to a piece of her. It was like wading through treacle just to order a meal. Take off in the Lincoln Continental or roar away out of town in the Transam and it was worse. Out of town she was a peepshow. "I feel I'm Barnum & Bailey with a freak on my hands," he said. The procession of people who, very sweetly for the most part, bobbed up to say "Hi" or ask for an autograph or make a genuinely flattering comment began to drive him crazy, that and the lack of sex. "I understand Howard Hughes," he said. "Dad met him a few times. Maybe I should get in touch and ask for some tips." Through his irritation and contempt for those remorseless public arrivals – "like some damn little Queen of England that the poor people rush to for a cure for evil or whatever the hell it was," he said – her own fears were activated. She would have no life of her own soon. Butterfield would offer a refuge.

But that was not the whole of it either. There was a savagery in Robert which in a peculiar symmetry matched the unadmitted pain in Mark. Just as she had almost succeeded with Mark – indeed on certain nights she had succeeded – in burying her own wound, obliterating that nightmare self which hounded her, so she sensed about Robert the force to beat the devil wholly out of her. There was no softness in Robert. He was not a crude man, she doubted whether he would be a violent lover, but he would be wholly tough and possessive and in that she might find equilibrium. Not to be sexually possessed, not to be taken over like some debilitated company, but to be matched, tested and forced to address the present flatly, without regret, without a backward look.

They took a trip through Nashville, cut across Texas, Amarillo, Lubbock, through New Mexico, Santa Fe, north across Arizona and into Las Vegas where Robert drove through the Strip and down to Glitter Gulch to find serious poker players. He arrived having driven, on drugs and alcohol, for eleven hours; he played through the night – although who could tell night from day in there? – lost a hard-fought $23,000 and, when he went to bed, found that at last Jen was ready for him. From the pit of his exhaustion he summoned that unsuspected scrap of energy which is inexplicable and can appear superhuman. They made love throughout the morning, stayed in Las Vegas for six days, took all the tests and married in a wedding chapel on the Strip.

Robert's family wholly approved. A Butterfield celebration was laid on in the Waldorf Astoria three months later. Mrs Butterfield III refused all interviews – charmingly – and confirmed that her television career was over, although another career might tempt her. She wanted marriage and a family. She was already pregnant.

It was a boy and on his first birthday the entire family was summoned to Colorado. Robert Butterfield IV would be introduced to the source of Butterfield strength. It was a ritualistic introduction taken with the utmost seriousness by the family. The original log cabin of the Butterfield ancestors was there. Three others – all of an equally modest size – grouped around it. Simplicity was axiomatic. You swam in the stream, cold as it was. You backpacked through the mountains and woods, all of which were owned by the family, who made up in land what they denied themselves in dwelling-space in this particular location. You fished and you ate the fish. You went out shooting. You remembered that this was where it had all begun and once a year you all came together for a week or so and paid tribute. The boy's first birthday added lustre to this year's event.

Robert had obeyed the family's imperative. The birth of his boy had banished all thought of useless activities. He was now building for a visible physical future and he would do his best to ensure that the boy's inheritance was even sounder, even grander, even more money-powerful than his own. This boy – who had all of Jen's physical grace, who was already Jen in miniature, which besotted Robert to a degree he could never have imagined – this boy would inherit just as big a portion of the earth as Robert Butterfield III could possibly command.

It was an occasion of affirmation, of powerful joy. Jen was the toast; the boy, the heir, was the pride.

On the next afternoon, Jen and Cally went out for a walk through the woods. Cally had been intimidated by the occasion and Jen wanted to give her a boost. She took her arm and they walked like two friends, equals, softly treading down the deep carpet of autumn leaves, sucking in hard the sharp clean air, stopping every so often to listen to the sounds in the deeper silence of the forest.

As they came back, Robert's helicopter came into view. The pad was at the bottom of the mountain, next to one of the three security lodges. From there a car would take you up to the cabins. Robert, who had just got his licence, had flown away that morning to a meeting he could not miss. Now he came back, no doubt triumphantly, ready with the story of the deal. In his delight and flying sense of invulnerability, he was approaching the cabin to salute the boy, his son. He made a pass across the small cluster of dwellings, wheeled and dipped down for a second pass. Some minute miscalculation nosed the machine down too abruptly. He could not control it. The large frightened furious bird of destruction, its blades beating hopelessly, landed plum on the cabins, which burst into flames. There were no survivors. There was only one photograph of Jen – at the funeral – and she looked so traumatised with grief that it was beyond comment.

SEVENTEEN

I

"MARRIAGE is unsatisfactory." Fred's delivery was loud and preening. "But promiscuity is worse and chastity is strictly for the angels."

"You don't have to marry," said Vivien.

"Non-married marriage is just a respectable way to have an affair."

"Is that so bad?"

"Having an affair is an admission of failure."

"How can you be so sure – about everything?" Vivien was quiet and genuinely puzzled.

"Would you like another drink?"

"Good idea!" Fred slung back his scotch and beamed around the large morning-room.

Mark hoisted himself out of the club armchair and padded across the rather worn room towards the bar. He could have rung for a waiter – or club servant – but he needed a break. Fred was so delighted to be in this gun-room of the Establishment that he seemed to have forgotten the purpose of his visit, decided to annoy Vivien, his university colleague, and address the world like a stage ham wit. It was at moments like this that Mark really liked him: but – as in Mahler concerts – intervals were essential.

Mark still felt rather shy about this – his – club. Colleagues had put him up and only recently levered him in and, in his bachelor state, it made all sorts of sense. But he was aware how often privilege excuses itself on the grounds of good value and still felt that a man who steered his own life ought not to be bound in clubs. He accepted it with the resignation of one who sees his life happening in spite of himself. His work was directed, it engaged him. The rest seemed to push him around and leave him beached, wondering how it had come about. People thought of him as lonely. No centre, that was the explanation, he thought, no marriage, no children, no home and no pack of close friends. Nick, Fred to a lesser extent, others from work . . . or was it just the usual Celtic melancholy? "Two large Bell's and a vodka and tonic." The very good thing was that you did not have to pay your bills until the end of the month. It made him feel like Beau Brummell or the young Tolstoy, and a touch of a con.

Fred was still on full volume when he returned – like a transistor on a private beach – unaware of the twitching grip on the papers as silent members burrowed into newsprint and emitted an unmistakable frisson of disapproval. If Fred noticed it – and that was on the cards – he chose to ignore it. Mark enjoyed that, it fed the subversion he felt he himself ought to express occasionally in this maximum-security institution.

"I was talking to young Vivien about the enduring strengths of Christianity."

"Were you?" The old leather chair was always lower than Mark anticipated and he landed in the seat – at about floor level – with a bump which caused a little spillage of the whisky. Vivien smiled, as if conspiratorially. Mark thought how attractive that made her look.

"Probably the most satisfactory moral *cum* spiritual schema ever invented." Fred gulped a large mouthful of the fiery substance and ignited into a racket of hawking and spitting. Mark noticed that he still managed to swallow most of it. This time it was he who sought out Vivien for a colluding look; again the smile.

"Yes." Fred did not falter and out of the coughing came the litany. "Buddhism, the Muslims, the Confucians, the myriad paganisms, the political credos – Marxism, I suppose, has some purchase here – none of them has the, what I would call, flexibility, the capacity to readapt that Judaeo-Christianity has shown again and again." He breathed deeply – cleared of all coughing and all names – a steeplechase well accomplished. "Except Hinduism," he concluded, happy to contradict himself.

"How did we get on to this?"

"Dorothy wants to be christened," said Vivien.

"That's why we're here." Fred looked rather snubbed.

"You didn't tell me that, Fred." Mark wanted to reassure him.

184

"You just said that you wanted the three of us to meet to talk about Dorothy."

"Ah. Well, what Vivien says is correct. She wants to be christened."

"She's . . ."

"Fourteen." Somehow the admission of her age made Fred instantly gloomy. Or perhaps he was visited by the memory of his miserably short marriage and the strain of being left with a seven-month-old baby. He had coped, Mark thought, outstandingly well, refusing all but minimal help and not seeking out a second wife or lover to share the burden.

"Fred wants us to be the godparents." Vivien, too, wanted to reassure Fred, Mark noted. So, a nice woman as well as an attractive woman.

"Does it matter that I don't believe in God?"

"No one," Fred was relaunched, "of any sensibility could '*believe*' in the English version of God, who is a cross between an insipid schoolteacher and a spanking matron. I wouldn't have you if you believed in him. The English Establishment has turned him into a retainer. The Englishman's God is his butler."

One or two newspapers crackled but it may have been the Test score.

"Jeeves for Jehovah. Not bad casting –"

"It's the age." Fred finished the whisky. "Fourteen. A questioning age."

"Well – of course – if you think – if she thinks –"

"Dorothy chose you. You and Vivien. I allowed myself no say in the matter. She must accept full responsibility."

"Well. Yes. Fine. Good. Right."

"Weekends are best for Dorothy. Sunday I think would be too sickly. Too much of a coincidence."

"I thought you were admiring the way Christianity survived and adapted."

"Intellectually, yes. Personally, I loathe it. Pain is at the heart of it and I cannot take the obscenity of the crucifixion. But there you are. Saturday the fourteenth, I thought. Will you be in the country?"

". . . I think so . . . yes . . . here we are – yes. Should be."

"Dorothy has chosen the church. The vicar says he rather welcomes atheists as godparents. Vivien is also an atheist. Dorothy has no objection. She says she will make your conversion her first task."

This time both Vivien and Mark avoided each other's eye: intimacy had developed swiftly.

"Why don't we go out and celebrate?" The prospect of an evening's club food and then a book back in the flat – which had seemed cosy – now appeared rather bleak.

"I have to catch the 8.13. Dorothy will have made supper."

"Oh . . . well," to Vivien, "could you? Would you . . . ?"

"That would be lovely," said Vivien, briskly.

"I'll send you the details in the post." Fred stood up abruptly and aimed himself at the door.

"He hardly ever drinks," said Vivien. "I think that three doubles went rather too quickly to his head. And this place, of course."

"It is rather impressive, isn't it?" Started as a boast, Mark's sentence ended as an insecure request for reassurance.

"It makes me feel ten and in church enduring the most boring sermon ever given. Fred deeply disapproves but he enjoyed it – hence the confusion. A typical class conflict, I'd say – or rather, he'd say."

"There are some places around the corner. We could . . ."

"Take pot luck. Lovely."

After dinner, as they meandered through the streets looking for a taxi to take her to the station, she slipped her arm through his in a rather old-fashioned but comforting way. Mark was surprised how much he enjoyed it: how much he had missed that easy common comfort, that affectionate link.

II

"Remember when I used to lie the whole hour and say nothing?"

The analyst said nothing. Jen let the silence register. Eventually the pressure of the analysis made her resume.

"You said – I'm sure you remember it – you said I was the most difficult patient you had ever had. You said that no one had ever resisted as much as I did. Did you say that to flatter me? Did you say that to soften me up? You're a cunning little bastard, aren't you? It's a bit like interviewing. I used that trick myself now and then."

The analyst smiled but the smile was unseen by Jen stretched on the *chaise-longue* in the splendid East Side duplex high in the Eighties, high in the market.

"It's very voluptuous lying here," Jen said. The slight slur in her

186

voice alerted the analyst. "Just draped on this Récamier sofa, gazing at the American sky through your tastefully positioned skylight, talking, talking like Scheherezade but with no threat greater than your scandalous fees which I can scandalously afford for ever and a day, a thousand and one days a year. I should be clothed in chiffon, a breeze blowing down from that bloody skylight, a touch of Isadora or naked maybe like one of those dirty French paintings where we all solemnly pretend it's a study of the female form – balls! – now that's what it really is. And what is this but a kind of oral onanism? I'm sure that's occurred to you, gratification through exhalation, the working of the mother-mouth or the mother-fucker mouth, as our brethren in Times Square correctly have it – drifting alone on this surf of self-indulgence, which is supposed to wash me whiter than white, to the shore of a sanity none of us would recognise, along this Old Silk Road of flux and flow talking as much absolute crap as I like. And you nary a word but just there like God or a sphinx – I prefer the sphinx, at least it demanded an intelligent question and it was probably female but beat not that drum today, feminism doesn't count when you're rich, not when you're rich-rich, that's the sauce that smothers all the flavours, especially in our little neck of twentieth-century time when money is on the rampage and even scholars, even artists, even priests, talk nothing else and everything is measured out in dollar signs. Being rich-rich means that you are allowed to have no incentive to try to be, to do anything else at all, why bother? *Why bother?* A career? Forget it – I can make more money in a non-career. A hobby – who the hell wants a hobby? It's treacle, this loot; lovely, lovely black treacle and we smear it on everything and love-a-dub-dub it all over us and then we're stuck in it and it's very nice, isn't it? I mean this is what the great American Dream is about. And I refuse to complain about being a poor little rich-rich girl. I like my sauce. I love my black treacle. Yum-yum. But I ask you, apart from coming here like some archangel fluttering into your punchdrunk mind, what more can you do? Forget it, forget it. Except you're paid not to. Do you know this one?

"Roses are red and ready for plucking
I'm seventeen and ready for taking to the pictures."
The analyst let the power shift back to him before he spoke.
"You took some again this morning."
"You bet."
"It is a waste of your time and mine if you come here high."
"How else can I make it?"

187

"It is a waste of your time and of mine."

"No coke, no talk. No talk, no pay."

"I'm very well able to survive without your fees, Mrs Butterfield."

"I'm not."

He withdrew into silence once again.

Jen tried to focus. For a few moments she fell asleep.

He made a steeple of his fingers. This was a sign of satisfaction.

"Try again," he suggested in his neutral voice when he judged she was awake.

"I'm high, I'm flying – I know what that means! OK? Writhings inside here, inside me, and lovely curlings of rose-tinted plasms and spasms and whatever rhymes with that and a bucket of coke a day keeps the home fires burning, best Colombian straight out of the coke face, support the Third World – buying coke could be a charity. That's the rich-rich hobby. Charity. Nothing to do with Christian charity. Show-off charity. Boast-a-lot charity. Look-at-me char-it-y. I do my bit through coke."

He waited. Her resistance, it was true, was formidable. It was almost a year since the tragedy and she had been persuaded to come. Broken then, stunned then, all but catatonic: and now? Though drugged, though somnambulistic, though driven by a need to the urgent and massive increase of her wealth which she used so little, he could sense a turning of the tide, an interest in taking on that tragedy. But he was very wary. Under the recent trauma could be a psychosis. She was a most remarkable woman, he thought – he had been one of her admirers when she had been on television. Her rambling confirmed how deeply being cut off from her career mattered to her, as it was bound to, he thought. Jen was an archetypical late-twentieth-century woman achiever – a pace-setter, a maker, a role model, at the head of the intelligent female cavalry advancing across so wide a field. The power marriage, the loss of the child, the avalanche of money had buried her deep, out of all that, out of touch with the self she had so audaciously invented, coming as she did from that backward, industrial, Northern, lower-class part of England. He had a perspective on all that. He had received messages from her on all that. But there was something even deeper. Even deeper than the death of her husband and her son? It seemed so. What it was he could not fathom, there had been no hint, but he knew now that she was blocking something which, his theory went, would prevent her self-fulfilment unless it was revealed. But what it was . . .

"I try to imagine his face. It already had an expression. He was like neither of us – not really. He was already like himself. What did he think was happening? What did he know? How long did he know? How long did he take to . . . How long did he take . . . How long – did – he – take – to – die?"

The pain and profound quiet cry of despair charged the room. The analyst breathed deeply and regularly to absorb it. Jen folded up and turned on her side.

An intervention was allowed here.

"All the evidence points to its being very quick, all but instantaneous."

Out of her rackingly subdued sobs came two words only: "All but . . . ?"

This she had showed him before. But what was the other thing? What was the deepest cellar here?

"A child meaninglessly destroyed . . ."

It was a risk: it was too much of a prompt, too crude – but the coke meant that he had to improvise and her present despair could be the gate to hope he had been looking for. He dropped in the sentence like a pebble in a pool and waited, on the bank, willing the ripples to reach out to him.

"That's not it," she said, "that's not near."

The analyst was alert as radar.

"That's not near," Jen repeated, "that's not it at all. It's the mother who – it's the mother. If, if you're, we're, talking about destroyed. What on earth is there anyone can do about that? Can't have another mother."

The effort and the drugs were causing her to fade.

He had no alternative but silence. Nearly there. So nearly there. But not yet. She would not yield that last secret.

She straightened out and rearranged herself on the *chaise-longue*. Every time she moved he was uncomfortably aware of her beauty. Perhaps that thought transferred itself to her.

"God, I'm cold," she said. "Look at those clouds. The weatherman said thunder."

He would get no more this day. The steeple suddenly collapsed and the fingers slotted into each other, a double fist, a silent, clenched, sculpture of disappointment.

EIGHTEEN

I

"HE will be called Seamus," said Sean, drunk and further intoxicated by the grandeur of his new role as father. "Seamus has been in the family for generations." He took a sip of port. "For centuries no doubt there have been Seamus McGuckians and now there is another." He waved his glass and hiccuped. His sister took this as a useful cue to scold him and usher him out of the bedroom. She had not wanted to stop his flow: after all he was the man and the head of this household. But the hiccup was the perfect excuse. Sean was not unhappy to be shooed away. The bottle was in the other room.

It had not been an easy birth and Valerie had taken to bed the moment she had come back from the hospital. Luckily it was during the holidays and Bridie could devote all her time to helping her. Valerie had crossed a threshold when Miss McGuckian had said that now they were related she must drop the formal address and call her Bridie. It was such a lovely name, Valerie thought. Yet for Miss McGuckian herself, rising forty now, a fast-ageing and old-country-style forty, Bridie had an association of sadness. About the province of her birth were spinster Bridies, drudges or worse. But, for Valerie, Bridie had been her butterfly gift out of the chrysalis of Miss McGuckian. She had embraced Valerie as a sister. It was as if she were meeting her for the first time – rediscovering a sister. Valerie replaced Bridie's unspoken loss of that tribe of a family she had left behind in Ireland. All the sibling sympathies from which she had been cut off grew again, bloomed stronger than before. Valerie was in a state of wholly unaccustomed security.

She dreaded to think where she would have been without

Bridie's influence over Sean. It was Bridie who steered and cajoled and ordered him to stick at the work in the factory, which seemed from his descriptions to be the worst of the satanic mills.

"I was not built for shutting up in a place," he would say. "I want to be out in the weather. I'm from the land."

"Listen to him," said Bridie. "Two or three acres of stones. That's the land. And what possible work could he get around here that would bring in the way that factory delivers the goods? I know about that place, Valerie: as factories go, it's decent. Don't you listen to him. Don't let it get to you. He's just trying it on and we must be wise to that."

As often as not Sean would retreat from "the women" with good grace. Occasionally, though, especially when Valerie was alone, there would be a sullen glint in his eyes which made her fearful. She did not know him then. She still loved him deeply, although she was long over the total adoration she had given to his every hop and skip. She knew about the drinking, the gambling, the preference for company which could be called roguish but could also be criminal. She knew about his moods and his hugely inflated sense of proprietorial splendour. A few times he had brought back his cronies who had sat around the bungalow drinking bottles of beer from the neck and appraising every item which Sean showed off like an auctioneer. She had made them sandwiches and tea – anything to get out of the room which seemed menacing and suddenly captured by an enemy. The familiar become hostile to her.

She discovered that she possessed a distressing sense of ownership of her own territory every bit as marked as Sean's lordly rule. Perhaps it came from having put so much time into that bungalow, time in which she had been forced to find ways and deceptions to achieve the respite of solitude; perhaps it came from a more profound sense of holding on to what had become solid and protective for her; but she was afraid of what she so soon saw as invasions. Bridie was a friend and she filled the house with warmth and order. Sean at his best – and it was for his best she still loved him – could make the place twinkle as if it had been dusted and polished to a 'T' and the sun was hitting all the waxed and shiny surfaces. But when Sean brought his new friends, she could not bear it.

And, although she struggled to admit it, it was much the same when too many of Sean's brothers and sisters came over for the holidays together. Then Valerie had to fight a panic akin to claustrophobia. It was an odd family. Valerie, in her starved family fantasy, imagined a romp of brothers and sisters, variety yes, but a binding, healing seam of common characteristics, gestures, looks, affections. Each of the McGuckians seemed a one-off and rather determined not to enter into any play of happy families. Bridie was the one who could whip them all together and she was more unlike them than any of them were unlike each other. Two of the much younger ones, the teenagers Fiona and Paul, were even somewhat insolent, which was a long way from the natural tact and courtesy of Bridie and the grace and manners always available to Sean. Left alone with them one evening as she was, and under heavy instructions not to let them go out into the town after a previous evening of misdemeanour and culpably late arrival back at the bungalow, Valerie had felt a build-up of resentment which had grown so intense that she had to leave the room. As she left, she heard them laughing and the sound of that laugh hurt and disturbed her.

Yet they were Sean's flesh and blood. And they were children. In the morning she pushed away the silly fears and took them out into the town, bought them new jeans and crazy T-shirts from the charming Indian trader in the market hall. They were happy, excited, grateful. Fiona kissed her. Valerie decided that she had to take herself in hand and stop being so selfish. They were just poor kids. And look at what she had!

Sean could be faulted – who could not? – but he had opened windows into her life and he could still make her feelings swell with happiness. She was no longer cribbed but a person in her own right in the town. Most of her friends from the church, while regretting her conversion to Catholicism, made a special point of being nice to her, even though it could seem the concern of the healthy for an invalid. No matter. And the Catholic community in the town, rather an ageing community now, suddenly appeared, as if she had joined the Freemasons – that was Bridie's analogy – and she found herself smiled at and nodded to by a sprinkling of people who had scarcely noticed her before. She went to Mass every Sunday; Saturday confession. Sean was not much good for anything on Sunday morning but, after a night shift, he would sometimes try to fit in a Mass.

As long as Bridie was there.

When the child was born, Valerie was badly weakened. It was a Caesarean, the thought of which terrified her although the reality was bearable. She kept worrying that the knife might slice too deeply and hurt the child. It was an absurd worry but it would not go away until the red, freshly swabbed life was put in her arms and she could feel its warmth, watch it for those first minutes, just watch, watch, look, seek, seek for any smallest sign of harm. No, it was fine. It was a healthy baby. He was a healthy baby.

"Seamus," said Sean, the moment he came into the ward, "Seamus it is."

But some obstinacy rose up in Valerie's tired, relieved, shocked mind. Seamus could indeed be one name but there would be another. She did not have to think about it. It slipped on to her tongue unsought.

"Harry," she said. "Harry as well as Seamus."

"Seamus," said Sean, loudly.

Weakly Valerie nodded. The small puckered face beside her moved her to tears and as she wept, silently, Sean was chastened.

"Harry it can be," he said, "to you. Seamus to me. Is that all right now?"

Valerie tried to smile. Sean looked around for a vase for the dozen white carnations.

II

"She never replied."

"How many times did you write to her?"

"Once," said Mark. "Twice."

"It is no consolation for you to know that I too wrote twice and I too received no reply," said Nicholas, lying to protect Mark's feelings.

"Unlike her."

"Not at all. Very like her. She was, she is, a woman who makes a move and casts off all behind her. The past is enemy territory."

"You make her sound cold."

"You would know that better than I," said Nicholas. "And I don't think of it as cold. It was her character. I found it intriguing and clearly very effective. He who travels without the baggage of the past travels fastest. It ought to be an ancient Chinese proverb. Let it be my donation to that ruined culture."

"I just thought . . ."

"Mark, my dear. We are trembling on the edge of the happy cliff of drunkenness. We have enjoyed a rare evening's intimacy. I have a pair at the House and so I need not return all evening. You have no dashing imperative to distract you. Except your marriage in the morning. Which leads me to conclude that we are spending rather a long time talking about the wrong woman."

"Who else can I talk to about her?"

"That is not, not quite, the point."

"Losing that child," said Mark, helplessly. "Imagine."

Nicholas poured out the last of the second bottle of St Emilion and looked around for the wine waiter. He had brought Mark to Green's in Duke Street, St James's, and, as it was a quiet evening, he had arranged to secure a booth which guaranteed privacy and was encouraging to confessions. Nicholas felt that he ought to behave as a true friend.

"Are you sure about tomorrow, Mark? More wine or brandy?"

"Malt. Of course." Mark paused. "Of course about tomorrow, I mean."

"You sound a little morose."

"Pre-match nerves. Don't we all?"

"One little problem I shall certainly be spared."

"But."

"But that is the received wisdom, yes. Cigars, please. Thank you."

"Viv is splendid," said Mark.

"I agree."

"Warm-hearted, decent, friendly, she doesn't fuss, she holds down a good job —"

"Are you writing her a reference?"

"You know what I mean."

"I do. Look, Mark. If you're not a hundred per cent sure, it isn't too late."

"We've been on and off for two years now. It isn't fair."

"I thought the Eighties had finally shaken off the marriage imperative."

"Not for Viv. And not for me, actually."

"Perhaps she wants it because she thinks it will finally confirm your feelings."

"Could be," said Mark. "Could very well be. And she could be right. Could very well be right."

"The bridegroom is not proceeding happily to the altar."

"It's all arranged," said Mark. "Cheers. And I will try to make it work. And so will she."

"Good luck," Nicholas said, rather solemnly. "She is a particularly attractive woman. Most men your age would say that you were very lucky."

"They would be right."

The two friends drank and fell into silence.

194

"But off the map. Off the radar entirely. For three years." Mark would not be sidetracked.

"I did hear a rumour that she was in the market with one of those junk bond johnnies."

"What does she know about the market?"

"We all have to learn about the market, my dear. It's the new place of worship. The new Temple. Wonderful how things come round again, isn't it? We have the Pharisees and the Pontius Pilates and the moneylenders. All we need now is Jesus Christ."

"I contacted Helen but she wouldn't say anything."

"Perhaps she doesn't know anything."

"She admitted that she had been to America."

"Ah."

"But she would say no more than that. She's become rather tetchy since her retirement."

"It was too abrupt. When the male super-bureaucrat retires he has usually sequestered the nest-egg of a high-sounding job, a quango where he can continue to boss the rest of us around to his heart's content. Women tend to get neglected or tokenised, and Helen would hate that."

"She wouldn't even give me an address."

"Mark . . ."

"Because, of course, our letters could have gone to an old address and not been forwarded. 'I'll do my best to get your note to her if you'd care to send it here,' says Helen, 'but I have to tell you that she wants complete privacy and isolation.' Helen tells *me*."

"You always were rivals."

"What?"

"Never mind. Mark. I have two conflicting responsibilities." He sipped at his cognac. Mark had already finished his Macallan. "As your best man my duty is to get you to the registry office on time tomorrow morning. As your best friend my duty is to tell you to call it off."

"Why? Time for another?"

"Of course." The signal was made. "Don't be disingenuous, Mark." He lit the large cigar very carefully.

"I just found that I wanted to talk about her tonight. Have I done this before?"

"Not at this length and not often but the eve of marriage is a rather significant occasion."

"I should have married her."

"Did you ask her?"

195

"Not – no."

"Well then. Mark. Drink up and I'll take you home."

"I should have followed her to the States."

"Did she ask you to? . . . Clearly not."

"I love Vivien."

"I don't doubt it."

"You understand, don't you? Things that lay about unsaid."

"Yes. I understand that very well," said Nicholas.

"Thanks for listening. All over now. Sorry about dumping on you."

"That's what I'm for."

"Especially tonight."

"You ran true to form. Maudlin, neurotic, sentimental; I'm told that's par for this particular course."

"Selfish. Not a word about you."

"I am not getting married in the morning. My time to shine can wait."

"Feel like a bloody idiot."

"That's the second malt. We have consumed much alcohol *ce soir*, old bean, and now it's time to go home."

They walked up to Piccadilly where Nicholas shepherded Mark into a taxi.

It was still warm enough and he decided to stroll around for a while. This had become his patch. Soon after getting his safe seat he had been able to move into rooms in Albany which suited him perfectly. He had bought a pretty vicarage – some of it dating back to the sixteenth century – in a well-placed village in his constituency and Albany in Piccadilly answered all his London needs, the greatest of these being respectability. It was not as interesting as the other flats he had enjoyed at different stages in his London life. Its collegiate air, its Oxbridge quadrangle character, its utter Establishment credentials were cramping, Nicholas found, one could be too tightly swaddled. Yet he had taken the rooms with gratitude. Albany was a place where wealthy and discreet bachelors of a certain age and class could safely graze.

It was a great advantage being near this hub of London, the Circus, the cesspit, the circuit, home of a daily more irrelevant Eros as the boys cruised and the pimps called their wares, the drugs moved around and the arcades swallowed up the dead-eyed. Nicholas rarely failed to find a sight which intrigued or saddened, in some way moved him, occasionally aroused him. The tackiness strewn at the feet of ancient grandeur, the surge of refurbishment beating against the tide of rubbish, the spokes to a street of theatres, a splendid swing of shops, a crush of cinemas, resonant London names clashing with garish shop signs, massive hoardings, the display of lights advertising to the awe-struck, the ceaseless kerb shuffle of West End life.

But, on tonight's stroll, he noticed little. That afternoon his cousin had passed on a disturbing piece of information. Currently he was being considered for a junior government post, the first step but well anticipated by a press who had picked him out as one of the brightest and best of the new intake. A murmur, though, his cousin had said, a ripple of doubt had gently cuffed his name off the table. It was difficult to track it down to source and even so what would be the point? He knew that Nicholas was discreet. He himself had never heard a word. Yet there was a whisper abroad and rather than risk it, at the moment, back burner, perhaps in a year or so, pity, unnecessary risk, next item on the agenda?

The chill still lay on his mind. It had not been warmed by the brandy nor had Mark's vulnerability shifted it. Someone out there was determined to get him. Nicholas's sex life had been so limited and so careful that it was not difficult to line up suspects. But of course it need be none of them. A word passed on, an innuendo and off the rumour would fly to take on its own life, independent of him, certainly out of his control. There was, he told himself, absolutely nothing he could do about it. He had to live through it and hope for the best. Some strategy.

But the only one. It was a curious world. At least one cabinet minister was known to be homosexually promiscuous. At least two others were heterosexually promiscuous. The sexual history of two more would not withstand much vigorous examination. Yet he, whose aim had been a quiet loyal life of affection and whose dallyings had been few, brief and heavily curtained from the world, would seem to have been selected as the suspect queer, the dodgy gay, the one they could not quite trust. Someone, somewhere, had rolled a pebble and the rumble of the avalanche had been enough.

It was strange, Nicholas thought, as he swung up Regent Street on his last lap, that towards the end of the previous century a great British Prime Minister, a man revered for his moral integrity and unbending public principles, would also stroll around these streets late at night. He would seek out prostitutes and talk to them at length, take them to homes for fallen women, urge them to give up the life of sin. And himself gain a deep and precious sexual pleasure from this. And never a damaging word.

III

"My very best wishes." Nicholas decided against an exclamation mark. As one grew older, he thought, less and less merited an exclamation mark. Moreover the absence of such a stroke when one was traditionally expected could be much more effective. Besides which, he did not know quite how enthusiastic he was – and was wary of being hypocritical. Nor did he know how enthusiastic Jen herself was. True she had married this monster, Lukas, and marriages call up compliments as babies call up inane smiles and gurgles. But it was an odd match for the Jen he knew and although she could well have changed – and her life since arriving in the USA had been dramatic enough to produce great change – yet he could only address the Jen he had known.

Moreover, in his more philosophical moments, he was convinced that she would not have changed essentially. Alteration, he thought, comes through the uncovering of pre-existing character; essentially "the child is father to the man". Before Wordsworth, the Jesuits, after him Freud; before and after them all, the mothers. So what could he say to hold the interest of the woman he had known so well?

Jen was the only woman he could make a fair claim to love. He had not declared this, not even in that sloppy theatrical throwaway phrasing which was increasingly rampant. Practical strangers calling each other "love"; embracing; showing far too much open affection; behaving loosely; a whole generation determined to overturn the well and hard won reticence of British social life and manners and declare they loved everyone on sight. Nicholas wanted nothing to do with that any more than he wanted anything to do with the gross and fashionable extension of the term "friendship". People nowadays claimed hundreds of people as their "friends". At most, Nicholas reckoned, and if you were very fortunate, you could manage three or four. Six at a pinch. As for love – apart from family – one, two if you were in or out of luck. Jen he loved.

He was fairly certain that she knew it even though they had never indicated any such betrayal of emotion. It was all the more powerful for that, Nicholas thought, and also the more powerful because Jen was not a fag-hag, nor was she a trendy, a sentimentalist, or a gooey liberal. She took everyone strictly as she found them and tested them hard. Nicholas was almost certain that he was the first homosexual with whom she had enjoyed a close and consistent acquaintance and he had been aware – and amused – that she had watched him closely. Any short cut for sympathy or short-comings excused by "special difference" would have been black marked. He remembered how she had cut off a writer at the knees one night in Bianchi's when the poor man had tried to explain to Mark and Jen and Nicholas how being an artist gave him, well, special agonies but also special insights and as a consequence of that, special dispensation of behaviour. The fellow – quite distinguished in his metropolitan way – had scarcely seen the scimitar swing. So Nicholas was tested by Jen and he in turn watched her. He was wary of the flirtation of over-sympathetic women, the barely concealed excitement of others, the insolent curiosity – all manner of under-standable reactions to which he was as fine-tuned as a Stradivarius. Jen passed all his tests and he, it appeared, all hers.

It was her astounding energy that he loved, that and her bold-ness. She went for it. Not for material gain – her arrogance would not stoop to the relatively undistinguished task of piling up money – nor for success. But because it was there. She could have been a mountain climber, an explorer or a Marco Polo piloting some route across lonely and desperate tracks. Nicholas – from an entirely different background – could yet feel moved and sympath-etic to the journey she had taken, to the guts and nerve and talent it took to vault so high and with such verve and good humour and appearance of ease.

Mark had disappointed him and yet, knowing of Mark's past, he had not seen it as a failure. Just that the man was not quite well enough recovered, not quite strong enough when the biggest moment came.

Butterfield he had not known. Lukas he had encountered half a dozen times in London and on Sam Spiegel's yacht in the Mediter-ranean. He had rather disliked him – the sharkish vitality, the blunt lust for money, the surface simplicity not very successfully masking a character of cunning and furious ambition. For Jen?

Perhaps she needed a protector and saw in the power of Lukas a force which would repel all other marauders. Her fabulous wealth, her Garboesque seclusion, her previous glamour com-pounded a most potent object of desire. Lukas would be her Horatio on the bridge. Or maybe there was a sexual synergy. That answered many puzzling questions. But insofar as he could judge . . . well, he would prefer it not to be the case. Lukas had a cruel laugh, savage teeth.

He looked at the sheet of paper – tore it up; inserted a fresh piece in the typewriter and put down exactly the same words.

What did he want to say? He heard the lessons of the school-room come back with all their terrible certainty. Decide what you want to say; summarise it; expand on the summary; come to a conclusion which reflects your original propositions; finish the essay. When and why had life and letters deviated so wildly from that perfectly satisfactory order?

He had written to her regularly over the years, at first with only the most perfunctory response, if any. But he had persisted, sensing that such persistence, such overwhelming evidence of continued and unremitting interest, was what she needed.

Quite suddenly, long and fluent letters had begun to come, not many but sufficient and intimate. For Nicholas this had been a great joy. He had told no one, not even Mark. There were no messages for Mark even though there were references to him and in his letters he talked of Mark as freely as he talked of himself. But something about Jen's tone encouraged his own tendency to secrecy and by skilful avoidance and one or two lies of omission he stuck to his policy.

He wanted to tell her that he missed her – but he had found ways of doing that before, ways which she had acknowledged subtly; to do so in a letter prompted by her marriage could seem rather crass. He wanted to tell her that Mark's marriage was breaking up – as painlessly as these things ever could (the absence of children and the fact that both of them were in their forties was perhaps a help) but it was still very difficult. Nicholas sought to find a way of communicating something which would let Jen know of Mark's true feelings without betraying him. As usual, much would be said of Mark's considerable career as an investigative journalist. As for himself, he would guy the party he belonged to, a party whose style and voice increasingly distressed him and he would lob over a fistful of rumours. The main news would be of Helen's lack of progress after her stroke. She had refused to go to America as Jen had wanted but had retreated to North Yorkshire to be nursed by her brother, a retired headmaster. Nicholas went to see her every three or four weeks.

And the letter would be rounded off with some wistful hopes and wishful thoughts. It would be a tour de force of tact and affection: a love letter camouflaged in laconic gossip. He began to write.

NINETEEN

SOON after Mary's birth, Bridie had to go away. She had held on but quite simply she could no longer afford it. The school had been forced to cut back and reduced her to two days a week. Private tuition in the town did not cover the gap. Her savings had diminished steadily over the two years and now there was a post in Derry which she had been offered and which it would be folly to refuse.

Valerie was panic-stricken but fought not to show it. Between the two women and the children had grown up one of those tender, unspoken, deeply loving relationships that entwine all hearts. There was a great deal of crying, of backtracking – "I won't go! I can't leave you. I can't leave Harry". Harry was in tears every night and Bridie sobbed at the prospect of losing him. Mary was a further pull but by then Bridie was afraid she would become a burden. She had to take this job at a big Catholic school, a distinguished school, a school that would bring out all her qualities.

Both women knew that part of the best of their lives would be lost. Hard as it was for Bridie, it was probably harder for Valerie, who was further and permanently weakened by the second birth, another Caesarean, and only too aware of the protection Bridie had given her against Sean and all his potential for careless hurt. Yet she did her very best. She called on resources of stoicism practised in the last years of her mother's life. She promised herself she would do various things – quite what she did not yet know – to occupy her time. And of course Bridie would come back for holidays and maybe, once matters were settled, they would all go over to Derry. It would be good for the children to see a big city.

But however hard they tried, when the time came to see her on to the bus, the women simply put their arms around each other and wept, broken-hearted. Harry tried to wriggle between them and they held him into their skirts while Sean looked on, embarrassed, holding Mary.

When she had gone and they were back home he said, "Well. The old prune won't be on my back any more. Thanks for that any road."

Valerie's fears were realised. The steady job went, to be replaced by digging roads for the council. Soon that too went and the drinking increased. A fine for petty theft. A tearful reformation with the dread visit of Bridie. But she could not stay more than a day and besides Derry was giving her a rich life now. Eventually the bungalow was sold to meet debts and, although Valerie managed to keep back a portion of the money, Sean saw it as an excuse for a spree. Valerie thought she would hate the council house where they were to live, but her neighbours were kind, it was still the same town, people understood. If only she had not been so weak and so tired now with this pain in her side, she would have taken a job herself. Harry was capable enough, although subdued before his father; afraid of the unpredictable moods and the violence which the man could take out on the boy. Mary was little trouble. Bridie's help now seemed so far in the past, sometimes she thought she had dreamt it.

Then there was the sentence for breaking and entering with several other burglaries to be taken into account. Six months was considered a harsh sentence.

After his release Sean would not come back to the town. Valerie must come and join him in the city where he could start afresh. He had one of his sisters and a brother there. They would see him right. The boy would like the city. Too many people minding your business in a small place. There was talk of another woman. Valerie's heart was broken.

Part Three

THE WAY
FORWARD

TWENTY

I

JEN found herself peculiarly reluctant to leave Harry. She refused the offer of help from Isabella. The boy was shaking all but uncontrollably. Eventually he tired and she led him back upstairs. His head lolled against the crook of her supporting arm and she wished for an access of strength which would let her sweep him off his feet, to be borne like a baby. That was it, of course. That must be it. She reacted as if she had been found out in a suspect act. She had been caught off guard. For years she had taken the greatest care to avoid any close contact with children, particularly with boys whose age would have been that of her own son. Harry was of that age. But there seemed something even more powerful than that.

When she entered his bedroom this puzzle made her determined to back off. What greater importance had her feeling than the accidental conjunction of her loss with his age and the seductive myths of mothers returning their children to sleep? She did not want to pursue it further. But he would not let go of her hand. It was that which eroded her will.

The smell of sleepiness about him and the child's half-conscious gaze of utter trust, utter vulnerability. The tucked sheet "down sheet lane", the comforting arrangement of the blankets, "and into the blanket shop", the stroking of his head, and finally the sound of sleep-breathing, filling the room like a perfume, the murmur from his lips as he made the last withdrawal, the small floppy dog which Isabella had found somewhere and which now lay beside his head, animated in the dusk into a companion.

Despite her resolution and the meaninglessness of it, despite what she would call self-indulgence and later question, she spun dreams about the boy and was drawn easefully and painfully into the world she had once feared could destroy her. For a long time she stayed there, through a fitful nightmare which tracked across his face like Morse code, past the beatitude of a half-wakeful smile, until he fell to the deepest level of sleep and his breath gently sawed the air, steady as warm, even waves on a shore. When she left the room she still accepted the accidental connection between them but felt moved – she would admit no more to herself – in a way she could not identify anything like as neatly as her first casebook conclusion.

"Asleep?" Nicholas smiled rather proudly.

"Dead to the world."

"I wonder if we ever are . . ." he poured himself another drink.

"It's very good of you," said Mark.

"Don't be so formal, darling. Do you find that he's become hopelessly formal, Nick?"

"Terribly. And a pillar of the Alternative Establishment. A great disappointment. Way down the road to becoming a Grand Old Man. We're still quite good at that. Not very; quite."

"Not so old." Jen kissed Mark smartly on the lips. "Not so old at all."

"I catch a whiff of hanky-panky," said Nick. "Shame on you senior citizens. Age has not withered him?"

"It can all be replaced," said Jen, pouring herself one of the stiffest drinks she had taken in years. "America is full of Frankenstein's females remodelled in the operating-theatre. Cheers!" She drank deeply. "How nice. How very nice. The three of us together again. Wasn't that a good time?"

For that sort of moment which seems far longer, the memories of their previous times together more than a dozen years ago surged through their minds. And the times themselves, the long gap, the consciousness of each one that the other two were revising some of the same experiences, and the shadow knowledge that there were still things there unrevealed, unexplained, that strange intimate association, like the sharing of a dream, bound them together as surely as the reaffirmation of an ancient Saxon oath of death-loyalty.

"It should never have ended," said Mark, able to use this public occasion to express clearly to Jen for the first time his regret and his awareness that the end of it was largely owing to his weakness.

"There you go," said Jen, after a pause.

"All good things," said Nicholas.

"No," said Mark, "it need never have ended. There was nothing inevitable about it."

And the silence, as each one thought what might have happened had Jen not gone to America. What brighter, better time might have been. What riches had been missed.

The two "moments" were brief and yet they were charged with promise for future meaning. They drew on the strength and sweetness of the past. They were the moments that good friends can feel, or lovers, when, as it were, a psychic snapshot is taken as they know that they are uniquely close. They each knew the others shared this apprehension. It was, although very brief, a spot of time which could grow into a reservoir of confidence and affection, already primed with its own nostalgia.

"If I am to operate on all cylinders tomorrow morning," said Nick, and finished his drink and prepared to go.

"I might have to go over to Belfast."

"I thought you were staying away for a while."

"Something personal." Mark pulled out one of his cheap cigars.

"What time shall I be round tomorrow morning?" Nick asked.

Jen considered. She had a wild idea that she wanted to take Harry to the shops and buy him decent clothes, sweets and presents, all the expensive junk of childhood's current addictions.

"Do you think I could buy him a warm coat?" she asked.

Nicholas shook his head.

"Not yet. Nothing that could seem like a bribe."

"A coat?"

"What do you think, Mark?"

"Nick's right." He drew deeply on the cigar: of the three he was still most deeply enmeshed in those insights from the past which they had just experienced. The major part of his energy and thought was still mourning his past cowardice. "We've got to play it absolutely straight."

"*Le mot juste*," said Nicholas, "*merci mon frère.*"

"Even though it's freezing out there?"

"There will be a time for coats," said Nicholas, firmly. "Before then there is so much trouble ahead that a hair's weight of miscalculation could tip the balance. The odds are very highly stacked in favour of his aunt or whoever she is. All she has to do is say 'I want him to stay: he made a mistake in London' and that's that. But *I* know from the boy himself . . ." He paused.

"And I think I know too – after that phone call," said Jen.

"– that they want to get rid of him. So. *Avanti!*" Nick decided against going up for another look at Harry: it would have too much the air of a "last look", he thought, and besides, the sooner he began to discipline his feelings the better.

Jen would have been quite happy for Mark to stay but, without making a fuss about it, he left with Nicholas. Jen felt that there was something unsaid between them; had she dug harder, she would have found that there had been an unusual sensitivity about Mark, faintly mysterious, even in the interludes of their love-making in the afternoon. It had nudged her but she had not yet registered it. When she did recognise it, it appeared as a very quiet plea for help. But she was far too preoccupied now. As soon as the men left the house she almost raced up the stairs to look on Harry again. His brow glistened with sweat. She wiped it gently. His breath was still even, the soft toy was clutched in the crook of his arm. She pored over him.

Jen stayed, immobilised in forbidden thoughts, and left only when the phone rang.

II

"It's their own bloody fault and why should *we* pay?" Rudolf paused. The dinner-party was down to a serious caucus of four after the early flight of the diet-conscious. "They go out. They, pardon the expression, bugger each other – they catch AIDS. Then they expect the whole bloody world to weep – no objection to that, the whole bloody world's stupid enough to weep over anything with the right publicity – but why should the Honest Joes pay their taxes for those gays to be given expensive treatment on your National Health system which ought to be looking after little old ladies, which it can't afford to do anyway?"

"Would you say the same about smokers?"

"Most certainly. And drinkers. I do both. I love it. I'm not going to stop. But I should take out a risk insurance for my pleasures and not expect expensive and unlimited surgery paid for by the rest of the community. But that's not my point, which is: one, I'm sick of the crap about AIDS; two, everybody's in on the act. Film

208

stars, royalty, politicians – why don't they come out for cancer of the colon or Alzheimer's? Why not? Because it's not fashionable, that's why not, and they wouldn't get their name in the papers. If the buggers want to bang away who am I to object? But let them pay for the consequences they have been warned about very clearly. A bloke goes hang-gliding and he knows he can miss a thermal and crash. He takes the risk. This other business is a risk. It's in their own hands – or cocks – and to add to it they spread it around. We're complete wimps. We deserve everything that's coming."

"What's that?" asked Alfreda, whose evening had gone particularly well. Rudolf's high-octane outburst was a satisfying finale.

"Oh – mayhem. Everybody wanting everything instantly. I mean *everybody* wanting *everything*. That is, those who can't work, won't work, aren't bright, can't think, still wanting goods, glamour, leisure, drink, and prepared to put that in front of all the other things that are sliding off the agenda."

"Oh God, Rudolf, you're not going to give us family values? It really is too late at night."

Rudolf smiled and switched off. There was often a stage with Alfreda where he saw that she considered him to be the entertainment. The old class thing, he thought: eat at my gracious table but you will have to sing for your supper. God how it rifted and rotted through England! That was why Jen was so perfect. English which, reluctantly, he liked; but one of a kind, maybe the American experience, maybe the Butterfield tragedy, something else as well though, something in herself.

He moved uneasily at the thought of Jen. She would not have burdened him with such an evening. First a cocktail party where he had been nobbled by one of those women reporters he both fancied and dreaded; then the whole stretch of an evening (time is money, still unbeatable he thought), most of which had been spent with celebrities brown-nosing each other. Now a final drink at Maugham's in his suite at his expense, once again, when he could have been phoning or faxing to his heart's content. He had been too soft-hearted with Alfreda.

His impatience with this rump of the party which looked planted for another hour or so, and the stab of unfair blame directed at Alfreda for arranging all this, touched off by the alcohol, suddenly and rudely catapulted him from his seat. Without a word he went through to the bedroom and only just closed the door without slamming it.

He rang Jen. The line was engaged. His desire was immediately fed by this obstacle and he considered whether or not to drive around to her place. It was only 1 a.m. The unexpected was his trademark. There was a separate door and he left by it. Alfreda would pick up the social pieces gracefully enough and the row in the morning would be a useful kick start to the showdown and break-up he now thought long overdue. His priority was to get Jen back soonest. It was urgent; it was instant; that was how he operated. To ignore it was to miss life.

III

"Yes, yes," said Jen with the forced calmness of the experienced counsellor, "I promise."

"You have to come *now*!"

"I will. Just as soon as we finish this call, I'm on my way."

"*Now!*"

"I will."

"But you're on the other side of the world."

"I can get there very quickly. We can meet halfway. I've already worked it out."

"Why didn't you understand?" Cally's question pierced Jen to the heart.

"I don't know."

"You say you always understand."

"No, Cally. You say that. But never mind. I'm on my way."

"*Now!!*"

Jen allowed a pause to develop. Cally's sobbing was hard to bear but she had to slow her down somehow. Eight thousand miles could not be surmounted in the split second which Cally demanded and needed. It was the longest period that Cally had stayed alone in Los Angeles. Jen blamed herself for becoming so determined on the reclamation of her own London life that she had let slip her charge.

Cally's sobs were replaced by a mantra.

"Please. Please. Please. Please. Please. Please. Please. Please. Please."

Jen worked her way back to the earlier conversation. She remembered dolphins. What else? What clue had Cally given her of this imminent collapse? What sign had she failed to read? If she could discover it, then some reassurance could be provided for the desperately chanting young woman solitary on the West Coast.

"I ought to have listened more carefully about the dolphins," Jen said. It was her only course.

"*Yes!*" Cally's cry was accusation. Somewhere, though, Jen knew, relief would follow.

"It's you," Jen said, very carefully, "you are the one – needing –"

"*Yes.*"

"I see. You were speaking about yourself, not about me. I'm sorry, darling, I've been out of touch for much too long. Out of real touch, I mean. Hugging you."

"You *have*. You have." These last two syllables were suddenly small and miserable. The tempest had passed but, Jen knew, it could blow up at any time at the suspected inflection of a single word.

"I'm on my way, darling."

"Yes please."

"It's the middle of the night in London, Cally, did you know that?"

"I'm sorry. Really. I'm sorry."

"That's OK. But planes don't take off from here in the middle of the night. It's not allowed, OK?"

"OK."

"So. Tomorrow morning, I'll get the Concorde to New York. I'll be there New York time about noon – maybe a little later but not much. OK?"

Jen went into gear. Cally was instructed which plane to catch. A car would pick her up from the apartment in Los Angeles. Dr Flavel or someone from her clinic would call almost immediately and accompany her to the airport, if necessary accompany her on the flight. Jack, the chauffeur and handyman, would be waiting at J.F.K. to take her to the house on Upper East Side. These arrangements were outlined swiftly and then repeated slowly so that Cally could copy them down.

"Now I'm going to put down this phone. I'll call Dr Flavel on another line – so that you can call me back on this line any time. And after I've talked to Dr Flavel and then to Jack, who'll fix the L.A. end and the tickets, I'll phone back to tell you everything's OK. OK?"

"OK."

"Sure?"

"Sure. I love you, Jen."

"And I love you. It's my fault. I've neglected you these last months."

"No." The tone was unbearable. "It's my fault. I can't hack it on my own, Jen. I've done things you don't know about. You won't want to know about. People. It's all over." Jen felt a *frisson* of foreboding.

"I'll make those calls and call you back."

"I just can't make it, Jen."

"You can. You can and you will. You've done marvellously over the years, Cally. It was terrible for you. You've done wonders."

"Have I?"

"Yes." Jen was genuinely emphatic. Cally had lost every relative in that log-cabin blaze – and at a time when she was in full spate of rebellion against the family, fighting it, quite spunkily, every centimetre, over her "rights". The shock had damaged her badly. However hard she tried, she continued to relapse into a state of suicidal hysteria. Over the last year Jen, the doctors, and Cally herself had thought she was definitely on the mend.

"Be brave now."

"I will."

"Remember that this line is yours. Shall I just leave it open or put it down?"

"Could you leave it open?"

"Yes. But if I put it down then the sound of it ringing – if you had to ring – would be a clearer signal. You know what it's like shouting down a phone when someone is a few yards away. Hopeless."

"Hopeless," Cally echoed.

"OK then?"

"OK."

"One, two – ring back immediately if you want to – and I'll ring you in less than five minutes – three. Soon, darling."

Jen put down the receiver, took the other line and gave rapid and clear instructions. She was about to phone Cally back when the door bell sounded. Her first thought was that it must be Nicholas. She let him wait, called Cally and told her what she had done. The door bell sounded more and more insistently. Jen worried about Harry waking up abruptly in a strange room. Isabella slept like a corpse. She explained her dilemma to Cally and asked for advice. Cally agreed, promptly and eagerly, that answering the bell was the best move.

When Jen saw Rudolf there she was too puzzled to be angry. "I have to make a phone call," she said. "Come in."

He had never been to the house. Jen waved him in – the wave telling him to fix a drink, find a comfortable seat, wait. She returned to the open phone and spent the next few minutes talking through the most recent events which had led Cally to her crisis. It was always the same. When the crisis hit the button of visceral fear, it was Jen who was sought out; the analyst, rather to her chagrin, was abandoned. But Cally had calmed down a great deal. The arrangements made by Jen, the pills she had undoubtedly slugged into her much-abused body and a certain rhythm of the terror had left her tired. She said she would try to sleep.

"But I can call whenever I want?"

"Yes."

"Like – any time *at all*?"

"Any time at all."

"OK then . . . You put the phone down first."

"No. I'm in no hurry," said Jen. "I'll just wait here."

"OK then." Cally hesitated. Jen could see her summoning the will to cut off the communication. "OK then," she said, finally, and a few moments later the phone went dead.

Jen felt weary. It had been a long day. The afternoon with Mark had thrown her into a turmoil of hope and pleasure; and then the arrival of Harry, Cally . . . and now Rudolf. She had forgotten about him.

She found him in her fantasy bedroom, walking around the place. When she came in he leered in undisguised excitement, as he thought, very sexily. Jen's weariness increased. Once, when he had been at the pinnacle of his incandescent global success, and she, in her drugged confusion, had wanted little more than a protector, he had seemed desirable and attractive. God knows, she now thought, what got into me, even for those few weeks.

"I'm tired, Rudolf."

"I'm game."

"Rudolf. I mean. I have a lot to do before morning."

"Can I join in?"

"Rudolf. What do you want?"

"You are my lawful wedded wife."

"Be serious."

"A scotch?"

"One. And then – out."

She led him across the first-floor landing to her study. Drink in hand – he had insisted on pouring his own – Rudolf straddled an armchair in a buckish manner and exercised his charm. Jen had survived his charm and her antibodies were still active.

"I am busy, Rudolf," she said. "So . . ."

"What the hell am I here for at this hour?"

"Something like that."

"I just fancied it. Thought – hell! When did I last see Jen? Why don't I see her more often? Can't think now what it was bust us up. My fault – no worries there – but damned if I can remember. And what the hell – we're still married. So."

"You came to save a broken marriage, Rudolf?"

"You put it beautifully."

"At . . . one thirty-five in the morning?"

"When needs must . . ."

"The devil drives. Did you remember it ended like that? What do you want, Rudolf?"

"Can't we just talk?"

"Not now."

"Tomorrow? Lunch? I'll cancel a meeting."

"You must be serious. Tomorrow I'll be in New York."

"I could switch the meeting there."

She explained the problem. Rudolf knew all about Cally. His view – expressed several times – was that she should get a job, preferably a tough, underpaid, physically demanding job, stop whingeing, stop crying on Jen's shoulder, stop enriching trick cyclists and while she was about it lose two stone and get a stud to sort her out downstairs.

This time he kept his opinion to himself.

"What are you saying, Rudolf?"

"You and me had a good time together. Admit it. At the start."

To speed up the conversation Jen gave a perceptible nod.

"Looking back I was probably a bit to blame." Rudolf knocked back a drink which all too clearly said "Who can say fairer than that?". Jen repressed the laughter which threatened to bubble through her tiredness. "But you liked me – anyway – we got on – there was something – right?"

Again, that was undeniable, though what that something was belonged to an age buried and gone.

"It was the business angle. The whole damned thing blew up just when I was within an ace. That scuppered me in more ways than one, Jen. You were a terrific sport about the money but all the rest went down the tubes while I wasn't looking."

"Rudolf. I'm sorry. I really do have a great deal to do."

"I admire you, Jen. There isn't another woman I'd give a toss for. You've got it all. You know shit from true. You don't ponce. You talk to nobody. There's not a bent bone in your body. And you still look great. No, I mean it. Whatever you do to hold together, you do it well. You look great. Why don't we see if we can give it another throw?"

"No."

"OK. So you need time to think about it."

"No."

"Fine. We'll talk it over when you're back from New York."

"No."

"It must be a bit of a shock. Late at night. Cally can drag you down like cement slippers, I know that. But I had to come, don't you see? I thought – she's my wife . . . Hell, I love you Jen or I haven't loved anybody. I wanted you to know right away. I wanted you to know I was serious. So. We'll talk."

"No."

"Fine. I won't push it until you get back." He smiled and as those predator's teeth clashed, Jen had to smile back at the imperturbable insistence of the man.

"Great eyes, Jen. Never seen eyes to beat them. The rest – great shape. But the eyes."

His voice softened. Jen made herself even more clear.

"It's over, Rudolf."

"The end of one deal's the window to the next."

"It's finished."

"There are no lines you can draw until the final line, Jen."

"I don't want to live with you any more."

For an instant, Rudolf thought of challenging her about Mark: some prudent whisper persuaded him to hold back.

"There's nobody like you in bed," said Rudolf, and waited for a return compliment.

"What I liked about you, Rudolf, was your energy and then I stopped liking it. I also liked the fact that you were self-made, vulgar, didn't give a damn, and enjoying behaving like a bastard. When I realised that you really were a bastard things began to change. After that – Rudolf. Go home. I have a lot to do."

"Still the old fire there." Rudolf grinned horribly. "I could always stir your fire."

"And that's another thing," said Jen.

"Yes?" Rudolf answered, after a pause.

"Never mind."

"Every rocket hit the pocket," said Rudolf.

"Home. Now."

She stood up. Rudolf came towards her – she realised – programmed for a crushing embrace. She held out a hand to prod his chest and offered her cheek. He accepted defeat gallantly.

"I'll be back," he said.

"I'll be gone."

"I'll find you."

"You won't, Rudolf. Goodnight."

He clicked his heels, bowed and then thumped down the stairs, whistling happily.

Jen knew that she had been lucky. That was Rudolf on his best behaviour. He would not come back so playfully.

She put the thought out of her mind. Her life had made her adept at that.

Nicholas would have to be phoned so that he could arrange for another woman to accompany him north. Mark would have to be told, of course. Neither of them could do anything at this hour and so she would call them first thing in the morning. Isabella was perfectly capable of looking after Harry on her own, although Jen was sure that Nicholas would be round as early as seemed reasonable.

It disturbed her a little that her concern lay more with Harry than with Cally. She put on her CD of Beethoven's last quartets, poured herself a malt whisky – a present from Mark – and lay on the deep sofa, too jolted by events to sleep, trying to sift through thoughts which cascaded through her mind without shape or order. She was aware that over the music she was listening out for any cry from Harry. She was aware that she was hoping for a cry.

TWENTY-ONE

H ARRY woke up in heaven. The only sound was of his breath which seemed such an imposition on the rich crush of silence that he held it, then exhaled as quietly as he could, wanting to disturb what seemed perfection as little as possible. There was a smell of lavender. The curtain had been drawn back a little when Isabella had glided in with the breakfast tray but the bleak outside weather made no impact on the centrally heated room. The sheets crackled grandly in his fingers. The walls of the room were immaculately white, wardrobes fitted into the wall, dark, shiny, expensive wood and mirrors which gleamed clean. The floor was just as polished, a paving of wood blocks. Two highly coloured rugs took his attention for a moment as he tried to unpick the patterns. Beside his bed was a table holding a very large cup of hot chocolate – Isabella's speciality – a bowl of cornflakes and toast – and biscuits! – all laid out on a tray covered with a thick white cloth. The knife and spoon were heavy and, no doubt, Harry thought, made of silver. There was no one else in the room so it must all be for him. He would have preferred to ask permission – so as to be sure he would not later be accused of stealing – but hunger overcame that fearful scruple and he had breakfast in bed.

He ate as noiselessly as possible, somehow convinced that any untoward disturbance would end everything and leave it as no more than a dream. There was a sense of unimaginable security and there was an apprehension of fragility. He knew that soon he would be moved on, but the room, and perhaps most of all the toy dog which he discovered on the floor, reassured some essential part of him and began to soothe the welts of the previous day. He had never tasted anything as delicious as the hot chocolate.

The next few hours were spent in much the same atmosphere of unnaturally luxurious and protected calm. He was constantly on the lookout for the catch. Isabella brought him his clothes – washed, dried, ironed and replenished from the store of her grandson. Jen – the most beautiful woman he had ever seen, whose eyes, whose intense look, had unnerved and enslaved him – gave him a warm, lingering hug and suggested he go out for a walk in the park with Isabella. She explained that she had to fly to New York. Harry's disappointment both pleased and fretted her and promises were made about a reunion when she returned. Harry had kept back the biscuits from his breakfast tray and he stuffed them in his pocket in case things went wrong.

Nicholas decided that he would not take his own secretary to replace Jen. He did not want to reveal his hand until he was much more certain of the outcome. Mark suggested Prue, who was delighted at the prospect of a day off. She was told that Nicholas had a tricky passage of business to conduct; that she was to pretend to be his secretary. "I can be his secretary for a day," Prue said, "take notes and things. MPs always want that. And it means I don't have to lie. I'm absolutely useless at telling lies except to Daddy or on the telephone."

Later in the morning, Nicholas and Prue called for Harry, and a taxi took them to Euston Station.

Harry had never been on a train. A few cars, Jake's van, buses galore but, largely because the depleted rail service offered no useful routes for his limited territorial forays, this was an adventure. The station concourse itself seemed as vast and importantly efficient as the airports he had seen in films. The seats were so comfortable – Nicholas travelled first class – that you had to sit upright so as not to fall asleep. Nicholas had bought him four comics including two computer games magazines which he had never owned first hand. And then they went to the restaurant and ate! Waiters served them. He was called sir. Was Nicholas a Lord? He felt panicky: was the man really taking him home? Suddenly he felt crushed by Nicholas's attentions. He looked away. Out of the window, at one stage, a motorway ran alongside the railway track.

"See those cars," said Nicholas. Harry nodded. "Let's say that they are going at – seventy-five, eighty, eighty-five – let's settle for eighty miles an hour. Now then. See how easily we are drawing away from them? So, we must be going at ninety, even a hundred miles an hour. What do you think of eating roast potatoes – or carrots –" a little admonition: Harry hated carrots "– at a hundred miles an hour?"

Harry stared at the cars for a few moments, seeming to measure Nicholas's words against his own calculation and then, with a little sigh of happiness, turned and simply smiled. Nicholas quickly turned away. Harry left all the carrots, guessing that he would get away with it. Then he read until they reached his town.

"How far is it from here?"

Nicholas was prepared to walk. Just as he had taken care to wear his dullest coat, so he was careful to negotiate past anything which would smack too overtly of privilege. It was a difficult question to answer. Harry had never made the journey from the station, which was on the right side of town, to his estate which was on the opposite side.

Nicholas interpreted the boy's silence correctly. He also noted that Prue – who was wearing the slight jacket she had slung on for work – was looking rather anxiously around this already darkening alien Northern place. The taxis, moreover, were merely cheap cars with a yellow plastic TAXI stuck on the roof. Nothing especially showy there.

As they approached the estate, Prue tried to keep the horror out of her expression. She was a charming, sweet, young English woman who had never in her life seen a run-down industrial town with its clamour of FOR SALE signs on shops, homes and acres of window-smashed factories. The taxi turned into the estate and, after several rows of well-kept gardens, newly embellished privately owned homes, slammed downhill to the sadder, poorer area beyond which, in a miasma of neglect, Harry lived. Nicholas tried – unsuccessfully – to absorb some of the boy's tension and fear. Harry had gone away from him. His face jutted in unconscious preparation for the inevitable bruising of re-entry.

"Where was you, Harry? Eh?" Jake grabbed him in a great show of affection. Harry flinched. Nicholas noted it and checked himself. "I was worried sick. Where was you? Here's me – all around Leicester Square – in and out the Arcades – I don't know what they thought – you seen Harry? I said, this boy, you know – I told them who you were – and then I thought – I told Fiona – I telephoned her up – he's a crafty one – he's worked out we've lost one another and he's gone and found a bus. That right?" Fiona nodded, using the occasion of Jake's babble to take in every detail she could of the curious couple standing so awkwardly in her sitting-room. Mary was standing beside her, on an invisible leash, not yet allowed to greet her brother. "So down we went to the bus station – believe me – we sweated – and then, you've no idea – when – tell them, Fiona – we got the phone call from – was it you?" Prue shook her head. "This other lady – we nearly gave a party. What happened?"

Harry looked about him uncertainly. He exchanged the swiftest of looks with Mary, whose demeanour advised "do nothing".

Fiona caught the moment and moved forward to embrace him. When she saw that the boy would not respond, she held back.

"Don't you ever do that again! You scared us all to death! Don't you ever scare us like that again."

She looked boldly at Nicholas.

"We can't thank you enough. You and Mrs Lukas?"

"Mrs Lukas had to go off unexpectedly. This is Miss Lewis-Jones, my secretary."

Prue smiled gamely, tugged out her notebook and gave a little wave with it. Then she flushed and stuffed it back in her pocket.

"You must have a cup of tea anyway," Fiona said. "Before you go back."

"I was thinking of staying the night," Nicholas said. "I have some friends nearby."

"Well that's lucky, isn't it? Still – a cup of tea."

Fiona, exquisitely aware of Prue's social discomfort, was swiftly beginning to ferret out the root of Nicholas's concern. With Mary – of whom she was a little wary – apparently frozen, Harry confused and Jake in pantomime, she was in full control and exploited it.

Tea was murder. Small talk came out like broken glass. Prue insisted on doing the washing up. At Fiona's command, Jake took Harry and Mary to get some chips. Fiona and Nicholas sat in the cheap armchairs beside the electric radiator.

"It's very kind of you to take all this trouble," Fiona began.

"No trouble."

"Others would have sent him to the police or at any rate just put him on a bus. Or asked us to come and collect him. So what you did was very kind. And a bit unusual."

"It was too late at night and frankly too cold to do all those other things. And Mrs Lukas . . ."

"Oh yes. The one who had to go off to America, was it, Harry said. Lucky woman. Chance would be a fine thing. She must have a very warm heart."

"Yes . . ." Nicholas had stood off for long enough. "May I ask you a little about Harry and his sister?"

"Of course."

"You are –?"

"Their aunt. The youngest. We're a big family on his father's side."

"And his mother's?"

"She died two or three years ago. There was nobody on her side. A very difficult person."

Nicholas nodded. Fiona interpreted the nod as censure and bridled. She lit a cigarette.

"Obviously I'm mistaken," said Nicholas, "but when I bumped into him he seemed rather more abandoned than lost."

Fiona stepped back. Nicholas's accent, appearance, manner and confidence were of that class which was so remote to her that she only saw its members on television but she knew that the country belonged to them. What they said went. Because he spoke softly he was no patsy. Because he was polite he was no less capable of crushing her.

"In fact," Nicholas continued, seeking out Fiona's eyes and looking hard at her, although the rest of his face and his posture retained an unthreatening amiability, "from what he said – fragmented, I agree, and understandably under stress – one could have put two and two together and concluded that – Jake, is it? – *Jake* had deliberately dumped him."

Fiona licked her lips. Before the trap closed, she struck.

"Where was it you met him?"

His hesitation irradiated her with hope.

"Just on the street. He was clearly upset."

The transparent lie gave her back all the swagger she needed. He had prepared a clever answer to such a question but it deserted him. The sight of Harry cringing before the expected violence from Jake and Fiona had unsettled him.

"Seems curious just to heave up against him like that. On a street."

"Not at all."

"I mean, in the middle of a busy street. People all around. You're walking along there and suddenly you see the boy – upset, you say. Not like Harry to show it in public. Still."

"Does it matter how we met?" Nicholas wished very hard that

he had not spoken that sentence. Fiona just smiled and inhaled deeply. "The fact is," he hurried on, "that we did meet and here he is: back with you."

"That's certainly the case. That can't be denied."

Prue popped her head around the door – literally, just the head. "All washed up," she announced.

"Thank you. Could you leave us for a while?"

"Of course. Right. Of course. Yes."

The head was whipped away.

"What happened to his father?"

"That's a mystery. We always think he's somewhere in London although they say he was seen in Birmingham a year or two ago. We tried to get in touch with him for the funeral but nothing doing. He sort of gave up on himself. She expected far too much from him. She drove him too hard."

"And you've looked after them ever since?"

"Me and Bridie." She explained who Bridie was. "But over the last eighteen months, since Bridie was made deputy headmistress, she's had no time for them. I can't afford to send them over to see her, and she hasn't had the time to come over since Valerie died. She has a terrible load of work and she won't let any of it pass her by. No one else in the family's got that fault. She was a cuckoo in the nest all right. So it's been poor old me and I've had my own troubles, I could tell you."

"Have you ever considered . . . ?" Nicholas paused: yet again, as so often in the last twenty-four hours, he was about to embark on a sentence which, he thought, could literally determine his life, "given that you're young, your life before you, could be a terrible burden . . ."

"I wouldn't be able to face myself in the mornings."

Nicholas feared he may have come too far. But instinct was not Fiona's monopoly.

"Perhaps I should talk to Bridie: as the older sister . . ."

"There's no need for that. Not now, maybe never. They were made over to me and my husband."

"Jake?"

"Don't be ridiculous."

"And your husband?"

"He did a bunk, didn't he?"

"I see." Nicholas regrouped. "Have you any children of your own?"

"I've been too fly for that."

222

"I see. So . . ." Sometimes the best way to proceed was to assume that the argument was over. "You're not totally averse to an arrangement . . . legal of course. Everything absolutely in order."

"The both of them or just Harry?"

"Both. If that's easier."

"It's just Harry you're interested in, though, isn't it, mister?"

Nicholas felt something like vertigo.

"Where *did* you meet him?"

"Perhaps this conversation has gone as far as it can today." He stood up and, noticing the flit of regret on her face, pushed on harder. "My suggestion was merely to help you out. My sister and I have been thinking of something along these lines for some time. It seemed a happy coincidence. But I can see I presumed far too much. I do apologise if I've trespassed on your feelings. We'd better leave."

"Now then, now then, you're rushing me . . ." She squashed out her cigarette. The action was not wholly successful. She stabbed the butt on the saucer several times with a force that fascinated Nicholas. "Why don't we . . . ? It's all a bit rushed," she said. Once again her instinct found the key. Nicholas had to concede the truth of that. From her point of view – whatever the nature of her behaviour – the arrival of a stranger who sat down and began to talk about taking away her nephew . . . whatever her circumstances it was a "bit rushed". Again his silence gave her confidence. He sat down.

"You see things are not easy here. Tell the truth, they're very hard." The beginnings of a sob entered her voice. "Just cash for little things is what we need. Everyday things. I mean, what are people like us going to do about Christmas? Nobody thinks about that. They'll be lucky if I can afford a present apiece for the kiddies. Not that we don't work when we can get it. But this town's dead." She paused and Nicholas found himself revolted by the sly whinge which now took over from the sob and coloured her voice. "I suppose people like you have no idea what it is to worry about where the next quid's coming from. There's near-starvation around here sometimes, no exaggeration, kids going to school hungry, coming back to a paper-load of chips, that's all. There's houses round here with less furniture than a squat. There's worse than tinkers. And in a place like this – but you wouldn't know, would you? I'm not criticising. But you try living in a godforsaken hole like this! Whoever built this estate knew nothing. He knew nothing about women, he knew nothing about what men want. Kids? They just hang about looking for trouble. There's no cash for anything."

He resisted the impulse to hand over his wallet to her but the pressure was felt. Fiona's words were both acted and sincere, real and exaggerated. She made her case.

"I'm saying this is very unexpected. I'll have to think it over. It needs a lot of thought, something like this, but I can see you're serious and of course you would want to do it through the proper channels . . ."

Nicholas nodded. Fiona gave him an old-fashioned look.

"There's a lot to be talked about. Maybe we should . . . ?"

What did he want?

What would he offer?

Was it a trap?

"I perfectly see your point." Nicholas did not quite realise that this solicitor's approach baffled and alerted Fiona more than any other. This was the voice from the "other side" against which there was no argument and no appeal. "In fact I have been far too hasty. What I suggest – if I may – is that I call you in a few days' time and we arrange to have a rather more formal meeting then – as might be lunch or – well – whatever you prefer."

"Time to think things over," said Fiona.

"Exactly."

"That's all right then." The brief abstracted look, the momentary thinning of the lips, told Nicholas that some calculation was in progress but he had no access to it.

"That's them," she said. She had heard Jake's van draw up. She managed to inform the words with the idea that Nicholas had been hanging on impatiently for Harry's return. Again, Nicholas felt a cold sting: Fiona could not be underestimated.

She led the way to the front door.

Outside, the street lights peered over the cold gaunt streets. It was already close to zero. In the peering orange glow, Jake and the two children looked spectral. All three were scooping chips into their mouths as rapidly as they could. Prue came out of the house behind them.

"Well," said Nicholas, "I'll call you . . ."

"If the phone hasn't been cut off by then," said Fiona.

"I'd better take the address."

"I've got it." Prue waved her notebook and then, embarrassed, plunged her hands deep into the pockets of the inadequate jacket.

"Cash is very short," Fiona said, almost absent-mindedly.

Nicholas nodded. He had to be strong.

"It's the children always suffers most," said Fiona, "that's the pity of it."

"We'll be in touch," said Nicholas.

He stepped down the cracked concrete path; Prue enthusiastically delivered her thanks and farewells in a tone which shivered against Fiona's deliberate indifference.

"I'm on my way back now," he said, to Harry, as lightly as he could.

The boy looked up. Nicholas was suddenly aware that behind him, from the boy's point of view, would be the sight of those bedroom windows replaced by cardboard and next to that an entire house boarded up, the boards scorched following a recent arson attempt. The cold seemed to knead into his face. Harry's anxious – yes, anxious – look instantly vanquished all fears about dealing with Fiona.

"You're coming back though?" he asked.

"Yes." Nicholas's throat was dry. "Oh yes, I'm coming back."

"Good." Harry smiled and held out his chips. If he took one, he would not be lying. Nicholas took one.

He had decided to walk back to the station. He needed to uncramp his feelings. Prue was game and sufficiently sensitive – and chilled – to wrap herself in silence.

As they moved through the wall of cold, the avenues of dirty concrete, between empty winter gardens, Nicholas remembered the time when he had spent a warm redolent evening on allotments beside a railway-line in a town not so many miles away. Although the circumstances and locations were very different, it seemed more than simply a few years away. A serious generation gap. "Once they took the apprenticeships away they ruined everything," one of the men had said. "There's nothing to hold them now. When they had six or seven years from leaving school working at a trade and working with men who would keep them in line, there was some hope. That's all gone and there's nothing to hold them together now – the ordinary lads, the less bright lads I'm talking about. Nothing for them to hold on to."

The memory was probably triggered by the sight, in the distance, of a party of youths around two cars outside what proved to be the community centre – a prefabricated bungalow on wasteland. As Nicholas and Prue approached, the adolescents took notice and huddled in conference. As the two drew nearer, it broke up as if a siren had sounded at Biggin Hill and they piled into the cars, drove off at ferocious speed, clashing gears, forcing accelerators, disappearing around the corner with a scream of brakes.

"Are you all right?"

Prue nodded.

"Thoughtless of me. I should have rung for a taxi. It's far too cold."

Prue shook her head. It was not the cold. The menace of the gang had hit a nerve and frightened her. Nicholas had felt no such threat: only a sad curiosity.

They walked on through the estate towards the low glow of the town. Nicholas felt as if the place were rubbing against a sore in his mind. What had they, he, others, the politicians, the bureaucrats, the makers and shapers, done about this? Here was a place, Nicholas feared, too easy to abandon, too easily out of sight, out of mind, in times of unemployment and economic difficulty, a breeding-ground for crime and riot. The only shops a small parade – half boarded up – which they walked past as the shopkeepers were pulling up the grilles for the night: not a pub in sight. None of that mixture of commerce and pleasure, habitation and work, intermingling of classes and trades which somehow humanises a place. Or was this no more than sentimental social claptrap? Was the real feeling much simpler but difficult for a liberal old-school conservative gentleman to admit: that he wanted Harry out of there? He wanted him where he would have more of a chance. Wanted him in his own, Nicholas's, upper-middle-class, privileged, facilitated world, the world of the officer class which had for so long managed to rule very nicely. Or was that too easy an essay in self-flagellation? No, it was even simpler: he wanted Harry to be secure and happy and near him, and that was how he knew to do it.

At the edge of the estate they took a bus to the station.

Nicholas put Prue on the train to London. She was tactful and sweet and Nicholas sensed that the outing had been a little like a safari for her. It was not impossible to imagine her, though sympathetic, regaling friends late that night in a little place off the Fulham Road about the sheer horror of that Northern estate. Prue would not be very much younger than Fiona: they lived on the same small island, comparable intelligence, good-looking women both. Yet for Prue the estate would be more foreign and more alien than any place she had been in her life, in London, in Hampshire, in the Dordogne where her parents had a place, or anywhere else in her travels.

At one time in his political life, Nicholas had believed that he could close, or at least bridge, such divisions, such inequalities.

He hired a car and motored across country, further north, to Harriet's, his sister's, where he was expected for dinner.

Harriet had married a shrewd baronet whose pleas of poverty were rather undercut by his understandable pride in the estate which had been in the family since the early sixteenth century. "We poor farmers" was his refrain. The land was over three thousand acres – there were another fourteen thousand in Scotland. The house – one of the documented places where Mary Queen of Scots rested on her passage south to her cousin and her death – was perfectly sound, having been restored with great care at considerable public expense. The return for this public money was, it seems, that for two afternoons a week the public was grudgingly admitted, stung for tea, barred from the most interesting rooms and heartily despised, its only redeeming feature being that it provided amusing stories of the rude mechanicals variety.

Harriet was a born-again snob – not, in Nicholas's experience, either common or currently fashionable among the richer and brighter aristocracy, but his sister was neither. Max, the farming baronet, had done extremely well out of the princely subsidies given to farmers since 1945. With his milk quota, his grants for forestation, his fixed prices, his grants for various buildings, his lucrative stretch of river, those most rentable grouse moors up in Scotland, the increased value of land, the rocketing of the art market which had multiplied by twenty in as many years the plunder of four centuries which trophied the house, his sell-up value would have made him a very wealthy man. But selling up was unthinkable. So cash was always a touch short, the three boys were at expensive public schools, there was the money for Harriet's horses, Max's little foibles, the winter sun and winter skiing, and the provision of a very good cellar. Nicholas always enjoyed staying there but not for long.

He arrived just a few minutes before dinner but a rapid wash and shower – he was a long soak, bath man but sometimes the sprinkler had its uses – and he was able to take a swift scotch first. Half a dozen neighbours had been invited round – the nearest lived about twenty miles away – and Nicholas knew most of them from previous visits. They were a jolly, healthy, superficially cheerful lot, and they had every reason to be. Their world was in very good shape. Nicholas, as a member of the political party which had led them into these fields of clover and gold, was welcome for that, welcome as Max's clever brother-in-law, and trebly welcome for the metropolitan gossip, the Westminster tittle, the clubland tattle which he invariably spread around a little ironically, although no one appeared to notice.

The talk was still on the overthrow of Mrs Thatcher. Nicholas's imaginative reconstruction of the alliances and conspiracies which had led to what all around the table (save himself) considered "the most ghastly tragedy" (although most said they "couldn't stand the woman"), was the evening's *pièce de résistance*. Indeed applauded. Harriet felt triumphant – not a sensation she enjoyed very often in this company where she had to fight hard for parity.

Then the conversation, under the influence of wine, descended from this lofty plinth and dwelt on country matters. It was a raunchy and detailed romp, which Nicholas enjoyed shamelessly. Such deeply layered confidence. The land, the island, really did appear to belong to them. Yet over the cigars he found himself discussing Uccello with a very intelligent woman on his right. It led to a wider discussion of the importance of experiment in Western art which was as enjoyable as any conversation he had had all year. She admitted to doing "nothing much: a bit of gardening". So they – we – could always surprise you – him.

The next afternoon, after Harriet had come back from the hunt but before Max had returned from the estate office, Nicholas put his proposition to his sister as succinctly as possible. He left nothing material out of his account.

Harriet was rigorous, ambitious and, particularly to her elder brother, fair-minded. She had long ago suspected his homosexuality. Plucking up all her courage, she had challenged him on it. Once "the air had been cleared" – her phrase – she never, never referred to it again. Nor would she have tolerated anyone else doing so. The only possible sign that the news had affected her was that she was rather more publicly affectionate to Nicholas – in her awkward, gangly way – than she had been before.

"It's out of the question," she said. "They would never fit in here. The boys" – meaning her three – "would be very put out – Jamie is a bit of a worry in the attention department already – and what would you do? Take a place nearby and ride over every morning to inspect the goods? I would love to help you, Nicholas, and I think that what you are doing speaks well for you. But I just know it wouldn't work out. And Max would go barmy."

"Why?"

"The whole thing would either baffle him or disgust him. Sorry. Possibly both."

"I hadn't expected you to be quite so adamant so quickly."

"I'm sorry. It's just one of those things that settles itself." They were having tea. She poured herself a second cup. Nicholas had not touched his. "Have you any fall-back plans?"

"Not yet."

"They could – of course – come here for a holiday. For Christmas if you like." That, Nicholas knew, was a real sacrifice. Harriet's Christmases were famous for their fanatical concentration on the core family. Carols, charades, church, mince-pies, jigsaws, close relatives, the hunt, the great Boxing Day supper and so on into a post-Dickensian world of intense, even orgiastic familial celebration. To allow two undoubtedly troublesome little strangers into this drama was generous.

"Christmas is probably out of the question. But I might take you up on it some time later." Nicholas sipped the tea, now cold, grimaced a little obviously, and put it down.

"Are you very angry with me?"

"Quite." Nicholas smiled. "Yes. Very." He knew his sister so well and aimed at the heart. "Very," he repeated.

"I find it . . ." Harriet paused. She was strikingly similar to Nicholas in her personal appearance but the large and elegant, rather haughty features which sat pleasingly on him seemed a little heavy, even lumpen on Harriet. Nevertheless when, as now, she was roused to intensity of feeling, Nicholas was disconcerted to see the near image of himself addressing himself so passionately, ". . . very hard . . . It is, Nicholas . . . please . . . it is . . ."

Harriet paused again and what looked like a gleam in her eye was really the first film of a tear. ". . . very hard to keep this place up and the family in line. Max isn't easy. It might look all very fine and dandy from the outside, I can sense that you disapprove of it a bit or anyway you think we all have it made down here. Well, we are very lucky and very fortunate in many ways – but that doesn't stop it being bloody hard. Sometimes I fear it may be beyond me. So it's not to do with – your feelings, do you understand? I'm sorry that this – well, I suppose you're not sorry, you're happy and I – well, that's none of my business. But what is my business is this family here, and Max. Max hates children. He's only getting round to the boys now when they can do things with him – like shoot – and, even so, he's beastly to them a lot of the time. I have my work cut out, Nicholas, for at least six or seven more years. This is in confidence, of course. And there's more but I prefer to keep it to myself. I mention it just to show that I hate letting you down, I absolutely hate it. But two small children in this house would be the end. I don't exaggerate. *I* wouldn't survive – not with Max – not with the boys. So that's the reason, you see . . ."

Nicholas put out his hand and she grasped it very tightly.

He blamed himself. It had been stupid to build his plan for the future on such unknown territory – for so it now seemed. He had embraced his own cliché description of his sister's situation.

"It was far too much to ask," he said. "I'll . . . I'll think of something else."

"For holidays – they can – any time . . ."

"I know. I know . . ."

He was already abstracted, his thoughts reaching back to the estate.

Harry was sitting watching television, still cold from roving around the town all afternoon and rather confused by the careful way in which Fiona now treated him. After Nicholas had gone she had asked him a lot of questions – where they had met, what he had been doing at the hotel, where Nicholas had taken him, what the other man was like. What the woman was like. He had been pressed hard for a description of Jen's house. "Like a palace," he kept saying. "Like a palace." Fiona's mood had been exultant.

She had given him some money to go into the town and play the machines.

Harry could not articulate his fears but as he sat watching the screen he had an obscure but certain feeling of danger: whether it was for himself, for the people who had helped him, for Nicholas in particular, he did not know. All he feared was that something terrible was going to happen.

Twenty-Two

I

"**M**ARK ARMSTRONG," the boy said, "you are a dead man."

The powerful Ulster twang made three syllables of the last two words. It was a locked-jaw sound, blunt as the South African butt, camouflaged as the Mid-Western drawl but with a certain music beguiling the latent menace. In the mouth of an eighteen-year-old it could be a foreign language: English words ambushed, bound and delivered into the eternal captivity of impenetrable local parlance. The Ulster accent took the conqueror's language with a grudge that would not shift out of the throat. These imperial words had been lassoed and the rope tightened around the neck with every deeper day of hopelessness that passed. Colin had known many such days in his brief half-lit life.

He was standing in front of the mirror in the room he had once shared with Tony. Tony's bed was still there, never slept in by anyone but Tony, even though over the past few years he had been at home so seldom. Everything to do with Tony was kept immaculate by his mother and revered by Colin who could not go to bed, could not climb the cheap stairs in the shoddy estate house to the handkerchief-sized room without praying that by some miracle Tony would be there. Tony was always kind to him. They would lie in the dark and Tony would talk away just as if Colin were his equal. He would never make fun of Colin. He would never be impatient that Colin's speech was so slow. He knew that his younger brother had "all his marbles". The slow speech, the limp from the gunshot in the foot, an error of discipline for which

Tony had made the perpetrators pay, these turned Colin into a rather isolated, sometimes comical figure. No matter how audacious he was at stealing the cars and joyriding and heading for the road blocks, he could not get rid of that. And Tony had stopped him doing that. Tony had said it was kids' stuff, save it for something worth the risk, don't play their game. So Colin had stopped, even though that alone had given him dignity in front of the others, who soon forgot his bold and reckless deeds and fell to ignoring him once more. But Tony was right.

He would lie there in the dark and across that prodded rug, so near that if both of them lay on the edge of their narrow beds and stretched out their arms, their fingers would touch, then he would hear the words of a hero. Oh, to be Tony's brother! Nobody knew the pure joy of that! It did not matter that the words would stumble and fail in public; it did not matter that he limped and made it worse by the strained effort to disguise it; he was Tony's brother and nobody on this earth was better than that. He was the man.

In the land of men, Tony was the man. In the land of guns and murder, in the land of revenge and honour, in the land of remorseless war and deeply woven codes of manners, Tony was the man. At least once a day and maybe more times someone would come up to him in the corner where he pitched his morning or around the few shops and pubs he made his beat and say "How's Tony now?" or "Tell Tony when you see him that I'm asking for him now" or just "Tell Tony we're all for him".

Colin would nod, act indifferent, like a toll-keeper collecting a fee so long that habit had worn down public acknowledgement. But, at night, on his own, in the bedroom, in the dark, he would recall every one of the remarks and revise them carefully, commit all to memory, every one available to pass on when the glorious day came that Tony would return home. Never more than for a single night. And then, in the back door like a rush of wind, muttered talks in the kitchen with their mother, and up to the bedroom where he would throw a few fake punches at Colin and into the bed to talk and bring to Colin the blessing of the Holy Spirit.

Everything Tony said was a wonder.

Sometimes Colin feared to breathe in case the coarse sound interrupted or deflected the words. Tony would always ask him his news and insist he tell it even though Colin knew that everything he said was of no account. Nothing, nothing compared with the world of Tony even though he was allowed into that world only through hints and allusions. Tony was trained to be utterly discreet and by nature he was modest, but for his younger brother who had so little he would lift a fraction of the curtain. He knew that Colin would never betray a word. Indeed the boy's savage loyalty would have made him a good soldier had it not been for the slowness of speech and now of movement also. The aspect he gave off of dimness Tony knew to be false; but the singularity of his speech and movement would have made him a liability, far too easily identifiable, a burden in any army. Particularly theirs.

Now as he stood before the mirror, Colin could have been a Greek warrior come out of an oracle, an Assyrian wanting blood for blood, a lieutenant of Saladin, an Elizabethan hot with revenge, for it was revenge he was vowing and looking across the narrow width of Tony's bed, never again to be graced with Tony's body, he stared the mirror into witness of his oath.

"I will find that man however long it takes me and then he'll be dead."

He knew where Tony had always kept a spare gun and ammunition. No one but he knew — Tony had told him that, for an emergency. He would find out how to get the weapon across to England — he could be patient, there were many ways, someone would tell him in time. He was already saving for the journey and scavenging for any job, any dirty manual task, any rain-sodden errand, any pitifully boring task which brought in cash which could be put in the purse inside his mattress.

Tony had met this Mark Armstrong. After he had been gunned down, Colin had heard his friends say that he should never have given the interview. The interview, they said, had put the finger on him. Armstrong, they said, was a man with too many connections. Tony had been too trusting. Whichever way you cut it, they had got on to him soon after that interview was given — weeks before the film went on to the television — and the week before it was transmitted he had been done for. Now tell us there is no link. It was your man Armstrong somewhere in the middle of it.

This gossip, this grief-stricken slack talk seeded in the shocked and bereft mind of Colin and the idea had been planted, immovable. He did not stay to hear more authoritative disclaimers. He did not sift the evidence or weigh the character of the loose-lipped whose blind resentments sprayed poison every which way. He had his course. He had the purpose he needed to put a spine into a life as blasted as his brother's bloody, unrecognisable face.

"If I don't do this thing," he said, holding in his right hand a smiling photograph of Tony, "God can strike me down."

II

A couple of days later, Mark was on a plane to Belfast. After a detailed conversation with the authorities he had persuaded them that it was the best way.

"There is nowhere I could hide even if I wanted to," he told the intelligent and courteous young officer sent to debrief him. "I have my own contacts. I must go back there now and unravel it." The man had put forward his objections – the element of risk seemed to him unnecessarily high; better, he thought, to give it a few weeks to see if it cooled off; perhaps the information came from the transient outrage of a fringe group or the short-term confusion of a single vengeful member. All the more reason, if that were so, for nipping it now, Mark said, and finally the officer was persuaded. Like others of his kind, he had respect for Mark and the dozen or so reporters who stuck to the unremitting subject of Northern Ireland: and this respect was returned.

Indeed, Mark thought as he shuffled through Gate 4A, the Belfast isolation wing at Heathrow, and submitted to the checks and scrutiny of the police, he was forever surrounded by decent people on his flight to Belfast. They were there in the lounge with its defiantly emerald green bucket chairs where the Ulster drawl was always punctuated by cries of children, never a daytime flight without a full complement; there on the plane, a belly-load of decent people soaring above serene tooth-drawn Windsor Castle, home of the emblem of so much savagery, across the short, nuclear-waste-infested strait of sea to the island now synonymous with hatred and insoluble vileness. Decent people every mile of the way. Decent people at Belfast Airport with a joke from the women at the desk, where he met John from the taxi firm that always picked him up – best to have someone you knew – out past the two stone eagles leading to a farm as handsomely and decently settled as any you would see on the mainland and the chat with John as sober and funny as ever.

It would be like that throughout the day and it had always been like that and it should have ceased to surprise him for, after all, why not? Most people in the province were peaceful, law-fearing, well intentioned and, as far as Mark could make out, most often better mannered, better behaved in public places at least, but also better at conducting themselves in personal civilities than their peers on the mainland. It simply was not so that a society which bred wickedness and bore the agony of unhealed wounds was rotten from skin to core. It never paid to generalise and yet the place teased out generalisations as easily as it provoked saloon-bar solutions.

His resumption of outrage for these decent people never failed to spark whenever he drove in towards the city, admiring the Antrim Hills. So like the Scottish Lowlands of his youth. Mark felt peculiarly at home in Ulster and respected the inhabitants, even those dipped and coated in the venom of bigotry. And, though the religious and political divide which so heavily informed the population still remained – and John, his driver, would rattle off his views on Wolfe Tone and Robert Emmet, on Presbyterians and the Battle of the Boyne as easily as his London equivalent would talk sport – Mark found himself drawn to the fighting families, and sometimes romantically considered whether in that nexus there was a story and a centre to this abscess, more Mafia than patriotic, more gang warfare than ideological terrorist rebellion, more heart and history than dogma and politics.

He had read a few months before the remarks of the Chief Constable of Northumbria, who had said that if he could remove two hundred families from his fiefdom in the North-East, then the crime rate would fall away to trivial proportions. As yet such a solution was unthinkable. Mark would be on the side of those who would fight to keep it unthinkable, but the way a society dealt with its own cancers was an indication of its health, and to fail to control the cancer – as was happening in Ulster – could be fatal.

John told him a couple of stories about the Dives flats as they passed by on their way to the hotel. "If they don't recognise you – you are the enemy. A sink drops on your car from the fourth floor – not nice! They take no prisoners, those boys!" There was a relish which could be found in New York, in Chicago, in Palermo, in Liverpool, in Singapore – the relish of those who are surviving in a tough city and ventilate their fear in boasts and the open naming of their fears. John's main talk was of drugs. He had a boy who was an addict, his second son, and he stated as unchallengeable fact his conviction that the two supposedly war-ring extremist groups, Catholic and Protestant – the IRA and the

235

UVF – were in collusion over this trade. "Every so often somebody runs up the flag," he said heavily, "but it's all in the money. They're prepared to ruin the youngsters of this province for the money. Don't tell me about religion. Don't tell me about patriots."

As if commenting on what he said, they passed a block of flats flying the tricolour, another flying the Union Jack, as if the buildings themselves were columns about to march in this ancient and knotted battle.

Mark realised that they had reached the Europa Hotel in the middle of the town without seeing a single soldier. He knew that they were de-escalating in the city centre but he was still impressed. The Europa had the same manufactured calm – like fake antiques – of any international hotel. Mark always noticed how much taunting glass there was in the building and the glass porch flaunted by the Grand Opera House next door and the glass in the new city centre. Fragility showing its contempt for violence.

He made a few calls, had a bath and then decided on room service. The events of the last few days needed thinking through but, as often happened when he sat down to "think through" his own career, he could summon up little interest. His attention was caught by the immensity of the problem in Ireland, a nut inside a nut like Israel surrounding the Palestinians and surrounded by Arabs. A place where so much had to be disentangled and reconstructed and forgiven that it was difficult to see hope. Dante was its truest poet. Involvement was like a bad marriage, and yet Mark found himself thinking about John and his son's drug problem and how that too was sucked into the larger, all-consuming dispute, while at the same time revealing the corruption of the conflict. It was extraordinary how John could stand up to all this but people in the province did just that every day. It was a place full of stoics faced by open-eyed terror.

There was a phone call from Michael Elliot, a friend from way back, brother of the man whose guest Mark was to have been at the opera in London. Michael wanted to tease him out of Belfast and out to his house – an estate would better describe it – where the rituals of upper-class and landed gentry country life went on much the same as in the Shires and the Borders, the rural counties and so many privileged enclaves on the mainland. Mark liked Michael but when he was out there in the Palladian house, he could see that the whole argument might well be rooted in land. For just as religion could seem to provide a key, and politics, and partition and family and social engineering, another unlocking was

236

in the land. It was one of the more remarkable characteristics of the province that so much land was still held in hands that had kept it to themselves for several centuries. Michael, charming of course and a force for progress and good in the province, was part of this and he welcomed Mark's questions as much as he valued his work. Michael himself was deeply connected with privileged sources of information and as such a most valuable contact.

"Are you over to do a follow-up to the programme?"

"Something of the sort."

"It was a marvellous piece of work, Mark. Everybody here was impressed. Even those who might not be thought to agree with you."

"Ah well." Compliments were always an embarrassment. It was a shame in a way, he might have drawn some sustenance from them but they never got to him; it was as if he had his own Star Wars system and the missiles shot them down before they could penetrate.

"I heard some loose talk . . ." Michael began, and waited for Mark to go on.

"That's why I'm here. Nothing serious."

"No point in telling a fellow like you how to handle it, but Gilly and myself would love to see you this time round."

"I'll try. There's quite a lot going on in London. But I'll try."

"Take care then."

"Love to Gilly."

He turned on the local news programme just after 10.30 p.m. There was a report on booby-trap bombings; a report on the funeral of an RUC officer; a report on a company which had yielded to threats to its employees and would no longer be supplying stores to the military. There was no indication that this was an exceptionally disturbing day.

At the end of the following morning, his calls made, waiting for his contacts to turn up with the underground meeting he was looking for, he went over the road to the Crown Liquor saloon. Painted windows, and glass, exotic tiles, mirrors, brass, polished wood, a mosaic floor, the close privacy of the snugs – a public house as rare as any in the world, "a many coloured cavern" Betjeman had called it and the commendation was proudly reproduced. Once again Mark was moved by the jewelled bar. In a city scorched and assailed as none other in Western Europe, in a place of barricades, grids, armoured tanks, was the frangible casket, untouched, and himself with two or three dozen young people quietly, politely drinking and peacefully exchanging the time of day. For gentle and civilised concourse in a rare and cherished place, it would be difficult to beat this scene anywhere.

From here he would, with luck, be led to a first meeting which, in a few days or a week or so, would take him to men, killers or with blood on their hands, who would grant him an interview for the chance to put their case, and along the way perhaps hint at what might be done to head off what local intelligence called "a maverick". It was they who had received the phone call and passed it on. The word was out but no one had admitted to it and no one seemed able to indicate any hopeful lines of enquiry.

It was something he could not yet absorb. He had now received the full message, that the man considered him responsible for a death, but the two actions – his filming of a "soldier" and, several weeks later, the death of that gunman – were so unconnected in Mark's mind that he could not see how they could be joined together in the mind of anyone else. Yet he knew enough to know that he was in a country where logic could be defied and imagination was at a premium.

The fact was, though, that when he had finished his Guinness and walked back across to the Europa he felt more exposed than he had hitherto experienced, even in the worst of the street fights. The authorities were in no doubt that the threat was serious and even though the initial enquiries – the man's younger brother (a backward type), those who had access to his colleagues – had yielded nothing at all, they had no doubt that Mark ought to stay away from the province for a time until it blew over or they came upon a lead. It was the sense of an unknowable enemy, some malign force out there somewhere, in any face, in anybody, which unnerved him quite suddenly on this simple street crossing. He hurried, all but ran, and then slowed down, feeling silly.

The urgency to find out for himself, and soon, was partly the rather arrogant response of outraged innocence and partly a wish to clear the decks at a time when he wanted to change his life decisively. Jen, he was sure, would live with him – whatever formal arrangement they came to. It was now, he knew, that he must strike to secure her: she needed to be pursued, to be insistently persuaded; any standing back would be regarded as lack of real desire.

He had decided to take Rudolf up on his offer, but give him the test of asking him to fund a three-part enquiry into the RUC which he knew he could place on Channel Four. For that, too, he needed this threat to be cleared up. Just as he could not think of asking Jen to ally herself to him if the prospect of assassination were real – the danger to her put it out of the question – so he could not continue on an active career in Northern Ireland if he had to contend with such a possibility: once again it would be unfair to everyone else. Nor did he know how he himself would stand up to it.

Better, he thought, the heightened danger of short-term risk than the extended paralysis of long-term uncertainty. He was determined to stay in Belfast until some sort of explanation was available. He went through the glass flaunting doorways of the Europa with a perceptible sensation of relief.

There was a phone message from Nicholas.

III

"And do you know what the slimy bastard did?" she demanded. Tim smiled and shook his head. He was devoting such energy as he had left, late on a Saturday night after a bitch of a week and the ultimately soporific treat from Martha ("on expenses: sod them") of a long liquid dinner at a local restaurant, to the made-for-television movie. Martha, lavishly into a "final drinkie-pooh" which was as usual driving rapidly towards a final bottle, took his indifference as the best she could hope for and soldiered on.

"First of all he lives in the most disgusting block of flats. Red Victorian rubbish. Bloody Bloomsbury! I bet he thinks he's in some holy communion with those prancing poseurs, pansified prats the lot of them."

"That's rather good," Tim murmured, his eyes not turning away from the screen. "You're very good, old girl, even when you talk."

"Especially when I talk."

"Yes."

"What I say is so much better than the written pose, the pritten, the prose – oops! – of all but a fingerful of my fannying contempt-ibles – try saying that when you're sober –"

"Contemporaries . . ." A murmur.

"I know what I said."

"Sorry. A fill-up?" Martha lunged to oblige and did not spill very much. She loved Timmy when he drank late with her. Loved him. When he listened to her. And drank.

"The lift was out of order of course. It would have to be, wouldn't it? To fit in with the style – man of integrity, no time for fancy flats or anything that could give away an interest in personal comfort. The vanity of the relentlessly modest – I hate it. Crap. So I had to walk up forty-two stairs. When I got there I felt like Gunga Din or whichever bag carrier it was who got to the top of Everest before the big white man. But do you know what the slimy bastard had done?"

Once again Tim's head went its pendulum way. What he was watching was such an obvious pinch from *Gunfight at the OK Corral*, even though it was a thriller set in downtown L.A., that he could not understand how any director would have the nerve.

"He'd gone out. Said he'd tried to reach me and only got the answering-machine – fair do's that was true – said his secretary was only part-time – why did he have to say that? Is he a Third World case? What is this? – all this was in a note and the bastard had tied it round a split of champagne and put beside it a glass full of what had been ice, now water, but still cold anyway. What about that?"

"I would have thought . . ." Tim could scarcely believe his eyes. It was *shot* for *shot*!

"Exactly. Creep! Creep! The creep!" Down went a full glass of claret. "*Toady . . .*"

"Did you . . . ?"

"Of course I bloody did!"

"He sounds as if . . ."

"He's yella! All those war correspondent bastards are the same. Standing there in front of a camera with the crew forming a kind of barricade and I bet two dozen policemen or gormless stagestruck soldiers hanging about while the Mark Armstrongs tell us it's been another night of violence and it's all made to look so dangerous and they are the bees' knees but it's CRAP!"

Tim nodded, gravely this time. Bed was approaching at an accelerating speed. Bed or unconsciousness.

"That's what gets me about him. About all of them. It was that stupid little split of champagne – not even half a bottle for Chrissake – that did it. Now I know why I want to get him. Getting him is getting all of them – telly plastic gnomes. Do you see?" The pitch told Tim that she needed no more contribution of any sort from him that night and he settled down to the final minutes of this copycat film which could provide a refreshing starting point for Monday's seminar.

"He thought he could bribe me," said Martha. "Or it was some sort of tip? A bloody tip!" Deep on the large sofa she poured the wine down and, in a fug of alcohol and bile, she went into the warm and embracing confusions of rich aromatic sensuous semi-conscious drunkenness.

IV

Some weeks later, Colin overheard that Mark Armstrong had been at the Europa. He thought it through very carefully. He walked past the hotel two or three times during the course of the next week and tried to imagine how he could have organised it.

It would not have worked. He could never go into the place – it was far too intimidating and the people on the door would see right through someone like him. He would never be allowed to cross the threshold. No. It would have been a botched job.

London – Tony had told him – was a place where nobody knew anybody. You could disappear around a corner in London, Tony had said, and all you would see would be an empty street or a new set of strangers. London was the place to pop out of a crowd and just let him have it. It would not be too difficult to find him. He had made a note of the television studios and he had the telephone number. He was very confident of finding him.

No, Belfast would be the wrong place for the execution. Get them on their own soil, Tony had said: that's what hurts the most.

TWENTY-THREE

"YOU love her more than you love me. I can see through you."

Harry felt that she could do just that. Fiona's savage look pierced through his own scared eyes, X-rayed the tense white thin naked body. He shivered and hoped she would think it was just with the cold. He had come out of the bathroom to seek a towel in the kitchen and Fiona had suddenly turned on him. He felt he might be sick.

"Admit it. Come on. Admit it."

Was she joking? Was she drunk? Would she turn on him if he told the truth or turn on him if he tried a lie? His shivering became more violent. Fiona held out the cheap pink towel tauntingly. He remembered the towels in the hotel.

"What's she like?"

"I've said." His teeth began to chatter. His hands covered his genitals. The thin shoulders shook.

"Is she beautiful?"

He nodded and quite suddenly he remembered her eyes. It was the eyes he saw when he dreamt of her. Eyes which made him not fearful but full of longing.

Fiona threw him the towel. He turned to go back into the bathroom.

"Stay here. That place is a bloody ice-box."

He began to dry himself warily in the one warm room. The early months of the year had brought unaccustomed snow. Low temperatures, burst pipes and the meagrely protected house had driven all life into the one room. It could have been cosy, but Harry felt isolated, on trial. On trial because of Jen who fascinated

Fiona, and Nicholas whom she despised yet, when he came on a visit, fawned over. That worried Harry. Should he trust Nicholas as much as he wanted to?

Harry was frightened of what she and Jake would do next. He had been back home for three months but he still expected, every day, that they would try to get rid of him again as they had done before. He had not been persuaded by their bombastic explanations. The shock of what they had done had only fully registered after a few days back on the estate and since then his sense of being unwanted and in some danger had intensified. Now there was Fiona's new fury, this craving for information about Jen; this relationship with Nicholas; and he was essential to her. In some way he understood that. She needed him to feed on and yet she would see him go without regret. He wanted to go. Whenever Nicholas came to take him and Mary, sometimes only him, out for a day's treats he wanted to say "Don't take me back to her". So far he had been unable, too shy, too much in awe, to say that.

"He'll be here in less than an hour," said Fiona. "Put on those new clothes I bought you from the money he sent."

"Can we wait for Mary?"

"God knows when she'll be back. Anyway – it won't bother the bold Nicholas. Maybe he even likes it better that way." And it would serve Mary right. Fiona had decided that Mary had inherited her father Sean's ability to wound and she enjoyed penalising her for that suspicion.

Harry rubbed the towel awkwardly over his chest and arms. Fiona's jibe alerted that secret instinct of recognition but it was so deeply impacted that it could find no light: yet there was a faint tremor – alarm, unease, pleasure, even pride – he could not distinguish. Why did Nicholas turn away so sharply sometimes when he looked at him? He knew that Nicholas liked him a lot, and he could warm greatly to Nicholas. But there was something he did not understand and occasionally feared. He studied hard to say nothing. Fiona poured him a cup of tea and plonked the packet of cereal in front of him. Such service was very unusual.

"Don't tell anybody you don't get a breakfast."

Still half wet, Harry sat down, the damp towel around his shoulders, and began to eat and drink. The radio had broken. For once the television was not on. The snow deep banked around the house and all over the estate added to a rare silence.

"She'll have all the clothes in the world," said Fiona. "Lack for nothing. She'll just whistle and it'll be brought up. She'll just say

243

– I fancy that or I want to try that and it'll come, whatever it is. Cost no object. No object." Fiona, once again wound tight with envy and lust, drew heavily on her cigarette. It was almost a sickness, an infinite longing for the material goods which flaunted themselves before her devouring eyes every day in television images which had utterly seduced her.

"So what was the house like? One of the houses. They have houses everywhere, people like that. So?"

Harry's throat went dry and he tried yet again.

"Big," he admitted, with difficulty.

"Of course it's big! All their houses are big. But were there antiques – old furniture that looks new because of all the servants' polishing – on a bloody pittance most likely. Were there?"

"I think so." His dry-throated unswerving honesty competed with the cereal which now threatened to choke him.

"And paintings on the walls?"

"Yes."

"Mirrors. A lot of mirrors?"

"Yes."

"Old golden, ornamented, twirly mirrors with candles – cost a fortune?"

"I think so." He swallowed and his eyes brimmed as he choked the cough.

"And her?"

He dared not take another spoonful. Her. The memory disturbed him. It had grown. It had grown, it seemed, every day and night since he had come back, sometimes merging with that of his mother.

"As good as she looks?" said Fiona, impatiently. "I've seen her photograph. I knew the name meant something when she said it but I couldn't quite place it at first. But they can do anything with photographs. Is she that good?"

He nodded. Fiona was relentless.

"Would you say it's natural or is it put on with the make up? Those people have more than make up. They have massage and jacuzzis every day if they want and saunas and people to do things for them and diets, skin grafts, face-lifts, and no bloody work, so how can you compete? Is it natural?"

"I think so," he whispered.

"How would you know?" She took out another cigarette.

Harry left the question unanswered.

244

"She's one of the richest women in the world but they say she came from nowhere. So much for her airs and graces."

But she has no airs and graces, Harry said, to himself, she just held me tightly as you have never done and as only my mother ever did.

"They despise us, people like that."

I'm sure they don't.

"They hate us. They're afraid of us because they know we can see through them. They're no better than us, that's what they don't like. For all their money and clothes and houses, they can't stand being seen through. That's why they lead such protected lives. They only want to meet people who bow and scrape and kiss their arse. They'll not take the risk." Fiona was no longer addressing Harry. He took a swift half spoonful of his cereal and, to be sure of swallowing, a sip of the milky tea. "It isn't as if they've done anything to deserve it," she said, staring ahead, abstracted, almost swaying as if drugged on her own terrible sense of the injustice. "They'll have inherited it or been given it or got it in ways you don't mention but they're no better than the rest of us. Just bloody lucky. That's what really makes me sick. They're nothing but lucky but you can see them – not just her, she's at the very top – but hundreds like her on the telly or going into restaurants, behaving as if we were muck. That's what gets me. Because they have what they have, we're supposed to be dirt. That's what sticks in my throat. Because they're no better than us – are they? Are they?"

She wheeled on the boy who shook his head.

"Get dressed," she said. "I want you ready when he comes."

Harry took a last dash of tea and left.

Fiona brooded on a change of fortune which ought to have made her happier but had just made her even more discontented. She was now getting money out of Nicholas. Oh, the pretence was that he was helping them out and just a few pounds and something for the children, but it was cash and substantial and most of it went straight into her pocket. She would assure herself that she played fair by Harry and buy him a new pair of jeans, a pair of trainers, a jacket and Mary got a warm coat, but such purchases did not take heavily from the crisp run of ten-pound notes which Nicholas handed over in a large white envelope.

Fiona had established her terms on his second visit. After the sparring, the children had been sent out with Jake and Fiona, holding all the cards, had laid it out.

"What is it you want?"

245

"My interest . . ."

"Is it to adopt him? Do you want to come to that sort of arrangement?"

"If – all things considered – it isn't outside the bounds of possibility."

"He's told me where you met."

Nicholas was finished. He could not deny it and from then on he was at her mercy. His only defence was unthinkable to utter. How could he persuade her that he had gone to that hotel and into that situation for the first time in his life? That he had not sought out Harry or any other boy of his age? How could he convince her of his determination to leave before doing anything at all but for the sight of Harry, the frightened, vulnerable, sweet sight of Harry which had flooded him with a tenderness he knew to be, and wanted to be, abiding?

He said nothing.

She outlined her terms. They were broke and in debt. She had no objection to his seeing Harry and Mary and taking them out for a treat every now and then. He could bring that secretary woman if he wanted to but he did not have to because Harry would always tell her the truth and anyway . . . she let the threat hang in the air.

Nicholas had wanted to talk it over with Jen – but she was locked in America. He considered Mark but decided against it. Mark would advise the sensible thing and he did not want that advice. His hopes of a solution in the short term were gone. His plan now – the use of the word plan dignified his course of action – was to keep seeing Harry, keep in with Fiona, and await his opportunity. It was not much but the alternative was nothing at all and, having tried to imagine that, he grasped at the mean deal on the table before him.

He was generous.

It was the generosity which built up her frustration. If there was this much without really trying, what more could be milked with serious application?

Nicholas arrived just after eleven. He had caught a very early train which had been unheated and unburdened by a buffet bar or restaurant. He had hurried through the station to grab a taxi because the train was late and so when Fiona offered him a cup of tea he accepted gratefully. She noticed his beautiful winter coat, the close tweed cross-hatching, the cut of it which seemed to swerve so gracefully around his body, the velvet collar. It would, she decided, savagely, pay for a fortnight's holiday abroad. She longed to be away, be in the sun, be one of those laughing handsome careless people on television who ate on the beach and discoed the night away.

Nicholas drank the tea scalding. He used the cup to warm his hands. His feet were remote frozen stiffnesses demanding concentrated stoicism.

"How has he been?" Nicholas asked.

"Right as rain."

"And Mary?"

"Mary's the more delicate type and in a place like this with the snow it isn't easy. She needs extra care."

"I'm sure I could help."

"Nobody knows how much help people like us need. It's like being down a deep hole. You get a few quid and you climb up a step or two and then the money's gone and you're back where you started, except worse because you had all that hope. Everybody around here's in the same boat which makes it worse. You think you're just this lump – whatever – this dump of people it's easier to pay off with social security than do anything for. You think it's going to be like that for ever. The world goes on – on television – you see all the ads and you think – there must be millions of people can buy some of that some of the time but what about me? What do I do? You're somebody who knows the answers, don't you? A Member of Parliament."

"I wish I did," Nicholas replied, uncomfortably moved by Fiona's desperation and, as before, half impressed, half intrigued by her eloquence which he ascribed to her Irish education and background. Should he give the formal answer he would unload on a constituent – the statistics, the "dependency culture", the decline of labour-intensive industry, the end of the apprenticeship system, the demise of religion, the whole despairing package?

"More tea?" she asked. He nodded and realised she did not want any answer.

With her back to him, as she put on the kettle, she said, so quietly that at first he thought he may have misheard her,

"Why don't you just take him? We could come to an arrangement."

A painful shiver possessed him and he found that he was shaking.

"Take him," she said, low-voiced and urgent. "You're a nice

man. I can see that. There's nothing for him here. I'll fill in all the forms."

This was so far from Nicholas's own imagined scenario for the day that he could not wholly take it in. He had come undermined by tabloid hints and threats of revelation. He was all but certain that Fiona had not leaked his story to the press but in his nervous state he had wanted to make sure and had braced himself for the unpleasant questioning.

Now she offered Harry like a parcel.

"Why are you saying this?"

"I've been thinking." Fiona turned and came over to pour him some more tea. She took her time about sitting down and yet Nicholas felt that this was not rehearsed or even prepared. An idea had simply flitted across her mind and she had netted it, liked the look of it, and was now absorbed in it.

"The things you could do for him," she said, "I could never do. At first I didn't think I could trust you as far as that door but I've seen you with him a few times now. You stand away. You're not all over him at all. People could think you were rather remote. They could think he was a bit of a nuisance you'd somehow got landed with and were seeing it through."

Even though that was what he had aimed at, his first fear was that Harry might share in this perception. His second – could he trust her?

"You want to know why I'm saying this?" Fiona paused and then a reckless expression came across her face. "I want money," she said. "Not just these little envelopes of cash. I expect you have one in your pocket now." Nicholas almost patted the relevant area. "I see this as fair. You get what you want. I get what I want."

Harry came in. Nicholas addressed himself to the moment.

"We must talk about it," he said and stood up to leave.

He had asked the taxi to wait outside. This was not his usual practice. His actions normally aped those of a secret agent and using the same taxi to bring him to the house and take him away with the boy was leaving much too easy a trail. But his earlier decision had made that less relevant. Moreover the snow and slush encouraged the retention of any hard-won taxi.

They drove into the middle of the town.

It did not look good even under the gracing mantle of snow. The mean High Street was a parade of large crude signs, usually in red or black, declaring FOR SALE, CLOSING DOWN SALE,

248

HALF-PRICE SALE, EVERYTHING MUST GO. The posters, Nicholas thought, were the most dynamic and alluring objects in the street. The slush swirled around the road, churned up and sprayed by every wheel. The pavements had not been swept and the cold made them treacherous. People walked in a huddle. Scarcely any of the younger people wore coats and their faces were hard.

Nicholas took Harry to the main amusement arcade, gave him some change and went to the phone. He had intended to go to the fish and chip restaurant and then to the cinema. But now that Mary had failed to show up, he had a better idea. His phone call was successful.

Harry was on a video game which involved guiding our hero through unimaginable scraps and battles involving over-muscular men, multi-coloured beasts and one absolute monster. The noise from the machine combined toyland gunfire and a perky little tune repeated continuously. Nicholas watched in genuine interest as Harry darted his man from one stretch of land to another, from street to street, never a second passing without some assault.

What effect, if any, he wondered, was all this having? The boy knew it was a game and it was the game to which he was addicted. Yet the incessant and unquestioned violence was always part of it. "Our hero" karate-chopped and kicked, socked, shot, knifed, all to the same perky little tune. All over television, grown men did much the same to each other accompanied by rather more sonorous music and Harry and his like watched, hypnotised. Was this imposing layer on layer of violence, however thin, even if all but invisibly thin, on their minds? Layers which, given the wrong opportunity, might infiltrate action, influence thought, poison emotion? Nicholas had become abruptly and intensely concerned about the society which his generation and those before him were bequeathing to the children of the last lap of the twentieth century. He wanted to do something to help it. Harry, in one sense, had given his career a focus.

Instead of going into the fish and chip sit-down restaurant, Nicholas bought fish and chips wrapped in paper – which Harry preferred – and the distinguished man and the eager boy ate them with their fingers while leaning against a small table jutting from the wall. Harry drank Coca-Cola, Nicholas orangeade. It was some measure of his devotion that the incongruity, though he was conscious of it, was not allowed to bother him.

He hired another taxi and they set off for the big city just a few miles to the south. When he told Harry where they were going the boy's face simply glowed with pleasure. No words could express it. It was so easy to make him happy and seeing the boy's happiness pumped pure oxygen through Nicholas's veins.

When he had taken Harry and Mary to the circus and to the pantomime, when he had seen them with the bicycles he had bought them for Christmas – all deliberately obvious treats – the joy he had gained from simply watching their faces had eclipsed most other pleasures in his life. He realised that he was free of all the hard stuff – sleepless nights, bonded years, fractious days – from the financial strangulations and all the other well-documented potential for the distresses of parenthood. But even that judicious disclaimer did not impair his zooms of delight at the expression in the eyes of the small boy now so jubilantly silent beside him.

They got to the football ground with a quarter of an hour to spare. Nicholas – bold to a fault – paid the taxi to stay and wait for them, partly because he was convinced that he would never be able to raise another taxi in the darkness which would follow the game, partly because the heaviness of the police presence and the crush of supporters suggested that he might badly need a line of escape.

It was the first time he had been to a major football match. This was a derby game, two of the great northern First Division teams lined up against each other. The mounted police, the circling helicopter, the growl and thrust of the crowd along from the stand entrance, moving in unsteady fat conga lines to the body-narrow turnstiles were all outside his experience. He rather prided himself on being English, but this was a mass section of, largely, English male life which was totally outside his ken. His own constituency boasted no football team that he needed to court and the few glimpses of the game on television had not prepared him for this. This was the nineteenth-century racecourse; the sixteenth-century London apprentices; Wat Tyler's peasant army; the circus of the streets – his mind flew straight into a romantic pageant of England which stirred him, moved him, both emotions heightened by a certain apprehension. Not for himself – Nicholas was a man of indisputable physical courage – but for Harry.

Harry loved it. He could have been bred for the crowd. As they climbed the stairs inside the large stand to find their seats in the upper east block, Harry held Nicholas's hand, but Nicholas was not sure who was leading when the small boy wriggled through the push and crush of men with the comfort of one to the manner born. Nicholas's well-developed courtesies were largely super-numerary.

Their Block – Block D – was on the top of what had, to Nicholas's eye, much in common with the more usual connotations of the Block system. His constituency did contain a large Victorian prison and the shoddy, cheap, cream-painted brickwork, the tramp of feet, the Blocks brought out more than a whiff of comparison. They came to a shop. Harry was perfect in this regard and Nicholas had come to love the boy's modesty. He had not quite spotted the element of desolate pessimism. It was abundantly clear that the grotto of football jerseys, shirts, socks, boots, balls, photographs, programmes, badges, scarves of several shades and varieties of wording, and surreal extensions of memorabilia, with its attendant display of monster chocolate bars, crisps, nuts, sweets and gum, was not a sight any boy could pass by without a second glance. Yet by neither a tug nor a flirt of the eye did he hint that a treat might be in order. Nicholas did not hesitate but stopped, queued, and came away with one scarf with "Champions" and the date printed on, one cap in club colours, one shirt ditto which the lady assistant said he would grow into, a very large Mars bar, a can of Coca-Cola, and a programme. Thus furnished they entered the stadium.

The pitch was so green that Nicholas reached for the word emerald. In the middle of the grey slush, barrack-bricked city over-loomed by low-bellied snow clouds, it was like a magical Persian carpet.

"Underground heating," Harry explained proudly, his wonder-struck eyes shifting over the ground like a sniper's sights. It was the first time he had ever been to any game bigger than a scrappy contest in the local park.

They sat down. Harry was on the edge of his seat and there he stayed; now and then he would turn to Nicholas and give or rather emit from some inner core of deep rock gratitude such a beam of happiness that Nicholas all but swayed at the force of it. The boy also conducted an intermittent commentary of encouragement. The home side was his favourite team and when the favourite players in his favourite team got the ball, a litany of prayers and exhortations issued. "Come on . . . Don't let him tackle you . . . pass . . . brilliant . . . oh *please* . . . brilliant . . . oh oh! . . . watch out! watch *out*! . . ."

Nicholas sat back. He did not feel as out of place as he had anticipated. They were in the most expensive seats of the stand, a few rows behind the directors' box, and he was relieved to see that there was a large number of large, well-wadded, uncheaply over-coated men, some smoking cigars, some with small boys, none con-forming to the football hooligan type which characterised the football crowd in the newspapers read by Nicholas. Indeed he wondered if he had strayed into a different game. But no, the two teams came out, music played, the large men leapt up to applaud, just as excited in their overcoated way as the younger men standing on the terraces at either end behind the goalposts who then took up the major part of Nicholas's attention: the lads standing on the terraces.

He was fascinated by them.

Their chanting, always rhythmic, sometimes deafening, occa-sionally rude, invariably rumbustious, boomed across the ground, often echoed or challenged by supporters of the other team and sometimes accompanied by the co-ordinated waving of the arm or other gestures which he found exhilarating in their precision. The police, yellow-jacketed, were placed like Roman walls between opposing Picts and Brits and, scan as he could, Nicholas saw not a ripple of "trouble". Of course, he realised, he could have been fortunate on the day or the "trouble" – the fighting between rival supporters – could now be located outside the ground or even (as he was to discover when he pursued the matter later) have shifted away from the game altogether. But the lack of it – given the game's associ-ation with hooligan behaviour – relaxed him.

This chanting. It was tribal, that much was easy – two tribes on ancient hills provoking each other to battle. It was also, he con-cluded, deeply humorous, a big daft joke, a happy expression of mayhem. It pretended to be intimidating from time to time but that soon petered out and the applause for a particular player or the generalised baying for victory would start somewhere deep in the stacked terraces and suddenly electrify ten thousand, fifteen, twenty thousand throats. The numbers were themselves impres-sive, Nicholas thought. These were the foot-soldiers, the cannon-fodder, the boys become men on frozen fields sent to rule and destroy and uphold, lashed together now in a common voice.

As the game rattled away and Harry's team moved towards a two-goal victory, Nicholas found himself increasingly immersed in the crowd and in the sensations and thoughts it set off. The force of it! Could it ever be – at such a size – as reliably friendly as it seemed? He dived into comparisons – the men in Nelson's fleet, the men on the Western Front, the Jarrow Marchers ... it was in a mood of rather sentimental euphoria that he left the stadium – or rather was all but carried along bodily by the satisfied crowd.

"That," said Harry, most emphatically, when they were settled in the back of the taxi, "was the best thing you've ever taken me to." He reached up and kissed Nicholas on the cheek and then swooped down into his programme. Nicholas, elated and alas – he knew the split instant after he said it that it would have been better left unsaid – seeking more of this innocent gratitude, said, "The best thing you've ever done?"

Harry's head started up and he looked ahead. Nicholas could almost feel the past surge through the small boy's mind – his mother, their time together – and the unnecessary obligation he had imposed on him somehow to square good manners with truth.

"Silly question!" said Nicholas. "Please don't bother to answer it. Look, it's snowing again. We were lucky."

"They can even play in snow on that pitch," said Harry, shaking his head. His solemnity caught Nicholas square on a funny-bone of feeling: it was so awe-filled, so full of a sense of the marvellous that he thought he might both laugh and cry.

By the time he reached the estate his mood had changed completely. Harry was asleep in the corner of the back seat, his scarf around his neck, the hat on, the brown paper bag holding the jersey clutched in his hand, the programme open on his lap.

Nicholas entered the estate as one broaching not only alien but enemy territory. His euphoria at the football had been, in part, he recognised, the expression of a wish that Harry's context was thus supportive. But the boy's section of this estate was a different case. These were what was increasingly called the underclass. This was where the trouble began and little wonder, Nicholas thought, but nevertheless it did. Began, continued and ended, with unemployment and violent boredom as the chief inheritance from generation to generation. This was the failure of Britain – and no doubt elsewhere in the industrialised world and no doubt worse in some places – but that was not the point. The point was that this was where Harry lived and how was he going to get him out?

Whichever way he interpreted it, he was yielding to blackmail from Fiona and she wanted more.

The tabloids had sent a sniffer around and although at present it was just a warning, his room for manoeuvre was severely limited. He was now convinced that the information had come not from Fiona but from Deuce. A Mr Voss had been telephoning his office and the one time he had returned the call the one-line enquiry "Still interested in the hotel trade, are we?" had been unmistakable. In a strange way – because he had thought he could control her

253

– he would have preferred the source to have been Fiona but the conversation that morning had eliminated that possibility.

His alternatives were few.

As the car drew near Fiona's house, Nicholas rocked Harry gently on the shoulder, easing him awake. He woke up reluctantly.

"Were you dreaming?"

"Yes." Harry's grumpy nod suggested that the dream had been a happy one.

"Good dreams?"

"The nice woman in London," Harry said. "Jen." He uttered the name softly as if it were presumptuous to be on such familiar terms with such a person – and yet he had met her as Jen, Nicholas referred to her as Jen. Nicholas caught the mood and again savoured the boy's delicacy.

"She is very nice," Nicholas said, "and she liked you very much."

"How do you know?" The question was rapped out hard. Nicholas regretted his blandness.

"I could tell," he said, sticking very strictly to the truth.

"Is she back in London yet?"

"No. She's still in America. But when she comes back – it should be soon – I'm sure she'd like to see you again."

As he spoke the words, Nicholas felt the end of his oppression. Of course. That was the solution! Jen. Jen and himself. Unchallengeable. But for it to work, he was certain, Fiona had to be wrong-footed. The plan revealed itself to him instantly and he immediately made his decision.

"I may not see you for a few weeks," he said, as they stood on the snow-swirling pavement. "But I will see you again whatever happens and whatever anybody tells you." He reached out and put his hands lightly on the boy's shoulders. "Whatever anybody tells you. Do you understand?"

Harry nodded, attempting to absorb the significance of the words but distracted by the cold and the thought that Fiona might be looking at them through the window, which somehow unnerved him. What did Nicholas mean? Why did he not stay if he liked him so much?

When they went in Fiona almost immediately suggested that Harry go and play with Mary. She and Nicholas had something to talk about. Jake had been sent out to the pub. Harry was alerted by her nervous, abrupt tone which chimed in with Nicholas's grim remarks just before coming into the house.

"So have you thought it over?" Fiona scarcely let the door shut behind the boy before she plunged into the business which clearly possessed her. "What do you think? It needn't be a lump sum although I would want some sort of lump sum to start with – that would be only fair – it could be in instalments – every month for a certain number of years until we got it all settled." She took a drink from a glass of beer: Nicholas had been mimed the offer of a similar can and had declined. "I thought £50,000," she said, or rather gulped out. "That seems fair. That seems about right."

"And after that?"

"After that?"

"After the £50,000 is spent."

"That'll get me out of here. That'll do it. I'll sign a form. Just get it drawn up. I'll sign."

"I doubt if that's possible."

"You could arrange it. It's just a matter of arranging it. There's nothing you couldn't fix in that way if you had a mind to it." She eyed him rather flirtatiously.

"I don't think it's that easy. I wouldn't want there to be a shadow on this."

"What bloody shadow? What are you talking about? You want the boy, don't you? You want to get him out of here? You want to give him a chance. Well then. Give me a chance along the way. And you can take him."

"Not on those terms."

"£40,000?"

"It's not a question of the sum of money involved."

"All very high and mighty of you to say that! That's what you lot always say. Money isn't the point! Money isn't the question! Money isn't all that important! Listen, mister. Money is the be all and end all. It's the way out of here. It's the chance for a fair crack at life. It's the only thing we've got and only those who have a lot of it can be so stupid as to say it isn't important. How much did you spend today on the boy? Tell me! The taxis, the food, the best seats at the football I bet, the presents, the this, the that – fifty quid? Sixty? More? A week's wages? You bought him that happiness, mister, and don't you kid yourself. And you can buy him as much more as you want – good luck to him – but you pay me too – or it's over. All over."

Nicholas was silent for an uncomfortable length of time but Fiona would not add to her threat and she dug in.

"Very well then," he said, eventually, "it's all over."

"You'll be back," she said. "You'll be back."

255

"I wouldn't count on it." He took up his gloves from the table. "I really wouldn't count on it."

"What for? What is it? What's the money to you? You could afford it."

"Yes. I could afford it."

"Well. Is he not worth that to you? Just the occasional treat, is that it? Is that all he means to you?"

"Harry means more to me than I care to tell you."

"A fine way of showing it you have. I'm offering you everything! Take him. Look at this bloody place. Look out the window. Take him!"

Her passion entangled avarice and a genuine plea for the boy's welfare. Nicholas hesitated. But he knew that to do this would be to put himself and Harry at Fiona's mercy for the rest of his life. Nor could he bear the idea of buying Harry. That was no way forward.

"I'm sorry," he said. "Not on those terms."

"Bastard!"

"I'm sorry."

"Get out. Get out! Bloody poof. I should never have let you lay hands on him. Queer creep! Get out before I call the police. Thank your lucky stars I don't want to drag the boy's name through the mud. Get out! Show your face here again and I'll make sure something gives it damage. Out! Out!"

Nicholas found himself pushed and harried through the one door and then another which slammed behind him. The taxi was waiting patient as a faithful hound. Nicholas glanced up to what he knew was Harry's bedroom. The boy was not to be seen. He walked slowly to the taxi and asked to be taken to the station for the London train.

Harry lay on the mattress, jack-knifed in misery. He had stayed by the door and heard all but the final words when he had scampered upstairs to join Mary. There was a pain like a weight on his heart. He heard himself crying – but quietly. Fiona must never find out. Mary lay beside him steeped in her own misery and bitterness. But Harry was deeply into himself. Nicholas did not want him.

"I'll save up," he said. "I'll save up and we'll go to Jen. She'll want us. We'll go there."

Part Four

NO CONNECTIONS

Twenty-Four

I

THE archaeologists who discovered that they were in the tomb of Tutankhamen must have experienced much the same, he thought, as analysts when the crucial but hitherto hidden is unexpectedly revealed. A revelation which makes a new pattern. A revelation which can redraft a history. Here now with this deeply distressed woman before him, he sensed the breaking down of a final wall, the entering into the forbidden tomb, the key to the trauma. Whatever was said by its detractors, the good analysts knew the impact, the positive and peaceful life which could come after the escape from such a bondage. There would be more work to be done. There was always more work to be done but the corner could be turned. Now this marvellous, strong, astonishing woman was curled in foetal wretchedness, helpless as a destitute child. She was finding, and holding to, the courage to break down the last wall and discover and take on the consequences which she had ignored and fought off for most of a lifetime.

He steepled his fingers and sat as still as stone.

"I should never have left her," she said and again she fell silent.

Cally had been dead when she got there. Her wrists slashed and pills enough to do the job alone. Jen had sorted things out in her usual efficient way and then collapsed. She had begged Mark not to come over; replied in one or two lines to Nicholas's letters; spurned her American friends, her New York acquaintances, all helpers but the analyst into whose hands she had for the first time utterly delivered herself. Yet despite her wounding need to find some relief it had taken weeks for her to batter through the skins

259

and shells and disguises which had so effectively cloaked and bandaged her.

"I was responsible for her. I don't care if they say that people will do it anyway. I don't believe that. She was – after the accident – she only had me – close – only I was close to her and yes she lived with me, and yes she seemed to get through it, but wasn't I too ready to push her off on her own? Why did I have to go to London for so long? Why didn't I ask her over? I know why. I wanted to see if being with, fucking Mark would help *me*, I wanted to help myself. I wanted to join in again and Mark would be the only man, and he is, but it was selfish. Anyway there was something . . . even with Mark . . . because it wasn't Mark I went back for really, was it? It wasn't even Mark. I was using Mark to blot it out again, wasn't I? I got as far as London and went as far back as Mark and then I stopped, didn't I? I was too scared to go on, even though the nightmares were scaring me more and more, but I didn't really think about Cally. Or I began to think about her as a liability, even a bit of a – even a bit of a joke. Talking about dolphins."

The tears now ran steadily down her face and her voice was forced through a throat constricting with fear and distress. "She must have known that. Those you love can always tell and she loved me. I know she did. But she must have felt that I didn't really, not *really*, not in the end, love her enough. Not enough. Not enough. Not enough. And so, she, so she, she just couldn't live any more, where was I? She just couldn't live – who was there to live for? Who? Not me. Not me thousands of miles away, building a life without her, she must have thought. A life without her. So where would she go, poor darling Cally, where could she go except into the dark? Oh God."

She curled up even tighter, trying to ease the pain which palpably twisted into her.

"And so," she murmured. The two simple syllables were spoken low but the analyst felt a thrill of hope at their intensity, their gallantry. "And . . ." She let a convulsion of sobbing subside and spoke with a remote, even dreamy, calm. "And it was not the first time. It was not the first time. I had – I had seen that before. I had. Seen. I had seen my own mother . . ."

He closed his eyes and felt the sway of relief, pity, admiration. The woman before him was now as still as he. He heard his own breath. She was as vulnerable as an infant.

"Help me," Jen whimpered. "Please."

As the Americans flowed east across the Atlantic to fight in the Gulf War, Rudolf flew west to gamble on remaking his fortune on the back of it. It could have been orchestrated for his single and particular benefit. As in ju-jitsu, what had seemed an impossibly weak position now became, through the luck of his timing and the power of his skills, a winning hold. From being a plummeted meteor of the Eighties he would be seen, he believed, as a real star, as immovable as any in that cold firmament of the money-making elite. Yet there was still a short-term problem. The cost of his debt had not diminished and his longer-term plans needed a breathing space to flourish, as they clearly would. To approach the banks for further restructuring of loans was psychologically dangerous. The image that would give him – of an ex-big league player still fatally wounded – would jeopardise the strategy he had, and needed, to re-enter the big league. Jen was the answer. She was still, after all, his wife, he repeated to himself once or twice too often on his flight from London.

He had not seen her for some months. Their few telephone calls had been brief and neutral. But she *was* his wife, damn it, and she had always been a sport. Better still, she had once been a serious gambler in a treacherous market. She would come round. It was stupid that they were not together any more. Just bad luck. The very weekend he had decided to turn to her and gone round to start the whole thing going – inevitably bumpy but a start had been made, he thought – she had rushed across the Atlantic to find that girl dead and acted like a widow ever since. That could not go on. Nothing did. Everything changed. You made your own luck. His fundamental commandments stood him in good stead just now.

Rudolf stayed at the Plaza where he commanded a special rate. He did not move in on Jen immediately – left a message – intimated that he would drop in some time during the next few days – played it casual. New York was hot on the war, now just a couple of weeks into its blinding computer-game stage. There had been no war like it: every mission a success; allied casualties so few it seemed unreal; technological know-how working and working well and all the time.

Communism had collapsed. American technology was beating the world. The wimps were gagged. For Rudolf – ace-in-the-hole. It was a new age and Rudolf could smell the scent of future profit on every news broadcast. Around Manhattan he was seen and heard, confident predator in suspiciously good form, teeth flashing, snapping up every gobbet of useful gossip. He had the air about him of a man with a big, big deal about to mature. Wall Street felt his energy and noted it.

Only once did he break out. It was at a small dinner-party given for him by the philanthropic Fieldings where wealth was as solid as the rock of the island. Rudolf could enjoy shocking the tolerance of the very rich. After Robert Maxwell had left for "a crucial international link up", the floor was his.

"The world has changed for good," he announced – he had been one of the very few to have taken more than one glass of wine. "Russia is bankrupt. Marxism is busted. Saddam is doomed. The Japanese can see America's power and know in their tiny Japanesy hearts that it could all be turned on them if they cross many more lines – why the hell they've been allowed to get so far baffles me – and now we can turn on those who are sapping everything inside our own societies. All the welfare junkies and the charity-dependents and the like. If you want kids – provide for them. If you smoke – don't come to me for money for lung cancer. If you eat like a hog, you can die like one. This isn't racist. It isn't elitist. I'm talking biological realism and everybody round this table knows I'm right. This will come. You can only go at the pace of the slowest if you don't want to win battles. The West has always wanted to win battles. You don't do that with half your army squealing and whingeing and raiding the stores."

As he gathered pace, he caught the merry blue eyes of the young-ish blonde who was clearly regarded as a star turn. Her smile and look of mischief encouraged him. Perhaps he went a little too far in his outline of a Darwinian universe but he felt that with her on his side he had somehow caught the true though unadmitted mood of the gathering. "We need fewer kids and more dumb jobs. The unemployed could turn their hands to domestic service for a start. The rest of the world should pay a tax for America's peacekeeping mission. Japan should be bust wide open. Money should be given to merit not weakness and then we'll motor." He smiled at his admirer. "Biological realism."

"Bullshit," she said, laughing all over him. "Complete bullshit! You should be stuffed and put in the Museum of Anthropology."

"As long as you do the stuffing, I'm on! Take me to your museum immediately."

The line saved him.

Eventually he calculated that it was the right time to visit Jen. She was perfunctory and rather downbeat on the phone but Rudolf had not made his fortune by being sensitive to individual moods.

As the door to the drawing-room opened, so he opened his arms to advance like a triumphant and welcoming lover.

"Jen! Jen darling! How are you? How are you?"

But even before that brief bark of a greeting was concluded, the arms were drooping in retreat, the tone lost its brio.

Jen looked terrible. Not ill – he had seen her ill; not depressed – that too. Just drained, dull, ordinary and unsexy. That was the most unnerving aspect. She had always managed to look sexy even at the worst times. On form, her erotic glow simply blew out most women, Rudolf thought. But who was this mousy, hair-clipped, slippered, plain-dressed, unmade-up, dull-faced person all but cringing in the corner of a large armchair beside the fire? She held up her cheek wearily, even Rudolf observed that. It was cold.

"There's whisky over there," she said, "or gin, or whatever it is you drink these days."

"Thank you, my dear. You?" She shook her head and indicated the half-full glass in front of her.

Maybe she was on the hooch, he thought, as he squirted a foam of soda into the tumbler of scotch. But when he looked more closely he saw no sign.

"How are you?" He sat down opposite her – man and wife, he clocked up – on either side of a good old hearth.

"Do you really want to know?" She smiled – but modestly, nothing that flirted or teased or dared as before.

"C'mon, Jen, don't play games with me."

"I am," she said, very carefully, "possibly more sane and more myself than I have ever been."

"More yourself?"

"More myself."

"What does that mean?"

"More honest. Less self-deluding. Much less. Not at all, I hope. Building on something which is true – not on a false image or an ambition or a fantasy about myself."

"If you're talking about the way you were before – I was all in favour of that, old girl, and so was every other red-blooded male on the planet. Cheers!"

"That's past."

"I'm very sorry to hear it." He took a draught. "I hope it's just temporary."

"It's not temporary."

"Nobody can change themselves just like that."

"I did once. A long time ago. And I'm doing it again."

"I don't understand."

"Never mind."

"Don't patronise *me*, Jen."

"I won't. Let's say I was living a lie."

"Fooled me. Fooled millions. And it was one helluva winner."

"It was an act."

"It's all an act."

"Do you think so?"

"So do you. What do you think we saw in each other?"

"I was mad then. I was out of it then."

"You were less mad than anyone I'd ever met. You'd had a shock. No doubt about that. But you'd bounced back. You'd handled the money like a genius. You were so hot you scorched the rooms you walked into. I have asbestos skin. That's how I got you."

"I thought you would do it."

"C'mon Jen, be fair. I did."

"But what I really *needed* was the security you can only achieve by yourself. I thought you were a short cut. Not a blind alley."

"That's all psychological guff. We were one great item in this town, and in every town."

"I mustn't think that it was all bad. I just find it hard now to understand the woman who acted like that."

"Maybe that was the real one. Maybe this is the dud."

"This is what I am."

"Back to basics?"

"Back to basics. Sorry, Rudi. No flash of stocking. No men's jokes. No oomph."

"It'll come back. You can't keep what you have in a bottle. It'll blow the cork clean out. And I'll still be the only man who can handle it."

"Your confidence," she said, smiling much more sympathetically now, "is truly awesome."

"It's my meal ticket, Jen, and I like to eat."

"So what's on the menu now?"

"I'm not saying – even to you. But – truly – it's very big. It'll take me right back up with the leaders of the pack. It'll give me a platform I've never had before. Let's just say this war came at the right time – it's the right kind of war – it'll last the right length of time – it'll leave the right sort in the shit and all my calculations will bingo out."

"Congratulations . . . So . . . why the *but* in your voice?"

"Clever girl. You haven't changed. Clever girl!"

"What do you want?"

"Short-term cover. Six – eight weeks will do it. Cash funds pronto, no publicity whatsoever."

"How much?"

"You have it."

"That much."

He named his figure. She could easily afford it.

"Six weeks." He was emphatic. "You have my word."

Jen got up and went across to the drinks table. She poured herself a modest vodka – her second and last of the day – a good measure of pure grapefruit juice, squeezed in some lime, placed two cubes of ice in the glass, sipped to test it and returned to her chair. This time she sat up, leaning back, legs crossed before her.

"If I don't?"

"I could miss the best deals of my life."

"If I do?"

"We are the business."

"I'm glad you came," she said and took out a cigarette. "It's time we talked." She drew on it deeply and relaxed. "We have to get divorced."

"Wait a minute."

"There's no argument. I want out."

"I thought we were ready to give it another round."

"No. It's over."

"C'mon, Jen. Who've you found better than me?"

He dared her. She hesitated.

"See?"

"That's my business," she said. "It's also off the point. I just want to start again. Back to basics. The odds are I won't marry again. I can't have children so why should I?"

"No children?"

"That's certain now. Positive. Or rather, negative." She sipped at her drink. "I'm the last of the Mohicans."

"Jen. We had good times, didn't we? You did everything you wanted. You met everyone you wanted to meet. What did I not give you?"

"You'll never know."

"I've warned you not to patronise me, Jen."

"I'm having a divorce, Rudi, and you're in no position to stop me. Marry Alfreda. She could use the money."

"She isn't you."

"Good."

"Is it Mark?"

"Mark and I were lovers in London – I'm sure you knew that. If it were anybody else it would be Mark, but it isn't. Not now. Maybe not ever. I just want to be my own woman and that does not include being your wife. Please don't argue, Rudi. Accept it. It's over. Let's do it nicely and stay some sort of friends."

"I don't have friends."

"This could be a breakthrough."

"What the hell is this back to basics, Jen?"

"I'm not up to telling you. I'm not hiding anything. I just have things to do to sort out my life, to get rid of all the stuff I never really wanted in the first place. To do a few decent things and join in with the century, with other women, with people who think, with everything this ludicrous wealth and ambition cut me off from. More than that, I have to find out something that means everything to me. Too private to tell – not to you, not to anyone. Don't ask."

Rudolf finished his drink and went to pour himself another. As he came back he paused and said, "The money?"

"Within reason you can have it. Six weeks. Standard rate plus two per cent."

"Bitch!"

"Done?"

He nodded.

"I need money," she said. "It has a destination now."

"I don't believe this."

"Your nightmare. Yes. A foundation. I'm locking up more than ninety per cent of it in a foundation to give grants and aid of all kinds to children in trouble."

"It's down the drain."

"It is being set up as we speak."

"Some bloated administrator con man will cream the lot."

"The director I have in mind will make as sure as humanly possible that every penny hits the spot."

"He doesn't exist."

"I haven't appointed the person yet but I will and they'll do it and it will be something good. That terrible hoard of money breeding money breeding money like some desperate egg machine, out of control, and every day's interest a success, every day a winner, more and more money for one person, but how can it be right when so many are so poor?"

"However much you've got it's a piss in the ocean. The poor are a black hole."

"No. That's the old excuse. Well directed, it will benefit enough individuals to matter. That'll do."

"It's criminal. You should use that money to make more, to make it stronger. Throwing it at the stupid people, all those feeble losers, all those ignorant shits, is blowing it. It's contempt. It's waste. Why don't you just put it on a lame horse? What the hell's got into you? All this crappy liberalism or socialism – I thought you'd grown up. That gets nowhere. Look at the mess it's made here and in the UK – and in Australia, in half the few habitable countries in the world. It doesn't work. What works is wealth. The more the better. Handouts threaten wealth. They say there's no need for wealth. They say Santa Claus and God Almighty and you can be a beggar and an asshole and survive. They tell people lies about what's really going on out there. You're chickening out, Jen. You're taking the easy, soft, harpstring route to the land of the goody-goodies. It's a pile of shit! The people are deceived. It teaches them nothing. What is this?"

"It's what I'm going to do."

"Who's been at you?"

"You don't believe that."

"So what happened?"

"Something. Something happened. And I'm going back."

Rudolf put aside his glass, half drunk, and stood up to leave.

"I get the money, you get the divorce."

"A deal."

"Two per cent above standard rate?"

"Right."

He nodded as if condemning her and walked rather stiffly across to the double doors.

"You know," he said, "this is the first time I've been with you that I haven't wanted to fuck you."

"I'm glad," she said. "It's a start."

III

Some weeks later Jen flew to London on a plane that was almost empty. The Gulf War had cleared the skies over the Atlantic. She slept most of the way. Sleep now had become an addiction. Never in her life had she sought it out so frequently and held to it so tenaciously. Sleep had transformed the pale, drained woman Rudolf had found wanting. There was a new glow about her – not the glitter of the former Mrs Butterfield, something softer and less designer-produced. She had put on a little weight. Her exercise routine had been relaxed. She had begun to read and rummage around old furniture and new fashions. There was a fearfulness still, easily startled, and the knowledge of pain, which had to be carried and fed by attention, only to be eaten by memory. Sleep soothed it. But it was good pain, she thought, pain which would move her to the action needed to resolve it and lead her into clearer waters.

Clarity was what she sought now. Clarity about her present intentions, about her friendships and the disposition of her future life; above all about her past.

Once in the house she confirmed her meeting with Nicholas. She had briefed him about the foundation in a long call from New York and he was sufficiently interested. He had mentioned a special reason for seeing her which was mildly intriguing. It might, of course, have been a flirt to cheer her up. Nicholas was such a good friend. She had now decided that friendship mattered more than anything: it must be kept in good repair.

Mark was not in. She left a message on the machine. She was concerned about Mark. Despite her self-absorption she had picked up something new and worrying in his tone. She had neither the evidence nor the energy to tease it out. She would see to it over the next few weeks. Meanwhile she wanted him to advise her of a good private detective agency.

Perhaps because of the flight – although she had never suffered from jet lag – she found it difficult to settle. She had decided not to go to bed until late for fear of waking up – after the displacement – at the hour when Cally had often called her – mid-evening Pacific Time with the West Coast night threatening – middle of the night, the hour of least hope and resistance London time. If only she had understood how lonely Cally had been. If only she had realised that she represented all Cally's family.

She talked to her advisors. Numbers were always soothing.

Rudolf had paid back only a modest percentage of the money. More encouragingly, the first steps were under way for the establishment of what would be an immensely rich foundation. Her lawyers told her that Rudolf was waving the divorce negotiations through. But for his debt, everything was as it should be. But she felt restless.

Isabella had brought hot milk and Rich Tea biscuits. Jen tasted neither. She wandered about the house. The brothel bedroom puzzled and amused her: what on earth had that been for? Mark or herself, or some hopeless nostalgia? She did not blame Mark, indeed she had often missed his sensuality, but all this plumage? What she longed for now was a hug. A close, tight, everlasting hug and Mark was the only one who could satisfy that deep need.

At the very top of the house she came to the room in which Harry had slept. As she entered, the boy's presence quite suddenly and firmly possessed her. She sat down on the narrow bed, confused by the force of it. On the table beside the bed was a neatly folded, washed and ironed white handkerchief. It must be Harry's, she concluded. Isabella would have found it, washed it and for some reason thought that this was the appropriate place to put it.

Jen took the handkerchief and pressed it to her cheek and stayed there for a while. What would her own boy have been like now?

Twenty-Five

I

IT was on the evening of the second day that the two policemen
went for him. Until then, although he had been threatened, he
had not been molested. Rough handling, certainly, when they
had come to his home just after six in the morning and thrown
him into the van which took him to the stockaded police station.
No niceties in the station itself, where he worked out that he was
one of several Catholics arrested after the murder of a Protestant
shopkeeper. Colin was accused of having been a lookout.

He had been in the area at the time, he admitted that immediately. He was no more a lookout than a murderer and yet he felt
guilty: there was murder in his heart. He had continued his steady
saving. He had made three further phone calls, one a month, to
Mark's office, once speaking to him directly, saying quite simply,
as he said to the answering-machine, that Mark was a dead man.
He had dug up the gun one night and cleaned it and buried it
again. As the winter bit through Belfast his obsession hardened. It
seemed to Colin that his was an honourable cause. He was to take
vengeance for the assassination of a great man, as they never
ceased to tell him, a brother in a million; family. It was something
he knew he could do. It fed him with a deep joy.

When they came to get him in the cell he knew he looked the
part of the guilty man. There was even part of him that wanted
to claim – yes, he had been a lookout, he had been part of it, he
was one of the elect.

"We want a statement from you, you bastard, and we want it
now." They came in almost on the run.

The bigger one took his head and banged it against the wall.

"You were the lookout, weren't you, you little shit? Look at his face. Look at it. Plain guilt all over it. Bastard!"

Colin experienced the shocked delay of pain and then the pain itself. The man was pulling his hair, attempting to lift him off the ground by his hair. Colin yelled out and the other man slapped him hard across the mouth. He was released for a moment and then a foot hit his privates and pushed him against the wall. The man standing there, one leg pinning the terrified youth against the cell wall. The other man boxed his head with hard palms, never ceasing the talk.

"Tell us now and we'll see you all right. Hold him there. Who was in it with you? You're Tony's little brother – we didn't know that when we picked you up but we know it now and we know *you* now, little bastard brother, and you were in it up to your neck, weren't you? No good for any fuckin' thing else but he'll be a lookout, won't he? Cripple. And sneak around and let the men go in and do the dirty job, won't he? Stand forward – forward from the wall and up with your arms now, up with your arms, straight up. Stand there while we decide which bit of you to mutilate – not your balls, you won't have any, will you? Little lookout – brother Tony not here to look out for you now, is he? He was to scrape up, wasn't he? You'll be hard to recognise by your own mother, if you ever see her again when we're done. Now." He got out a pad. "Statement. C'mon. Statement."

Colin felt the thick sludge of blood running down his throat. He feared that he would choke. Was his nose broken? The back of his head ached so badly he shut his eyes. It was hard keeping the arms high above the head. Was the clammy feeling on his neck a spread of blood?

"I did no-no-nothing," he stammered. Then he heard himself sobbing. "I was out for a w-w-walk, nothing else, I swear it." His arms drooped.

"Up. Up. Up those lying arms, you lying bastard. Up! Up! So who was it who contacted you?"

"No-no-no-nobody contacted me."

"He's crying. He's bawling like a big wet baby. Where's your brother now, eh? Six feet down and that's not far enough for scum like him. So. Who was your contact? Up! Up!"

He told the truth because he was too frightened to lie, too shocked to make anything up. But they rejected his innocence. The sense of panic began to make him breathless. This was the truth.

271

This was all he had to say. What more could he say? He wanted to scream.

"Up! Up! Keep those arms high, you lying bastard. Up! Up! So. Who contacted you? C'mon. We know. We have the name. We have the place. We have all that we need to put you in H Block for life but if you make a statement it will go easier. It will go easier if you make a statement. So. Who was the contact?"

It went on. He felt his mind sink like lead and clench tight on the hatred he would later and surely express. The revenge he would take. The world he would surprise and shock: a world that now shocked him into baby whimpers and squeaks of agony.

He began to feel that he was floating. His arms and shoulders were cramped in pain and up, up, up, they had to be held. He tried to make his body click them off. He wanted them to be separate. Where was Tony? When he began to sway they pushed him upright. They made a game of it. Up! Up! Pushed from one to the other. He fell flat forward, cutting his face on the floor.

The doctor insisted he stay in the hospital for two days and two nights. Colin watched the clock all the daylight hours and through the night he sweated. They were sure to burst in on him. The doctor had said that they would not arrest him again. He had said that they realised he was telling the truth. Colin knew that he was lying. He said nothing. That's what Tony always said. Say nothing. And then – get the bastards. He would get his man. His vengeance was now poisoned with malevolence. Give him the guns and he would kill them all. All, all, the bastards! Tony was on his side. Tony had helped him to say nothing.

II

Mark was in Belfast during that week. He had gone there in an increasingly desperate attempt to find a clue to the problem which threatened his life and career.

There had been three more phone calls – one a month since December. All in the office. The one left on the answering-machine was clumsily, self-consciously dictated but resolute and un-equivocal.

The two Special Branch officers who had come to see him in London had been courteous. It could be a hoaxer. The country was full of them. He was on television: that made it worse. It could be a loony. Again – all over the place, place stiff with them. Harmless, most certainly. Or it could be the real business. In which case the only way was to track him down. Who was his enemy? Who was it likely to be?

Mark was unable to reply. The truth was – everybody and nobody. Not very satisfactory. Certainly nothing much to offer two young, sensible, fit security men idly dangling the mugs of coffee he had made them. He knew that Northern Ireland was riddled with information. Information in the Province was as rife as the corruption which swept down from the government quangos to the backstreets of West Belfast. Sometimes it could seem that everyone was on the radar. Yet even so, he had not yet found a lead who knew it well enough to root out this apparently isolated disturbance which was intent on his death.

The officers told him to take care. The local Bloomsbury station would keep a special eye on his block of flats. Not to travel in his own car. Try not to have a regular timetable, a routine, especially not predictable times of departure and arrival. Anything suspicious, let them know. If the calls continued, let them know anyway. He felt more edgy after they left than he had done before they arrived.

He would have loved someone to talk to. But Jen had withdrawn into isolation in America and, sweetly but firmly, she had dissuaded him from visiting her. Nicholas was abstracted, burning away at some scheme of his own over the boy, and also Mark did not want to appear alarmist. Nicholas, he was sure, would have brushed the threat aside, probably engaged the caller in conversation and flaunted himself.

Mark went to Belfast ostensibly to take stock of the overall position. It was a good time to do so. The Gulf War had subdued the Province somewhat and there was a sense of pause. After three or four days, Mark found the calm illusory. The prospects for the new peace talks seemed to generate a worrying optimism, almost guaranteed, he thought, to produce a backlash of violence. The individual gangs of extremists on both sides, it was reported, were more often than not out of control. The gory, intense, almost family warfare which Mark still – often to the amusement of his colleagues – raked in from the long past on the English–Scottish border – was increasingly dominant, he thought, and likely only to escalate. As socialism cracked in Eastern Europe and Russia, the ideological fanatical socialists at the core of the IRA vowed to continue their struggle. In this potent mix of great optimism and deepening entrenchment, Mark's enquiries seemed picayune, his anxieties simply off the map. No one knew anything.

Before he left for London, he met one of his most reliable contacts. The man tracked back the first call. He dredged up what had happened in the few weeks before that call: what Mark had done, what television had shown, what had occurred in Northern Ireland. It was a bit like consulting a shaman with his cowries, but out of it, he said, he had got a "sniff". It was serious. He advised Mark to keep clear of the place for a few months.

When he got back to London, there was a message from Jen and he went around immediately. They held each other close, standing, simply hugging, for a long time as if they needed to recharge each other.

"That's better," said Jen, eventually. Still with her arms around him, she leant back and examined what she saw. "You're tired," she said, "or down."

He smiled a little, trying to accustom himself to the difference in her. It was not the plainness of the make up or the slightly but noticeably fuller face. It was much deeper. There was something here he had never seen before.

"You've had a hard time."

"On the mend."

"Sure?"

"Oh yes."

They went across to the chairs beside the fire which murmured around the edges of large beech logs.

"Long time," he said.

"It was difficult."

With some relief she talked about Cally's suicide, about her own despair, the analysis, the idea about the foundation, the decision to divorce Rudolf. She did not expand much on her request for the name of a firm of private detectives. There was something she needed to find out, was all she said. In the context of a life which was being wholly reorganised, it seemed a matter of little consequence.

In turn, as she sipped at a spritzer and Mark took to claret, he puzzled out his mystery in Northern Ireland.

"But what do you think?" she asked.

"In the end," he paused: he was sure of his conclusion but he was a little embarrassed by its self-dramatising nature, "I think there is somebody out there who is determined to kill me. Whether he is competent, whether he is armed, whether he is serious enough to persist – I don't know. But at the moment, yes, there is some-body who wants to carve my initials on to a bullet. A lot of people live with that. Anybody who has been a minister in Northern Ireland lives with that."

"But they get protection."

"Even so."

"Do you have to go back there?"

"Do fish have to swim?"

"Mark. That's not like you. That kind of half-ass smart quip isn't you."

What he wanted to say was that he was besieged, quite over-whelmingly and intensely, by a feeling of almost unbearable loneli-ness, akin to the feeling which had penetrated him on that night walk in Edinburgh so many years ago. The feeling which work, conviviality, drink, anything but solitude had fought. Now it sud-denly occupied him. But how could he blurt this out? Everything in his past choked it back. More importantly, it was Jen who was finally responsible. For he knew, as surely as it was possible to know, that in some profound sense she had moved away from him.

"We could go to bed," she said, intuitively.

He shook his head. "You don't want to or you wouldn't ask like that."

Jen nodded and said, "It was so lovely – last autumn – when I was here. I thought I would never have that again."

"And now?"

"It's different. You know that. But if I love anybody, Mark, it's you. And I can't bear to see you so miserable." She tried to help him shake it off. "What's happening about the franchises and Rudolf and your man – Bagehot –?"

"Bagshaw. He's not so bad. I blew up about him but it isn't him. He's just one of those who can't help moulding himself to the shape required by those in authority over him. He's always been with us. He's the new-style civil servant, the pretend business-man, the programme-manager with not much of a clue about management, programmes, business or public service. He writes a mean memo."

"It sounds like his epitaph."

"The Bagshaw has to be circumvented. Circumventing takes so much time and effort one of the things about getting older is a growing sense of urgency. Young people are impatient. We are desperate."

"And Rudolf?"

"I think he may be deciding to pull out. It sounds great fun running your own television station but now he's seen some of the demands being made, he's not so sure. It's not a licence to print money any more – if it ever was. It will cost him another half million at least to trigger the deals and vet the offer document – and he has to agree to that within a few days. It will cost him time. And he might lose. The two companies he is going for are strong – perhaps not as strong as he is, but it is not a no-contest. And it is local. British. Our rules. Lots and lots and lots of rules. I may be wrong but I think he is irritated by that. I think he will pull out. We'll see."

"And you? What will you do?"

"I'll manage. I pulled out a fortnight ago."

"Why?"

"I want to stick to Ireland. If I can't go over there for some weeks – or months – then I can read about it and write that book instead of a couple of articles. I want to see it through. My life has been a fair old shambles – no complaints, self-inflicted wounds, all of them – but I am involved in this problem the way some people are involved in the Middle East, in the future of Russia, in the drug trade in Colombia – whatever. I've spent years on it and what I realised – while you were away – my mind a little concentrated no doubt by the death threat (first time I've said that aloud – the claret's working – no, you are) – was that the reporting could be the best part of my life. It's what I will have done. I want to go on trying to understand and explain why people in that little clump of the world, so many of them such lovely people, will assassinate and destroy without cease and so far resist all temptations even to take a small track that might lead to a road that might have peace at the end of it. And I'm bound up in it in other ways. I feel I know those men and women now. I have lived with them. What is it in their psychology, in their theology if you like, in their tradition which lashes on to this insatiable and so efficient destructiveness? How do the others, the non-players, cope? Where does all that hatred come from? How do they take their kids to school, sleep at nights, have a drink, go to a party, shop, walk, love each other? This voice that tells me it will kill me is bringing me into the middle of it all. Which is why we can't live together even if you wanted to. I want to see it through myself. But – to tell you some of the truth anyway – suddenly I thought – wouldn't it be good just to live with you? We could have such a life! You know that. I know that. But the thought was blacked out when I met you just now because the life I had dreamt of, to be honest, was not available. You don't want it." Jen knew that he was making a greater effort to speak his closest thoughts than he had ever done before and she wished she could have given him all that he wanted. But it was not possible.

"Not yet. Not yet. I have something to finish too before I can start again." She did not encourage him to question her.

"So that's my life – to end this true confession. And what luck, the chance to work on something important. There's the problem of getting stuff on the air and into print but I've managed that before and I'll take my chances. Frankly, there's a lot to be grateful for." He hesitated for a few moments. "I wish you loved me, Jen."

The sudden declaration moved her greatly. She stood up and held out her hand. He took it and followed her to a plain, spare bedroom. Her eyes had flooded again with that indescribable lazy search of desire.

It was the tenderness of old lovers.

III

When the man had gone, Colin went to his room and lay down to stop the shaking. The man had only been kind. He had been a friend of Tony's, he said, Tony was the number one. They knew he had been picked up and they knew he had said nothing. That was right, wasn't it? Of course it was. Tony's brother, say nothing. He could be trusted. They wanted him to know he could be trusted and they would be keeping an eye out for him in the next few weeks or months or so. For Tony's sake. No trouble. Keep up the struggle.

His hand was taken in a hard grip, the elbow also held.

They would be watching him.

TWENTY-SIX

RUDOLF made one of his fabled entrances. The door banged. A curse was hurled into the air. A secretary was bawled for. The jacket was torn off. The shirt wrenched loose at the collar. The whole pantomime most enjoyable and relished by all in the know. It was Rudolf playing with the biggest train set a boy had ever had – being Rudolf the Mogul.

Then he noticed Martha. What he took in was a plumpish smile, an ample, accumulating body and sheer black (as it turned out, stockinged) legs crossed, very shapely he thought, dimpled knees peeking out from the tight velvety feel-appeal plum-coloured skirt, and, Rudolf nodded approvingly, very serious tits, boobs, paps, he loved those words, bosoms.

He was a little drunk and somehow impressed. She was not beautiful or even pretty as others were in one of a hundred bid-dable or buyable ways. She would not look too good on the arm but there was some sort of oomph about her. He had been cheesed off throughout lunch by the worst of Alfreda's arcane English friends, aristos or poofs, the lot of them he reckoned, not a gram of oomph on offer.

Halfway through the lunch he had taken a call which had pre-dicted a positive move forward in one of the biggest deals of his career, a deal which would hit the headlines on every business page worth a Deutschmark – and he had come back into the room to listen to some terrible story about a wooftah ballet dancer and the least interesting member of the Royal Family. Although he wanted to explode with it, he kept his own news to himself. It was wasted on this lot. Alfreda had told him he had behaved badly and she would see him later. But she had let him go.

Raced back to his temporary HQ in Maugham's. Wanted, wanted, wanted the phone and the fax and all things fast and technological. And there she was. Ready to eat, he thought. To gobble up like a big cream bun, the sort you loved when you were a kid and everybody tried to stop you eating ever since. He wanted to go back to big cream buns. He could be on top again. He could be out of all this fragile furniture and posey paintings and Society. He sensed it and he just wanted to eat.

"I have an appointment," she said, looking at her watch. He was late. "For an interview. For the . . ." At the mention of the paper his memory was activated. It had been part of the campaign dreamt up by that PR ponce to deepen or widen – or whatever damn stupid word he used – his image in preparation for the franchise battle. His news was "Fuck the franchise". His public line was that he did not need it now. He would wait a couple of years and then move in and buy a station if he still felt like it. Why should he fill in all these balls-aching English Establishment namby-pamby do-gooding questionnaires and forms when the whole scenario would change soon enough and he could walk in and buy anything he liked without the fuss – only the clean and clear exchange of money?

Why not give her the story? Hell! Serve that PR ponce right – blow-dried, overcharging, oily-tongued barrow boy looking to brown-nose half the world for a title or an invitation to one of those stately homes that captured his sort and then spat them out.

"You wait here," he said. "I'll be back."

He gave her his most sharkish smile and thought he might have seen her somewhere before. Through in the next room he roared away, sending his secretary tumbling out with a scroll of imperatives, and then fell to silence as he checked and double-checked and treble-checked and Marnerly miserly counted over his present fortune again and again and again. It could be there! In which case he was *back*. This he would tell no one, he decided. This he would let hit the newspapers through the back door. This he would acknowledge, later, modestly but from a great height. Oh, a great height!

His secretary returned, he ripped through half a dozen faxes, declared himself out of action for a short time and swept Martha into yet another room – the anteroom to the master bedroom. Sit down. She wanted a drink? Good grief. Yes, Martha said, it was five o'clock.

"I can't believe you can behave like some caricature mogul and not burst out laughing at yourself," said Martha.

Rudolf burst out laughing.

"Cheeky bastard."

"Nobody behaves like that," she said.

"Cheers!"

"Cheers. Nobody."

"Depends whom you know . . ." He flailed for her name.

"*Martha*. We've met although I wasn't going to admit that."

"I knew I'd seen you. Never forget a face."

"Oh Christ!"

"Martha."

"Whom do you try to impress when you do that routine?"

"Me."

Now Martha laughed. She had not meant to. What he said was not particularly funny but the man's energy and blind boyish roller-coasting delight in himself was like a big wave: you surfed on it or you were knocked over by it.

"What happened today? Why are you so high?"

Rudolf was checked. She noted that. But there was no way, no way she could know.

"You're a clever girl."

"I'm a clever woman."

"I won a bet."

"You're a liar. It's more than a bet."

"Martha . . . ?"

"Yes. It's Martha. How many times do I have to tell you? Christ!"

"Names . . . I don't want this interview."

"I've waited for one hour and forty-five bloody minutes!"

"I don't need it."

"Thanks. I mean – shit!" She had been just about to start her tape.

"The world has moved on."

"I don't believe this. You talk like a burnt-out cliché as well."

"I am considering pulling out of the franchise race."

"So?"

"That's news. You don't need a tape for that. That's the interview."

"I'm not interested in that sort of news. I make people news."

"You can have first crack at the story."

"Keep it. I couldn't give a stuff about the franchises. Television!"

"I only agreed to this because of that."

"Do I get another drink or have we left licensed premises?" His PR had told her that he had agreed to the interview because of his admiration for her work – and she, stupidly she now thought, had swallowed it.

"I don't – that enough? OK – want an interview in your paper at this stage. Period. The world *has* moved on and if you think that's a cliché that makes you a writer and me a man who knows when the world has moved on. And maybe a man who helped it along – just a bit."

"That's the best thing you've said so far."

"This interview is over. Why don't you stay and we can have a drink? Off the record."

"Off the record" was a red rag to Martha. Lots of her best stuff had come from people foolishly saying "off the record" and then blurting out what, in all "conscience", she could not resist transferring into print. On temptation as on much else she agreed with Oscar Wilde. "Off the record" was her entrance to the local notoriety she craved and adored. If she wrote a book she would give it that title. If she had a television programme, she would give it that title. If she got a title she would find a way to anagram or echo or allude to "off the record". Nobody was ever off the record with Martha Potter: off the record was buried.

Then Rudolf put his hand on her knee. *On her knee!*

Martha looked down, as if some lump had fallen from the ceiling.

He squeezed. He squeezed so hard that she yelped and spilt her drink.

"So," he said. "How about it?" And glanced at his watch.

"*How about it?*"

"There's an empty bed through there and I'm roaring for it, Martha." He stood up.

As Martha finished her drink and her eyes looked longingly at the bottle for another, a considerable number of thoughts went through her head at very high speed:

She fancied him which is why she had fixed the interview. No point in being hypocritical
It looked as if he fancied her
That looked like a good bulge. Eye level. A growing bulge
She remembered her longing for his, well, arse, at the party which he had forgotten, months ago
Oh God she wanted a change

Tim, Timmy, Timmo was a sweet, loyal, undemanding husband to whom she had never been unfaithful

To her own astonishment

One more drink and she would be able to think straight

His behaviour, his language, his attitude, his very existence were everything she hated about men. He could be the sole cause and justification for feminism. He could be the only begetter of all the jock women in the West

Tim, Timmy, Timmo. Good taste. Domestic purity

Oh God! He was turning away and taking that terribly (was it real?) attractive thing with him

Would anybody ever find out?

It could be a personal commitment not an ideological surrender. It could be a way to steel herself for the greater battles to come. One bonk with Rudolf and feminism, which in truth had begun to go off the boil, Martha thought, and certainly ceased to be any fun, but after one bonk with Rudolf her feminism would be born again as fundamental and powerful as Islam.

He was in the bedroom. He was sitting on the edge of the bed tugging at his shoelaces and getting them into those tight, mean, nail-splitting little knots

Had he a condom?

Had she?

Look at *that*!

Could she use all this in the interview?

"Are you any good with shoelaces?"

It happened that she was. The call for help and the shoelaces took her into the bedroom where he was sitting on the edge of the bed and then – *she knelt at his feet*! Years of struggle and history had been wiped out in the last fifteen seconds. She tugged away and tugged away while his meat-feeling hand roughly but not untenderly moved about her hair – a little as if it were seeking small alien objects: but on the whole well meant.

"Well," he said, "that's the bloody shoes!"

She stood up. He looked up. Then he wrapped his arms around her bottom and pressed her to his face.

"This velvety stuff," he said, the voice was muffled – whether with emotion or the velvety stuff wasn't clear. The large hands had slithered around the large bottom. "Christ!" he said, twanging the suspenders, "the works!"

282

Was this a leader of men?

"Come here," he said and having pressed her to him, now crushed her to him. For a moment Martha thought that she might topple over him and nosedive into the bed but she managed to keep her balance.

As he mumbled and rubbed at her thighs she felt rather stranded, high above him. There wasn't anything constructive she could do, but she wanted him.

Suddenly he pushed her away, looked up with strain and effort deep on his face, and said, "I've got an erection like a power drill."

Even as the confession was being made he was heaving off his jacket, popping the buttons of his shirt, loosing his trousers, hopping around to tug off the eternally undignified socks, all watched with bemusement by Martha. Should she be flattered? Horrified? Excited? Somewhere else? At last, gasping with the effort, he was down to the tasteful regency-striped boxer shorts bought for him by Lady Alfreda.

"You've kept your clothes on," he groaned. "How did you know that's what I like?"

And then Martha was flat on her back on the emperor-sized bed and he was lying on top of her showing off the length and strength of his erection, his hands invading her clothes like Mongols looting a city. And suddenly Martha wanted him. Everything else had to be erased from the computer. She wanted him and she was honest enough to know that she wanted him for good – this was more than a fling – and she went for it.

First she took his penis which was in a dangerous state of imminent explosion and, using methods refined well before Timmo, she deflected its eruption while maintaining its erection. Delayed pleasure was practically unknown to Rudolf and he thought it was a sort of ju-ju.

Then she gorged herself on it – again, working him carefully so that he did not, yet, come. While he was in and out of her mouth and being teased and primped with her expert fingers, he pounded the bed with his arms like a wrestler wildly resisting submission to a most excruciating hold.

She left him alone for a few moments, took off her skirt and blouse and pants. Left on the rest of her carefully chosen underwear and a large loopy necklace which she then wrapped around him.

"Oh God," he said. "Oh God. Oh God. Oh God. Oh God!"

Having tied him up, she took one of his hands and guided it, accompanied by her own, into her vagina.

"Christ! It's bloody enormous," said Rudolf, reliably.

"Come on," said Martha. "Come *on!*"

Making a mould-breaking effort to give real attention to the other person in bed, surmounting a culture as stiff and trussed up as his own still erect and miraculously unspent member, he dug into her and found the juices sweet. She rode his hand, bent down and pressed her great breasts into his face and then unwound her necklace from him and slowly lowered herself down on to him like a very large and armoured medieval knight being lowered into the saddle. Once down she socketed in. Rudolf was held. She did not move. He waited. It was already way, way beyond his normal wham-bam time. It was virtually uncharted waters, because, although with Jen he had enjoyed it vividly, it had soon resolved itself into more of the same. Jen, in fact, seemed a bit like him after the first few weeks, just keen on banging away fast. And there had been call-girls but he had never felt comfortable or, more importantly, safe, with call-girls. This woman was serious and she was seriously asking him what he liked. Whether he liked that. Or that. And listening while he tried to scramble together a reply.

Then she began to drive down on to him.

This time he yelled aloud. He was so deep inside her it hurt, but he did not want it to stop hurting. She grunted like a man and he heard his own grunts, grunting echoes of the primitive battle as he started the inevitable move which heralded his ejaculation. But he was trapped. She drove on, down and up, down and up and there was roaring in his ears. He roared aloud, he came hard and it hurt but, twist as he could, Martha would not stop and, for a moment or two, the pain razored his mind and then passed . . . and still he would not stop and still he was hard, erect as a guards-man, at attention inside her as she strove for her climax and again took his hand, guiding it to her clitoris, and he understood! It was a moment of love. He made love to her. When she came, clawing at him, gasping, unco-ordinated, blubbering, helpless, he was proud of himself. And he stayed inside her. No rolling away. No race for the shirt. Not even a glance at the watch. That was the most surprising thing of all.

They dozed.

She went next door for the bottle, took a swig out of it and passed it across to him. He swigged too, vaguely remembering that bohemians and students did this. Then he looked closely at her.

There was a lot of Martha just as there was a lot of him. The bum was a bus end but so was his. The boobs were hefty but they suited the black bra. The belly was not as lardy as his own but there were serious comparisons. He was deeply happy with her. She was slaggy and homely. She was a relief. And she had done things to him already that nobody had done with much enthusiasm ever, not even Jen at the hopeful beginning of their time. Things that he knew now that he wanted and wanted to do again and enjoy more and more.

Martha too saw his bare, over-big, inelegant, strong, hairy body and saw nothing wrong with it. Rather there was pleasure in both their sumo acres, a sympathy with the bulk and wobble of flesh, an understanding of the complete impossibility of "keeping in shape" and simultaneously staying sane or cheerful. Unselfconsciously and then flagrantly they stretched and lolled their bodies over each other, gambolling – in slow motion – heavy-happy and each feeling that a secret had been cracked. Lovely liberated flesh, and lots and lots of it. At last! To be enjoyed.

Rudolf was overwhelmed with this sense of liberty. He had still not looked at his watch. He had finally decided not to leap up and rush for the office. He was swigging at the wine and somewhere in the hinterland of his groin he felt the head lift, the scent quicken, the promise that more could be on the way.

Martha grasped him firmly and then hard. She rubbed her half-clad body against him. She held him gently underneath. He half sat up and put a pillow behind his head so that he could look down on this cultivator of delights. He searched for the *mot juste*. It had to be appreciative: "Best interview I've ever had?" Too flippant, perhaps. "This is the second jump start I've made today?" Somehow, not quite right. Martha suddenly went into action. He flung back his head, banging it on the pillow and said it.

"Oh God. Oh God. Oh God. Oh God. Oh God!"

It was at that point that Alfreda walked in.

She paused for no more than a blink.

"How embarrassing," she said, quite loudly enough, and clearly.

Martha's face, scarlet with effort, swivelled around instantly like a puppet's head.

"Oh God," said Rudolf, who saw Alfreda but could not, would not, break Martha's spell. "Oh God. Go on! Go on!"

With a mimed look of apology, Martha turned back to him and plunged on.

"How disgusting," said Alfreda, and left with great dignity, closing the door quietly and firmly behind her.

Twenty-seven

I

THE announcement that he would not stand for re-election was the last item on the *Nine O'Clock News*. It was as brief as could be. A photograph showed a much slimmer-faced Nicholas ten years ago. Jen switched off the television.

"I'm still not convinced."

"There was no alternative."

"It said in the *Standard* that you were in line for a good job with the new lot."

"Perhaps." He paused.

"Sad?"

"Yes. A bit. Remembering why I went in. The things I wanted to do. The little I have done. There are people I'll miss."

"You can see them socially."

"Oh – politicians, yes. I rather meant the people in the constituency."

"Can't you keep your house there?"

"Perhaps. It'll be someone else's patch soon. We'll see."

"So there's nothing at all to stop you taking on my foundation."

"Let me think about it."

"What else will you do?"

Nicholas reached out for the gin – not his usual evening drink but it seemed an occasion which permitted one or two gestures.

"What most bothers me is whether Harry is thinking I've abandoned him."

"He'll have received your gifts – she couldn't exactly send them back."

"She could."

"She wouldn't. The two letters you showed me suggested to me that she knows she overstepped the mark and wants you back on almost any terms."

"It has to be my terms. For his sake."

"Still feel the same?"

"Oh yes. It'll never change." He hesitated. "Just as the love I feel for you will not change. Or for Mark. They are different from each other, of course, and both are different from what I feel for Harry." He paused and spoke with unusual intensity. "One of the penalties with regard to Harry is not being able to see it in any way publicly acknowledged as a legitimate feeling. I suppose that makes me believe that the feeling is outlawed. More than that – it's unacceptable. It's illegal. It's dirty. It's obscene. It's evil. Yet it's the finest feeling I have ever known. What I feel for him is chaste, it is loving, it wants to look after him – and Mary, and she is no makeweight; she is there because she is like him. This love wants to do the practical loving things like seeing he gets a good education, eats his breakfast, plays fair, has manners, speaks truthfully – as well as just wanting to be near him more than I want to be near anyone else on earth. And I think about men and boys in our literature, and I think about the boys sent away to court and into battle and ask if all of them were – 'corrupted' is the word. All of them?

"And do all those fathers who are clearly – I can see it in some of their eyes now, I can see it in the streets – clearly in some sort of love with their sons – are they corrupting them? Yet I have to live under this threat. To get what I want, which I think, I believe, is good for the boy, I have to deceive and manoeuvre and manipulate and be manipulated. Certain sorts of love automatically receive censure and sometimes you have to ask why. I'll not have the courage but someone will some time soon. And will he be supported by all those who know what he is talking about but fear for their own reputations if they admit it? I doubt it. So what I have to do is find a way which is good for him and lets me have the minimum: to see him cared for and to see him, if only now and then." He sipped at the gin and Jen poured some more.

The room was silent but for the flickering fire. They could have been in the deepest forest. "What I've done over the past few months – and this ties in, curiously enough, with your foundation – is to look around at what we are doing to our kids. Not to the well-off or even the moderately well-off, but to those who need

help. It's hard to believe we're not breeding a substantial generation of addicts, thieves, emotional criminals and wholly streetwise
anarchists.

"I met this man who calls himself Deuce. He was in charge at
that hotel I went to – you remember that. Well, he's alerted one
of the tabloids – I'll be surprised if there isn't the sniff of a story
out soon – 'The real reason for de Loit's resignation' – *che sera*.
But I sought him out. I'd given in to Fiona's blackmail – mild
though it was, it deserved the name – but this man . . . I wanted
to tell him that he could do his worst. He doesn't want to do that
– to accuse me publicly would be to ruin himself – but he was
working out a grievance and I thought that if I saw him and, as it
were, stared him down – he could see that there was nowhere to
go. He reminded me of that afternoon in the hotel – the intolerable
compound of feelings, so bad, so good.

"Anyway we met – he blustered a little. I suspect I blustered a
little. He looked uneasy but I suspect so did I. I asked him where
he got the boys – of course he thought I was seeking information
for my own purposes – which was true in a way – or for the police
– which ought to have been the case. So he said nothing – just
'They are much better off than where they come from'. Where did
they come from? From the provinces, from the Borstals? No, he
said, from everywhere, for instance from just down the road. From
Southwark.

"I followed that up. I contacted someone I know in the force and
asked about Southwark and went to Southwark. Just across from
St Paul's. Almost up to Waterloo Station. Chaucer country. Shakespeare's Globe Theatre. Blackfriars and the neighbour of the City.

"Southwark is a warren of drug routes run mainly by thirteen-
and fourteen-year-olds *for* thirteen- and fourteen-year-olds. The
handlers are older. The big bosses might be any age, even my age,
you never see them, they never touch the stuff. But in Southwark,
around the estates, there are boys with a £250-a-day habit. There
are other boys on mountain-bikes zipping down the side-alleys,
hopelessly outrunning the police, delivering crack to the pubs.
There are fences who make Fagin seem a relatively harmless old
man. To feed their habit – the boys – it is mostly boys – steal.
They say that ten car stereos a day can feed a big habit. So ten car
stereos a day it is. They'll ring the police station and report a crash
in the south of the borough – say around the Elephant and Castle
– and the police will roar down there – they know there's a limited
number of police on patrol – and, while they're in the south, the

boys will do the north – cars, flats, shops, offices. If they're high they'll just smash everything as well. £20,000 computers – a hammer goes through the screen.

"And by the time they're seventeen they're old men. Their parents don't know most of the time, I was told, and they don't believe it when it finally comes home. Out there I've found a world suddenly – as it seems – hostile to everything I want a boy to have. There may come a time when governments and councils tackle it head on – but what happens until then? The church has lost its Sunday School attendance – vanished in just over a generation – and we have to concede that those schools may have helped. The social workers, rightly, devote themselves largely to the victims. What about the growing underground army of the predators? Why should they stop in Southwark? Why not, some time soon, march across the bridges and through the squares up into Bond Street and Oxford Street and Regent Street and loot the shops which keep no more than a plate of glass between themselves and what another plate of glass promises them and urges them to buy every day and night of the week?

"So where are the fathers in Southwark, Jen? Meanwhile – there's Harry. And Mary. And a private life to be lived. I want to and I will do something for as many of those children as I can – but you see how tainted I am. How suspect. Like all scoutmasters are now suspect, all vicars who take choirboys out for a day's walking on the hills – 'the finger of suspicion' – you remember that song? – points all the time at men who not so long ago were admired as selfless, public-spirited people. That was not all it seemed, of course, but nor is this wholesale condemnation by association.

"I would like to help those lost boys in Southwark, but I know, in our present state, that the odds are I will be hounded for my pains. I want to give Harry a life he could value, a life of value and I know that for that I could and quite likely would be pelted as a pederast. But I am not a pederast, Jen! You know that. I am a man who has enjoyed very little love from anyone and even that chiefly unhappy. I want to have his hand slip in mine, to observe and experience – sometimes, not always – the sense of welcome when I arrive, however momentary, I don't care – sadness when I leave – and to know that I would never harm, never hurt him in any way. Yet I risk seeing myself banned and potentially vilified, perhaps about to be put in the public stocks of cheap print, quartered in the name of purity and in the pursuit of readers and sensation, money and greed. So, my dear Jen, so, you offer me the opportunity to direct your foundation which could be a mighty instrument of change. I offer you the chance to adopt Harry and Mary."

Jen, who had been intent on what Nicholas said, recognising throughout the pulse of trust and love for her which let him unload what was clearly – even within his reserved sentences – a terrible weight on his mind and spirit, was shocked.

"Adopt?"

The word popped out, inadequately.

"There are two or three variations, but let 'adopt' stand in for them all. Adopt."

"And you?"

"I would hope to be around," he said. "With your permission."

"Don't be silly." Jen was so taken aback that Nicholas sensed that he had unexpectedly penetrated deeply.

"I would certainly be prepared to consider it," she said, finally. "But not yet. There is something about my own life that I have to settle, Nicholas. I have to. Until I do that I can be relied on for nothing much except pushing money around and organising things. Certainly I can't take on anything as important as what you are suggesting."

"How long?"

"I have to give myself as long as it takes."

"That may be too long."

"I'm sorry. I am sorry."

"I know. Is this . . . ?"

"Please believe me."

"Of course. I meant – is this something I can help you with?"

"I don't think so. It's something I have to find out first. And then see if I can face up to it."

"I knew the plan was too perfect," said Nicholas. "Sorry. That's too near self-pity."

"It could still happen."

"That's the really maddening thing about it. It could. But – never mind. You must have been through the mill with Cally. And then whatever it did to you – a lot I would guess." Jen nodded. "And you don't want to talk about it."

"Not yet."

"Not yet." He reached out and poured himself another glass. "I suppose this is as good a time as any to tell you, at last, that if nature had deployed my constitution, my hormones and my genes marginally differently and if I had been possessed of the energy and talent to win your affection – as they say, did they ever say that? – then I hope I would have sweated blood for it because of all the women I've known you are the only one I could say I love." He raised his glass.

Jen was moved. She could have shown it in a way which was somehow falsely modest, she could have taken his tone and pushed it the very short distance to sentimentality. She could have acted in many ways which would have been ultimately self-serving. Instead of which she got to her feet, went over to him, kissed him hard on the cheek, held him tight and said, "I'm taking you out – now – for the best meal you've had in London for years. Give me five minutes and easy on the gin. I want to start at the beginning. We'll celebrate your freedom from Parliament."

II

Harry swerved wildly. The front wheel slammed against the kerb and the weight of the bag of newspapers threw him to the ground. The car sped on, whoops and cries from the open windows signalling another joyride, another car stolen by the estate kids and driven on the brake and the accelerator to perform stunts for the estate community. He had banged his knee and the sick feeling in his mind made him dizzy. There were few working street-lights on this part of the estate and the dark emptiness – once the car had vanished – rather disturbed him. He had only taken on the evening round to build up his savings. Fiona and Jake were making him frightened. Mary's hostility was provoking Fiona further by the day.

He went up the paths and stuffed the tubes of print into the letter boxes. Sometimes, learned by now in the ways of the dogs, he just threw them at the door. Some of the gardens were well stocked and he could smell the first scents of spring. Now and then from the burnt-out boarded-up houses would come threatening sounds which tightened his stomach. Yellow lights behind drawn curtains as far as he could see. He was always pleased when the last paper was gone and he could flee on his wonderful bicycle back to the main road to give up his paper bag, buy a packet of crisps, ride back easily, no hands, while he ate them. His knee still hurt.

Jake and Fiona were having another row. Jake, Harry concluded, was on his way out. Whatever he did, it was not good enough and he was no match for Fiona. He kept threatening her, but until now she had always stared or shouted him down. This time Harry sensed a difference. Jake was well drunk, although it was early in the evening. Fiona was bitingly sober. Harry was instantly enrolled.

"You made me do the dirty work, didn't you?"

"Shut your face. Harry – get upstairs!"

"Stay here!" Jake grabbed the boy by the collar and pulled him into the kitchen. "You stay just there, Harry – you should hear this."

"Keep your bloody hands off that boy."

"Oh. Oh! Listen to her. She's the one wanted me to lose you in London, Harry. You ask her. You ask her."

"You're drunk. You don't know what you're saying."

"Don't I? Don't I? Harry knows – don't you? Harry knows I'm telling the truth. Didn't I try to lose you? Didn't I?"

Harry knew that he had to say nothing. Only by saying nothing could he keep from being hurt. He tried not to catch the glare of either of them. He had learnt that, too.

"Let the boy go upstairs. His sister wants to see him."

"Oh no you don't! His sister said nothing about him. Why d'you bring his sister into it? Because you want rid of her as well, that's why." Jake opened yet another can of lager. "That's why." He gurgled it down. "Because you don't want to hear the bloody truth which is you hated him so much, you hated him so much you sent me in the van to London to get rid of him. It was your idea, bitch, all of it was your bleedin' idea."

Harry knew that Jake was telling the truth. He screamed silently to himself to get out, but stayed, frozen. It was going to get worse. He had to pretend he was not there.

"He's drunk, Harry. I never hated you. He's just pitiful. He's useless, that's why he's pitiful. Look at him, dribbling down his chin. Near falling down. No use to no woman – get out! Get out, you bastard, I've had enough of you, anyway. Leave me with my family."

"Family! Family. Ha. It's only because of the old poof, isn't it? And you chased him off because you were so bloody greedy and so fucking stupid and such a bloody cow, weren't you?" Harry felt a stab of relief.

"You've a mouth like a lavatory."

"Otherwise why'd he go? He couldn't do enough for Harry but you didn't want that, did you? No, you wanted money, money, money, didn't you?" He drank another deep draught, which finished the can. Another was opened immediately. A cigarette was very clumsily lit. "Bitch!"

"I want you to go out of this fuckin' house now."

"Who'll make me?"

"You'll go."

"You and whose army?"

"You'll get nothing from me again, Jake, not a sniff. Not a touch. I'll have you up for rape first."

"Call the police then. Go on. Call them." He drank more. "Ha!"

"Harry. Go out and get me some help from next door. Just say – Fiona needs some help. They'll understand. They know what I've had to put up with."

"You? You? You're the one wanted rid of him. Don't you deny it. You're the one spent all the money he got left in that will. You're the one won't let him go to Derry to see that aunty school-teacher because you know she'll find you out. Don't make me laugh. Ha! Don't make me laugh!"

"Harry!"

The boy gathered himself and then edged towards the door. Jake's arm shot out across his chest. Harry looked at the glistening tattooed butterfly.

"Leave the boy alone."

"He'll not leave this house without my say-so." Jake spoke quietly. The sudden drop in his voice scared Harry even more. The tone was thick, almost a growl.

"I'll leave it then."

Fiona moved around the table and made for the door. Jake let her open it and then grabbed her hair, pulled her back cruelly, and slammed the door hard.

Fiona turned on him, her nails going for his face, her shoes for his shin. Jake held her off for a few seconds, seconds perhaps of regret or of the last remnant of chivalry, and then he smashed the lager can into her face. She staggered back, picked up the half-empty bottle of milk from the table and, faster than he could defend, cracked it down hard on his skull. The milk splashed down his face. As he surged forward, she hit him again. The sound was sickening. But Jake reached out and grabbed her arm. With his other hand he simply slammed out at her, hitting everywhere, face, neck, shoulders, breasts, stomach.

Harry pressed himself against the wall, waiting for any opening he could find. The yells from Fiona electrified the house. Jake just kept hitting her until she was on her knees and then on the floor

– blood and milk all over her. "Please Jake," she kept saying, less and less loudly. "Please Jake. Please Jake." He was captured in a vice of oblivious, violent rage. Hit her. Hit her. Hit her.

The banging came from their front door. Fiona looked across to Harry, her eyes both weary and imploring. She was utterly defenceless. Harry levered himself from the wall, wriggled out into the hall, opened the door and was pushed aside by three of their neighbours.

"He's killing her."

"They can hear it a mile away!"

"Grab him! Get the bastard!"

Jake kicked and struggled but only half-heartedly. These were three men who had every justification for beating him, which they would have enjoyed and he knew it. Besides, his venom was spent. Fiona was on the floor. Her face a terrible mess. One of the men helped her up.

"I'll get the lasses to come round."

"Steady now."

"Bastard. You bastard!"

Fiona whispered to one of the men who sat her on the chair.

"Out!" He jabbed at Jake. "She says 'out'! And don't come back. Out! And don't show your face here again!" He prodded Jake with a blunt forefinger. Grinning hideously, bloodied hands, Jake lopsidedly made his exit. At the door he turned and pointed at Harry. He still grinned but now the expression became vindictive and sinister.

"You," he said. "You!"

The boy's face was consumed with fear. Jake laughed and banged the door exultantly behind him. Harry felt that he would never be safe again as long as he lived.

III

"I don't know anyone who could help . . ." said Mark. "Maybe . . ." He paused. They were in his flat which always seemed rather scruffy when Nicholas turned up. "There's Fred's daughter – Dorothy – she would know people . . ."

"It isn't strangers I want," said Nicholas, who had met the high-minded Fred but not his cause-espousing daughter, "though I suppose, if it came to it, I would have no option."

294

"Dorothy's a very nice, an admirable young woman – helps other people, worried about the planet, a bit comical to some, but . . . fine. I saw them both last week: she's a very decent young woman."

"I hope she has better sense than father Fred."

Martha's article had been largely uncomplimentary. Fred had featured prominently as the frank old friend and talked about Mark's self-doubts, anatomised his intellectual limitations and spun out his recollections of Mark's worst moments, the first divorce, the subsequent depression, the drinking, the failures. As he had said on the telephone the next morning – he could only tell the truth. He assured Mark that he had told her much more but she had only chosen the negative side.

"Fred's not to blame," Mark said. Nicholas reached across, smiled, and tapped his arm.

"Have you any notion of Jen's – preoccupation?"

"None."

"In some ways she's changed a lot," Nicholas said. "I've been trying to work it out. It isn't as if she's gone back to being the old Jen or rather the young Jen we met – twenty years ago? More? Dear God. And it isn't that she's emerging as a different figure altogether. One mustn't overemphasise it. But what it is, I know not. Of course there was Cally. And she went back into analysis. I'm still not quite sure about all that."

"Yet she can still sometimes appear to be the same."

". . . No . . . Even the eyes have changed a little – have you noticed? They're not as perpetually demanding."

"I feel that I've lost her," said Mark.

"I don't think so. It's an obsession. Something matters to her so very much that she dare not or she will not reveal it."

"What will you do?" Mark reverted to the question which had prompted Nicholas's visit.

Nicholas hesitated.

"I think I ought to see him again. Otherwise he's bound to think I've just abandoned him. It's not much good and I'm not proud of myself but I'll have to pay the Danegeld. Until I come up with something I can't just walk out on him."

"It can't work out like that."

"I know."

"Your sister just won't . . ."

"Can't."

"And you . . ."

"If I went for the guardian role – even if the local authority countenanced a homosexual, one word from Fiona about the hotel, one call, and I'd be hounded out of the country. More importantly, Harry would be thrown to the jackals. But I've got to get him out of there, Mark. The world is closing in on those kids and at least I can help one of them – him."

"The foundation?"

"Most likely, yes. I want to settle this first. But yes – it could help. Once again, though, I could be suspect. But that foundation could change a lot."

"There must be somebody . . ." said Mark.

"There are times when you wonder if you really know and really trust more than a couple of people in the whole world." Nicholas smiled, quite unexpectedly. "Thank God for you, say I."

"You're going back to see him then?"

"Yes."

Mark raised his glass.

"Good luck."

IV

The bus left at ten o'clock in the morning. Fiona would think they were at school. Harry told the man they were going to their aunty's in London for a special treat. He put them at the front near the driver. Both of them were wearing the clothes Fiona had reluctantly bought them out of Nicholas's money.

It would get into London Victoria at three-thirty. They would still have plenty of light to find Jen's house. Harry had copied down the address including the postcode. He would ask at the other end. London was full of buses.

Mary was bright-eyed with excitement. She sat very still but Harry could feel the excitement. He was going to look after her. He had twenty-one pounds and fifty pence over.

When the engine started up they looked at each other, suddenly frightened.

Part Five

A SEARCH FOR THE PAST

Twenty-Eight

I

THE arrival of Harry and Mary startled her. Isabella brought them into her study rather proudly as if Harry had been drawn back by the particular sweetness of her hospitality. She had long ago come to the conclusion that the house of Mrs Lukas and the life of Mrs Lukas were strange and unpredictable matters. Two children appearing on the doorstep at dusk seemed perfectly in order. She left them and went to the kitchen to make hot chocolate and boiled eggs. Jen remained seated. Although she felt an instinct to go over and hug Mary and Harry, who stood before her, the shock she experienced immobilised her.

Harry was smiling — that lovely smile — quite confidently. She took his confidence as a compliment and was grateful. Mary fascinated her. That quiet old-fashioned grave look — or was it defiant? — the level gaze in the eyes. Standing close to Harry but as much his protector as his dependent. Over the next two or three days, Jen was to be deeply drawn to the two children, discovering the despair behind Harry's smile, the spikiness in Mary's character. But their survival was impressive.

It seemed to her that in the memory of their dead mother they had found a power which preserved them, keeping them younger than their years in some ways, wiser in others. Most of all her death and the subsequent trials with Fiona and her lovers had reinforced their sense of being a tiny republic which must stay independent to survive.

Haltingly, his confidence evaporating with the breath of every word, Harry explained that they had run away. When questioned as to the reason for this, he fudged it. Jen guessed, correctly, that he would not be drawn into detail and her affection for him grew even then: it was a curious loyalty, but she respected it. Mary was silent. Jen thought that the girl might speak more readily than her brother but not in front of him. Jen did not want to challenge them. The hope and even joy with which Harry had set eyes on her were threatened by fear. Now she did go across to them, hugged them – finding Mary stiff in her arms – told them everything would be all right and delivered them to Isabella in the kitchen.

Harry looked around proudly and kept glancing at his sister, wanting her to share in his appreciation. Mary refused to react to such direct requests but when she knew he was not looking she squirrelled away her impressions. So many folds in the curtains! Paintings on all the walls. Carpets on top of fitted carpets. Everything so comfortable and everything so posh. Even the kitchen was big and somehow a furnished place with lovely cupboards and a fridge as tall as she was . . . Mary took it in very carefully. She had followed Harry's plan because she had sensed the pain inside him and she too had been scared after the fight between Jake and Fiona. But they had never turned on her in quite the way they had turned on Harry; and they did not frighten her as much as they frightened Harry. Harry would get into a state and say things like he wanted to be dead, he hoped he never woke up, and she knew he meant it. She was not like that. She just hated them. The man who came now and then with presents would cheer Harry up but Harry had gone very quiet about him lately. After the row, though, he had started to talk about him again – and the lovely woman. He was sure she would take him in, take both of them in . . . and she had.

Mary had found it difficult to look directly into the woman's eyes. They seemed to look right through you. And when she had touched her, she couldn't bear it.

Harry looked so contented at the kitchen table. He sat there, smiling, glancing around, answering all Isabella's questions, offering to help. He had pulled it off. They had changed at Victoria and caught another bus and the conductor had put them down nearby. Harry had no more plans and no more stamina. His smile was the last energy he had. He knew that she would take him in. He knew it. If she tried to send him back . . . he would never go back. He would just run: it was all worked out. Just run away for ever.

300

Nicholas was in the House. Jen left a message with his secretary. Mark was out – Prue was not sure where. Jen wanted to contact Fiona immediately – to demand an explanation, to give vent to the gusts of fury which swept through her, to tell her – not that she deserved to know! – that the children were safe. She schooled herself to wait for Nicholas.

Jen was very touched to see the manner in which Harry and Nicholas greeted each other. It was casual and yet intense. Nicholas stayed in the kitchen with Harry while Jen took Mary into the sitting-room. She felt absurdly formal with the little girl and somehow on trial, as if the conversation were a test which she could not fail. Mary sat dwarfed in the armchair next to the fire, her head inclined to the floor. Only by the sort of effort she had never had to make did Jen lift the small girl's head, as it were, introduce her to the things in the room, claim her attention. She was a controlled little creature with a habit of pausing markedly and calmly before each answer, which made Jen grieve that already she had been forced to learn the manoeuvres of appeasing the powerful adult. She wanted to hug the slim little girl but remembered the stiff resistance which had met her earlier effort and decided against it. Besides, she was confused about her own motives.

An hour or so later, the children were still being bossed around by a happily overactive Isabella and Nicholas and Jen sat down to talk.

"I can see even more clearly now what a remarkable boy he is," said Jen.

Nicholas glowed. "Isn't he? Isn't he?"

"And Mary . . ." Jen paused. "She quite . . . disconcerts me."

"She's every bit as remarkable as he is," Nicholas said briskly. "There must be thousands like them – fine kids needing no more than a bit of help or a break. Good kids too. A very firm moral sense despite so much going against it."

Jen nodded. She did not want to dwell on them too deeply just yet. Her own thoughts were in too much confusion. The arrival of Harry and Mary had finally steeled her to pursue the course she had avoided for so long. She would set off within the next few days. No more hesitation. No coward soul.

Between them, they pieced the story together.

"You must phone," Nicholas said. "She will be suspicious of me and try her old tricks and I'm not reliable there, I'm afraid. I've made a hash of it and – no. You have to do it. She's intrigued by you. Whatever Harry told her about you and this house has alerted her. I'm pretty sure she knows all about you. She's nobody's fool. And you're not compromised."

"What should I say?"

Nicholas shook his head.

"I have nowhere to go. I'm no help," he said. "I have no cards but the old cards, and they didn't work."

"Even if I could, even if I wanted to, I can't, I just can't adopt or whatever, not yet. Maybe never. I don't know. Looking at them reminds me . . ." She tailed off. "It's just very strange," she said. "I don't understand it myself. Perhaps, when I do . . ."

"We can't just put them on the next bus back."

"We may have to."

"Oh no. Harry would never get over that. It's difficult enough as it is for him to believe anybody cares for him at all. Besides, Fiona would love you to keep them for a few days. That would give her leverage."

"Is she really such a witch?"

"She's one of those people who stumble into wickedness."

"What do I ask for?"

"Ask if they can stay for a week or so. Say you'll see that they go to school locally if necessary, although the holidays are coming up quite soon. Don't say anything about me unless pressed . . ."

"What will you do?"

"I don't know. Find out what can be done. Have a last throw. He, they both, need to be rescued."

"I have to go away, Nicholas. I can stay for a couple of days to settle them in but then I have to – I have to go away."

"For how long?"

"A day or two – less than a week. Isabella can cope."

"I would visit them every day."

"Nicholas?"

"I know it could be dangerous but I will be careful. And a week for me, Jen, is – is gold." It was a plea and he took no pains to conceal it.

"Give me half an hour to think it through and then I'll phone."

When Jen made the call, she was cool, direct, and unthreatening. The children might have just strayed in from around the corner. She would be happy to send them back immediately but they seemed rather unsettled and might benefit from a few days' change . . . it was all agreed, even charmingly.

Fiona's acquiescence resulted from a mixture of being fearful and being flattered. And there was bound to be money at the bottom of it. The MP would be seeing the children again. Maybe it was time for herself to take a trip to London to confront him again and, while she was about it, meet this rich and beautiful lady.

II

Despite all her promises to herself, Jen put off the departure for one last day which she spent with Nicholas and the children on a switchback tour – the Science Museum, Harrods, a Pizza Express, the cinema . . . She saw Harry's sudden clutches at the hand of Nicholas and began to understand from that the reservoir of devotion, the desperation that it would be denied. Mary grew – just a little – in trust; Jen was wary and watchful.

She drove north in a hired, unostentatious car. Her clothes were equally unremarkable. As the names on the signs came towards her, she felt sick, and, at one stage, drew into a service station not for fuel or food but to get out of the car and walk. Deep breaths. The air was cold, late snow still clinging to the fields, patched white puddles of it – an early spring aborted. She drew into the city while it was still daylight but, by the time she had checked into the hotel and turned the car towards the small town, dusk was thickening.

Dusk suited the town she sought. Once a coal-mining centre, its industry had been removed from it and the jerry-built sentry lines of cottages stood at attention, in battle order, but the campaign had moved on. This place, this hilly windswept hard-rocked place, these few rivulets of brick petering out into ghost shafts, slag heaps and then the sudden open heart of woods and countryside, had been the buried terror of her life. Perhaps its dynamo. But now, it was a deep and secret burden which had to be excavated and examined and cast out.

She was through the town in minutes.

It could not be that small. She circumnavigated a Tom Thumb roundabout and drove back into the town, as slowly as she could. It was now about six-thirty in the evening, a weekday, and the main street was as empty as if there had been an air-raid warning. The dim yellow light from the fancifully decorated pubs suggested an intimacy from which she withdrew. As far as she could see, every single shop had some form of SALES poster slashed across its window. She turned the wheel and let the car drift down the brick back-to-back canyons, the low yellow light softly strobing her face.

The place should have more impact than this, she thought. It *has* to have more impact than this.

At the bottom of one of the rivulets was a little islet of a terrace seemingly cut off from the rest of the hill-swarmed settlements. Here she stopped, turned off the engine, turned off the lights and simply looked. She had thought that so much would instantly leap out at her. She had hoped for that. She had wanted such an engagement. She was sure that she was ready for it.

But nothing came.

Yes, that was the house – it was the correct address. That end house. Could she remember? Was she imagining it or was this image still somewhere in her mind? Did the house look the same? The house looked the same.

The street-lights would be different – about forty years ago? – Or would they? Why could she not remember more clearly? Her feelings had been so clear – why was the actual place not helping her more? Her feelings were less clear now than they had been in New York. Why was that? A tremor of panic began in the terrified roots of consciousness. She had to repel it. She wound down the window. Took deep breaths – held the breath as she had been taught. Why was it not more clear? That was the house. The end house. The same.

What if someone came out of it?

(What did that matter?)

And came up to her and asked her what she was doing?

(What would she say?)

What was she doing?

(Is this when people prayed?)

Did she want a face to appear in the dark? Oh yes. That face, that loved and ravaged face: and that other face, that loved and grave, innocent face – yes, she wanted those faces to appear in the dark. She had come to find those faces. She had run and run from those faces all of her life since then, and put all the miles and matter she could invent between herself and those faces, but they had to be rediscovered or she would not be able to live any life at all. They had not been given their due. She had simply run. Spurned them and cast them off and yet those images were the

most essential and the dearest she had. The darkness was un-
broken. A car engine started up.

Abruptly she turned on her own engine and headed back to the
city.

But the next morning she was once more in the town. A long
call to the agency she had hired to help her had keyed up her
anticipation even more highly, but she did not quite know what
to do.

She had come to this place to face a death and find a life.
She had come to make amends. To make her peace. To let the
untouchable part of her heart be touched, if necessary assailed.

But in the daylight the numbness persisted. If anything it was
worse, because of the embarrassment. The shops were few and
small and little in them encouraged loitering. The pubs seemed
bleak in the daylight – the preserve of young men, loud music and
dogs. She read a few newspapers in the library but the librarian
was soon a little restless. The first church she tried was locked.

In the second – a church she had never visited and could not
remember – she sat in the back pew, commanding the length of
its chilly late-Victorian interior, and concentrated.

There was the blood. That was the woman. Where was the
man? And the girl. Had the man died? Had he done something
terrible? Was he in another room ready to leap out and do something worse? There must have been screaming but she could
remember no screaming. She could hear nothing of what had happened. But she was certain of the house and the blood and the two
faces and the absence of the man.

It had been her fault. The woman – the ravaged woman – had
said so: she was sure of that. She had said "Get out! Get out!" or
was it something else – and had she shouted? – but something
followed which said "It's you" or "you're all right" or whatever
but it meant – "You are living and I am not and so you are to
blame". That's what it meant. That's what it had always meant.

Jen tried with all her strength to focus on that past terror.

She began to shiver and was soon in a spasm of shivering. Even
when she walked up and down the empty nave she shivered wildly.
And in the middle of this was the silly social fear that someone might
come in and discover her shivering and want to help, ask questions.
She left the church and hurried to the car. Once inside she turned on
the heater and shook, shook with the force of her shivering. What
had she said? "Get out! Get out! You're all right!"

She had been all right.

She had got out.

Now she was back and there was nothing there.

In the afternoon she drove down once more to that islet of terraced cottages. An old man was up a ladder cleaning windows. A woman with a pram manoeuvred her way through a narrow front door. Two schoolboys suddenly raced past her, yelling, making for the end house – her house – but they ran past it, into a no-man's-land.

She went away.

That evening she stayed in her hotel bedroom, phoned Nicholas, talked to Harry and Mary, talked to the private investigator. It was agreed she would move on to the other town the next day and then to the city.

In the middle of the night she woke up and dressed quickly. The night-porter let her out reluctantly and with ill-mannered curiosity. She drove the car straight back to the end house, her house, and got out and stood in front of it.

There were only three street-lights before this isolated row. But the moon was up in a cloudless frosty sky and the light pooled the place so that little was hid. Jen simply stood there, longing, longing to go back. She had dressed warmly and the night air bit only into her face; she welcomed that. Faint sounds of the night – a distant lorry, high up an aeroplane. She willed it and then just waited. There was nothing more she could do.

Oh God, that ravaged older face, the woman so desperate, her mouth open – crying? Hurting, crying – the most loved of all faces and only, only ever to be seen through blood and crying. And that other small grave face in the next room in the corner, stunned, just stunned – that face never seen again – reminders, a leap of the heart, but gone – abandoned, wilfully, by her, abandoned; wilfully cast off and put behind her and cast out.

But that lovely older ravaged lovely face, never to be seen again. In that house. The end house. Her home. Never to be seen, her mother, her lovely lost mother gone in front of her eyes, gone. Killing herself.

As the tears came down her cheeks she felt the life since then wash away and there in the dark she sobbed, childhood, lost childish sobs, at last the mourning.

Twenty-Nine

I

HE was sure now that no one was on his tail. At the station he had feigned exhaustion and sat on the ground as some student-looking types were doing, his back to one of the pillars, pretending to doze. But he was alert to every move and his arm was looped tightly through the straps of his bag. It had been Tony's bag when Tony had been a student. Maybe Tony had even been in this station – bound to have been if he came over the cheap way: that gave Colin some comfort. Now that he was on the mainland and in the big city he was experiencing a severe drop in confidence.

He had gone over his plans so often that he had somehow assumed that they would take him over and do the work for him. But he felt exhausted. The pains he had taken to cover his tracks, the care over the money, counting and recounting his savings, the excitement of bringing the gun into the house and concealing it in Tony's bag . . . Then the boat, avoiding everyone, the long train journey, pining with hunger but too scared to lose his seat by going to the buffet bar.

He got up. It could be hunger. A large cup of tea, well sugared, and a big and sticky Danish pastry made the difference. He went down into the Underground – limping badly, tired – and carefully negotiated himself to one of the parts of London where he had been told you could get cheap digs. He had enough money for about a week, he reckoned.

It was outside the rush hour and the Underground was not crowded. Colin studied the map and made a note of where he had

307

to change trains. Buying his ticket made him feel that the operation was now under way. There was even a contentment about him as he sat on the comfortable seat, staring fixedly at the floor, hugging the bag on his knees, listening to the tunnel sounds of the train. Somewhere up above there, in a building or on a pavement, was the man Mark Armstrong. Colin nodded to himself and began to mutter quietly. People avoided him.

II

"What should I call you?" Harry asked. His nervousness had killed his appetite. He wanted to take the edge off the significant silences which he sometimes encountered with Nicholas and found stifling.

"What have you been calling me?"

"Nothing really." Harry tightened his lips. Would Nicholas be angry? Nicholas tried to recollect: as far as he could remember, the boy was speaking the truth. The boy always spoke the truth.

"Nothing?"

Nicholas boomed the word – just a little. Harry, he sensed, liked it when he made a bit of a clown of himself. Sure enough, the boy gave that swift grin which made Nicholas soar with pleasure.

"Well, I always call you Harry," he said, gravely. "Never any other name at all."

Again the boy smiled. It was moving how much he liked the very childish things. So much of his own childhood had been shut in a cage. Now the bruises and the demands of those caged childhood years were coming out, hoping to play.

"That's because I am Harry."

"You're the Harriest Harry I could imagine."

"What does that mean?"

"Well: there are big fat Harrys who are usually very jolly – they've Harried their lives away. And there are mean Harrys who used to be good Harrys perhaps but then let the Harry side down. There have been King Harrys of course – eight of them – and President Harrys, Flash Harry, Hari Kari and Harry the Horse, but whenever I think of a Harry I think of you. You are the true Harry."

"Hm." The boy's eyes danced at this nonsense but now he was interested in his own initial question. What should he call him? Hoping that Nicholas would ignore the uneaten food. He sipped through the straw and the garish drink slid down the long glass as he worked on his next move.

They were in a Burger King near Leicester Square. Harry had wanted to go to a film and the fact that it was in Leicester Square did not seem to affect him one way or the other. Nicholas was nervous of encountering Deuce – although he sensed that the tabloid attack would not now appear, the optimum moment come and gone. He was also worried that the Crystal Rooms might trigger uneasy memories but Harry merely pointed to it and said, "You aren't allowed in there until you're eighteen."

Nicholas's rigorous public attitude of detachment got in the way of his quicker sympathies. Harry in fact had been so upset by the sight of the Crystal Rooms that he felt stunned. A rush of sour and frightening memories had seized him. And Nicholas, the nice kind man beside him, Nicholas was seen again in that hotel. The pink bathroom. The crying of Doug. The men dancing. That terrifying look in the eyes of Deuce. He did not know where in his mind to find refuge. No Fiona; no Jake. Nicholas – he knew Nicholas liked him but what had been happening at the hotel? The pit stomach sickness at Jake's last threat, after his fight with Fiona, to get him, rushed into his throat and he thought for a moment that he would indeed disgrace himself and annoy Nicholas and perhaps put him off for good by throwing up all over the pavement. Maybe even on his new shoes. Where was he to go? His mind began to cry in a bewilderment of miserable loneliness. Where would he end up?

The cinema was salvation. In the crowd, other children, the queue for ice-cream, the big, big screen making you think of nothing else, wiping out everything in your own mind, all the others feeling the same, on your side, and then the dark, the lovely dark which was not really dark because the screen lit up in front of your eyes so that you went from the dark into the light – with everybody else – all of you, all the other kids and you – went together into the big screen, into the film, into the laughing and holding your breath and in the end the crying. Despite all his efforts, Harry could not prevent himself from crying.

The director of this film had devoted great skills to making the young audience feel like crying. He drew on the children's fear of losing their very best friend, their only protector, their first great love, of losing this for ever. The watching children were caught in the glare. Harry turned away so that Nicholas could not see him.

But Nicholas too had been enmeshed in the manipulative emotionalism. He deplored the forces involved – the mechanical plot, the hugely sentimental music, the lingering on small crumpling faces, but he was caught. He was also embarrassed that he too might weep. Children manipulated everywhere, so effectively.

When Harry came out he felt very tired, even weak, but the panic had been in some way, for a time, shriven.

They had walked rather somnambulistically out of Leicester Square and drifted down Charing Cross Road rather aimlessly. There was no rush to be back at Jen's.

Mary had gone out with Jen, whose general manner and attitude since her visit to the North puzzled Nicholas greatly. She would not respond to direct questions, nor was she prepared to be confessional. Sometimes Nicholas thought that she was disturbed, sometimes that she was overexcited. It was not a mood he recognised. With the two children she seemed excessively nervous, now snatching, now retreating. Nicholas was rather put out that she so firmly excluded him from this secret. There was even a little jealousy that she might have confided in Mark.

Yet he could not pay it a great deal of attention. He was absorbed in the present. This, he guessed, was one of the benefits or consequences of love. That you could be alongside your life as the seconds trickled through your fingers. There was a giant sensation of pause. No retracing or reviewing of steps taken, no scheming for the future, a sense of simply being there. And being there with someone for whom you felt the most tender emotion imaginable. Not wanting to be anywhere else, with anyone else, doing anything else; just watch this boy, slowly thawing out, sipping his drink in an all but empty fast-food house in the West End.

"I don't want to call you 'uncle'," Harry said, finally. Nicholas was growing aware that it would take a long time for him to get used to speaking his thoughts freely before adults, without fearing a rebuff or a lash of the hand.

"I quite agree," said Nicholas. "I am not your uncle."

"I wish you were," said Harry, longingly, eyes straight ahead, avoiding Nicholas, intent but abstracted. "But you aren't and so I can't use it, can I?"

Nicholas was moved. It was not a game to the boy. But he could not resist teasing it out a little more.

"We've got on very well without you calling me anything, haven't we?"

The boy nodded tentatively and Nicholas was once again reminded of how far there was to go.

"So why the rush?"

"It's just that . . . when I want to shout for you . . . I want a name, otherwise . . . it's just shouting."

"I see." And Nicholas did understand. It was manners, it was need. It might even be affection.

"So." Harry took a very long sip and finished the drink. He gave one last look at the uneaten food. He could not take it. Nicholas would have to be angry. "You decide."

Nicholas took his time.

"You needn't eat that burger if you can't manage it," he said, and then added, "Why don't you just call me Nicholas? That seems the easiest thing."

Harry smiled.

"Do you think it's funny calling me by my Christian name?"

"Not funny. Sort of . . . difficult."

"Try."

Harry nodded.

"Nicholas," he said with a faint giggle, "we should go home soon."

If only, Nicholas thought, if only. One day, we might do just that.

The next morning was a Saturday and Nicholas came round at about twelve to take Harry out. Jen had gone shopping with Mary. Nicholas wanted to take Harry down to the Thames, perhaps catch a boat or amble across one or two bridges. But the boy plucked up his courage and asked to go to the park to knock a football around. Nicholas was not an enthusiastic participant.

"Wouldn't you rather go and see something?"

"No."

"If not the Thames, we could go for a ride on the top of a bus or pop into the Science Museum. You'd like that, I promise."

"Could we play football?" Harry was obstinate – which was rather unusual for him. But Nicholas, just in time, recognised it for the new confidence it was. "I think you're being a bit lazy, Nicholas."

"But I am lazy."

"Well, you shouldn't be. Come *on!*"

Once in the park, Nicholas put down his coat as one goalpost. Harry's jacket made the other and the boy practised shots against a sluggish middle-aged unathletic goalkeeper whose good humour and affection was sometimes in close contention with his basic distaste for physical sports and his sharp sense of his own utter inadequacy.

"You're not very good, are you?" said Harry, quite kindly.

"Sorry."

"No. It's not your fault. Probably you didn't get a chance to be good, when you were at school."

Again and again the ball sped between the coats and Nicholas would trail rather mournfully away to retrieve it.

Soon after they had arrived a gaggle of boys, almost a dozen, mostly about Harry's age, set up a game nearby. The slower Nicholas got, the more Harry's attention was drawn to the real game. Their ball landed in his patch and he returned it. The same thing happened a couple of minutes later. This time he stood nearby, clearly yearning to be part of their game. Nicholas picked up both coats and trudged across to him. He stood beside Harry for a short while and then boomed out,

"I see you're six against five. Can Harry here join in – make it six against six?"

One or two barely perceptible nods. Harry looked anxiously at Nicholas. Was it allowed? Could he really do it?

"Away you go," said Nicholas. "Away you go."

The boy sped off and was soon one of the mêlée. Nicholas watched him intently for a time and then relaxed. There could be many days like this. Harry near him . . . himself looking after the boy. A benediction.

It was a rather dull spring morning in London. People walking and running in the park, the city at bay, but a great and complex engine forever on the move. Discordance, discontent, unfairness, wickedness. But also such life, he thought, and sometimes harmony, a sense of battling on and reaching out, of opportunities and possibilities – just look at the city itself working like the most intricate yet contradictory mechanism imaginable – such hopes, he thought, as he felt his senses soar with gratitude and a rare sweet access of security, such peace.

"Nicholas!" The man smiled at Harry's imperious tone. "Could you get the ball, please?"

It had been kicked past him. He gave Harry a mock salute and turned to do what the boy had asked.

She wanted Mark with her as well as the private investigator. Mark had not been told what it was about but he turned up at 4 p.m. in the foyer of the National Theatre as arranged. They set out immediately.

The Thames rippled swiftly under a mild spring sun. The Embankment was loosely populated with idlers. Above them Waterloo Bridge ferried its cargoes and around them was the evidence of a great and handsome city. The Palace of Westminster a few score yards upriver, St Paul's much the same distance downriver, Somerset House across the water. From the National Theatre, past other palaces of culture, they went by way of a narrow lane of concrete into the area which supported the Waterloo roundabout, Cardboard City.

Even though it was afternoon, the gloom of the place was its first impact. A dismal, stained, concrete misery. The three men around a brazier. At this time of day only a few of the cardboard "homes" were out, the majority was stacked away until the roving homeless should come to claim them at nightfall. But there was a busted old sofa, three armchairs, several free-standing and large black plastic bags looking not unlike the two stout bag-ladies who regarded Jen and the two men with hostile curiosity.

While the investigator went to ask his questions, Jen looked around, trying not to pry. But what privacy could there be here? Yet when a set of stony eyes caught her own she realised that whatever little privacy there was, it was heavily guarded. Your own space could mean a square yard and when you had nothing else, it would be fanatically defended. The eyes were fanatical eyes. They threatened you to look into them. They dared you to divine their misery and hurt. They challenged you to try so that a connection could be made, if only in a reaction of violence. Up above the traffic of a metropolis sped along. Nearby preparations were under way for comfortable, engaging leisure. Jen marvelled at the discretion of the homeless here, that they tucked themselves out of sight, finding literally an underworld to see out the nights. Almost as if they did not wish to intrude. Why did they not march across the bridge and storm the capital? She remembered the girl who had stolen her money and wondered what had become of her. Should she find out?

The private investigator, still heavily protected in a thick winter coat and a very large grey scarf which wound around his neck a couple of times before being shovelled down his chest, came across to Jen and beckoned her away. He had a tendency to bend his head when he was speaking, as if everywhere were bugged or as if information would appear more authentic were it muttered mouth aslant. Jen leant down to pick up the words.

Mark, wishing he too had kept on his winter coat as the gloom and sullen nature of the place accentuated its coolness and sent a shiver down his skin, smiled and thought they looked like nothing so much as a pair of suspects – spies? – uneasily exchanging shady information in the underpass. He could see them at the opening of a thriller. The two of them meet – an attractive woman, a dumpy nondescript man – in Cardboard City, pass on intelligence or state secrets (were there any any more?) and are observed by someone with powerful German binoculars from whichever tall building gave the view. (That could be checked out.) Meanwhile he, Mark, was the man who had penetrated this deadly network or – better – an ordinary citizen who was about to stumble into it accidentally; or was he the ex-lover, ex-agent acutely aware that the discussion they might be having could be about himself, his future, if any, his cover blown . . . ?

"Mark!" Jen called him over. "Do you ever see any men drinking around the Shaftesbury Theatre area?"

It was quite near his flat.

"Top of Endell Street," he said, "there's always a gang of them there – next to the French Church."

The investigator looked at him and Mark experienced a touch of guilt. Had he crossed a demarcation line and done the man's job?

"We'll go there now," said Jen.

She had left her car near the National Theatre. It swung out, went around the roundabout – over the heads of the homeless below – and across the bridge into Covent Garden.

Mark and Jen were left to one side while the investigator went up to the group of men sitting on the steps, glazed-cheeked, raw-faced, alcoholic and derelict. In time he found one of them who would engage him in conversation. It was again to Jen alone that he transferred the information.

"There's a hospice in Bethnal Green," she announced to Mark. "I think that might be where I'll find the answer. And there's absolutely no need for you to come with me. It seems stupid when you're only five minutes from home here."

"You know I'd come with you if you really wanted me to . . ."

She had not given him any explanations but he had been pleased that she had needed him for this quest.

"I just wanted you to be with me in Cardboard City," she said. "I had a feeling about it. Wrong, as it turned out, but I was very glad that you were there. I was convinced I would . . . I wanted you to be there."

"You still can't tell me?"

"I will – soon, I hope. It's just too important for me. I have to be absolutely certain. Then I'll tell you. I'd rather be on my own now."

She came close to him and he kissed her on the cheek.

"Take care," she said.

He watched her go and turned north. Even such a short and well-trodden walk as this could perk up his spirits. The dusk of spring in the city charged him with unfounded optimism. He glanced proprietorially at the lit shop windows, appreciated the complex flow of people and traffic, began to see a shape to the evening – catch up on the latest from the Gulf, watch out for other instalments from a world which seemed to be collapsing for the benefit of television cameras – and after that some reading of reports he had been sent about the RUC. He would have to return to Belfast soon if he was to carry out his longer plan of writing the book and producing the series – but a weariness was holding him back.

Perhaps it was the tug of disappointment over Jen. However fond they were of each other, however close they could be, the love that he had wanted was not available. He had been once offered the chance once and failed to take it. Years before but the chance had been there. At this level of need, you only got the one chance, he thought, and if you muffed it then you sailed on and on in some sort of outer space of infinite emotionlessness like a rocket which has missed its destination. And then there was the business of making a living. He was of an age when the struggles which had given zest to the job were irksome. Indeed the whole television game seemed inappropriate for men his age – better left to younger talents. And it was all becoming so electronically as well as administratively overcomplicated. Not much comfort for a man who had considerable trouble pre-setting a video and no patience at all with bureaucratic memos.

As he turned into the street he noticed a young man in front of him, walking ahead of him, limping a little, peering up at the flats. The numbering could be very misleading for a stranger. The flats were in block numbers and it was easy to get confused. The young man was shabbily dressed, clutching something in front of him. Just before the entrance to his own block, Mark caught up with him.

"Can I help?"

The young man turned, startled.

"Is there any particular flat you're looking for?"

The white cold face was stiff with inexpression.

Mark felt uncomfortable. Central London these days was host to numerous stray and beaten-looking people – old, young, menacing sometimes, pathetic, some plainly mad, howling. Mark felt that he had interrupted the man's important private world. "I'm sorry," he said, and went rapidly into the flats.

The lift was on the ground floor and in working order. He was in it and had begun on his ascent before Colin had time to tug out his gun – wrapped in layers of socks and vests and a towel – and get into the hallway.

"But I know where you are," he said, aloud, as the lift clanked higher. The echoing of his voice gave him some pleasure. He spoke again, much more softly this time.

"You're a dead man, Mark Armstrong," he said, slowly. "You have my word."

IV

A sense of injustice had engorged Deuce when he spotted Nicholas and the boy – "Norf" – wandering across Leicester Square nice as you please to the Odeon. Deuce was a firm believer in Justice as laid down in the laws of Hammurabi. He deplored the softness of the liberal state. He would have brought back hanging for all sorts of murder, reinstituted the lash for juvenile crime, disallowed those social workers' reports which let young hooligans laugh at the law, and made all criminals contribute directly to the income of their victims in perpetuity. He also believed in total licence for individual tastes, including sexual tastes, including all known perversions. He had no doubt that except for his rather professional acceptance of perversions, his opinions could speak for the vast majority of his fellow citizens. If they did not, he did not give a sod. His fellow citizens had never given a sod about him. Nor did he want them to. By and large they were rubbish.

Deuce would have been offended at being called complacent but so he was. His dumb certainties brought him the yeast of eternal self-righteousness and the compulsion for revenge. He had tried over the past few months to get his own back on Nicholas but had been careful not to go too far. These things could backfire. But a grudge was a grudge – one of his stock sayings which he delivered as a model of reason and reasonableness. A grudge was a grudge.

He was on the telephone to a contact who knew the burgeoning world of the London paparazzi and, when the man and the boy came out of the cinema, he pointed them out. Deuce and the photographer then tracked the pair to the restaurant.

Nicholas and Harry were plainly to be seen in a window-seat but Deuce would not have it. They must be in the street – that would be far more effective. He had noticed that the boy held the man's hand – that was good.

When eventually they left the restaurant it was growing dark. Out of the glass doors they came and Nicholas fussed over Harry's scarf before drawing on a pair of leather gloves. The boy then took his hand and they turned in the direction Deuce had anticipated.

"Norf!" said Deuce. "Fancy bumping into you again! Well, well, well."

The flash caught two scared faces. The man beginning to ward off the photograph with a half-raised arm, the boy suddenly locked in panic, holding the man's hand but looking as if he were desperately trying to escape from the grip. A second and a third flash completed what landed up on Nicholas's desk the next day as a sequence wide open to the worst possible interpretation.

Deuce and the photographer had already worked out their line of retreat. There was no point in pursuing them. This part of London was Deuce's territory.

Now he was quits.

V

She was too late. He had died almost three weeks before. The name, however, was verified. She had all the information she needed. She ought to have felt relieved, justified even, eventually, exultant. But a tiredness overcame her. A sense of wasted lives. Lives then and now, in her past, in the present, Cally, under the

317

roundabout, the girl, in the streets, in cities and countries all over the world a sense of wasted life. And so much waste of love and hope, of the chance for goodness and fairness. The man who had died – a waste – and his wife, as it now seemed, wasted because of him.

She wanted her child back. She knew it was mad to want the child so long dead but she wanted it to make something of her life. She was totally silent as she drove home, London flicking past like a guttering candle.

But her tiredness, as sometimes happens, released a rare clarity: she saw what she must do with her life. She saw how she could find her way back to the sort of ideals personified by Helen. There was a lightness in her mind which promised relief, even fulfilment, perhaps even the possibility of happiness. She was back to the heart of herself and now she could begin to forget about herself and act. There was a sad contentment about her. But there was also a deep sense of resolution. Now she had to act.

VI

The mistake Colin made was in trying to get too close. He was back outside the flat just after dawn and he sat on some steps opposite, hunched and attendant, but to any passer-by just another stray soul. He expected Mark to come out every minute that passed, but it was mid-morning, a chilly morning, before he did emerge. Colin heaved himself up right away but Mark was already bouncing along with a good brisk stride.

Then Colin began his limping run, unzipping the bag where the gun now lay unwrapped, ready for use. His legs were shaky-stiff after the long squat on the cold steps and the loud sound of his own breath disconcerted him, but he made ground and the man's broad back drew closer. Now he had the gun out and now he threw away the bag – maybe it was that, the sound of the bag hitting the ground, which alerted his man, because Mark turned and, for an instant, Colin ran on, caught in the hunted, suddenly targeted look on the man's face.

The man's hand came forward as he pulled the trigger and the bullet went down into the thigh. Another shot missed altogether and now the man was grappling with him – much bigger and stronger, shouting, "For Christ's sake drop that gun! Drop it!

Drop it for Christ's sake!" There was another shot and a cry from the man and then Colin's head was slammed against the pavement, his ankle twisted violently, a last shot blew into him, into him. The guts of him suddenly swimming, large and heavy, somebody standing over him, the sound of the siren, his hands on his belly and then a hand to his face sticky with blood. The man beside him groaning, but still alive, still alive. He had let Tony down, he had failed to be a true brother. He closed his eyes. They could do whatever they liked now. For this there was no forgiveness.

Part Six

HOME

THIRTY

A
S the van slalomed down on to the motorway, Fiona felt
free. Going south, open highway, hungry cars racing in
treble lanes, London at the end of the road, glamour. Out
there. It was time she had some of that. Way beyond time.

Jake knew that she loved speed and he pushed the van to its
limit. The speedometer swung up to seventy-five, which more than
compensated for the noises and the strain, the rattling. He lit two
cigarettes at the same time and was pleased when she thanked
him. That was a bonus. She had kicked him out and kept him out
for weeks and then got in touch for this visit to London and he
had dropped everything to do her a favour. Anything to get back
with her.

He had expected to be treated like dirt. But she had been very
easy-going. She gave him a cup of tea and asked him which skirt
he liked best – not the one to travel in but the one she was going
to wear in London when she met that rich bitch and had the
showdown. Taken off the skirts and put them on right there in
the kitchen in front of him so he itched for her – she knew that,
she was a great tease. He'd often told her she could have been the
greatest stripper of them all. And she'd come up close to him
(him sitting, her standing) and pushed it right against his face and
rubbed around a bit. Then backed off. Black, she'd decided. (He
was sure she'd already decided – which made what she was doing
even better.)

He had brought the transistor so they listened to music and
Fiona even hummed along once or twice. She had worked it all
out. Jake did not know Jen's phone number or her address. Fiona
would get to London, somewhere in the West End, say she had to

make a phone call, send Jake off to park the van and, once he was out of sight, go down into the Underground and ride along for a couple of stations before hopping out and telephoning Jen (as arranged) and thus dumping Jake. She intended to travel back alone, later, and in style. Jake would be dumped. The thought gave her much pleasure and made her smile. Jake caught the smile and reached out to squeeze her thigh. She allowed him to do this and even wriggled a bit for his benefit. By now she had wholly convinced herself that the original losing of Harry in London had been Jake's idea enacted for reasons best known to himself. He deserved to be dumped. She reached across and patted his crotch. Jake was already aroused. She let her hand graze there for a while as the van rattled on.

She left him at Baker Street and even blew him a kiss.

Jen was very apologetic, but could Fiona wait until about six? It was just that some unexpected business had arisen and it would make it far easier if the later time could be met. Doing her a real favour. Many, many thanks. Fiona put down the phone with a sense of triumph. The woman was clearly on the run! She made for New Bond Street and sucked in the wealth of the shops thereabouts throughout an afternoon full of anticipation. One day soon, maybe tomorrow, she would be able to walk down this street and go into the shops and buy. No worries. Just sail in where the snobs sailed in and say, "I'll take that." She would milk them dry.

Jen phoned her lawyers. In one of the tabloids there had been a hint about Nicholas, a whiff which tortuously, unlibellously, made a reference to his homosexuality.

He had been sent copies of the photographs and brought them round to Jen. She was doubly alarmed, for Nicholas, of course, but also for Harry. Nicholas had come for help but he was stunned at the energy and the ferocity of her response.

Her case was simple and she did not deviate. The boy was a child in whom she had considerable interest, in whose future she would play a substantial part. Very delicate and private negotiations were going on which, if disrupted, would do nothing but bring this child, who had suffered, yet more suffering. Her great and dear friend Nicholas had taken the boy out to the cinema and then for a hamburger at her express request. Any innuendo read into the photographs, clearly taken with the basest of intentions, would be fought with all her resources through to the very highest courts, however long it took, however much it cost.

324

The lawyers confirmed that the editor had denied any intention of ever using the photographs. The lawyers had also alerted other tabloid editors. Mrs Lukas could accept the reassurances. There would be no follow-up to that glimmering of a smear.

Her fury had exhilarated her. The anguish she had felt at the possible harm to Harry was appeased; she was deeply pleased to be able to reassure Nicholas, yet there was now a glint of caution where once there had been the open country of simple optimism. Nicholas had looked scared. He had known himself to be vulnerable. In the present context, he was. It would not, then, be such a simple matter to have him head up her new foundation. She would need him to organise its finances, set up its structure and control its operations. But someone else would have to front it.

She left a message on Nick's answering-machine and confirmed that he should come round just after five. Over the past two days, Rudolf had called five times and five times she had let him dictate his brusque message on to the tape. She did not want any complications from that quarter at this time. But finally she decided that his persistence would be as bad as anything he had to say and phoned his private line.

"Jen! Jen-Jen! My old Jennie with the light-brown hair. How are you?"

Barking bonhomie. She kept her grip.

"Busy."

"That's my girl."

"Very busy, Rudolf, and so what is it?"

"They should put you in charge of the Middle East. What is it? I like it."

"Rudolf. I'll count to five. One . . . two . . . three . . ."

"Money. In a word. Dosh. There we have it. Filthy lucre – love the stuff. Money-money-money. Another very short-term loan of the same."

"Rudolf. You still owe far too much from the last loan." She gave him the figure even to the nearest thousand. He laughed very loudly.

"A temporary blockage."

"I am told that you are telling that to all the girls."

"For you – the truth. I need three weeks. Twenty days. The truth."

"And then what?"

He outlined a fantastical series of financial manoeuvres. This

325

wizardry had beguiled many bankers, many heads of corporations, many government departments, many prospective partners. Unfortunately, Jen had seen him do it and seen him put down the phone and yell with laughter afterwards and all but gallop across the room shouting "I got them! They fell for it! I did them in! Ha! I put it over on them. Is there anything, Jen, tell the truth, anything in the world I cannot sell and anyone on earth I cannot sell it to?"

She listened for old times' sake. If you allowed yourself to be carried along it was mesmerising stuff.

"That was very good," she said, when he had come to the Klondike of a peroration.

"Yes?" Rudolf appreciated the compliment coming from Jen.

"Oh yes. But I want my money back fast. I have plans for it."

"Jen!"

"Rudolf!"

"Jen. Listen."

And once again he drove her around a world of deals and time zones and debt restructures and prime opportunities, but she listened with a different interest. There was desperation there. And anger. Anger at her for not doing his will, the anger which more than once had made her physically fearful when they were together – of course he had always apologised, and blamed stress. But, once or twice, she had gained the clear impression that he had come within a moment of striking her, which was no small part of her decision to leave him after such a short time.

She would not budge. He cursed and derided her foundation. She would not budge. He promised her even more wealth if she went along with him now. She was adamant. His anger broke. She did not respond.

Always true to his instinct that the only way to survive was to live to fight another day, Rudolf dropped the subject abruptly. He wanted to leave Jen with their contact still warm. He made an attempt at small talk, failed and then stumbled on a subject which suited his needs.

"Your boyfriend. How is he?"

"He may limp a little but he'll survive."

"The papers made him a hero."

"Made a change."

"You mean Martha's little article? Besides – he asked for it. You mess with my girl and you don't wait for the gloves to go on."

"So you are an item."

"That's what it says in the gossips. Always believe the gossips."

"Martha looked very pleased to be on your arm, Rudolf, in that photograph. It was almost as if she had you in an advanced judo hold."

"Some girl, eh?"

Over the past few weeks the papers had been full of Martha and her relationship with Rudolf. Alfreda's name had been whacked across the columns to add spice. Taking her chances well, Martha had made an open declaration of Republicanism in an article which had gathered unexpected intellectual sympathy as well as approval from the smart crowd. Only a few accused her of a most cunning pitch for an invitation to lunch at Buckingham Palace. And there was her article on "AIDS and the Immaculate Princess".

After having declared her sympathy for all those with HIV/AIDS and her admiration for the Princess of Wales's well publicised concern over the issue, Martha pointed out that many of the most public victims had led lives of the utmost promiscuity which was OK, perhaps, but somehow sat uneasily alongside the current and Royal craze to make martyrs of them all. This was especially true, she had written, of the homosexual community. They were asking for it, she wrote. They were promiscuous in a way which would make any heterosexual the legitimate target not only of feminists but of any woman rightly suspicious of a boastful one-night-stand merchant. Their divorce of sex from anything but instant and passing gratification was disgusting and deplorable, she judged, and what it had to do with the home life of dear Princess Di eluded Martha's understanding. She was venomous and young Stephen had given her some useful names.

The reaction was most satisfying – the very best she had ever provoked. Her notoriety was glorious. Her glee uncontainable. And she continued to do things to Rudolf's willing body which provoked eruptions of joy.

"Are you going to marry her?"

"I could do worse, Jen. She's a helluva lot of fun. What do you think?"

"I think you're made for each other."

"Do you? I appreciate that. While we're being cosy – are you taking Armstrong on?"

"Not yet. Perhaps not ever, formally. We'll see."

"But you . . . ?"

"Oh yes."

"I wouldn't like to think of you going without."

"By which I take it that you are being very well served in that department," said Jen, glad that he could not see her smile.

"Best ever. No disrespect. Sorry."

"I don't mind. Truly. Shall I get Bob to phone you about the money you owe us?"

"I'll phone him now, OK?"

"OK. Well . . ."

"Jen. Maybe we could . . . ?"

"No. It's much better that we don't meet at all."

"Jen?"

"Yes?"

"I'll be back."

Rudolf's self-control lasted only until he had replaced the telephone on the receiver. Then his rage at being denied the money by Jen possessed him in a way which would have alarmed any observer. Fortunately he was alone, but those hurricanes of rage were no respecters of company and reports were awesome. It was as if he was about to explode. As if the blood rushed against the bone and pressurised it to near break point. He held on to the arms of his chair and roared aloud. He could have ripped Jen to pieces, torn her limbs from their sockets, swung her around the room by her hair, and forced her whimpering to his feet to apologise for denying him what he wanted. What he had to have. What he needed to survive. She was trying to murder him. She understood how bad things were – she, above all women – but she had denied him. His sense of justice was outraged. He saw himself victimised, unfairly condemned, unsupported, cast out, abandoned and betrayed. He would have his revenge. Somewhere along the line – squash any remaining thoughts of a deal with Armstrong for a start – but any chink he could find he would be in there. She had to be hurt.

Where the hell was he going to get the money? She must have realised – she must have read – that all the odds against him were shortening – by the month, by the day. What could he do next? He roared aloud in bull-wound as Martha came into the suite and found herself assaulted with a ferocity which impressed but also rather frightened her.

Jen had one more long phone call to make, and then she called Mark.

He was back in his flat now. He had resisted all her suggestions that he move into an hotel. He had decided to catalogue all his books and found instead that he had begun to reread many of them. Not for years had he had the free time to immerse himself in the worlds of crime and espionage, of hurt and guilt to which he had been addicted since adolescence. This, together with his blues records, made him happy in a truant boyish way he thought lost to him for ever. There was also a steady supply of claret – a couple of crates from his former office which had produced a long, conciliatory and flattering letter from Bagshaw, hoping to meet and discuss a new contract. The franchise bids were due in within a few weeks, and now that the Rudolf Lukas possibility had gone, Mark was again a valuable player in the market.

Jen was worried at his determination to go and see Colin in the hospital. Both men had been taken to St Mary's Paddington and Mark had been wheeled along to see him two or three times. Colin would not talk but he had not asked for Mark to be forbidden to come. Jen was worried but Mark was determined to press on. "If I can talk to him – who knows? Some little thing might be achieved. Anyway, I'm going to try." She was both annoyed and moved by his obstinacy. She would go round to his flat later in the evening. "And thanks again," she said, "for listening last night."

She took Harry and Mary across to the park and, as promised, let them row her around the Serpentine. Mary was becoming a little more friendly now and Jen's occasional caresses – she schooled and rationed herself strictly – were no longer rebuffed. Harry was growing less tense by the day and when he saw Nicholas back at the house he beamed rather cockily and called him "Nick".

For a few moments the four of them were together, and Nicholas was struck again, as he had been several times over the last few days, by Jen's great gust of energy. He had not seen her like this since those first wonderful years in London. It was almost as if she was on a high – although he knew that she had totally given up the drugs which she had reached out for after the death of her son. But her manner was fierce, strung; she all but trembled.

"I'm afraid I want to talk to Nicholas alone for a while," Jen said. "Do you mind? You can watch the television in the upstairs room or whatever you want."

Whenever bidden to do anything, both children responded immediately. Their deference grew from fear and it pained Jen to see it. Did they still so deeply feel that they were on trial? That they would be sent away if they misbehaved? That their own personalities had no weight? She had to change all that.

329

And she would start now.

"I'm still rather nervous about what I have to tell you," she began. "Even though I told Mark last night . . ."

"He said you'd been a bit shaky."

"Did he say why?"

"Not a word." Nicholas settled himself into the middle of one of the large sofas, spread his arms along the back of it as if bracing himself, and said, "He said you were worried about him seeing that young terrorist. Let him do it. That's his life."

"I know. But . . ." She lit a cigarette and sat opposite him. Isabella had decreed it was still cold and there were a couple of logs burning in a sable mound of ash. The light outside the room was brighter than inside.

Jen began most hesitantly.

"I don't know whether to start by coming straight out with it or going back to the beginning. It's been difficult keeping it to myself over the last few weeks but I had to until I could settle it. It mattered so much to me. It wasn't until I went back – to the town – that I could really go forward. I hadn't been there for – thirty-five years, more – but I knew it so well."

Nicholas waited. Jen quite uncharacteristically suddenly jumped up, went rapidly over to the drinks and brought back two long whiskies. Nicholas sipped and waited.

"You and Mark are – well, I trust you, both of you, more than anyone. Anyone." She put down the whisky, untouched. "And I think I love Mark – certainly I don't want anyone else – and you and I have always loved each other in our fashion, haven't we? I know."

Nicholas nodded. She was silent for a few moments.

"I have to get it out. Perhaps I should have told you and Mark together but I thought that would be too formal. I thought it would be embarrassing. Make it a public announcement when it's the opposite – I thought it a private confession? Yes." She sipped her whisky.

"When I first met you in London, in the Sixties, I told you – if you asked, I would have told you – that my parents were Dennis and Marjorie. I was not very kind about them. I was particularly unkind about her – patronising about him. Even when I married and there was all the money, all I did was send them money. I should have seen them. I should have made the effort. I was selfish and now they are dead and it's too late. It's painful, isn't it? Never to be able to make amends. Never. They were good enough people

– in some ways they were very fine people doing their best. I was the problem, not them. The older I got the more I turned on them – on her particularly – until, when I was sixteen or seventeen, I could have murdered her. Sometimes I dreamt that I did. That I actually murdered her. And I almost attempted it – one Sunday – the Sunday dinner, it was a rigid routine even though there were only the three of us. We had been arguing for days and it had festered and I picked up the knife and – lunged at her. She was so frightened she jumped back and knocked the pan of sprouts off the cooker. Sprouts all over the floor. And near-boiling water. And there was I, standing with a knife, not knowing how it had got into my hand and what for but I had lunged and – another few inches – it would have cut her. It was soon after that that they told me: I was adopted."

Jen found it unexpectedly difficult to emit that last word. It checked her. She paused and Nicholas could see that she had to collect herself. She went on.

"Although it seemed to make sense of everything that had happened, especially between Marjorie and me, it also drove me mad. I just wanted to get away from them – as fast as possible, as soon, as far as possible. Just get away. I asked questions and Dennis, my 'father', honestly told me the answers but I felt there was something else." Here she breathed in deeply and then went on more firmly. "Whatever it was, it frightened me so much that I dreaded it – I dreaded it until just a few months ago. Dreaded it. I just cut it out. Ran from it. I did anything just to keep it away. It was always waiting for me like an assassin around the corner. Maybe it was why I did what I did. I turned myself into another person so that it couldn't get me. You know how frantic I was. Maybe . . ." And now she said it.

"I finally forced myself to remember that my mother killed herself. And I saw it. I was five and I remembered. Dennis had told me – something, not the whole truth but something. I'd blocked it out completely. After he told me, I buried it. The only time I could let it out with any feeling of security was when my child, when he was born – just after that, a few weeks after that. I thought I could live with it then. But after he had gone I buried it again – let it haunt me if it would. And it did. But I pushed it down so deeply – until Cally died – you never met Cally – same way, wrists – and then it was a wall that just collapsed.

"I saw Cally's body in the morgue and I knew that I had to face

331

my own past. I had to look at that and take it on. I had to talk about it and admit it. The analyst helped me to get there.

"One of the things I did for myself was to go back to the place. The house is still there. I looked at it and looked, not knowing what to feel, and then I really *did* see – her: my mother. I'd never seen her since that day. I saw her face. It was there, in the dark, in that cottage. She was desperate and kept saying 'You'll be all right' – I think, I think it was that, or 'It's all right for you'. But whatever she said – her face was so tired, Nicholas, it was in such pain, it wanted release." She paused and took a sip. Nicholas was as still as he could be, forcing down the instinct to go across and comfort her, knowing that she wanted to tell him all of this and something more.

"There was another face," she said. "I saw it again the other night. But I saw it clearly on that night too. It was a small, terrified face, my younger sister, in the next room when I rushed through screaming for an ambulance or a doctor or help or whatever – this other face in the big chair by the fire. Terrified. Terrified. Paralysed." She hesitated. "Mary's face." Nicholas held his breath.

"I'd known about the sister for years, I suppose. But I had blocked her out. And Dennis failed to tell me about her even though he was as honest as he was able to be about my real mother's death. But after Cally's death I remembered the sister. And since I've been back I've tried to track her down. She was adopted somewhere else and I never saw her or heard of her again."

Jen took up the glass of whisky and then decided against it.

"I was convinced that Mary and Harry were the children of my sister. I was sure their mother would turn out to have been adopted. Mary looks so exactly like her. The thought almost drove me mad." Jen hesitated again and spoke more slowly now, almost dreamily. "I was so shaken by this that I did not want to do anything in case I did the wrong thing. I hired the private investigator. He tracked down the mother – her name was Valerie, not my sister's name, but that was a small matter: parents who adopt a child often give it a new name. He went to the town where she had been brought up and married. When he phoned to tell me that he had found out everything about her parents, I just told him to come around immediately. I couldn't bear to hear it on the phone. By that time Mary and Harry were more important to me – my niece and nephew, my own family, my only family, the only family I could ever have – more important to me than anyone and anything on earth. I think I went slightly crazy waiting for him to arrive. Why had I not let him tell me on the telephone? I wandered around this place, touching things, plumping cushions, tidying unnecessarily – anything, anything – and praying, Nicholas. Oh God, I wanted them to be hers and now to be mine. I wanted that, I swear, more than I have wanted anything else in my life.

"But I couldn't have it. Valerie was not my sister. Either Mary did look like my sister as a girl or I misremembered or wanted to misremember. So that was it. No children. Not my own." She paused and caught her breath. "My real sister is alive and living in Canada – childless, like me. But her own choice. We've talked on the phone. I'm flying over as soon as this is sorted out. It will be wonderful to see her. Won't it?"

Jen began to sob. "It will. It will be wonderful to see her," she said, but the words were scarcely audible as the wrenching pain of the sobbing increased. Nicholas went over to her and knelt beside her chair. She put her arms around his neck and sobbed, shaking, the tears hot on his neck, the pain all but unbearable.

Eventually Jen composed herself. Went out to bathe her face. Came back and this time did take a deep drink and lit another cigarette.

"But then I thought – so what? These are two children who need love and care and I can give them that. And I want children to look after. So. I was adopted. I hated it. I hated those who adopted me but maybe I can get it right for them. Maybe it will prove that I'm not going to cave in to self-pity if I take on what I fear most – adoption. If they need it, of course. If they want it." She looked directly at Nicholas, her still-swollen eyes affecting him to tears of his own: those eyes, still the lasers of some deep truth. "So I kept the investigator on and found out more about them.

"Valerie, their mother, died a few years ago. Her husband had left her by then. He became a serious alcoholic. We heard that he was still alive somewhere in London but by the time we got on the scent, he was dead too. He was Irish. Sean. One of us will have to tell the children that he is dead. I've taken advice about it. They suggest that you tell Harry, I tell Mary – over the next few days. When we judge the time to be ripe. But we have to co-ordinate it." The plans gave her a briskness which fortified her.

"One more very important point," said Jen. "There's a sister of Sean's in Derry, Bridie, a deputy headmistress. She had not realised what Fiona was doing to the children. She's quite awesomely busy – a very impressive woman, but when she believed me, she was mortified and wholly on my side. Then I went into the legal aspect. I have a right to adopt them – it will take time, of course, but Bridie is in favour. Fiona could be an obstacle. But if we succeed – and we have to – you can be near him and with him to your heart's content, Nicholas. You'll do him nothing but good."

Nicholas got up and walked across to her. This time she stood up to meet him and they embraced warmly, closely. "Thank you," he murmured into her hair and again, "thank you."

Then the two close friends sat for golden minutes talking about short-term and long-term plans and hopes, looking at their new luck like old prospectors who have finally stumbled on gold, unable to credit it, unable to ignore the evidence, knowing their world had changed. In those few minutes they drew out plans and expressed hopes, not only about Mary and Harry but also about the foundation which Nicholas insisted – independently dovetailing with Jen's decision – that he could not head. He had considered the risks from a tabloid press devoted to smear and the wrecking of reputations would be too great a liability. In any case, he would much prefer running the show in an unobtrusive way. It was more fitting for charity work. And he wanted time to attempt to track down and destroy Deuce's business. Nicholas was fully aware of the dangers but in some way it was part of his responsibility to Harry and he could not duck it. It needed time and a plan and he needed help. To be a more anonymous figure – no longer an MP, certainly not the leading name in a massively funded foundation which would undoubtedly be greeted with peals of publicity – all this would help. Now he knew what his life was for.

"Well," said Jen, "there's one more problem."

"Fiona?"

"Yes. She could make it very difficult."

"She knows all about the hotel."

"I'd guessed that."

"In some way I'm sorry for her," said Nicholas. "I even find that I can sympathise with her."

"Why?"

"Her background, her . . ." Nicholas trailed off.

"Rubbish. Tens of thousands of people far less fortunate than her don't do what she wickedly tried to do to Harry. There are some things you must not excuse – you can try to cure them, OK – but you must not excuse or the whole point of trying to lead a decent life, let alone a good life, is redundant. Some people, some acts are bad. They have to be called such and they have to be condemned. The alternative is brutality." She heard the voice of Helen, and smiled to herself.

"I suppose," said Nicholas, ruefully, "that my own experience has made me more sympathetic to those outside accepted morality. But I admit – a line has to be drawn. You are right."

"Fiona will be here quite soon. I – no, we – have to tell the children."

To make it less formal, the adults went up to the room in which the children were watching television. But their attitude instantly alerted Harry and Mary who turned and were silent, reconciled to being judged or found wanting.

As clearly and briefly as she could, Jen explained that she wanted to try to adopt them. She told them why; she told them that she had spoken at length to their Aunt Bridie; she told them that it would take some time. She wanted them to consider whether they wanted it. Meanwhile their Aunt Fiona was coming to see her, very shortly, and perhaps she would want to take them back to live with her.

"We'll run away again," said Mary, promptly. "Won't we? I hate her."

Harry nodded but something else worried him.

"Will I be allowed to see Nicholas?"

Nicholas checked the pricklings of emotion he felt at that simple question which seemed, to him, as much a declaration of love as he could ever hope for.

"Oh yes," said Jen, "yes. Every day."

Then something rather strange occurred. The two children, who had been orphaned, terrified, starved of care for years and survived through the support they had found in each other, just looked at each other, silently, as if the adults were not there. It was done very deliberately and unselfconsciously. It was a moment of intense, private communion. After a pause, and without looking at Jen, Harry spoke, obviously for both of them, and said, "We think you're like our mother."

THIRTY-ONE

FIONA had found it difficult to discover Jen's house in the riddle of back alleys. She had anticipated something altogether more grand, something colonnaded and freestanding, something like a stately home which arrested the flow and huddle of cramped London brick. For a few moments she had thought that Jen had conned her, that this was not the address of "one of the world's richest women" but a trap. When finally she found the small black door which indisputably carried the number she had been given she pressed the bell in short nervous jabs. Nothing happened. She jabbed again several times and in her impatience banged on the door. It opened.

The courtyard reassured her. There were statues. The house looked suddenly quite grand after the back alleys and the small black door. She remembered that Mrs Lukas was said to have several residences. Probably just lived in this one for a week or two. Typical.

More certain now, she walked across to the steps and mounted them carefully; her new shoes were pinching a little. Another bell. This time the door was opened for her by a dumpy, firm-looking woman who repeated her name as if she were testing a guinea on her teeth. Fiona stood in the hall while Isabella went to bear news of her arrival to Jen.

Now Fiona began to see where the money was. There were curtains of materials she had never seen before, thick, heavy, brocaded in careful patterns, costing, no doubt, the earth. The Persian rugs which glittered on the floor could have been the gold once fabled to pave the streets of London. Real paintings, landscapes, portraits, around the hall and then ascending the gently spiralled staircase like a framed and privileged guard of honour. From the high ceiling a chandelier hung down, petalled in purest glass. Even the walls were painted in a way she had never encountered but sensed was exclusive and unbelievably expensive. It was the biggest and incomparably the richest place Fiona had ever set foot in and she ached to the pit of her stomach to have some of it for herself, some piece of this deep wealth. Why not? Why them and not her?

"Ah, there you are," said Jen briskly. "I'm very sorry to have kept you waiting, especially after asking you to come a few hours later than we originally planned – come through, please – Isabella will take your coat – I'm Jen Lukas." She held out her hand.

It was easy to show off with all this flash of manners, easy to be smarmy and polite when you had the cash. But she was beautiful. Anybody could look good in those clothes, which must have cost a ransom, but you could not deny that she was beautiful. Fiona summoned her own resources: much younger, lush hair, jet-black, which she kept long, and swept now and then with her hand to draw attention to it, a creamy Irish skin and a sexiness that the likes of Mrs posh-voice Lukas in a house like this could neither fathom nor compete with.

She let Jen usher her into the ground floor drawing-room, her mettle keen. Nicholas was an unpleasant surprise. He stood up and they shook hands before Fiona could quite work out what it was all about.

"Nicholas has an interest in this, as you know," Jen said. "I thought it better if he join us. Drink?"

Fiona's eyes were directed to the drinks arranged both casually yet impressively on a highly polished cabinet in the corner of this magnificent room which had quite taken her breath away. The furniture, the lights, the carpets, the ornaments, the mirrors, she scanned the place so fast it became a blur of utter unattainable luxury and once more she experienced a gut-deep envy and rage that this had all been denied her.

"Do you have a vodka and tonic?" She spoke with care.

Jen nodded. While she fixed the drinks, Nicholas asked her about her journey up to London and Fiona was grateful for the ordinariness of his chat: it gave her time to recover her balance. She must not be intimidated by all this. She was just as good as them. Better in some ways, she had no doubt. And how had they all come by it? You couldn't tell her that all this, and all the much much more she had read about, came without fiddles and doing other people down and a great measure of cunning: no way could you get this loot honestly. Just no way. By the time the large cold crystal tumbler of vodka and tonic was in her hand she had regained her poise on the back of a strong sense of moral superiority.

"Cheers," said Jen. "Shall we sit down?"

A large armchair was indicated for Fiona, so deeply plumped that she felt herself too comfortable, and at a disadvantage. She perched on the edge of it. Nicholas occupied a large sofa. Jen sat in the armchair facing Fiona.

She explained that she wanted to adopt or become the legal guardian of Harry and Mary. She told Fiona that she had lost her only child years ago when he was no more than a baby; that she had discovered that she could have no more children and that it would be marvellous for her if she could help Harry and Mary. It could also, she suggested, be of benefit to them, given that they were – as Nicholas had told her – rather a burden on Fiona.

Fiona had taken a couple of drinks in a wine bar after her walk down New Bond Street. She had gulped her first mouthful of the vodka too greedily. Now she put it aside on the table placed, she noticed, so perfectly beside her chair.

"I love them," she said. "Nobody can know what those kids mean to me. I swear to God."

"I see," said Jen. She glanced at Nicholas but he was determined to keep silent throughout if he could. He felt he had no leverage with Fiona and was there only as a witness.

"They were a sacred trust from my brother Sean and now that he's dead –"

"You know?"

"The police contacted me the day before I set off here. I'll have to break it to the children."

"He's been out of their lives for a long time – in their terms."

"He's still their father. I'm still their aunt. You can't get away from blood. We were all very close even after we came over here."

She lit up a cigarette. Jen also took one out and Fiona felt vaguely rebuked for not having offered her one; and then resented the feeling.

"I've spoken to your sister Bridie," said Jen. "She seemed to think it was quite a good idea."

"Bridie would. Bridie's never lifted a finger. Sean relied on me. All the talk – there always was with Bridie – but when it came to it they were dumped on me."

"Bridie seemed to think that you had welcomed them. And there

338

was something about money – in their mother's will – what Bridie described as a 'fair old sum' which all went to you for their upkeep."

"If it all went to me it went away from me soon enough. Kids destroy money. You'll know nothing about that sort of thing."

"But nevertheless . . ."

"Look, Mrs Lukas – the money our Bridie was talking about wouldn't buy a picture on one of your walls. So don't come talking to me about money. People like you don't know what money is. Money doesn't enter into it with you, sure it doesn't. Money for food and clothes and rent and holidays – you never give it a thought – money to pay bills, money for a night out, money for kids – that isn't the sort of thing you have the slightest notion of. When you want, you get, and what you want, you get and money's dirt. So don't you talk to me about money and don't Bridie talk to me about bloody money either with her posh little school-mistress's flat and the salary and the trips abroad with the senior pupils all found. Talk about money when you have no money or when you scrape the barrel every other day of the week and then you'll be talking about money."

Jen paused. She understood why Nicholas had been outgunned by this woman.

"Are you saying that you want to keep Harry and Mary?"

"I am. By Christ I am."

"Despite the fact that you tried to have Harry abandoned in London?"

"That's a bloody rotten lie."

"Despite the fact that they ran away from you the other day?"

"Jake had upset them. He beat me up and threatened them. I won't hold it against them."

"Despite the fact that you told Nicholas here that Harry was available for a price?"

"Is that what he told you? He's not much of a help to you, is he? Did he tell you where he came across Harry?"

"I did," said Nicholas.

"In that case that settles your game."

"What you are saying –" Jen began.

"You seem very keen on telling me 'what I am saying' . . ."

"Nevertheless, what you are saying is that you feel that you are perfectly capable of looking after them well, that you love them and that you will resist all suggestions to the contrary."

"Right!" Fiona finished her vodka. She was winning. She had them. She had them on the run!

"Another drink?"

"I don't mind."

Nicholas motioned to Jen, took Fiona's glass and recharged it, moderately. Jen let the action be an excuse for silence.

"Don't you think," she said, when Fiona was resettled with her vodka, "that they would have a better chance in life here?"

"That's not the point, is it? The point is they are my family."

"What if I said that they did not want to live with you?"

"I'm sure you've bribed them. But that'll pass. Truth always floats to the surface," said Fiona and drank.

"My lawyer says that Bridie alone could give the authorisation."

"I'll fight that. Bridie's been useless."

"Fiona," the name was spoken gently. "You don't like them. They don't like you. You don't want them. They are afraid of you. You have done them positive damage and there's no reason to believe that you would not do them more damage. You are very clever and very plausible but you have behaved wickedly to these children and now you sit there lying about it and asking us to sympathise with you in some way because you do not have all the money you somehow believe has been denied you by a vindictive act of injustice. All you are here for is gain. Not for Harry or Mary but for yourself. You want money. You don't want their welfare or their happiness – those two children are no more than bargaining-counters to you. You want money. How much?"

Fiona's head jerked back but she did not give anything away.

"That's not the sort of talk I expected to hear."

"Isn't that what you came for?"

"I'm sure it suits you to think of me as dirt. Your sort always does."

"Very well. What if I say I'll fight you in the courts over the children? I have Bridie on my side – what if I take it through the courts?"

"That would bring your friend Nicholas out into the open."

"It might. But I'd risk that. So would he. What would you do?"

"I wouldn't let them be taken away by the law."

"You would fight it?"

"I would."

"Even if it meant dragging the children through it? Even if it meant taking them through the courts?"

"When you've right on your side," said Fiona, "and it's family – God help us, there's nothing can stop you."

"Would you take those children through court to oppose your sister Bridie, the children's wishes and the opportunities I can provide? This could be my last question, so take your time."

Jen took out another cigarette. Nicholas glanced at her asking if she would like another drink, but she shook her head. Fiona finished the vodka. If only she could take her shoes off.

"I wouldn't want to do anything that would harm the kids."

"I see."

"But there's the matter of how much I'll miss them – and whatever they say, everybody has their ups and downs, don't, they? – they'll miss me. Things were very hard. All I need is a good push start and I could get myself sorted out once and for all."

"Yes."

Jen knew that the battle was won but felt only sadness and some tinge of pity. It would come down – in Fiona's case – to money. She would be generous. Her lawyers would ensure that she was totally protected and Fiona, after the payment, would have no comeback. But it seemed so mean.

And then Jen found that she managed a feat of imagination. To be Fiona. To see yourself as she saw herself – eternally pressed to a pane which would never yield the abundance displayed on the other side. A circle of hell. A perpetual torment. She, Jen, was in danger of becoming much too grand about money. Surely the point of her new life, her life after that visit to her mother's house, was to scrape off as many layers as she could from the coatings which had hidden and for a time suffocated her? If she was to live a life unencumbered by the magical realism of her great wealth then an understanding of Fiona was important. She would not condone what she had done. She reserved the right to condemn it. She need not confuse understanding with forgiveness. But she was being offered a deal over money and given the deals which had been done with the money she had garnered, it little became her, she thought, to be too superior.

"Nicholas mentioned £50,000 as the sum you had asked for."

Fiona's tongue darted out to lick her top lip. Was it too much? Too little? Would she be somehow giving evidence against herself if she admitted it? Was Jen serious? She kept perfectly still, her head slightly bowed, a submissive posture.

"I think that's a fair sum. If you care to stay in London overnight, I'll have lawyers draw up documents for the payment of that amount tomorrow morning. Say ten o'clock?"

"And the kids . . . ?"

"That will take much longer. Much. And perhaps your payment will have to be delayed for reasons to do with that. We'll know tomorrow. But you will get the money. And that £50,000 buys your agreement."

"You can buy anything, can't you?"

Jen paused and thought of her past and then, more passionately than she would have wanted, said, "Oh no. Oh no. You cannot, no one can, buy anything."

For the first time, Fiona smiled. So it was not all roses, was it? There was hurt there, she could feel it come off the woman like heat. And deep hurt most likely. Good!

She stood up.

"Ten o'clock in the morning then."

"Yes."

"I'll see you to the door," Nicholas said.

Fiona was about to give him a mouthful but then she decided against it. She had got as much as she had hoped for at one go and a survivor's instinct told her that the boundary had been reached.

When he came back into the room, Jen was standing by the window.

"Well?"

"It's a beginning," she said, rather sadly, and added, "Did you notice – she didn't ask if she could see them?"

"It seems strange now that it might happen."

"Yes." She turned from the window. "Do you think we are rather an unlikely couple?"

"Many couples are," said Nicholas. "Or so I'm told."

From the upstairs window, Harry and Mary had watched Fiona leave – limping slightly. When she had reached the door, she had looked back and spotted them. Even from that distance her stare had chilled Harry. Then she had raised her hand, almost a wave, and was gone.

"I think that means we can stay," said Mary.

Harry waited a while. Then Jen came in and the relief when she hugged him was so powerful that he felt that he could sleep for ever.